Seductive Santino

Anne Marie Citro

Copyright © 2020

All rights reserved. No part of this publication may be reproduced, distributed, or transmitted in any form or by any means, or stored in a database or retrieval system, without the prior written permission of Anne Marie Citro, except as permitted under the U.S. Copyright Act of 1976.

Editing by C&D Editing
Cover created by: Ravenne Villanueva
ravennedesign@gmail.com

This is a work of fiction. All names, characters, places and events portrayed in this book either are from the author's imagination or are used fictitiously. Any similarity to real persons, living or dead, establishments, events, or location is purely coincidental and not intended by the author. Please do not take offence to the content as it is fiction.

Trademarks: This book identifies product names and services known to be trademarks, registered trademarks, or service marks of their respective holders. The authors acknowledge the trademarked status in this work of fiction. The publication and use of these trademarks is not authorized, associated with, or sponsored by the trademark owners.

This book contains mature content not suitable for readers under the age of 18. This book contains content with strong language, violence, and sexual situations. All parties portrayed in sexual situations are over the age of 18.

Dedication

To my older brother, Joe. I wrote this series based on a family that has gone through tragedy and had to survive because you have no other choice in life. Can you relate? Yeah, I thought you might. Through the absolute worst and the absolute best times in my life, you have stood beside me, my husband, and my sons.

So often I have been at a funeral and heard the eulogy and thought I wished I had known that person better because they sound like someone I could have been really good friends with. The things said about the person, who never got to hear them, is the saddest part to me. Well, I need to tell you how I feel, and, seeing as this is the only part of the book you will read, I better make it good.

I'm lucky because I got to know you as not just a sibling but also a damn good friend. You have the biggest heart of anyone I have ever met. You also have the most inappropriate sense of humor of anyone alive. And you get away with it. I have heard the phrase a million times that someone would give you the shirt off their back, but you are the only one I believe truly would.

It's not often that men in their twenties would drop everything for their uncle, but I know my sons would sell everything they own for you.

On Wednesdays, you host Pals' Night (guys only), which has always been a burr on my ass, except for the one night I was allowed to go. They look forward to it, and nothing could interfere except a death. That's dedication. There's a reason. You're a great man worth knowing—smart, funny (matter of opinion), dedicated, loyal, and generous to a fault. It has been an honor to be your little sister and friend.

A lot of people outgrow their siblings, but my respect for you continues to grow. The brothers in this series are loyal to one another, and I learned that from you.

If you haven't met my brother, I feel sorry for you, because he is a real-life superhero and has an amazing little sister. LOL! Love you, bro!

Table of Contents

Title Page
Copyright Page
Dedication
Note to the Reader
Chapter 1: "Angel" by Sarah McLachlan
Chapter 2: "Nobody Knows" by The Lumineers
Chapter 3: "Crash This Train" by Joshua James
Chapter 4: "In The End" by Linkin Park
Chapter 5: "Mad World" by Gary Jules
Chapter 6: "Wake Me Up" by Avicii
Chapter 7: "Broken Girl" by Matthew West
Chapter 8: "Lullaby" by Dixie Chicks
Chapter 9: "Head Above Water" by Avril Lavigne
Chapter 10: "Shadow Days" by John Mayer
Chapter 11: "Speak to a Girl" by Faith Hill & Tim McGraw
Chapter 12: "My Life, My Love" by ABBA
Chapter 13: "Heaven" by Kane Brown
Chapter 14: "She's Stronger Than Me" by Garth Brooks
Chapter 15: "One Man Band" by Old Dominion
Chapter 16: "Concrete Angel" by Martina McBride
Chapter 17: "Con Te Partiro" by Andrea Bocelli
Chapter 18: "Some Of It" by Eric Church
Chapter 19: "Miracle" by Foo Fighters
Chapter 20: "Happiness" by NEEDTOBREATHE
Epilogue: "Blessed" by Elton John
Thank you
Acknowledgments
Sneak Peek

Note to the reader:

I have included a small glossary of Italian slang words. Some Italians might disagree with the meaning, but it is slang and regional. The meanings used in this book are what I grew up knowing.

Bambini – Babies
Bambino/bambina – Baby boy/baby girl
Basta – That's enough
Bella – Beautiful
Bellissima – Gorgeous/very beautiful
Capisci – Do you understand?
Ciao – Hello or goodbye
Cara mia – My darling
Castagne – Chestnuts
Coglione – Asshole or male testicles
Cucciolo – Cub/puppy
Dolcezza – Sweetness
Dio mio – My God
Famiglia/famiglie – Family/families
Fanculo – Fuck
Il mio amore – My love
Pazzo – Crazy
Piccola amore – Little love
Shamo – Stupid/idiot
Stunad – Moron
Scustumad – Stupid person
Strega – Witch Additive Alessandro
Stella/Stellina – Star/little star
Squisita – Exquisite/delicious
Topolina – Little mouse
Va Bene – Alright
Vaffanculo – Fuck it

Chapter 1
"Angel" by Sarah McLachlan

Santino's heart slammed against his ribs. He had never seen such an incredible creature.

He examined her from his vantage point at the bottom of the stairs that were adjacent to the reception area. She was a beautiful young woman, but not in the trendy sense, with too much makeup and dressed to impress, like most of the girls her age. This little nymph was fresh; the innocent girl-next-door type with a side of adorable sexiness.

All the other women in their party wore short skirts or skimpy sundresses, whereas she wore a lilac scoop-neck T-shirt with white jean capris and white Keds. Her flawless, sun-kissed skin made him want to reach out and run his finger down the side of her face to confirm whether it was as soft as it looked. And her hair was silver-blonde, cascading halfway down her back in gentle ringlets. Having curly hair himself, Santino knew if he pulled on one of the loose corkscrews, it would extend down past her waist.

Feeling someone staring, the woman shifted her head toward him, and it was like a punch to his gut. Her eyes were like luminous, blueish-silver twinkling stars, becoming falling stars as she dropped her gaze from his. All he could think of was the Italian endearment Stellina, for little star. That was how he would secretly refer to her.

She stood beside an all-American jock who Santino was sure had been every college girl's dream. He even wore a college football jersey. Although handsome, he had a coldness emanating from his stance. If their roles were reversed and Santino was beside her, he would have had a possessive hand at the small of her back to let the world know Stellina belonged to him.

With a second look, he noticed the young woman stood slightly behind the jock, like she knew her place. It irked Santino that he didn't introduce her to Luca, who was checking them in, simply stating he was the groom, Jacob Moore.

Luca smiled at the young woman. "And are you the bride-to-be?"

The corners of her mouth tilted up as Stellina nodded, but she didn't give her name.

Oddly, Santino noticed the whole bridal party stood slightly away from her. Usually, the bride and the bridesmaids would be giggling and whispering together. Not this group.

Before they completed registering, each guest had to read and sign the terms and conditions of their stay, such as the rules of conduct and awareness that they could lose their damage deposit if anything was broken. Luca then handed out keys. Surprisingly, the bride-to-be and the groom were sharing a cabin, while the rest of the party shared cabins with the standard guys in half and girls in the others.

For over four years now, the Savage family had been successfully running Savage's Buck & Doe, a resort devoted to bachelor and bachelorette parties. The resort was located in the foothills of the mountains near New Tripoli, Pennsylvania. It was his mamma's dream and his dad's brainchild.

Valentina Savage, Santino's mamma, had wanted to open a bed and breakfast when her husband, Shawn, retired from the music industry. Unfortunately, both Shawn and Santino's oldest brother, Marcello, died before the resort opened. Therefore, the other four sons stepped into their dad's shoes and made their parents' dream a reality.

His three other brothers were all married now. Sabastian, the second oldest, had married Emmy, who was one of the chefs at the resort. They had an infant son named after the grandpa he never got to meet. Luca, the third, was married to Brooklyn, and they had a five-year-old son named Eli. Alessandro, the fourth, had just married Ava not too long ago. Santino was the fifth son, and the only single one left. He knew his time would come, but it definitely wouldn't be with Stellina.

In the years the resort had been open, Santino had never laid eyes on a female guest and felt such an overwhelming attraction. He knew it was not only against the rules for the staff to get involved with a visiting guest, but it went against his morals to lust after another man's fiancée.

He gave his head a shake. He had a job to do. So, pushing thoughts of Stellina away, he went to offer his assistance with the group's luggage, and to find their cabins. Theirs was the largest wedding party staying at the resort this weekend, and thankfully, the men offered to carry their own luggage, so Santino and Luca only had to take the women's.

Santino had just dollied two of the bridesmaids' luggage to their cabin and was heading back for more when he saw Jacob carrying his luggage with one hand. Irritation and disgust swept through him when he saw Stellina limping behind, carrying her own suitcase with a knapsack slung over her shoulder. He wondered if she had injured herself.

What kind of inconsiderate stunad didn't help his future wife, especially if she was hurt?

Santino reminded himself to stay neutral. They were his guests, and their relationship wasn't any of his business. However, when he was finished, he was definitely going to the kitchen to thank his mamma for raising him right.

When his task was completed, that was exactly what he did—

stormed into the kitchen. Alas, most of his famiglia was there and felt his tension.

"What the hell is wrong with you?" Sabastian asked.

Santino took a minute to think before speaking, knowing his mamma would fly over the counter and cuff him in the head if he used the language he wanted to right then. "I just can't believe how some guys are brought up. You would think they were reared by a pack of wild animals." He dropped himself onto a stool at the end of the large island and rubbed his hands down his face.

Luca, who knew exactly to what he was referring, explained to everyone what they had witnessed.

"Valentina, I can't tell you how thankful I am that you raised your sons with respect and kindness," Brooklyn, Luca's wife, responded first. "Now, speaking of being a good mom, I have to pick up Eli from his riding lesson."

Smiling, Valentina countered, "Thank you, dolcezza. I tried my best, but I still question myself on a daily basis." She had raised five sons basically alone, since her husband had traveled a lot with his job.

Still unsettled, Santino stood. "If it's okay with you, Brooklyn, I'd like to go get Eli. I need a break from all this crap, and nothing makes me feel better than spending time with either of my nephews."

When Brooklyn nodded, and before anyone could say a word, he pushed out of his chair and stalked out of the kitchen.

***

Chloe followed her fiancé into their cabin after a delicious early dinner, thankful she hadn't run into either of the brothers in the restaurant after they had seen her dragging her own luggage in.

The looks on their perturbed faces had been humiliating. She hated when people saw her limp, yet she couldn't very well hide it with the weight of her suitcase. And though Jacob wasn't gallant by any stretch of the imagination, she knew he loved her, and it had been so long since anyone had.

Chloe had been plagued with loneliness since her mom had died a month before she had started college, leaving her with no family. Everyone said you couldn't die of a broken heart, but Chloe was convinced that was exactly what her mother had died from. For seven years, she had watched her mom, Lori, slowly whittle away until her heart couldn't sustain her anymore.

With that thought fresh in her mind, tears stung the back of her eyes. She wouldn't allow them to fall, though, having learned years ago that her misery was hers alone. Instead, she compartmentalized her emotions and tried to think of the good things in her life. Except, she then thought of Jacob and how he was moodier than usual, which confused her.

Although he had a good heart, he was the type of man who was extremely hot and cold. For weeks, he had been excited about this trip. All he could talk about was the resort and this weekend. When she had mentioned how she wasn't sure if her boss would allow her time off, he had flipped out, so Chloe ended up trading several public holidays in order to get half of Wednesday, then Thursday and Friday off.

The couple had met in their last year of college. He had slowly befriended her after sitting beside her one day in their Understanding Stress Management class. He had talked to her each day about the course workload and his future plans. They had both been getting a Health Sciences degree. His father was the vice president of a large pharmaceutical company and wanted Jacob to follow in his footsteps, which meant starting from the ground up in sales. He had graduated eighth from the top of his class.

On the other hand, Chloe had become a mental health technician. She worked for an outreach program for younger veterans who needed help assimilating back into the workforce. Her job consisted of recording data of the veterans' abilities and willingness to participate in group therapy, as well as their demeanor. With the data she collected, she tried to find jobs they could be retrained for, in environments better suited to their changed personalities and comfort zones.

Most of her clients were reserved and unwilling to share emotionally. Chloe understood and respected their need for privacy, as well as their resistance to socialize. She worked around it, which had made her success rate skyrocket in the six months since she had been hired, to sixty-eight percent. In her mind and the project manager's, that was a huge success. Only time would tell how true the numbers were if the retraining was successful.

Her immediate supervisor was a bully, and because she was quiet and kept to herself, she had become an easy mark. Therefore, her time at the resort meant she wouldn't be getting off Labor Day, Columbus Day, or Veterans Day. In her mind, that was a contradiction in terms, seeing as how she supported veterans.

"Chloe? I called your name twice," Jacob said, coming out of the bedroom.

She shook her head, responding softly, "Sorry. I was lost in my head."

Slightly miffed, Jacob snapped, "I'm going with the guys to the bar before karaoke. The girls are pre-drinking in Brianna's cabin. They just ordered a shitload of booze. Why don't you join them?"

She looked down, moving the area rug with the toe of her shoe. Chloe wasn't like the girls in the wedding party, which consisted of Jacob's friends and family. Loners like her didn't have a big circle of companions to include in the mix. She didn't watch the latest TV shows, absolutely hated clubbing, and couldn't cook to save her life.

"You know I don't like drinking. I think I'll go for a walk. If that's okay?" She glanced up through her eyelashes, knowing she didn't need his approval, though she desperately wanted it. He had saved her from her lonely existence, and she didn't want to rock the boat.

Jacob softened for the first time in weeks. "Sure, babe, whatever you want." He moved forward and pecked her lips. Then, catching a hold of her shoulders, he told her, "I want this weekend to be something we'll both always remember. I know I've been a little off, but I've been stressed out about the big launch for the new antidepressant next month. I lost my focus planning our next four days, but I'm sure I'll be rejuvenated and raring to get back to work by Sunday."

She giggled. "Uh . . . said no one ever."

He grabbed her by the waist. "You even giggle softly; has anyone ever told you that? I've never met such a soft-spoken woman. Everyone you meet thinks you're so sweet and innocent, but I know the little devil that lives inside your unearthly image." He winked as he gave her ass a hard slap.

Jacob had a wicked sexual side. The things he made her do still had the power to embarrass her in broad daylight. He was domineering and liked rough sex, and she would do anything to please him.

Jacob was a charismatic, gorgeous-looking guy, the life of every party, a take-charge man with an outgoing personality. Girls were constantly making passes at him in front of her, but he never strayed. He was very opinionated and wanted control, but he would be a good husband and father. She would live comfortably in his shadow.

She still couldn't believe he was interested in a wallflower like her.

When Jacob had asked her to marry him, she had no problem agreeing to his friends' girlfriends being part of her wedding party. She would have preferred a quaint, small wedding because of her lack of friends and family, but Jacob wanted the whole nine yards. And since she loved him and wanted the future he promised, she had conceded.

After the wedding, Chloe would finally have what she had longed for—a family of her own and, God willing, lots of kids.

It had been so long since she had been part of a family. The exact moment she had lost everything replayed on an almost-constant loop in her mind.

Chloe and her sister were laughing and playing hopscotch at the end of the driveway. Harper had just jumped three spots, standing on one leg, when their mother stormed outside in tears, screaming at their father.

The girls stood frozen, listening to their mom threatening to leave for good.

They turned toward their father, who came to the door, screaming that she would regret it. They stood completely still, transfixed by their father's rage as their mom jumped into the car, backed up without looking, and instantly killed her sister.

There wasn't a day that went by when Chloe didn't miss her sister, Harper, who had not only been her best friend but also her identical twin.

Harper had been the vivacious, funny twin, whereas Chloe had been, and still was, the shy, reserved one. People had instantly fallen in love with Harper, and Chloe had lived vicariously in her sister's shadow. For ten years, they had been inseparable.

The void left after losing her twin had never lessened. She hoped having lots of children would fill it.

After one final kiss, her fiancé left. Then she grabbed her running shoes from her knapsack and her phone. She put her earbuds in and shoes on.

With thoughts of Harper fresh on her mind, she pushed the playlist devoted to her sister. Fresh tears gathered as Kenny Chesney sang "Who You'd Be Today," something Chloe had often wondered regarding Harper.

One of her greatest pleasures was walking and listening to music. Chloe had spent almost a year not being able to walk, so she viewed it as a privilege, and she did it as much as possible.

She had twenty-eight playlists and put them all to good use. Growing up, music had become her only constant companion. Today was all about country music, like most days, but she also liked classic rock and pop.

Heading off toward the trails she had heard about from Luca, she was rounding a bend when the song ended and the sound of guitars trickled through. She looked around and saw the man who had been staring at her in the reception area playing guitar with a little boy. She paused her playlist to listen to them as they relaxed under the shade of a tree.

The man played a chord, explaining what he was doing, and then he encouraged the child to repeat his actions. The little boy was concentrating so hard his little tongue was poking out of the side of his mouth.

Chloe saw the minute he messed up and lifted his frustrated eyes to his teacher.

"You're doing great, Eli. Try G again. Once you get these basic chords down, everything else will fall into place. You've got E minor and C major down pat, so just be patient. G major is a little more difficult."

The strawberry-blond head looked up at the man like he was his hero. "I want to play as good as you, Uncle Santino. I've being practicing E and C. Tonight, I'll practice G with Daddy."

Santino ruffled the little boy's hair. "You're way more advanced than I was at your age. Before you know it, you will be playing better than me."

"Weally? Cool! Wait till I tell Daddy." The boy then focused on getting his fingers in the right position.

Santino glanced up, seeing Stellina watching them. He smiled through the hair that fell in front of his eyes, and she smiled back, fiddling with her phone. He didn't want her to leave yet.

"Hi. Did you need help with anything?" Placing his guitar down, he rose to his feet, while telling the little boy that he would be right back.

The guy was well-built, tall, lean, and probably the hottest man she had ever laid eyes on. He stood about six feet tall with curly dark hair, heavy brows, and deep brown eyes that smoldered.

Chloe became more flustered the closer he came to her. "Uh . . . No. I'm just going for a walk." Looking over at the beautiful little boy, she said, "I didn't mean to disturb your lesson."

Santino followed her eyes to Eli, while battling with himself about keeping his distance. This woman made him want to break all the rules.

"That's my nephew, Eli. And I'm Santino." He smiled at her. "I'm sorry. I didn't catch your name when you registered."

"Um . . . Hi, I'm Chloe." She turned to leave. "Well, I better let you get back."

"Chloe?" He waited for her to turn back around. "You only have about two and a half hours of sunlight left, so make sure you don't go too far, and stay on the designated paths."

She bestowed upon him a heartfelt smile. That was the first time a stranger had actually cared for her well-being. "I will. Thank you, Santino. That was very kind."

The sound of her soft, feminine voice did funny things to his insides . . . and so did the sway of her retreating hips, even with the slight limp.

Shaking his head, he couldn't help wondering why all the good ones were taken.

Heading back to Eli helped remind him that he had to be the kind of man a young boy could look up to and respect.

Santino had been blessed with the best male role model growing up. His dad had been a gentleman through and through, and highly regarded by friends and family alike. Nothing was more important to Shawn than his wife and sons.

His dad had believed in love at first sight and was convinced that, when each of his boys met the right woman, they would also fall hard and fast. It had held true with his brothers.

His dad had often told the story of how his parents had met when Shawn traveled to the Umbria Jazz Festival in Italy. Shawn had heard the eighteen-year-old hometown favorite sing, and then saw her in the crowd. One look and he was hooked. Then, in less than six weeks, his parents had fallen deeply in love, married, and had moved to America.

As much as Santino knew his dad loved his sons, their mamma had been his world. Valentina was a beautiful spitfire who had raised five sons with an iron fist and an abundance of love.

Shawn Savage had been the best musician Santino had ever heard, and had taught his sons everything he knew. His dad's job had been exciting—traveling with bands that needed a larger stage presence while touring. He had never accepted any offers for a full-time position in a band, though. He had loved music in all its forms and had loved the limelight for only limited spurts. However, he had hated the drama and invasion of privacy that accompanied fame and fortune.

After touring with one band, he would come home for a month or two, then start a new tour with a new band. He had kept to North American tours so he was always a short flight away if Valentina had needed him. Santino had to give his mamma credit. Not many women would put up with such a grueling schedule, but they had somehow made it work, and his absences only made their hearts grow fonder.

As the boys had grown, so had their musical talents. Shawn would take one or more of the boys to accompany him on tours during school breaks. The bands were so impressed with the young Savages' talents, always including them on their tour for any length of time they were with them. Many times, they had requested one of the brothers during the summer.

Shawn was very proud of his sons, using the time they had together to teach them life's most important lessons. On the top of Shawn's list was respect and loyalty for famiglia and women. By showing the boys the pitfalls of fame, he was able to take the lust and lure away, ensuring they could have successful careers in the industry without sacrificing their morals or integrity. The times Santino traveled with his dad had been some of the best of his childhood memories. But, as they say, all good things come to an end.

Santino had learned that lesson the hard way when a narcissistic psychopath shot and killed fifty-eight people at a music festival. Santino wanted to believe the shooter was ill, but he didn't believe the monster who had gunned down his dad and oldest brother was anything except pure evil. Even the authorities and the psychoanalysts had tried to convince the public that the asshole was depressed or mentally ill. However, Santino had times in his life when he was depressed, and a lot of people suffered from mental illness, but they didn't gun down innocents.

Santino would never buy into that explanation. He believed the shooter was a nefarious, depraved man who didn't have a good bone in his body or an ounce of love in his heart. He was the devil, born from evil people, and had probably transferred his vileness to the next generation.

The only time Santino ever believed he could possibly be capable of murder had been not too long ago, when Mamma had confessed she had tried to slit her wrists shortly after the murders, when the weight of her sorrow had become too much to bear. She had cried during her confession, mad at God and the world. Mamma had said, if the shooter hadn't died, she would have spent every dime they had making sure she stalked and killed everyone he loved, and then slit his throat. That was what evil could do to a good person.

It was hard to imagine he could have lost yet one more person he loved to that evil man. He would forever search for answers as to why.

Santino remembered going to his dad's gravesite and asking him if a good person could become evil or was it in their genetic makeup. One look at his dad's picture had made him realize that, even if the shooter had survived, his mamma could never have done those things.

Recently, his mamma had shocked them all when she had started dating Quinn, their famiglia therapist. She had sworn she would never love again, but she was so lonely, and time had started to heal her wounds.

Quinn had to pass their case on to another therapist after realizing his attraction to Valentina. Although Santino had another therapist, he still referred more often to Quinn. The man was caring, smart, and genuinely led them to discover their own answers to most problems.

Everyone was moving on and creating new bonds for themselves in the aftermath of the massacre, except for Santino. Maybe he was looking too hard. His dad had sworn he would have that magical moment when he would know the right girl had come along. The problem was that he automatically searched for that elusive feeling with every girl he dated, yet it never happened. He had met so many single women at the resort, exchanged numbers, and dated a few after their visit, but he never felt any sparks. He allowed his friends to set him up, but still nothing. It was just his luck that the first time he felt anything real for a woman, she was engaged.

Half an hour later, Eli was begging him to go swimming in the resort's pond. Santino couldn't think of anything he wanted to do more, as it was hotter than usual for an August evening, so they raced to Eli's cabin first to change, then to his, and were in the water in under fifteen minutes.

They had been horsing around for an hour when Santino spotted Stellina again. She was sweating from her walk, still oblivious to the world around her, lost in her music. Her limp was a little more pronounced.

Seeing her stirred those feelings again.

Disgusted with himself, he looked away.

"Eli, we have to get out. I have to get ready for tonight's event with the guests."

"Aw . . . Can we swim tomorrow?"

"I can't make any promises yet. I have no idea what your parents have planned. But if we're both free, I'd love to. We'll have to hurry up, because I didn't realize how late it was."

He bundled Eli up in a towel and took him back to Brooklyn and Luca. Thirty minutes later, he was dressed and setting up for karaoke outdoors.

All the different wedding parties were attending, so he had the staff stock the outdoor bar.

He loved when they could do it outside, opposed to the dance studio, because drinks inevitably got spilled.

When Alessandro joined him, they started the music. It didn't take long for groups of guests to gather.

Alessandro started the karaoke by singing "Paradise by the Dashboard Light" by Meat Loaf. Everyone went wild, joining in, and singing out loud while dancing.

Santino then started a list of groups or singles who wanted to sing, cueing the machine. It was amazing to him how the same songs were requested each week.

The first group of girls came up to the microphones. They butchered Beyoncé's "Single Ladies," but they were having fun, and that was all that mattered. The guys in their group countered the girls' song with "Born to Run" by Bruce Springsteen. It was game on after that, with all the bridal parties requesting one hit after another, trying to outdo each other.

Three hours later, Jacob Moore requested The Rolling Stones "(I Can't Get No) Satisfaction," and his bridal party went crazy. The song was like an inside joke that only those closest to him were privy to, except Chloe, who sat back on a log bench, shoulders curved in and hands between her knees as she bit her lip. The drunken party laughed louder and kept looking from Jacob to her, encouraging him on. Chloe was confused, and it showed. They were making a spectacle of her, making her insecurities flare.

Alessandro nudged Santino and nodded toward Chloe.

The hair on his neck prickled at seeing her so defenseless, a need to protect her burning through his body.

He looked back at Alessandro. Something wasn't right, and they both knew it. They both agreed to watch the group a little closer as the weekend unfurled. But right now, the only thing Santino could do was use music to make a point.

With a click of his fingers, he replaced the next song with his own choice, and when Jacob was done, he snagged the microphone and lifted his index finger to the group waiting next. They understood when the instrumental for "Better Man" by Pearl Jam started. Santino's baritone growl was a perfect fit for the song.

He looked at Stellina and sang her the first verse, then the second to Jacob. Jacob smirked at Santino like this was exactly what he had been hoping for.

Not getting any satisfaction, Santino looked at each member of the jerk's bridal party, who were as smug as the groom. For the life of him, he couldn't figure out what was going on.

When he finished, he passed the microphone to the next group as a few people converged to tell him how amazing he sounded.

When he made his way back to his brother, he whispered in Alessandro's ear, "They're up to something, and I have a feeling Stellina is the brunt of their plan. I just don't get it."

Alessandro pulled back, looking at his brother like he had grown an extra nose. "Stellina? I thought her name was Chloe. But you're right, coglione. I feel it too. It's like nothing I've ever felt before with any guests. Trouble is definitely brewing."

"Right, her name is Chloe. I made a mistake."

Alessandro gave him a look like you're shitting me. "Oh, I can see how Stellina sounds like Chloe." Then he got serious. "I think we should have an emergency meeting tomorrow morning; let the famiglia know to keep an eye open. There's way more going on here than a group celebrating an upcoming wedding."

"I'm afraid to let her out of my sight. I swear, if they hurt her—"

"Don't do anything stupid, coglione. We could be wrong."

The next song was ready to start when Jacob asked them to stop, grabbing the microphone. The brothers watched as the man called out to his fiancée.

"Chloe, I know you hate being the center of attention, but babe, I want you to sing me a song."

Chloe shook her head, eyes lit up like a deer caught in the headlights, fear written all over her face.

"She's doesn't want to," he defended the poor woman. Santino couldn't figure what he was up to.

Jacob glared at him, then turned back to Chloe. "Please. I never ask you for anything."

The bridal party started to chant, "Chloe, Chloe!" and the rest of the parties joined in.

Chloe was so uncomfortable, but he was right; he had never asked her for anything. So, she stood as they all clapped, her legs shaking so badly that she stumbled and fell back to her spot.

Santino's knee jerked forward, ready to assist her. However, Alessandro grabbed his arm as Jacob went to help her up.

"You can do it, babe. I've heard you sing; you're good. Sing this for me. I need to hear it from you."

Stepping up, Chloe took the microphone with shaking hands, keeping her eyes on the karaoke screen. The song was "Angel" by Sarah McLachlan. She had it on her Harper playlist and knew every word by heart. Nodding to Alessandro to start, she took a deep breath, then sang the first verse.

Santino stumbled back, bumping his hip against the table that held the equipment. Stellina's voice was amazing. It was soft, light, breathy, but most of all, angelic. Everyone standing there was affected by it and the words she sang.

Santino looked at Jacob, stunned that the man looked completely floored, with fury in his eyes. Then, as Chloe finished the last line, Jacob turned and walked away without a word to anyone.

The Savage brothers were mystified as they watched Chloe just stand there, uncertain of what had happened. Whatever it was, it was big, causing a chill to travel down both their spines. There was a storm brewing, and they were frightened about who would be left standing when it was over.

Chapter 2
"Nobody Knows" by The Lumineers

The famiglia had their early morning emergency meeting. Now all of them had been made aware of what had happened the night before, and that the young woman needed to be watched.

She had barely touched her breakfast and now stood in the kitchen, taking Valentina's cooking class. Chloe was exceptionally quiet, and the girls of her wedding party seemed extremely arrogant with her unease.

"Carina, do you have any cooking experience?"

Chloe shook her head, while tucking her hands deep into the front pockets of her jeans. Valentina could tell she was beyond self-conscious.

"Carina, it's not a sin, and I can teach you a few things that you could cook for your future husband. I'm a firm believer that the quickest way to a man's heart is through his stomach." She smiled at the hopefulness in Chloe's eyes.

The snickers from the other girls annoyed Valentina. She knew without a shadow of a doubt that these young women were bullies, and that didn't sit well with her.

"Her name is Chloe," one had the audacity to chirp.

Valentina spied the mouthy one. "Yes, we know who all of you are. Carina means cute or cutie, and she certainly is that. A beautiful little angel."

"Harrumph!" The mouthy one wouldn't let it go. "Oh, I think we all have a little bit of evil in us." She looked directly at Chloe. "Some much more than others."

That comment triggered the others to agree with quiet chit-chat, whispering behind their hands to each other.

Chloe wished she could disappear. Everything had gone sour after her karaoke performance last night. She couldn't understand the hostility that the wedding party was tossing at her. Jacob had asked for the song, yet the anger pouring off him when she had returned to the cabin had been baffling. She had made sure to stay clear of him until he had fallen asleep.

When Valentina asked about the women's cooking experience, everyone except Chloe had some foundation. It broke her heart when Chloe confessed to living off frozen dinners and take-out. The girls were all too happy to tattle that she couldn't even boil an egg or cook that boxed macaroni and cheese stuff with any success. They continued laughing at her, asking if she expected Jacob to live off frozen meals.

Now Valentina understood her sons' concern regarding this group. Something was off.

The need to protect this young woman was overwhelming as she handed out tasks to all the girls, keeping Chloe beside her, teaching her how to make meatballs. At one point, she led Chloe into the pantry to grab some ingredients.

"Carina, I'm not trying to butt into your personal business, but I'm not entirely comfortable with how your friends are treating you. It's not right. You don't have to put up with it."

Embarrassed, Chloe whispered, "I don't have any friends. They are Jacob's friends. They mean a lot to him, and I want to make him happy. They're right, though; what girl doesn't even know how to make boxed mac and cheese?

"My mom didn't cook when I was small, and we used a

microwave a lot. We didn't have cable, so I didn't watch cooking shows. But I want to be a good wife to my husband. Please, Valentina, teach me how to cook. I don't have a lot to offer my fiancé."

The tightness in Valentina's chest was staggering. Chloe reminded her of Reece, Brooklyn's brother, when he had been a teenager. Like him, this little carina had not had the best life, and it crushed her that she was so insecure. The girl was starving for acceptance and love from anyone. She was sure there was a story behind those sad eyes.

"You have a beautiful soul, and that is much more important than anything else. I want you to remember that."

By the time they got back to the kitchen, the other girls had obviously also had a private discussion. They acknowledged the favoritism Valentina showed Chloe, and even encouraged it. That was another red flag for Valentina.

When the class finished, she was even more concerned. She would need a week to teach Chloe enough to prepare a decent meal. The girl didn't have a clue, and everything Valentina had demonstrated hadn't been absorbed because she was so inhibited.

The guys in their party joined the girls in the dining room for lunch, to enjoy the fruits of the women's labor. Valentina watched from the door as the bridesmaids told Jacob that Chloe was the teacher's pet.

With condescension, he turned to Chloe. "Using your shyness to get out of work won't make a good wife."

Clueless as to why Jacob had become so exasperated with her, and embarrassed at the attention, she tried to pacify him, answering softly, "I want to learn to be the best wife I can be to you."

"Sometimes, wanting something isn't enough. At least you're pretty."

The mouthy girl grinned. "Beauty fades, and then what are you left with?"

As Chloe's eyes filled with tears, Valentina geared up to go to battle on her behalf, but Santino blocked his mamma from stepping out of the kitchen, forcibly using his body to guide her back inside. "Ma, back off. You won't be helping; you'll only make it worse."

Santino had witnessed the whole exchange too, and was also furious, but he knew if his mamma said anything in her current state, it would only be detrimental to Stellina.

Valentina slapped her son's arm out of frustration. "Shamo, someone needs to stand up for her. Those people are heartless. I've never seen such disrespect for another person's feelings. If she marries him, her life will be hell. It makes me sick to my stomach." She stepped toward the counter and slammed a few pots around.

"I get it, Ma. I feel the same way. Something weird is going on." He ran his hands through his hair. "Give us a couple of days to keep an eye on her. Don't get involved. It isn't going to be easy, but you have to give us some time. We think the groom might be physically abusing her, but Sabastian called Keith this morning, and he said the police can't legally do anything until we see something. Don't give them a reason to pretend in front of us. Please, Ma."

She threw the sauce pot into the sink with more force than necessary. "What is the world coming to? She's like a little bird with a broken wing, being tormented by a group of cats. It's killing me. How can she think that's acceptable?" She turned the faucet on full blast, the water hitting the pot and spraying everywhere. She quickly grabbed the handle, turning the pressure down. "I think she was abused long before that monster zeroed in on her demeanor and decided to continue the cycle." Valentina turned toward her son, her eyes swimming. "We have to help her."

Santino went to the sink and turned off the water before gathering her in his arms. "I know, Ma. But we can't give him reasons to make it worse on her. She's way too complacent. It's obvious she doesn't know any different.

"Chloe likes to walk, so I'm sure she'll head out after her photo shoot with Brooklyn this afternoon. I'll catch up and see if she'll confide in me. If I find out he's hurting her, I'll offer for her to stay at my cabin until she can get a clean break from him."

Valentina pulled back. "No, I want her to stay with me if you can convince her. I want to teach Chloe that kind of treatment isn't acceptable from a boyfriend, husband, or friends."

"You're right. Look at how Emmy blossomed under your affection." Santino kissed the top of his mamma's head. "I know it's wrong, but honestly, Ma, I'm attracted to that woman. I could easily fall in love with her. I have this desire to take care of her and show her how a man should treat a woman. I've never felt like this before."

Pulling back, Valentina brushed a curl of hair from his eyes and said tenderly, "Santino, you're not falling in love with Chloe. What you're experiencing is empathy toward a woman that you suspect is in an abusive relationship. You want to save her from herself and him.

"Quinn and I talked about abuse after watching a TV show. He said domestic violence is complicated, and most women go back an average of seven times before they escape. It's honorable you want to help Chloe, but don't confuse rescuing someone for love. Realistically, we have to accept she's engaged to that man and, in all likelihood, she'll leave here and marry him."

His mamma might be right, but he had been attracted to her even before he thought Stellina was being abused. He knew the way she was being treated had nothing to do with the attraction he felt for her.

In order to avoid an argument, Santino said, "You're probably right. I just feel so helpless. I know she's in love with that coglione, so I would never overstep. You raised me better than that." Pacifying her, he kissed both of her cheeks, then went to shower, since he had just returned from taking the guys fishing.

Meanwhile, after lunch, Chloe passed on the massage that had been booked for her and opted for a manicure and pedicure instead. Now that her nails were dry, she was hoping to go for a walk to unwind. However, she couldn't have been more surprised when the spa girl whisked her into a boudoir studio inside the spa.

The photographer, Brooklyn, had met with Jacob in the reception area while the girls were having their spa treatments. Jacob had said he was surprising his fiancée with the photo shoot, requesting a sexy book with beautiful, risqué outfits he was providing. Handing them over, he had explained that Chloe had some scars she was self-conscious about, but he wanted her to embrace who she was.

Everything he had said went against what Brooklyn had heard from her husband and brothers-in-law about this man. Brooklyn decided to believe Jacob had the best of intentions and promised she would do everything in her power to make it a good experience for Chloe.

The petite woman entered the studio, her body language screaming terror and self-consciousness. Brooklyn wanted to put her at ease.

"Hi, Chloe. I'm Brooklyn, the photographer. I know this can be intimidating. Most girls who walk in here are nervous, but I promise to make it fun for you."

Speaking softly after taking a big gulp of air, Chloe said, "Nice to meet you, Brooklyn. I'm really scared. Jacob didn't tell me that I'd be taking erotic pictures. I want to make him happy, but I'm not sexy. I'm . . ." She dropped her head, wringing her hands. How did she explain that she didn't have a sultry bone in her body?

Brooklyn saw the insecurities overwhelm her. "I understand. Please sit down, and let's talk for a minute." She gestured to two chairs. "Most girls who come in here feel exactly the same way. I promise you that I will make the pictures classy and beyond alluring.

Jacob will absolutely love them.

"I met with your fiancé. He bought some very beautiful pieces of lingerie for you. I've hung them up behind the screen. He seemed very enthusiastic and wants you to embrace the experience and be proud of your body. The way he talked about you, he thinks you're gorgeous and thinks this is a way for you to see yourself as he sees you. He even picked the poses he wants. If you put your trust in me, I promise it will be the perfect gift for you to give him."

Chloe sat a little taller. If she swallowed her pride and did what he wanted, maybe it would change the hostility he seemed to harbor against her.

She agreed, moving behind the screen to change. However, her confidence plummeted again when she tried on the first piece. It was a skimpy bustier with laces and a see-through thong with garters. She looked down, panicking, then changed into a see-through, lace, baby doll nightie with ribbons. It was even more provocative, putting everything on display.

Chloe stood behind the screen with tears welling up, angry at herself for being so childish. She needed to prove to Jacob that she was a woman and not a baby.

Finally, she stepped out from behind the screen, wearing a short satin lace robe that covered up the see-through nightie, knowing that she would be nearly naked and would never relax when she took it off.

"Ready?" Brooklyn asked softly. The poor girl was shaking.

Chloe shook her head, close to falling apart. "I can't do it. You'll never understand. Your body is beautiful. Mine isn't. I don't know why Jacob loves me. I can't cook, I don't talk much, and my body is repulsive." She lowered her eyes, pulling the tie tighter around her waist. This whole weekend was a disaster. If Jacob had been having any second thoughts before, they would be cemented now. She was going to lose the only good thing that had happened to her.

"Chloe, things aren't always as they appear. My body has been my nemesis my whole life. It brought me all kinds of unwanted attention. People never saw the woman behind the boobs.

"Your beauty radiates. If you put just a little bit of faith in me, I will take the sexiest, most tasteful pictures you have ever seen. I promise your fiancé will be blown away."

Not knowing what else to do, Chloe nodded.

Brooklyn positioned her against the bedpost. "Lift your left leg and rest it on the bedframe. Now extend your arms down, holding the bedpost. I'm just going to lower the side of the robe to show only your shoulder." The fear in her eyes was tangible, so Brooklyn tried another approach. "Close your eyes and just lean your head against the post. Chin up."

Chloe bit the inside of her cheek, which added to her sexy look.

Brooklyn stood back and took a few shots.

"I'm going to reposition your hair so nothing is exposed as I remove the robe." Brooklyn shifted the material down, letting it pool on the floor around her feet. Then she adjusted Chloe's long locks so some of it hid both her nipples. She snapped a few shots from different angles.

Looking at the viewfinder, she was thrilled with the results. "Look at these."

Chloe opened her eyes and looked at the viewfinder. They didn't show the nitty-gritty and actually looked really good. Brooklyn was right; they were sexy.

She smiled. "Maybe I can do this."

A satisfied smile bloomed on Brooklyn's face. "Work with me, and I promise everyone will be happy with the results." She turned, opening an antique armoire and asking Chloe's shoe size. "Here, put these on."

Not being able to stand in stilettos because of her bum leg, Chloe lost the little bit of confidence she had gained.

Her frustrated mumbles about her leg were so soft that Brooklyn had to concentrate to hear what she was saying.

"I'm sorry. I didn't know your leg gave you trouble. Don't worry about the shoes. Take them off. I'll work around it. Trust me; I do know how an impairment can make you feel. I had a tumor and was mute up until two years ago."

Stunned and feeling silly for making such a fuss, Chloe relaxed.

When she got comfortable again, Brooklyn started asking questions, hoping to get some insight for the famiglia. "Do you mind if I ask what type of injury you had?"

The half-truths she had been spouting to different doctors her whole life fell out naturally. "I was caught in a fire and had to jump out a third-story window when I was eleven. I broke my hip and my leg in two places."

"Oh my goodness, I'm so sorry. That must have been so painful." Brooklyn's raspy voice was clogged with emotion.

"Yes, it was. But against the odds, I survived. The pins in my legs and my partial hip replacement don't allow me to move as freely as I used to. I'm sure you can see my left leg is disfigured. Can you hide it?"

Brooklyn nodded. "I can, but it's not that bad. I really think you should embrace those scars. You survived something horrific and should be proud. The fact that you can walk at all is a miracle.

"I'll take shots both ways. I won't share any with your fiancé until you approve them. We can delete anything you don't like. How's that?"

"That would be great. Thank you. You're really nice."

"I had a bit of a rough go before I married Luca, and I don't have a lot of friends. Just my sisters-in-law and my ex-dance partner, Raimer. I would love to be your friend. How about after you leave the resort, we keep in touch?"

"Really?" Chloe's eyes expanded. "I don't have any friends, and I don't have any family left. I'm sort of a loner."

Brooklyn lifted her hand for a high-five. "I hear ya, sister. That was me three years ago. Do you live in Allentown?"

Chloe smiled, slapping Brooklyn's hand. "Yeah. I'm originally from the South, although my maternal grandparents lived in Allentown before they passed away. Jacob was from there, so after college, I moved here into my grandparents' old abandoned house outside of town. I made it livable and hope to sell it before I get married."

"Where in the South?"

Chloe squirmed. "I was born in Texas, but I moved to Alabama when I was young."

"I would never have guessed. You don't have an accent," Brooklyn told her as she moved around to set up the next shot. "Let's not forget to exchange numbers before you leave. Maybe next week I could bring my son over to meet you."

Chloe's lips spread into a beautiful big smile when she realized the connection. "Is your son Eli? I met him when Santino was giving him guitar lessons yesterday. He's adorable. Such a happy, outgoing little boy. I would really like it if you both would visit me. I love kids."

The smile Brooklyn gave her back was comparable. "Thank you. He is the light of my life, and he thrives at the resort with all the male attention. We would love to visit. Give me your address, and we'll come by on whatever day works for you."

Chloe felt like she was going to bust with excitement. "I want as many kids as Jacob will let me have. I want nothing more than a big family. Are you going to have more?"

Stopping, Brooklyn decided to confide in her new friend. "Can you keep a secret?"

Chloe nodded.

"I'm pregnant, but no one knows yet."

Awe covered Chloe's face. "Wow, congratulations! That's so exciting. I bet your husband will be thrilled."

She laughed. "Maybe for two seconds, until he finds out we're having twins. Then he might feel differently."

Chloe's eyes filled with pain. "I had a twin sister. I loved Harper so much. That's so exciting. I would give anything to have twins."

Dread filled Brooklyn. There was no doubt in her mind that this poor girl's twin and the rest of her family had died in the fire.

Quickly turning the conversation away from Chloe's sadness, she said, "I bet that because you are a twin, the odds are pretty good that you'll have them too. I've been planning a special date for my husband on Monday night to tell him. I'll definitely let you know how he reacts to the news. I'm nervous, so thanks for listening to me and for being a good friend. Now, why don't you change into the bustier ensemble, and we'll take the rest of the shots on the bed with the heels."

Throughout the rest of the shoot, Brooklyn continued to put the young woman at ease, and near the end, Chloe conceded to a few more risqué shots. Brooklyn then showed her a few, and even promised to print three super-hot ones so Chloe could give Jacob a little tease before the book was finished.

After Chloe changed back into her own clothes, they looked over the shots on the computer. Chloe was thrilled, not believing the woman in the pictures was her. In the end, she let Brooklyn choose the pictures she thought were best. Then Brooklyn handed her the printed ones in an envelope before giving her a hug.

Chloe left the studio after thanking Brooklyn profusely in her gentle, whimsical voice, proud of herself and convinced the teasers would go a long way in smoothing the waters with Jacob.

Relieved the bridesmaids had left the spa and she wouldn't have to see them, she went back to her cabin to leave the pictures on the bed for Jacob before escaping on a walk.

Santino was in the reception area when he saw Chloe happily leaving the spa. He went straight to Brooklyn to see if she had managed to gather any information, quietly entering her studio and nearly swallowing his tongue when he saw the pictures Brooklyn was scanning. Stellina looked so fucking sexy that he couldn't hold back the whoosh of air that escaped his lungs.

Brooklyn twisted around, seeing his expression. Then she quickly turned back, shutting the lid of the computer. "That's an invasion of privacy. Did you forget how to knock?" she snapped in annoyance.

"Sorry." He knew he had screwed up, because Brooklyn never got mad. "I saw Chloe leave and wanted to catch up with her, but I wanted to know if you learned anything first."

Still vexed, she responded, "You can never tell anyone you saw those pictures. Chloe would be devastated."

He ran his hands through his hair. "Of course, I would never hurt her like that. Really, I'm sorry. I'm just worried about her."

Brooklyn softened, knowing intrinsically that Santino was one of the most stand-up men she knew. "I know. I overreacted. I'm sorry too. It's just . . . Chloe and I became friends, and I feel like I have to protect her. I learned a lot about her, but most of it is private. I also talked to her fiancé before the shoot . . . Maybe you guys are wrong. He seemed really caring. I think he loves her, and I know she loves him."

Santino didn't expect the blast to the gut he felt at hearing that. He rubbed his hands through his curls, then down to his goatee. "I wish I believed you, but you haven't seen them together. The way the guy treats her is disgusting. I feel it in my bones that something is terribly wrong. Don't ask me how I know. I just do. If someone doesn't step in, something very bad is going to happen to Chloe."

Standing, she went to him and placed a hand on his shoulder.

When he lifted his eyes, Brooklyn spoke. "I hope you're wrong. I admire that you're trying to help her. Without you, I don't know how I would have survived Reece's death, and we wouldn't have Alessandro home. I know you, Santino. You have the biggest heart of any man I've ever met, but you have to accept that Chloe might not need saving."

Santino shook her hand off as he stood. "For Chloe's sake, I hope you're right. But I have a gut feeling he's abusing her, and if I find out he is, there is going to be hell to pay."

Brooklyn wasn't convinced after her time with Chloe, but she also knew the family never got involved in guests' lives. "If it helps, we exchanged numbers, and she gave me her address. I'm going to visit her next week with Eli. I'll try to find out more then."

He tensed. "You shouldn't go there if Jacob is there, especially with Eli. I don't trust the guy as far as I can throw him. You might think he's a good guy, but Brooklyn, the guy is a mean prick who has no respect for women." Turning toward the door, he looked over his shoulder. "The whole situation is fucked up."

As he stepped through the threshold, she said, "Wait. I don't think it's a secret, so I can tell you that she doesn't have any family. There was a fire when she was younger; that's how she hurt her leg. It sounded to me like that's how she lost most of her family."

That was a blow to his heart. He knew firsthand how hard it was to lose your famiglia to a tragedy.

Turning back to look at her before walking out, he said, "That only makes me want to protect her more. She has no family, and her fiancé and friends treat her like shit." He trudged away, knowing he didn't have much time if he wanted a chance to speak to Chloe alone.

As luck would have it, he saw her heading toward the path up the mountain.

He had almost caught up when he called out to her. It took a couple of shouts before she heard him over the music playing in her earbuds.

She startled and turned. "Were you calling me?" she asked, taking one of the earbuds out.

Smiling, he responded, "Yeah, I saw you going for a walk, and it's such a nice day, so I thought I'd join you. We worry about guests walking alone in the mountains."

Chloe knew in her heart that Jacob would not approve, but she wasn't sure how to tell Santino that. "Um . . . I guess. Or maybe I should just go back."

He picked up on her uneasiness, which made him want to know even more if it was because she was afraid of her fiancé. "It's up to you, but just so you know, I'm the guide your group will be hiking with tomorrow. I know these mountains like the back of my hands, and I like to check the path before I take a group. If you're uncomfortable with me alone, I understand. I'll go early tomorrow and make sure the path is clear of falling trees or rocks. Have a nice walk, Chloe." He turned, heading back toward the main lodge.

"Wait."

Santino twisted around, looking at her.

"I'm not trying to be rude. I just don't think my fiancé would like me being alone with another man. I know it's stupid, but I would feel the same way if he was alone with another girl. I hope you understand."

That irked him. "I don't, actually. I believe you should trust the person you're going to spend your life with. If you were my fiancée and I knew you enjoyed walking, I'd go with you."

His holier-than-thou attitude and his jab at Jacob made Chloe mad. "I do trust Jacob, and he trusts me. I just don't think it's proper. Call me old-fashioned. I don't care. He's out with his friends and doesn't know I went for a walk. I'm a big girl and can walk by myself.

Have a nice day." She swung around and headed back up the path.

Santino could tell by her body language that she had taken offense to his comment, but her soft voice made it hard to take her seriously. He was happy to see she had a backbone.

He jogged up to her retreating back. "Wait, Chloe." He didn't want to insult her beliefs or make her time at the resort worse than it already was. When she looked over her shoulder, he continued, "I'm sorry. I was out of line. It just makes me crazy nervous when people hike alone, especially a woman, because there are black bears, three types of venomous snakes, coyotes, and even mountain lions in these mountains. I always carry a whistle or air horn to scare them off and a knife just in case. I'm not trying to freak you out. It's rare that you'd see any of those animals, but I think you should have someone to walk with; that's why I offered. It's better to be safe than sorry."

Her beautiful eyes were huge. "I had no idea. I guess you think I'm an idiot for not considering the wildlife. I just really needed to unwind, and walking is my salvation."

"Then let me walk with you, and I can check the path for hazards. We'll kill two birds with one stone." Hopefully.

He waited while she chewed on her lip with indecision.

"Okay, but I have to warn you, I'm not much of a talker." She pulled her earbuds out.

"No problem. If you want to listen to your music, go ahead. And I hope you sing along because your voice is amazing. We're a famiglia of musicians, but my older brother Sabastian is the best singer out of all of us."

She smiled as she walked. "I figured that out when I saw you giving lessons to your nephew and heard you and Alessandro sing last night. That was the first time I ever sang in front of anyone. I'm more of a closet singer."

Santino chuckled. "So you sing in the shower?"

Blushing, she answered, "No, I've never sung in the shower, but I love to crank my radio up and sing my heart out when I'm driving. Of course, the windows are up. I'm sure I look like a nutbar."

"Oh, I don't believe that for a minute. What were you just listening to? I heard you softly singing when I walked up. I swear I had the title on the tip of my tongue."

"I didn't even realize I was singing out loud. It was 'Nobody Knows' by The Lumineers."

She stumbled on a tree root, and he caught her forearm before she face-planted.

"Be careful." Steadying her, he then knelt so she wouldn't be embarrassed. "Let me cut that out before someone else falls and breaks their neck. By the way, I love that song. I used to listen to it a lot after my brother and dad were murdered." Santino heard her gasp. "Music really helped me when I lost them. It kind of makes you feel not so alone." He stood up, seeing she was struggling not to tear up.

"I'm sorry for your loss. I lost my family, too, so I know what you mean. Music has always made me feel better. I think that's why I love to listen to it when I walk. Somehow, I feel closer to them."

"I'm also sorry for your loss. I guess we have a lot in common." Now he needed her to relax and to gain her trust, becoming the friend she deserved. "Tell me some of your favorite songs."

A gentle giggle escaped. "I couldn't begin to list my favorites. I love them all, and have hundreds. I should have bought shares in iTunes. I think it would have been cheaper than purchasing them all."

"Me too. I'll give you the first five that pop into my head, and then you give me five of yours."

They walked for a couple of hours, sharing their love of music, which was very similar.

When they got back down the mountain, Santino wished her a good evening, happy that the seed of friendship was planted. If anything happened, he might be able to convince her to stay at the resort.

Chapter 3
"Crash This Train" by Joshua James

The famiglia kept a close eye on the Moore wedding party. Thankfully, no one saw any evidence of physical abuse, although everyone felt the tension surrounding the group as it grew in leaps and bounds. The air felt the same as before a thunderstorm—charged, ready to ignite. Consequently, almost all the famiglia had decided to attend the bonfire sing-along scheduled for that night, just in case. Quinn was also there. He had started attending every week, never getting enough of hearing Valentina's singing. Emmy was the only one missing, having volunteered to babysit Eli at their cabin with little Shawn.

Jacob had given his future bride a beautiful white sundress the night before, and had asked her to put the white daisies he picked in her hair. When she came out of the bathroom, he was blown away.

"Holy shit, you look gorgeous, like an angel."

Feeling beautiful for the first time in so long, Chloe radiated, lifting the floor-length dress up and spinning. "It's the dress. It's heavenly, and I feel amazing in it. I hope I can find a wedding dress that makes me feel exactly the same way."

Jacob pulled her into his arms, hugging her tightly. "You'll get exactly what you deserve, babe. Always remember that. I want to hear you sing tonight. Knock their socks off."

Chloe stiffened. "I don't think that's a good idea. I upset you last time. I want our last night here to be perfect."

He pulled her back to look in her eyes. "Everything will be perfect. That's why I want you to sing. I got emotional last time because you sounded so beautiful. I could feel myself welling up and didn't want to look like a wuss in front of my friends, so I took off."

"Why didn't you tell me? Of course I'll sing if it makes you happy. Maybe we can make love tonight. It's been so long." Chloe felt him tense up.

"Babe, it's as hard on me as you. I've just been under a lot of pressure. Don't worry; I have something special planned for tonight. Satisfaction guaranteed."

Chloe giggled, excited that they would connect later. She missed the closeness. "I can't wait. I love you and can't wait to marry you."

"Love you to death, babe. Let's get going. I don't want to be late." He grabbed her hand and proudly walked out to the bonfire. They were some of the last ones to show up, but their friends had saved them a spot.

Just as they were getting ready to sing the first song, Santino saw Chloe approaching, and a rush of heat traveled through his body. It was like a magnetic force; everything about her made it impossible for him to ignore.

These feelings were exactly what his dad had said he would experience when he found the girl that he was meant to spend his life with. But how could he be so attracted to another man's future wife? It was sick and demented, and his dad would have been so disappointed in him.

He stopped staring when Brooklyn kicked his foot.

"Perfect timing. Glad you could make it. Grab your seats," Sabastian welcomed the couple to the bonfire. "We would like to thank you all for coming to Savage's Buck & Doe to celebrate your upcoming weddings. It has been a pleasure to host your bachelor and bachelorette parties. We hope you enjoyed your stay as much as we enjoyed having you."

The groups clapped, hollering their thanks.

Alessandro took over when everyone quieted down. "Tonight, we encourage you all to sing along. We heard you at karaoke and know you can carry a tune . . . some more than others." Everyone laughed as he continued. "The first song we'll play is 'Brother' by NEEDTOBREATHE. It's a tribute to our brother Marcello."

The four brothers started after Santino tapped the side of his guitar five times. Hypnotically, the crowd listened and began to sing along, while Valentina, Brooklyn, and Quinn handed out the sticks and marshmallows.

Santino did everything in his power not to look at Chloe, but he couldn't keep his eyes from traveling her way. She was beaming, singing away as Jacob cheered her on. The guy had been such a dick the other night when she sang, yet now he was all lovey-dovey? It didn't make sense to him.

The odd time Santino picked up her beautiful, angelic voice, it was like she was speaking to his soul, causing a chill to travel up his spine.

Once the tribute was done, they started taking requests.

The brothers sounded so good that the bridal parties felt like they were at a concert. The music, drinks, and laughter didn't stop for hours. Near the end of the night, Jacob stood up.

"Can I request 'My Old Man' by Zac Brown Band?"

"We'll definitely play it," Luca addressed him, "but it's always our last song. A tribute to our old man."

"You lost your father and your brother?" Jacob asked.

Santino got another type of chill as the air crackled and the group silently waited for the answer.

The boys looked at Valentina before Sabastian answered, "Yes, they were both killed in the Las Vegas massacre."

Jacob shook his head. "No way! I lost the girl of my dreams at the massacre too."

Chloe shot her head up to look at him, and she paled as she began to tremble. This was the first time she had heard he had lost someone in the Las Vegas massacre, or that he had been in love before.

"Nicole was the sweetest girl to ever grace this earth. I grew up with her and planned to marry her one day. It seems the asshole who murdered the ones we loved got off too easy. I bet you wish you could kill everyone related to him. That kind of evil just breeds evil."

"Amen to that," Valentina said. "I understand how you feel, but luckily, you've moved on and you're marrying Chloe now."

Jacob curled his fingers into tight fists. "Moving on? That's what you think this is?" With more disdain than anyone could believe, he went on, "I wouldn't marry that crippled bitch if she was the last woman on Earth. And do you know why, Valentina? Let me tell you."

Chloe's deepest, darkest secret paralyzed her with fear. How did Jacob know about her father?

Would she ever escape the man who had made her life a living hell?

Each of the brothers exchanged confused looks, though they knew this was what they had been waiting for. One by one, they put their guitars down and stood.

Jacob pointed at Chloe. "This little whore you're so fond of is the devil's spawn. Chloe is the daughter of the man who murdered your husband, son, and my Nicole. She looks innocent, but she's really a wolf in sheep's clothing, bred by the devil himself."

Everyone's eyes and bodies swung from Jacob to Chloe.

"Is it true?" Valentina screamed. "Are you the devil's child?"

Quinn tried to grab her as she leapt from her seat and started attacking Chloe.

"Why in God's mercy did you come here? Why do you want to

hurt me?" Screaming louder, she shook the frightened, crying girl's shoulders, causing the flowers in her hair to fall from her jarred head.

Chloe chanted through her tears, "I'm sorry. I didn't know. I swear, I didn't know."

Alessandro got to Mamma first, right behind him was Quinn. "Mamma, stop. You're hurting her."

Valentina halted, stretching her head around and responding with venom, "I'm hurting her? What about how she's hurting me? All of us? She has the same vile blood in her veins as the man who murdered my famiglia!"

"Mamma!" Sabastian yelled, coming up to her other side and yanking her elbow.

Valentina dug her nails into Chloe's arms, leaving marks as she let go.

Sabastian released his mamma, thinking she was backing off. Before anyone could stop her, though, she raised her hand and slapped the young woman across the face with enough force to knock her off the log bench.

Alessandro locked his arms around Valentina's waist, pulling her back, but not before she screamed, "Puttana!" spitting in the sobbing girl's face.

As Alessandro twisted her away from Chloe, Quinn got right into her frantic face, calmly but firmly reprimanding her. "Valentina, that's enough. You need to get control of yourself. Chloe didn't shoot Shawn or Marcello."

Valentina fell into his arms, sobbing, and Quinn waited to straighten her up until he felt her strength come back. "I'm taking you inside to talk." Tucking her under his arm, he looked at Luca. "We all need to talk. I want all of you to come to her apartment after you sort this out." He then guided the weeping woman away.

Santino stood stock-still, trying to absorb the scene in front of him. How many times had he wished he could seek revenge on the shooter's famiglia? But this was Chloe, not the monster he had envisioned.

"You bastard! You set us up. Do you see what you did? Why would you want our mamma to suffer more?" It hadn't taken him long to figure out this was why Jacob had brought her here.

"Valentina had the right to know," he answered cockily. "All of you should know that this little bitch is living her life as if nothing happened, while our loved ones are rotting in their graves. The rest of you only had to deal with her one weekend. I've been the one suffering for months to get her here.

"I had to get her to trust me and convince her I wanted to marry her. It sickened me to touch her, so I punished her during sex, my hand burning from the spankings I gave her. She thought I liked rough sex, while the joke was on her because every time I wrapped my hands around her neck, I had to stop myself from snuffing her out like her father did to Nicole."

Santino charged him, jumping over the dying fire and attacking like a madman. His fists flew as fast as the words coming out of Jacob's mouth.

Luca and Sabastian jumped in, pulling them apart and holding their berserk brother back with his arms behind his back.

The cruel nightmare unfolding in front of everyone was destroying Chloe by the second. Each word and action were like knives plunging into her heart. Then the realization hit that her fiancé had never loved her. Everything he had done, all the time they had been together, had been nothing more than his sick way to seek revenge.

No one would ever love her because she was the Devil's spawn.

Jacob looked down at the woman he hated as much, if not more than, her father as Alessandro helped him up from his knees. "Stand up, bitch, and stop acting like a victim." Spittle flew from his mouth. "You should have warned somebody—the police, doctors, anyone—that your father was psychotic. But did you? No! You safely hid and didn't say a word, like the useless whore you are."

Santino was struggling to get away from his brothers when their eyes met. Chloe had to look away from the hatred in his eyes. There was no doubt he believed that she bore some responsibility. What could she have done to change the outcome, though?

She had to tell him the truth.

Chloe wiped the saliva from her face, shifting to her knees and pushing herself up to her feet. Shaking like a leaf, she breathed out in front of everyone, "I didn't know. I swear, I hadn't seen him in years. I had no idea."

"Liar! You'd say anything to absolve your accountability, but their blood is on you." He pulled back a bucket that nobody had seen one of the bridesmaids hand him, tossing the goat's blood all over her. It was just like the scene out of Stephen King's movie Carrie.

Chloe stood wide-eyed, covered in blood from head to toe. Her heaving breaths caused her to taste the metallic flavor, inhaling the blood through her nose, where it traveled down the back of her throat.

Huffing in and out, petrified, she saw the hatred in each person's eyes staring at her. It didn't matter that she hadn't seen her father in years; they blamed her and always would.

"Why should she get to live when Nicole and your family died?" Jacob continued.

"Please, stop." Sobbing, shocked by the tragic events unraveling, Brooklyn came to her friend's defense. "It's not her fault. You should be ashamed." On one hand, she felt sick for her husband and his family, having their pain ripped open again, but she was also appalled for Chloe.

"Brooklyn!" Luca yelled, afraid she would get caught in the

crossfire. "Stay back. Don't get involved."

Stunned, she stopped dead in her tracks and shouted, "You can't possibly blame Chloe!"

While everyone was distracted, Chloe took off, running toward the dark forest, terrified that Jacob or someone else would kill her before the night was over.

She hated that the Savages were fighting because of her. She had to hide until everyone left, then she would find a way to escape. She would pack up, leave Allentown, and start all over somewhere else . . . again.

Even though it was a warm night, she trembled as shock set in. The stench of the cold blood made her want to throw up, but she pushed it down so no one would hear her retching.

Running as best as she could, she reached the edge of the forest, where she would hide until daylight. She crawled into the middle of a big bush, scraping and scratching the soft skin of her face and arms.

Chloe covered her ears, tears tumbling down as she heard punches being thrown and the women screaming for them to stop. She pulled her bloody knees closer to her, wrapping her shivering arms around them and rocking back and forth as Jacob screamed, "Chloe! I'll find you, and when I do, you'll pay. Do you hear me, Satan's spawn? You'll pay!"

Chloe heard Ava, Alessandro's wife, move closer to her hiding spot, calling the sheriff and begging him for help, and telling him to hurry. She then listened as Sabastian told the crowd that the police were on their way and everyone would be charged if they didn't leave the resort in the next thirty minutes. Everyone was suffering because of who she was.

She slammed her eyes closed, remembering the look of pure hatred in their eyes. Santino's look had hurt the most as it had turned from disbelief to repulsion when he realized he had defended the shooter's daughter. The memories were staggering, causing her to heave, and almost giving away her location.

After the sheriff arrived, things calmed down.

Chloe listened as they called her name, wondering how she was going to pick up the pieces of her life again. She had built her life around the man she loved, and had thought loved her, too, when the truth was that he hated her. He found her repulsive in every sense. Would this nightmare ever end?

She wished for the thousandth time that she had died with Harper that fateful day. Why had she been left behind to face the sins of their father? Why did God hate her? Maybe they were right; she was evil because she carried his blood in her veins. Maybe she was meant to live a life of misery because he hadn't paid for his sins.

Having no luck finding Chloe, the brothers stood with Keith while he and his deputy recorded the IDs of all the members of the Moore wedding party. Then he informed them all they should not leave Allentown as the group gathered their belongings and were loaded into their cars.

The brothers were relieved to learn that the girls had only pretended to drink, knowing how the night would end. However, Keith gave them breathalyzers, making sure it was safe for them to drive before letting them go. The other two wedding parties would check out in the morning.

Once they were gone, everyone continued to search for Chloe. Keith finally suspended the search after a couple of hours up the mountain because it was too dark. He promised he would be back in the morning with a search party.

Sabastian, Luca, Alessandro, and Santino all watched as Keith drove away. It didn't sit right with them that Chloe was still missing, but the sheriff was right; they would never find her if she didn't want to be found.

Silently, after hours of searching, they walked to the main lodge, knowing they had to check on Mamma and collect their wives before this horrific night was over.

One by one, they filed into Mamma's private apartment on the third floor of the main lodge. Ava and Brooklyn sat in the chairs with tissues, facing Quinn as he comforted Valentina on the couch. Valentina didn't lift her head at hearing her sons coming into the room, making each of the boys feel like they were reliving the days following the massacre, when they didn't know if their mamma would survive their losses.

"Are you okay, Mamma?" Santino asked in a strangled voice.

"Did you find her?" The hostility in Valentina's voice was as clear as day.

Alessandro crossed his arms over his chest, unable to hide his disgust at her tone. "No, she's still missing. That terrified, tiny woman is all alone in the forest."

Valentina made a noise of distaste.

Santino couldn't keep his anger contained. "How can you blame Chloe? She's as much a victim as we are."

Valentina snapped her head up. "Victim?" She narrowed her eyes at her youngest son. "How dare you call that puttana a victim? You can't tell me you're still attracted to her after knowing who she is? Grow up and start thinking with your brain. You're too old to be thinking with your penis."

Everyone in the room gasped in shock.

"Valentina, please." Quinn used his therapist voice to reason with her. "Lashing out at Santino because you're hurt isn't helping you or them. They understand your torment. Attacking them is crossing a line."

Jumping to her feet, she snapped back, "Don't tell me how to deal with my children when they're being shamos."

Ava stood up. "Valentina—"

"Everyone, shut up!" Brooklyn yelled, not able to take it another minute.

"Amore mia, please." Luca moved to his wife, who was usually the calmest person he knew. He had never seen her disrespect someone she loved.

"No. You are all going to listen to me. Chloe is a victim." She shook her head. "I can't believe what I'm hearing. Valentina, I love you like a mother, but you're wrong. That young woman was attacked and terrified. How can you judge her for an act her father committed? You all told me that Reece and I weren't responsible for our parents' actions, yet here you are, blaming a girl who had no control over her life. Has anyone stopped to wonder what her life was like? What she might have suffered at the hands of that bastard? Let me tell you because I became Chloe's friend—nothing has changed."

Shocked, Valentina shot back, "How can you say that? She's the devil's spawn."

"Please, everyone, sit down and let's hear what Brooklyn has to say," Quinn implored, guiding Valentina back to the couch.

Sabastian grabbed chairs from the kitchen for himself and Santino, as Alessandro sat with Ava, and Luca sat with Brooklyn.

Sabastian squeezed Santino's shoulder for support as he sat, and Santino gave him a look of thanks. "Brooklyn," Quinn said, "please tell us what you know that will help us understand Chloe better."

Luca gave her strength by kissing the side of her head.

"Chloe told me that she has no family. Her sister and mother died. I thought they died in a fire because that was how Chloe said she got her injuries, but that doesn't make sense because there were no blister scars on her body from a fire."

Valentina couldn't censor her thoughts. "You just admitted you think she's a liar. That woman isn't innocent; she's an evil puttana."

Santino stood. "That was brutally uncalled for, Mamma. My whole life I have looked up to you and admired how you always defend the weaker, but tonight, I'm ashamed of you. I can't listen to another word out of your mouth. I get that you're hurting—we all are—but I never thought I would live to see the day you would be that cruel to a person whose demeanor screams how severely she has been abused. It's sickening. What happened to the woman I had to hold back from defending Chloe in the dining room from those animals? Everything changed because you decided she should be held accountable for something her father did. You disgust me. I'm leaving.

"Brooklyn, if it's not too much to ask, would you mind coming to my cabin and filling me in? Anyone else is welcome who wants to hear the truth." Heartbroken and furious, he stomped away.

"Santino, please." The accusation burned like a hot poker in Valentina's heart. Why couldn't he understand?

Not looking back, Santino slammed the door shut on his way out.

Valentina started to cry, but when Brooklyn, Luca, Ava, and Alessandro all stood to leave, she whipped her head to the only one still sitting. "Sabastian, you understand, right?"

He shook his head. "No, Mamma, you raised us better than that." He then turned to Quinn. "Will you stay with her tonight?"

As Sabastian stood, Quinn answered, "Yes, of course. You all have to understand she's just in shock and exhausted. She doesn't mean it."

Valentina shook her head.

Answering her counteraction, Alessandro sadly said, "Mamma, if you truly can't see how wrong you are, you're going to lose another son, and rightfully so. This hatred you harbor isn't healthy, and will grow until you destroy everyone you love. You told me when I hit rock bottom that the only man responsible for Dad and Marcello's death was the shooter. Did you lie to me?" Without another word, he turned and walked away.

Valentina sobbed harder as she watched all her children quietly file out of her apartment.

When the brothers and their wives filed into Santino's cabin a few minutes later, they found him sitting on the couch with his elbows on his knees, head in his hands. Everyone knew he was trying to control his emotions.

He had always been Mamma's champion and the foundation of their famiglia. He had put every ounce of his being into helping them through their individual crises. They all knew he felt something for Chloe, and that he was fighting between his loyalty to his famiglia and the woman who needed him to survive. It was going to be one hell of a battle, but they would all support him.

As Sabastian and Alessandro sat beside him, Alessandro said, "Bro, we stand beside you. We'll support you and will do everything in our power to help Chloe."

Santino heaved out a gut-wrenching sound, trying to catch his breath.

Sabastian slapped his back, then rubbed it. "Don't feel bad. It had to be said. You're right; Mamma will never really heal until she lets go of the hatred."

Santino lifted his face, utterly destroyed by the events of the night. "How could I have said that to her? What if she tries to kill herself again? How will I live with myself?"

Luca came forward. "She won't kill herself. And she has to be accountable for what she did tonight. If you hadn't said it, I would have. Mamma is wrong. Chloe's in danger, and we have to help her. Now we have to figure out how to do it. Brooklyn, tell us everything you know."

Brooklyn recited what Chloe had told her, and then she clarified why she thought parts of it weren't true. "I used to lie about where my parents were because I was embarrassed, since they abandoned Reece and me. Also, Chloe didn't have any marks to indicate she had been close enough to a fire. I could be wrong, but my gut is telling me that her dad hurt her, and maybe that's how her twin sister, Harper, died."

Alessandro suddenly sat up straight. "Did you say her twin was named Harper?"

They all looked perplexed as Brooklyn nodded and asked, "Why?"

Alessandro got up, starting to pace. "Gesù Cristo, I don't know, but something is gnawing at me."

"What are you talking about?" Santino asked, as confused as everyone else.

Alessandro rubbed his temples, racking his brain and trying to make sense of something. "I don't know, but I feel like Chloe is in more danger than we thought. Did anyone check the new cabins?" He remembered something about a dream he had the night before his wedding.

"With the lights around the property, we would have seen her near the cabins. She has to be in the forest," Ava said.

Santino got up and sprinted for the door.

"Where are you going?" Sabastian called out as Santino reached for the doorknob.

"The new cabins. She wouldn't go anywhere near the occupied ones. Chloe might have gone there after we stopped looking. I have to find her before anything else happens."

"I'm coming," Alessandro said as he ran after Santino.

The rest of the group followed, most thinking it was a dead end.

The first scattering of light before dawn changed the sky from black to mauve, making their race to the new cabins easier. They could hear rustling in bushes and the trees as the nocturnal animals settled in for the day and the birds greeted the morning with happy chirps.

"Let's try the newest cabin, then work our way back," Alessandro said, catching up to Santino.

They raced up the steps of the shell of the cabin that they had erected just weeks before. Santino grabbed the handle, whipping the door open. It was pitch-black, so Alessandro felt his way to the temporary construction lights hanging from the hook. They both heard a squeak, and assumed it was a mouse.

Ava, Sabastian, Luca, and Brooklyn had just cleared the doorway when the light flicked on. That was when Ava and Brooklyn both screamed at the horrendous scene in front of them.

"Chloe!" Santino hollered in a horrified voice.

In agony, Chloe opened her swollen eyes, trying to decipher the blurry, upside-down figures in front of her. The pounding pressure in her head from the blood that had rushed there had her squinting against the blinding light, distorting any definition.

She flexed her body and tried to scream past the gag, afraid they had come back to finish the job by killing her outright. She groaned in pain as her body protested against the bindings holding her in place.

Chloe's battered and almost naked body hung upside down from an X made from two two-by-fours. Her limbs had been crudely tied with thick ropes that were nailed to the X. Her wrists and ankles were bleeding from supporting her weight ten feet off the floor. Under her hanging body, a Satanic inverted pentacle had been painted on the floor. Four feet above her, secured from the peaked roof rafters, was a severed goat's head that was dripping blood, covering her body in streaks of red. Across her naked belly, written in goat's blood, were the words Satan's Spawn.

"Help me get her down!" Santino wailed.

Sabastian ran for one ladder, while Luca grabbed the other.

"Wait! Don't touch her until we take pictures. We need evidence," Alessandro yelled.

"Fuck that! We have to get her down before the ropes give way and she breaks her neck."

"Santino, wait!" Alessandro insisted. "Ava, quickly take some pictures with your phone. We can't let these bastards get away with this. Brooklyn, call Keith. Tell him to get an ambulance here as quickly as possible."

Still not coherent enough to understand what was going on, Chloe cried between painful moans.

"Stellina, please don't cry. Hurry, Ava. Alessandro, grab me something so I can get up to her," he said from underneath her. "Stellina, listen to me. You're going to be okay. I swear, I won't let them ever touch you again."

Alessandro moved a workbench over, and Santino climbed up, but it wasn't high enough to reach her face.

"Give me something else, quickly. She's panicking."

Chloe was twisting and turning, trying to pull away from his reach.

"It's me. Santino. Stellina, I won't hurt you." He expanded his legs so his brother could place the box of tiles down. Meanwhile, Sabastian and Luca climbed up the ladders fixated on either side, trying to untie her.

"Alessandro, I need the box cutter," Luca demanded in frustration, unable to undo the knots.

Santino climbed onto the box, trying desperately to untie the gag. Giving up, he tried not to hurt her as he pulled the gag over her chin. "Chloe, it's okay. We have you."

Her terrified, strangled scream weighed heavily on everyone in the room.

"Ava, run and get a blanket. How much longer, Luca?"

"I'm almost there. You've got to keep her from moving. I'm afraid I'm going to cut her."

Her hair was a tattered mess, caked with both dried and fresh blood. Santino wouldn't have known the color if he hadn't seen it before. He pushed it away, cupping her cheeks while leaning in and whispering, "Shh . . . Calm down, Chloe. You're going to be okay. Please stop fighting us. The more you fight, the higher the chance of you getting cut."

"I got it," Luca said as her leg started to fall forward. He quickly grabbed her foot, then tossed the closed blade to Sabastian. "Alessandro, after Sabastian cuts down her other leg, you're going to have to cut the rope off her wrists while we hold her legs up."

Sabastian finished, then quickly grabbed her leg. They all struggled to hold on to her slippery body.

Ten minutes later, Alessandro finished cutting the last ropes off her wrists.

"I'm done. Santino, make sure you hold her shoulders until I can get up there and stabilize her." Alessandro jumped down from one of the ladders, then leapt up beside Santino and reached for her hips as Luca and Sabastian started down the ladder and Brooklyn moved forward to support her head. Luca then jumped down to hold her thighs so Sabastian could let go of her other foot.

Ava rushed back in, covering Chloe as Santino repositioned her into his arms. As they heard the sirens in the background, Brooklyn and Ava took off to meet the sheriff and the ambulance.

"You're safe, Stellina. I'm not letting you go," Santino tried to soothe the whimpering woman in his arms.

Chapter 4
"In The End" by Linkin Park

The unfamiliarity of her surroundings and the sound of the sirens frightened the disoriented, traumatized young woman in the ambulance that was rushing down the country roads toward the hospital.

Santino sat in the attendant seat at the head of the stretcher, running his hands down the sides of Chloe's thrashing head, offering comfort.

"Ma'am, do you have any allergies?" The paramedic tried to wipe the blood off with sanitized wipes so he could insert an IV.

She didn't respond, moaning painfully because the tingling in her limbs had become unbearable as the blood circulated back to the areas that had been denied for so long.

"Sir, do you know if she has any allergies?"

"No, we only met her four days ago. But we know she doesn't have any family." He couldn't believe her battered body was looking worse by the second. Bruising was popping up in front of his eyes. "How could anyone do this to you?" Bending closer, he whispered into her ear, "I'm sorry I didn't keep looking for you." Santino felt sick at the fact that she had been hurt on their watch at the resort.

The rest of the trip was quiet as the paramedic worked on dealing with superficial injuries, while Santino prayed that she would be okay. When they arrived at the hospital, a team whisked her away.

Keith, who had come in right behind the ambulance, intercepted

Santino before he could follow the doctors. "Son, let them do their jobs. I need your statement."

After following Keith into the waiting room, Santino recited the events since they had parted ways. Pacing the room, he angrily stated, "It was Jacob and his friends. You can't let them get away with it. She's innocent. Chloe didn't do anything to provoke them except be born."

"I suspect you're correct. And my team is gathering evidence as we speak."

Santino told him about the evidence they had been smart enough to take, then texted Ava, telling her to send the pictures to the sheriff. Keith uploaded them.

It was one thing to hear the story; it was quite another to see it.

He left the room a couple of times to make some phone calls in private.

A few hours later, the doctor walked into the waiting room just as Luca, Brooklyn, and Alessandro arrived. "Sheriff, are you here for Chloe Marsh?"

Keith stood, nodding. "Yes. She doesn't have any family, so I will be her advocate."

The need to protect Chloe had Santino blurting out with conviction, "I will. I got to know her and would like to help."

"I believe you, son," the sheriff said. "But, from all the reports, I don't think Chloe will be comfortable with any of the Savages. I'll ask her what she wants, and if she is unable to make decisions, I will advocate on her behalf." Keith placed a hand on Santino's shoulder, knowing he was a good man.

Brooklyn stepped forward. "I'm Chloe's friend. Can I help?"

Keith didn't want to offend the young woman he had grown so close to a few years ago, after her brother's murder. "Brooklyn, you know I think of you as another daughter, but I think she is going to be gun-shy. I will definitely tell her that you're all out here and wanting to help. Doctor, let's go."

The sheriff followed the doctor out as the doctor explained that Chloe hadn't sustained any major injuries and was insisting on being released. Keith wasn't aware of Santino and Alessandro treading quietly ten feet behind them, listening.

The lawman's hardened shell cracked when he rounded the corner of the curtained-off examination room. The nurses had wiped away the majority of the blood off her battered face and body, so now he could see that her wrists and ankles were rubbed raw, and were now wrapped in bandages that were seeping blood. She looked like a frightened little girl curled up in the bed, with big, haunted eyes staring at nothing.

Keith took off his hat as he approached the bed. "Chloe, I'm Sheriff Keith Brown, and I'll be investigating your assault."

She lifted her frightened eyes to him but didn't say anything as she tucked herself into a tighter protective ball. Meanwhile, the two brothers continued to listen outside the curtain.

"I'm sorry you've been through such a traumatic night. I promise you, darlin', I won't rest until I bring everyone responsible to justice. Can you tell me who did this?"

Panic set in, and her heart rate accelerated as she remembered the threat Jacob had repeated to her. *You say one word, and they'll never find the pieces of your body, whore!*

In a gravelly voice, she answered the only way she could, "I don't remember anything before, during, or after the attack."

Keith knew she was lying. It was written all over her face. Fear of retribution kept victims silent.

He pulled up a chair, sitting beside her to try another approach. "Darlin', the doctor said you don't have any broken bones or internal damage. Your memory will probably come back with some much-needed rest. I understand you're asking to be released. I have notified victim services, but is there anyone else I can call?"

She closed her eyes in shame. Then, shaking her head, with the gentlest voice the sheriff had ever heard, she responded, "No, and I don't want victim services. I'm fine on my own. I don't have my car, though, so if you could drop me off at my house, I'd appreciate it." No matter how bad she felt, she had to disappear the minute she gathered everything that would fit into her vehicle. She would wait for things to blow over before thinking of selling the house.

"If you insist on leaving this hospital, I can't in good faith let you leave alone. I'm either sending a deputy to stay with you, or you have the right to go with victim services to be placed in an undisclosed woman's shelter." Although she looked like a child, she was a woman with rights, and Keith had to treat her as such. "I have issued person-of-interest warrants for Jacob Moore and the rest of the wedding party that checked in to the resort with you. Until I sort this out, you're not safe alone."

The alarm on her face escalated.

"Chloe, I've seen that look before, but you can't run. We have to deal with this head-on. I want the people responsible put away. Once you remember everything, all you have to do is give me a statement. You don't have to show up at court if you don't want to. It will be the state against the defendants. I know you think you're all alone, but some of the Savage family are in the waiting room. Brooklyn and Santino want to help you."

Blindsided, her eyes sprang open. "No!" Her voice was soft but hoarse. "They hate me now that they know who I am." Tears escaped her swollen eyes as she pulled herself up, fiddling with the IV. "Please don't let them hurt me. I just want to go home by myself and forget this ever happened."

Santino's chin fell to his chest as he pressed his fingers against his ribs. It felt like he had just taken a hard hit to his sternum.

Stellina was terrified of him and his famiglia. How was he going to convince her that he wouldn't hurt her?

"Darlin', I won't let anyone hurt you. Usually, they're a good family." The lawman's shell broke a little more. "I heard what Valentina did. She had no right to attack you. Would you like to press assault charges against Valentina Savage?

With a strained voice, Chloe told him, "I don't blame Mrs. Savage. I might have done the same thing in her shoes. I don't want to press charges. But I also don't want to see any of them ever again."

Deep down, Keith didn't want to charge Valentina either. The woman had suffered enough, but she had broken the law, and Chloe had every right to press charges against her, if that was what she wanted to do. "If you change your mind about charges, the option is there. I understand that you are frightened of the rest of them, so I will send them home. Do you want victim services, or a deputy?"

With everything that had happened, unease scrambled her thought process. Who would she have a better chance of escaping? She needed her car and some clothes before moving on. "I'll take a deputy, but I don't want him in my house."

He placed his hat back on his head and stood. "Nobody has to go in your house. If you feel better with a woman, I can have a female deputy watch you. I'll call and have her meet us at your house while you get ready." The poor girl didn't even realize she had admitted to remembering Valentina hitting her. The sheriff ignored that fact, though, hoping she would come around and tell him everything after a day or so of rest.

"Thank you." Dropping her eyes, she self-consciously admitted, "I don't have any clothes."

Trying to preserve her dignity, he didn't turn around as he walked toward the exit. "I'll send the nurse in with some scrubs you can wear home. I'll also ask if any of the Savages grabbed your luggage before I send them home. If not, I'll arrange for one of my officers to bring it to your house."

"I need my music. I mean, my phone, please. I don't care about anything else."

He turned at the desperation in her voice. "I will make sure you get everything. As soon as the discharge papers are signed and the IV is removed, the nurse will come get me, and I'll take you home."

Alessandro dragged Santino away before they got caught. They didn't utter a word until they reached Luca and Brooklyn in the waiting room.

"How is she?" Brooklyn asked with concern.

Santino walked to the window, filled with rage and helplessness.

"Chloe's going to be fine. They're releasing her soon," Alessandro answered.

The conversation stopped when Keith entered after speaking to the nurse.

"Chloe is banged up pretty badly, but no major damage. I'll be taking her home when she is released."

Santino stared at the people walking in and out of the hospital with the weight of the world on his shoulders. He would never forgive himself for not searching for her harder. If Jacob had found her, then he could have.

He failed her once; it wouldn't happen again.

"What about my offer to help her?" Brooklyn asked.

Dismayed, the sheriff answered, "I'm sorry, honey. She doesn't want to see any of you. I'm going to have to ask you to leave the hospital and not contact her. Believe me when I tell you that Chloe is a lot stronger than I thought she was. Give her some time. She's scared and doesn't know who to trust. If Valentina hadn't attacked her, the outcome might have been different. The good news is, she isn't pressing charges against your mamma.

"A group of officers will be at the resort, collecting evidence for probably another four to eight hours. Once that's done and your statements are filed, you probably won't hear anything else until you're called to testify. It's over. Go home, folks. Take care of your mamma."

"That's bullshit, and you know it." Santino twisted around to face Keith. "After you arrest those bastards, their rich parents will get them out on bail, and then where will she be? Chloe needs to be somewhere safe until the trial and, let's be honest, your department doesn't have the funds to watch her until then."

Keith sympathized with Santino, but the young man was crossing a line. "That isn't any of your concern. She made it abundantly clear she doesn't want any of you near her. You can't force yourself into that little lady's life.

"I'm warning you, Santino, you go near her, and I will charge you with stalking. Do I have your assurance, or do I need to instate a restraining order?"

"You do what you have to, and I'll do what I should have done to begin with," he seethed, while stomping out of the waiting room.

Alessandro called out to his brother as he slammed out the door.

"Santino would never hurt her. He feels responsible for not protecting her from the attack," Brooklyn said, trying to soothe Keith's anger, reaching for his forearm.

The lawman lifted his hat, running his fingers through his thinning hair. It had been a long night. "I have the utmost respect for your family, but Santino's done all he can. You know I will do everything in my power to protect Chloe. I promise you, darlin', no matter the cost, I won't leave her defenseless."

Brooklyn's face softened. She knew better than anyone that this man's word was as good as gold.

Luca stuck out his hand. "We know. Please understand that

Santino was just blowing off steam. We're going to head home. If you need anything from us, please don't hesitate to call."

As the three of them left the waiting room to look for their youngest brother, Alessandro waited until they were out of hearing distance before telling them, "Santino's not going to be deterred. Let me stick close to him. I'll keep you guys informed."

Luca glanced at Alessandro, the look saying everything. He also had every intention of offering his help to Santino, but, knowing how she felt about the sheriff, he didn't want Brooklyn to know.

Brooklyn pinched his side. "If you think for one second that I don't know what just transpired between you two, you've been smoking something funny. I love Keith like a father, but Santino has been my hero from the second I met him. I know he feels something for Chloe. I also believe he might be the only one who can help her. He'll help her just like Luca did for me when I needed him most and thought I was alone. I'm also helping, so don't even think of pushing me out."

Locking arms with the tall beauty, both men grinned.

"You know, if any of my buddies heard about us falling in love at first sight, they would think we were crazy," Alessandro responded. "But it really is part of the legacy Dad left us. Now, what are we going to do about Mamma?"

"Nothing," Luca answered. "This is something she has to come to terms with on her own. It was her who taught us all to fight for the underdog. She just needs time to figure it out."

Brooklyn smiled. "Bet you guys are happy she's sleeping with a therapist now."

The brothers stopped dead, making Brooklyn stumble as she was yanked back.

Luca narrowed his eyes. "Amore mia, you ever say shit like that again, I'll take you over my knee."

"And I'll watch." Alessandro waggled his eyebrows. "She's our mamma. What you said is sick."

Brooklyn rolled her eyes. "Oh, for goodness sakes. None of you were immaculate conceptions. Why does it freak you out to think that your mamma has sex? It's the most natural thing between a couple, yet the four of you get your boxers in a knot with even the slightest thought. I know for a fact that at least one of you is a dirty birdie."

"Damn Ava—she has a big mouth," Alessandro answered devilishly.

Luca barked out a laugh as he slapped Alessandro's head. "She meant me, coglione." He nodded his head suddenly. "There's Santino."

Their youngest brother was leaning against a tree, smoking a cigarette, unaware they were heading his way. His face was screwed up with the storm brewing in his mind.

"Not a great time to form a bad habit. Trust me; bad habits have a way of taking over when your energy is best spent elsewhere."

Santino took the last drag before flicking it away. "I need a vehicle."

Alessandro pushed his shoulder. "Somehow, I knew you would, but you got a driver plus a vehicle. Let's go. I brought Ava's clown car, figuring Keith wouldn't recognize it. You can thank me later for tinting the windows."

Santino cocked his head in confusion.

"My strega insists we take her car sometimes, and I don't want anyone to see me in it."

Santino couldn't help chuckling. "Thanks, bro, but all I need are the keys and a crowbar to get me into her Mini."

"I remember asking you to leave me alone in New Orleans. Did you? No. Payback is a bitch. Let's go," Alessandro answered soberly.

Brooklyn stopped them. "Be careful. She's delicate. And don't piss off Keith. Once you know she's safe, come home and get some sleep. Stronger minds always prevail. Oh, and I'll text you her address. That way Keith won't see you following."

Santino hugged his smart sister-in-law. He had thought he was going to have to battle her too. "I'll take care of her. I promise."

She pulled back. "I know. Just like you always do."

Alessandro led him to the car, and then they moved the car to a location where they could see the hospital's entrance. While they waited for Keith to come out, Santino put Chloe's address into the GPS.

After about fifteen minutes, they watched Keith pull his car up to the entrance. He got out of the driver's side as an orderly wheeled Chloe out. He helped her stand, holding her arm as she heavily limped to the car. She looked so fragile and further withdrawn.

As they drove, leaving before Keith so they had time to find a place to hide, Santino was lost in thought, his legs moving restlessly. It was going to take a miracle to convince Stellina that he would take care of her and would never hurt her.

Swearing as the guilt thickened in his chest, he looked up into the bright sky. Dad, I need you now more than ever.

Turning, he asked his brother, "Do you think she jumped out of a window because of a fire?"

Alessandro glimpsed over before turning into another lane. "No more than you do. I can't imagine the life she must have had. But I truly believe, if anyone can help her, it's you. If you thought saving my life was hard, this is going to be ten times worse. Are you sure you're up for the challenge?" He kept checking the rearview mirror, making sure the sheriff's car wasn't in sight before looking at Santino.

"No choice. She's the one. Millions of women out there, and I have to fall for the daughter of our dad and brother's murderer. How fucked up is that?"

"Like you said, it's not a choice. I never in my wildest dreams thought I'd end up with a prickly speed demon strega." He shrugged. "When it's right, it's right."

"Do you think it's possible that I somehow knew she wasn't really Jacob's? I mean, I've been disgusted with the thought of being attracted to an engaged woman. I'm not even sure I could have walked away if she married him. I probably would have had to bide my time until the marriage fell apart. Which it would have."

Alessandro didn't answer right away, because the GPS interrupted him, telling him to get off at the next off ramp. "All of us knew from the minute we met Chloe and Jacob that they weren't meant to be together. Nobody who loves a woman would treat her so badly. So stop beating yourself up. Your instincts were spot on."

After traveling another twenty minutes to the outskirts of town, the GPS announced they had reached their destination.

Both men looked left at the isolated house surrounded by trees; the closest neighbor was about a mile up the road. The house was in desperate need of fixing up. On closer examination, they noticed not only was it rundown, but it had been vandalized.

"Goddammit," Santino cursed when he spotted her car. The windshield and rear window of the black Ford Focus had been shattered, all four tires had been slashed, and Murderer's Daughter was written in white spray paint across each side. Most of the windows in the house were broken too. And on the front door, what Santino had first thought was a wreath, was an inverted pentagram in black paint. It sickened him to see the hateful words and destruction.

Alessandro dragged his eyes away from the hideous scene when he spotted a car approaching in the rearview mirror. He shifted gears and kept going, turning left on the side road that bordered her property. Making a three-point turn, he then pulled off the road and onto the shoulder, positioning the car so the trees kept it hidden from Keith's view. Then the two men climbed out of the car and carefully made their way through the trees, until they found a spot to watch undetected.

The car Alessandro had seen wasn't the sheriff's. It had driven right past them. But just as they crouched down, the sheriff pulled into Chloe's driveway.

They could see Keith raise his hand, telling Chloe to stay in the car. Getting out, he pulled his gun out as he surveyed the foreseeable damage, then peered in the windows. When he determined there was no immediate danger, he headed back to the car, heavyhearted.

Chloe struggled out of the car, tears streaming down her face. Her life was in shambles with no means of escape.

It took every ounce of his strength for Santino to not run to her and shelter her from the mayhem.

Alessandro stopped him by whispering, "Don't move. If we get caught, who'll be there for her?"

Santino whipped his head around to glare at his brother, barely holding it together as he seethed out, "God Almighty, look at her! She's hurt, completely alone, and has nothing left. I swear, I'm going to kill them."

"Be smart about this and stop talking stupid." Alessandro could feel the tension in his brother. The man was a hairsbreadth away from sprinting forward. "If Keith hears you talk like that, he'll lock you up." He dragged out his next words. "We'll be there for her. Just be patient."

Santino took a few deep breaths. He knew his brother was right, but every fiber of his being was screaming to help Chloe.

Dismayed, Keith faced the young woman. "I'm sorry, darlin'. The house has been vandalized. It's a crime scene now, so you can't stay here. Unless there's somewhere else I can take you, I'll have to call victim services."

Sniveling, she asked, "Can I get some clothes?"

"Sorry, darlin', but I can't let you in yet. Maybe tomorrow."

Just then, another police car pulled into the driveway, and a female deputy got out. Keith went to talk to the officer.

Chloe lowered herself back into the car, leaving the door open with her feet on the ground. She couldn't hold back the gut-wrenching sob that escaped. Bringing her hands to her face, she wondered how she was going to pick up the pieces of her life. She couldn't go back to work with no clothes, no car, and looking like she had been hit by a Mack truck. Thankfully, she still had a few thousand dollars in the bank. It would have to be enough to start over. She would give herself a minute to lose it, then she was going to have to pull herself together and consider her options.

Keith walked to the passenger side of his cruiser and saw the poor little thing crying. "Chloe?" He watched as she wiped her shame away, then lifted her head. "Julianne brought your things from the resort. She's going to take you to the shelter. I'll stop by tomorrow afternoon so we can talk further. Today, I want you to relax and get some sleep. I promise I'll protect you, sweetheart. You're not alone."

He was such a nice man. "Thank you. Would you mind helping me get to her car?" Crying had depleted the last of her energy.

He looked down at her tiny, little feet in the thin, blue booties. "Don't move. Julianne will bring the car up, and I'll help transfer you. I'll make sure someone from the shelter helps Julianne get you into the house."

Alessandro nudged Santino. They had to get back to the car so they could follow the deputy.

Santino took one last look at Chloe trying to stand. His heart splintered when he heard her yelp of pain. The beating she had received had taken its toll on her bad leg.

He vowed to himself that he would do everything in his power to heal her body and her mind. No one deserved to pay such a high price for a crime they didn't even commit. Especially not Stellina.

***

When they arrived at the shelter, Chloe put her arms around Sheila, a woman from the shelter, and Julianne. Sheila carried Chloe's purse in her free hand, while the deputy said she would come back for Chloe's bag after they got her settled.

Alessandro and Santino parked across the street and watched as they brought Chloe to a bedroom facing the street.

While Julianne went back for Chloe's bag, Sheila handed her a box full of personal care items, like soap and shampoo. Then Sheila showed her the door to the bathroom and the remote for the TV. The men watched as Chloe shook her head.

After Julianne brought in her bag, both women left the room, closing the door on their way out.

"Let's get out of here before the deputy catches us. We know she's safe for the rest of the day and night. We'll come back tomorrow morning," Alessandro said as he started the car.

"Wait. Please." Santino watched as the beautiful, broken girl tried to get up twice. Finally, with the aid of a chair she had dragged closer, she stood and limped into the bathroom, repeatedly wiping the tears from her face. "Alessandro, I can't go home yet. I need to know she was able to shower and is lying down before I leave. Drop me off at the coffee shop up the street. When I'm ready, I'll call an Uber."

"Bro, if you're not ready to leave, I have nowhere else to be. Let's go grab a coffee then come back. That way, the deputy won't see us sitting here."

"Thanks." Santino had to swallow the urge to bawl after hearing his brother's compassion.

They grabbed a croissant and a coffee, then sat at the window. Five minutes later, they saw the deputy drive past them. Stuffing the rest of their breakfast into their mouths, they headed back to the shelter.

At the shelter, Chloe was thankful that the bathroom was fitted with handrails and a seat in the shower. The bandages would get wet, but she had to sacrifice something to get clean.

After three good washes and half a bottle of shampoo, her hair was finally clean. It took all the hot water the shelter had to wash everything away.

Forty-five minutes later, Chloe limped heavily out of the bathroom, fully dressed. She was unable to stand long enough to dry her hair, so she tossed the dryer on the bed before edging her way carefully to sit down. All her muscles were screaming out with soreness.

In the shower, she had devised a plan to sleep away the day. Then, as soon as night fell, she would sneak out, head home to collect her belongings, and move on. Chloe knew it would have to be somewhere completely new. She couldn't head back to Alabama, where she had gone to college, because Jacob might look there. He knew so many people that one of them might spot her and give away her location.

Thoughts of Jacob brought terror and regret upon her. He had never loved her. It had all been an elaborate plan. It would have been so much better if he had just beaten the living shit out of her the day he had discovered who she was, instead of leading her on. He had been so charming. Her knight in shining armor, the one who had rescued her from a life of loneliness.

If she was honest with herself, deep down, she always knew something was off. Little hints of anger and rage would surface, but she had brushed it off. Her father had always been violent, so she assumed every man had a little bit of uncontrollable rage. That was a mistake she wouldn't make again.

Some people were destined to be alone. It was time she accepted that she was one of them.

She grabbed her phone out of her purse. Swiping the screen, she saw five calls from her supervisor. She clicked on the voicemail, listening to the first message.

"Miss Marsh, this is your boss, Albert. Don't bother to come back to work. You're fired. Our office received an email with an attachment of naked pictures of you. When you signed your contract, it stipulated a code of conduct that we expect from all employees. Your lack of discretion has put the project in jeopardy. Don't bother coming in to collect personal items either; they will be boxed by security and sent to your address. We will not be writing a letter of recommendation."

The color drained from Chloe's face. Naked pictures? How was that possible? She had never allowed anyone to take pictures of her. Then it hit her like a ton of bricks. The boudoir pictures she had taken with Brooklyn and left for Jacob.

She quickly went to Jacob's Facebook profile, and there, posted for the whole world to see, were her pictures, along with a story about her being the daughter of the infamous Las Vegas murderer. There were already hundreds of hits, and it wouldn't be long before it went viral. How would she ever get a job with her name and pictures all over the internet?

Chloe collapsed on the bed. There would be no rebuilding her life after this. Jacob had made sure she couldn't possibly start over.

Santino watched as Stellina fell apart. When she didn't move for half an hour, he assumed she had finally fallen asleep. He and Alessandro could leave knowing she was safe. Besides, he would come back tomorrow.

Chapter 5
"Mad World" by Gary Jules

When they got back to the resort, Alessandro went to the main lodge and brought food to Santino's cabin, so he could avoid Mamma in the kitchen. After eating, Santino then showered and lay down.

Santino woke up with a jolt, a bad feeling overcoming him. Everything in him was screaming to go to Stellina.

He glanced at the clock, seeing it was nine seventeen in the evening. He had only slept for a few hours after not being able to fall asleep because of the vision imprinted on his brain of Chloe hanging upside down from the cross.

As long as he lived, he would never be able to comprehend how a man could take his vengeance out on an innocent person to the degree Jacob had. Especially a woman as fragile as Chloe.

Santino couldn't deny that he had thought of retribution more than once, but common sense had always prevailed. However, Jacob had spent months preparing for Chloe's forced penance. It led Santino to believe the man was mentally unstable. That kind of rage wasn't normal by any stretch of the imagination. The more he thought about the situation, the more unease crept into his bones.

After throwing off his covers, he shivered, and it wasn't because of the air-conditioning. He needed to check on her.

Santino grabbed his pants, nearly falling in his rush to get them on. Then he threw his T-shirt on, while racing to grab his car keys.

The sun had completely set by the time he skidded to a stop in front of his Alfa Romeo, realizing he couldn't take his car because it would stick out like a sore thumb. He reached into his pocket for his phone and called Alessandro.

With a gravelly voice, his brother answered with, "What's wrong?"

Santino released a breath he hadn't known he was holding. "I need the keys for Marcello's truck."

"Where are you going?"

Frustrated but determined, he started heading toward his brother's cabin. "I have to check on Chloe. I have a bad feeling, and I can't chill out until I know she's safe."

"Give me five minutes. I'll come with you," Alessandro said, untangling himself from Ava.

His wife mumbled, "What's going on?"

Feeling stupid for panicking, Santino said, "No, just give me the keys and go back to bed. It's probably nothing. If I need you, I'll call. I swear. I'm at your front door."

Two minutes later, Alessandro opened the door with the keys, and Shamo, Alessandro's dog, jumped all over Santino, thrilled with his sudden visit. Santino bent down to give the pup a quick scratch before getting up and reaching for the keys.

"Promise me that you'll call if you need anything." Alessandro held tightly to the keys, not releasing them until Santino nodded in agreement. "Bro, I mean it. You call me."

"Thanks." Santino shot down the stairs, running toward the truck.

On the drive over there, he had to remind himself to keep just slightly over the speed limit. The last thing he needed was to get stopped by the sheriff.

Forty-five minutes later, he was sitting in front of the shelter. Chloe's light was off, which wasn't surprising, but still unsettling. The drapes had been closed, too, so he couldn't see if she was in bed. His chest tightened with anxiety as he sat there, watching the house like a hawk.

At eleven, Santino saw the next shift arrive. The woman who had helped Chloe came out, then got in her car and left.

Ten minutes later, he saw movement at Chloe's window. The room was still dark, but the drapes were moved aside, and then the window was opened. He then saw Chloe push the screen aside and throw her purse and her overnight bag out onto the ground.

His natural instinct was to go and help her, but on second thought, he figured he had better just sit still for a minute and see what she was doing. If he moved too quickly, she might call for help, alerting the staff inside.

He held the steering wheel so tightly that his knuckles turned white as he watched her struggle to get out the window. Finally, she hoisted herself completely through the opening, dropping to the ground. There was no doubt in his mind that Chloe's fall had hurt her already injured body, especially after it took five tries for her to gain her footing. She ended up having to drag herself with a heavy limp to the corner. Once settled, she then made a call. Five minutes later, a car pulled up and she climbed inside.

Santino turned the truck around, following the car, which had an Uber sign in the back window. It didn't take long to figure out they were heading back to her house.

Instead of turning onto her street, he continued driving straight, making a three-point turn after a safe distance. He waited for the Uber driver to pull away before he turned onto her street, driving past the driveway a few yards before shutting the truck off.

In the meantime, Chloe dragged her bag as far as she possibly could before leaving it in the driveway. She then broke through the police tape on the door. The lock had been broken, so there was no need for her keys.

Inside, she felt around for the light, flicking it on. All the color drained from her face, and her heart rate accelerated when she saw the magnitude of the damage.

This wasn't vandalism. This was a hate crime of epic proportions.

She cautiously meandered around the destruction, going from one room to another. Every piece of furniture she had bought at second-hand stores and painstakingly restored were reduced to piles of rubble. The couch and chairs had been butchered, stuffing hurled everywhere. Every wall was covered in slanderous profanity. The kitchen had also been ravaged—every plate, glass, and mug smashed into a million pieces. The pots and pans looked like someone had taken a sledgehammer to them. Jacob and his friends had made sure there wasn't one useful thing left in the house.

The farther she walked in, the more a stench increased. Opening the refrigerator door, she squealed, jumping back when she saw animal guts over every surface.

Chloe quickly closed the fridge, backing away, knowing she had to get anything salvageable from her bedroom and get the hell out of there.

She stumbled on the cord of the shattered coffeepot in her haste, nearly falling on her face. Reaching out, she grabbed the table, cutting her hand on a piece of broken glass. It hurt like hell, but not as much as the realization of the hatred it had to have taken to obliterate not only her home, but to also commit aggravated assault. The chill over her skin moved deep into her bones.

Chloe went from her hands shaking to full-on body trembles. She had always known the world was a dangerous place, but right here, it felt beyond vicious and hideous. The malicious attacks were so conclusive that she knew she would never again feel safe or trust herself to care for another living soul.

Little droplets of blood from her hand made a path to her bedroom, where she ever so slowly pushed the door open. Up until this point, Chloe had been so shocked and scared that the tears had remained at bay. That all changed the minute she saw the picture of her and Harper taken out of the smashed frame and tacked to the wall with two butcher knifes through their ripped faces. Above it were the words, One down, one to go. You can run, but you can't hide. Die, whore! In the middle of the bed lay all of her photos, burnt beyond recognition.

A cry of agony escaped from her shattered heart. She had nothing left except for the clothing on her back and her memories. Every tangible piece of her history had been destroyed. If everything in front of her wasn't enough, Harper's little stuffed lamb had also been shredded.

Wobbling, she bent to pick up the treasured stuffed animal that had been her solace in the worst of times. Then, looking heavenward, she cried, "I'm sorry, Harper. I've lost every connection I had left of you. I trusted the wrong person. Why didn't God take the stupid twin instead of you? I miss you and don't know how to pick up the pieces."

Santino stood outside, peeking through the corner of the window as he listened to the horrific scene in front of him. He realized at that moment that Jacob had no intention of killing her. No, killing would have been more humane. Torturing her to a point of breaking was far more debilitating, and much crueler.

Santino knew he couldn't wait another minute. He had to convince her that she had someone on her side. He would help her pick up the pieces of her life, even if it meant he had to walk away from his famiglia to do it.

He slowly made his way to the front door, where he quietly pushed it open. He was astounded at the scene in front of him.

He had heard many stories of how police officers sometimes took their lives after years of exposure to the evilness of mankind. He now understood some things could never be washed from your memory.

It took longer to reach the bedroom than he had first anticipated because every room caused him to stop to take in the immensity of what seemingly normal people could do.

Santino was moving toward the bedrooms when he heard a scraping sound farther down the hall. He stopped at the bedroom she had been in, finding it empty, so he followed the noise that led him to another door at the end of the hall. Being an old farmhouse, he assumed it led outside.

Before he opened the door, he heard muffled crying. He cautiously turned the knob, not wanting to scare Chloe. The room turned out to be a garage that was also in disarray.

Santino's heart just about leapt out of his rib cage when he saw Chloe standing high on a stack of wooden crates with a hangman's noose around her neck. He froze mid-step when she started to speak.

"Is this what you wanted, Jacob? A noose around my neck?" The pitch of her voice became higher with simmering rage. "For me to have nothing and no one to live for? No options but to take my life and save you the trouble?

"The noose fits, by the way. But I'm sure that was calculated, like everything else you did. Unfortunately, I did have to drag another crate over. You didn't consider that the pins in my leg wouldn't allow me to stretch high enough to climb up here. Shame on you for giving me time to change my mind. Guess your perfect plan had a few flaws after all. Although, not many because here I stand, in your trap."

Santino looked frantically through the dim light to see if Jacob and his friends were there. He was relieved for a second at seeing no one, until he heard the elevated stress turn into debilitating sobs.

Chloe choked a couple of times with emotion, her voice vibrating with gut-wrenching pain. "I'm sorry, Harper. I can't do it anymore. I can't live another day surrounded by so much hate. I know you're disappointed in me for giving up. The weak one couldn't prevail while the strong one had her life taken. What you don't understand is, I can't live without you." She held the noose loosely around her neck with shaking hands.

When Santino saw that her quaking caused the unstable crates to wobble, he entered quietly, fearful of startling her and causing her to fall.

"I tried so hard to come out of my shell and live my life to the fullest, because you didn't get the same chance. But I failed miserably. I'm a mess, Harper. Everyone hates me." She was talking through her weeping. "I'm so scared, and completely alone. I have nothing left."

Santino saw the exact second that she heaved in too deeply for a huge breath, causing the crates to crumble. He screamed, "No!" watching her fall as he sprinted with all his might to reach her. Thankfully, Chloe's hands were still tangled in the noose, stopping her neck from snapping.

He reached her as she fought the inevitable, grabbing her hips and hoisting her up.

"Hold on, Chloe."

Panic-stricken, she fought, wiggling and gasping for breath.

He wrapped one arm around her hips, using the other to loosen the rope. It was like fighting a wild animal caught in a snare.

"Stop moving!" he screamed.

She froze at the command as black dots flashed behind her lids.

Finally, he was able to yank back the knot enough to drag it over her head.

"Gesù Cristo, Stellina, what were you thinking?" He lowered them both gently to the ground.

Chloe flopped down, limbs hanging loosely, making Santino think she had died. Panicked, he moved his fingers to her neck to check for a pulse. The strong thumping assured him that she must have unknowingly held her breath during the struggle. Lack of oxygen had caused her to faint.

Santino brought her slack body to his pounding chest, hugging her tightly. Tears gathered in his eyes, threatening to fall with the enormity of what could have been a different conclusion.

He felt her stir as consciousness came back. Adjusting her gently on his lap, he cradled her head with his left arm and watched her lashes flutter open.

He ran his sweating hand down her bruised face and calmed his voice, hoping not to scare her. "Chloe, you're okay. I promise you're not alone. I won't let anyone hurt you from this moment on."

Confusion filled Chloe's mind for a minute before awareness set in, along with terror. Her fight-or-flight response kicked in, and she started to struggle, but it didn't last long before he reprimanded her.

"Chloe! Stop and listen for two seconds. I swear on my dad's and brother's souls that I will never hurt you. I'm trying to help."

Pushed past the point of caring, she managed the courage to shout back, "Really? The same people my father killed? Tell me again you want to help the daughter of the man who murdered your family." Her beautiful voice was strained.

He gripped her struggling body tighter. Through clenched teeth, he seethed out, "You're not accountable for your father's actions. Stop buying into Jacob's bullshit. You're not alone, goddammit!"

"Let go of me!" She struggled with all her might, but when she realized he wasn't letting go, she gave up and started to cry. "Please, Santino. I can't take any more. You can't get blood from a stone. I have nothing left." Chloe totally gave up, her cries turning into soft whimpers.

Santino cradled the defeated girl closer to his chest as he lifted himself up to his feet. He walked back through the house, stopping to collect the ruined stuffed animal from her bedroom before carrying her to the truck. After lifting her into the passenger side ever so gently, he buckled her in. Then he locked her door, hoping to keep her in the truck until he got in on the other side.

Climbing in, he noticed she hadn't moved a muscle. Either she had withdrawn into herself, or simply didn't care what happened anymore.

By the time they reached the resort, Chloe was sleeping. He carefully carried her to his cabin, knowing this was the last place she would want to be, but he didn't have an alternative right now. Tonight, they would stay here, and in the morning, he would come up with a better plan.

Santino was juggling her, trying to fit the key into the lock, when Sabastian startled him into nearly dropping her, cautiously asking, "Are you all right?"

The last thing he needed was the compassion in his older brother's voice. It ruptured his resolve.

"No. No, I'm not. Look at what they did to her." He slowly turned with the precious bundle in his arms, hearing not only Sabastian's intake of breath but also his two other brothers'. "If I hadn't been there, she'd be hanging from the rafters from their hangman's noose. They not only broke her spirit but also everything she owned. How could anyone do this to . . . ?"

As the brothers saw the minute the anguish of the last twenty-four hours became too much, Luca stepped forward. "Careful. Let me take Chloe."

He reared back. "No. No one touches her, understand?" he venomously barked out.

Luca backed up with his hands raised in surrender. "I understand. Relax, bro. We're not going to hurt her. We only want to help."

Alessandro took the keys out of his hand and opened the door.

Then they all watched as Santino carried her to his room, took off her shoes, and tucked her into his bed. When he was done, he signaled for them to follow.

He left the door open, moving one of his leather club chairs so he could sit and watch her, protecting her completely from outside forces and herself.

Luca whispered, "We can't talk like this. We might wake her. Let me go get Eli's old baby monitor." He dashed out the door before anyone could answer. Five minutes later, he returned, going into the room with Santino hot on his heels.

Luca hooked the monitor up on the nightstand beside Chloe, then carried the other half into the kitchen, where the rest of his brothers were sitting at the table. He turned on the viewing screen and sound.

Santino relaxed, listening to her steady breathing as he watched her sleep.

"Talk," Sabastian said.

Santino reiterated the whole story, stopping at times to look at the monitor and to rein in his emotions. Alessandro got up a few times, cursing softly while pacing. Luca and Sabastian sat stoically, arms crossed, listening to every word.

When Santino was done, Sabastian reached over and clasped Santino's clenched fist. "You know we're with you one hundred percent, right?"

Santino kept his head down, swallowing a huge lump in his throat. After a minute, he lifted his devastated eyes. "Thank you, but that's only one of my problems. I can't stay here with her because of Mamma."

"Not your problem," Alessandro rebuked, still pacing. "For years, you've taken it upon yourself to be Mamma's guardian. As of right now, your first priority is Chloe. Let us deal with Mamma."

He pushed his chair back swiftly, getting up. "You know she isn't going to allow Chloe to stay here."

"Allow?" Luca stood to match his younger brother's height. "She doesn't allow us to do anything. These are our homes. Mamma is wrong; no two ways about it. Besides, you're going to need help."

Santino went to the fridge to grab a beer. He lifted it, silently asking if anyone else wanted one. Everyone shook their head.

He twisted off the cap, then took a long pull. After he let the cool liquid soothe his parched throat, he continued, "But she will. You know that as much as I do. Mamma hates Chloe, and given the chance, she'll hurt her. Maybe not physically, but no one here can stop the sharp edge of her tongue. Chloe can't take another hit of her crazy shit. She's not strong enough. I don't even know how I can help her. What happened to Chloe is straight out of a Stephen King novel. That's gotta fuck with her head."

No one had a chance to answer before Chloe cried out.

Santino rushed to her side, realizing she was dreaming. Kneeling one leg on the bed, he ran his hand over her head, soothing her gently with soft words of comfort. She was almost settled when she suddenly jackknifed up, screaming at the top of her lungs.

Santino seized her shoulders, trying to gently shake her awake. The three brothers filled the room, distress bleeding from their pores.

Chloe saw the room full of big men and panicked, screaming at them to leave her alone, bursting out of Santino's hold and throwing herself off the bed. As she dragged her injured body across the floor, she was so disorientated that she smashed into the night table with a yelp.

"Chloe, stop!" Santino yelled.

She stopped dead, heaving deeply as she rolled into a protective ball.

Alessandro stepped out of the room to text Quinn.

Alessandro: We need your help. Whatever you do, don't tell

Mamma. We're at Santino's cabin. Come quick!

Quinn: I'm on my way.

Meanwhile, Santino went to Chloe, sitting on his haunches and speaking softly. "Nobody is going to hurt you, Chloe."

Mewling like a kitten, she crunched up tighter.

"Please, Chloe, you're killing me. I want to help you, but I don't know how. Tell me you hear me and that you understand what I'm saying."

She didn't answer, rocking back and forth.

Santino continued to try to reach her as the other two stood, dumbfounded. A few minutes later, Alessandro walked in with Quinn.

"Santino, Quinn's here to help."

Santino whipped his head around, ready to kill his brother.

Quinn stepped into his view. "Santino, come with me for a minute. I need to understand what happened before I can help her. Trust me, Santino; I know what I'm doing. Chloe isn't the first PTSD victim I have worked with. Please follow me. Luca can watch over her while we talk."

Getting up, Santino furiously slammed into Alessandro's shoulder as he walked out of the room.

Not deterred, Alessandro followed.

When they cleared the door, Santino's anger exploded. Turning, he grabbed Alessandro's shirt and pushed him against the wall. "What the fuck did you not understand about Mamma not finding out, coglione?"

Quinn tried to muscle his way between them as Alessandro answered, "Did you see Chloe freak out? She needs professional help before it's too late. Quinn is her best chance to make it out of this with her mind intact. He's got the expertise; you know that. Trust him."

"Santino." Quinn took over as he slowly peeled Santino's fingers from his brother's shirt. "Anything Chloe and I talk about is confidential between a psychologist and his patient. I have never broken the rules of the American Psychology Association."

"She's not your patient because she doesn't have money for a psychologist," he growled back, "so you could tell Mamma anything you wanted."

Miffed, Quinn calmly responded, "You know me better than that. I love your mamma, but I would never cross a professional line, even for Valentina. Earlier today, Sabastian told me everything that happened after the bonfire. That young woman desperately needs professional help. She doesn't need to pay me. I'll take on her case pro bono. Tell me what happened since she left the hospital. I need to know the best way to proceed with her."

Santino lost all his bluster. If he wasn't so tired and distraught, he would never have challenged Quinn's ethics.

"Okay, but Chloe is my responsibility. I'll pay you."

Quinn's forehead creased in annoyance. "Now you're insulting me. I didn't go into this profession to get rich. There are times people can't afford my services, and I'm more than willing to help for free. I consider us as close as family, and if I can't help my family, well, then I might as well hang up my hat. Set your ego aside for one minute, and let's work together to help Chloe."

Chastised, Santino apologized, then told Quinn a short version of the last few hours.

After listening intently, Quinn asked the hard question. "Do you think Chloe meant to end her life?"

Horrified, he spat out, "No, I don't think it was her intention at that moment. She slipped."

Relieved, Quinn answered, "Good. Santino, do you trust me?" He waited for a nod. "Take me into your room and introduce me to Chloe. Even if she seems despondent, carry on like you got her acknowledgment. Once I start, I might need you all to leave. I assure you that she is safe with me, and I will be gentle with her."

Agitated, Santino started to tap his fingers against his hip in increments of five. He didn't want Chloe to think he was abandoning her like everyone else had. "What if she needs me?"

"I promise I'll call you."

Conceding, he said, "Okay, follow me." He led Mamma's boyfriend to Chloe.

Quinn looked at the young woman curled into a ball and rocking. Her body had definitely taken a severe beating today.

Santino crouched down beside her, brushing the hair from her face. "Chloe, I've brought someone to help you. He's a psychologist. He helped me and my brothers. Chloe, this is Quinn. You might remember him from the bonfire. He wants to talk to you. He thinks he can help. If you want me to stay, just say so and I will."

She didn't answer, but Quinn carried on like she had. "It's nice to meet you, Chloe. I know you had a traumatic couple of days. I'm sorry for everything you've gone through. Right now, everything seems overwhelming and insurmountable, but you're not alone. Santino has vowed to help, and I would also like to help you, if you'll allow me?"

Chloe heard the man's kind offer, but she was done talking. This wasn't the first time she had heard empathetic words from strangers. Every time she had lost someone close to her, some professional had uttered the same hollow words that had never changed the circumstances of her life. What was left to say? Culpability was hers alone, because she was the only one left standing. Her feelings didn't matter.

The man who fathered her had murdered innocent people, ending the spree by taking the coward's way out and killing himself. The devil had left her behind to pay for his sins. The evilness lived in her veins. Now she would pay for his crime time and time again, until her final breath. She had been trusting too many times and lost.

Yes, the time for talking was over. Chloe now had a decision to make, but until she decided if she would end the suffering herself or allow Jacob to take her life, there was no way she was trusting another living soul.

Quinn talked to the hollowed eyes of a woman who had retreated into herself. He knew her withdrawal was a protection mechanism. It wasn't something he would break through tonight, or maybe anytime in the foreseeable future. Only time and gentle caring would help this poor soul.

Quinn turned to Santino. "Chloe is exhausted. Let's concentrate on getting her body healthy, and then we'll move on from there. Let's get her up and into bed. Do you know when she last ate?"

"No. I assume they served her dinner at the shelter. I have no idea whether she ate it or not," he answered softly, taking the cue from Quinn's soft-spoken mannerisms.

Together, the men each took an arm and lifted her, guiding Chloe to Santino's bed. She couldn't subdue the sounds of pain she made as they transferred her back to the bed, and each moan, groan, and mewl nearly took Santino out at the knees. He vowed again to help heal Chloe. He wouldn't rest until he saw a real smile and heard a belly laugh that she'd be unable to contain.

He watched two tears trail down her cheeks, knowing they were one percent physical pain and ninety-nine percent sorrow.

Once she was tucked under the covers, Quinn said his goodbyes. "I'll check in with you first thing tomorrow. Try to get some rest."

Santino nodded his thanks before kneeling beside the bed, listening to Chloe breathe. She had instantly fallen back asleep.

Santino was beyond exhausted, but terrified to close his eyes even for a minute, fearing she would wake up disorientated and afraid.

All his brothers walked in undetected.

Luca moved to the chair beside the bed, whispering, "I know what you're feeling. You're afraid that if you sleep, she'll need you and you won't hear her. I went through exactly the same thing during Brooklyn's crisis. Trust me, brother, you'll hear her. Your body will be so in tune to her breathing that even the slightest change will make you aware. Sleep while you can."

Not looking at him, Santino answered, "I'm not sure I can, but there's something I have to do before I even attempt to sleep. Can you go to Marcello's truck, get the stuffed animal on the seat, and bring it to me? Then I want you all to go home to your famiglia and hug them for me. Peace won't come for me tonight, but I want each of you to remember the gifts you have been given and hold them tightly."

Each man was humbled by their youngest brother's words. They knew the gift of their famiglia was not something to be taken for granted. Santino had a long road ahead of him, but they would ensure he didn't walk it alone.

Luca did his bidding, bringing the severed toy to him. Then they all said goodnight and left.

Santino sat quietly with a pair of scissors, a decorative pillow, and a sewing kit that his mamma had put in his cabin. He had balked at the time, telling her if something needed sewn, he would either take it to the dry cleaners or throw it out. Now he was thankful for the single needle and two colors of thread.

For two and half hours, he painstakingly ripped the pillow apart, taking the stuffing out and putting it into the little lamb. His stitches were crude at best, but inch by inch, he repaired the old toy. When he was done, he got up and stretched his muscles before walking to his closet, where he ripped two black buttons from the cuff of his best suit jacket. They would be perfect. However, he didn't fail to notice it was the same jacket he had worn for his dad and brother's funerals. In his heart, he knew they would approve.

Santino moved back to the chair and finished sewing on the eyes.

He then lifted the pathetic little toy, turning it over and over, inspecting every part of its body. Chloe had lost so much in the last twenty-four hours, but the two things that had seemed to break her were this little lamb and the photos burnt on the bed. He couldn't save the photos, but he could her little lamb.

Exhausted, he laid his head back on the chair, but not before he tucked the little lamb under her arms. Unbeknownst to Chloe, she was not alone. She once again held a connection to Harper, and had a man eager to help her survive the pain and find a way to move on.

Chapter 6
"Wake Me Up" by Avicii

Chloe awoke, cuddling the familiar feel of Lambie tucked in her arms against her collarbone. Every muscle seemed to ache.

It took a minute for the memories of yesterday to filter into her consciousness, and when they did, her eyes sprang open. The first thing she saw was Santino, sleeping on the chair beside the bed. Terror seeped through her, yet she was aware enough not to make any sudden moves to wake him. A torn apart pillow and a needle with thread stuck into the arm of the chair drew her attention. From the little she knew about him, it didn't make sense, until it hit her.

She was holding Lambie.

She shifted quietly, lifting the invaluable toy up. Lambie looked how she felt—battered—but he was still carrying on. Santino had sewn Harper's favorite toy.

Unbelievable happiness swept through her as she turned the little lamb in her hands, tears streaming down her face. It was the nicest thing anyone had ever done for her.

"Sorry it looks like Dr. Frankenstein did the job. I've never sewn anything in my life."

Chloe squeaked, frightened by his voice.

"I won't hurt you. You're safe with me."

"Thank you. You'll never know how much this means." Although she had promised herself not to talk to anyone, the man in front of her had just given her the best gift of her life. Sniffling, she tried to slow her beating heart.

He didn't move a muscle, afraid to lose the little bit of ground he had gained. "We need to talk. But first, I think we need to eat something. How about a cup of coffee or tea?"

This man confused her. He should hate her even more than Jacob, because he had lost two family members in the massacre, yet every time she turned around, he was trying to help her. Why?

Santino saw the wheels in her mind turning. "Please don't overthink things right now. If I wanted to hurt you, I had ample time and means. If you believe nothing else I say, I want you to believe I would never hurt you. You're safe with me, Chloe.

"Let's take it one baby step at a time. I need a coffee badly, so I'll put a pot on and the kettle if you prefer tea. The washroom is that door over there." He pointed. "Do you need help up?" he asked as he stood, stretching his tight muscles. He reached out to help her.

Distressed and unable to stop herself, Chloe released a sharp cry, pulling back as her body protested. He was such a big man.

The wounded look in his eyes made her feel bad. Dropping her eyes, she apologized.

Santino smiled. It was a small step, but it was still a step in the right direction. "No need to apologize. I moved too fast. Sorry." He moved back a few steps. "Try to see if you can get up by yourself. If you think you can, I'll head to the kitchen. If not, I'll figure out how to get you there without touching you."

Chloe lifted her eyes to judge if the sincerity in his voice matched his expression. It did.

He moved the chair to give her a clear path, and then she slowly edged to the side of the mattress, swinging her sore legs and feet to the carpet. She balanced a hand on the nightstand and one on the bed. It took five very frustrating tries to lift herself up. She wasn't strong enough to sustain her weight with her bad leg, so she fell back down to the mattress, blowing out a discouraged breath.

"It's okay. We'll figure something out," Santino said, heading for the walk-in closet. Chloe heard him moving things around, and then he came out with a bat. "It's not a crutch, but it will work like a cane." He moved to the end of the bed, avoiding her personal space, and laid the bat down so she could reach it. It was ingenious.

She used the nightstand and the bat as she stood on her second attempt. Chloe took her first step with the help of the bat, then grinned up at him.

"Be careful when you reach the hardwood floors; it might be slippery. I'll leave when you reach the washroom. Coffee or tea? Oh, and I should warn you, I can make toast and a mean bowl of cereal, but that's where my cooking skills end." He lifted the edges of his mouth in an innocent smile.

Chloe couldn't help tittering. "Me too. Although, I can also make a mean microwavable dinner."

That half-suppressed laugh went straight to Santino's heart. Never in a million years had he thought she would even crack a smile in the next month. He prayed she was starting to trust him. But he had to remember not to put the cart in front of the horse.

When she nearly slipped with her second step on the hardwood floor, he lurched forward a step before catching himself and stepping back when he saw the alarm on her face. "Sorry, knee-jerk reaction."

Chloe nodded once before concentrating harder to keep her footing as she licked her dry lips. She finally made it to the door.

Santino didn't say a word as he left the room.

She breathed a sigh of relief, did her business, and then leaned against the sink to wash her hands and face and run some toothpaste over her teeth with her finger. She avoided looking in the mirror, not needing a reminder of the last forty-eight hours. Her aching body was reminder enough.

Santino was surprised when he walked to the kitchen island and found three containers of food, accompanied by a note.

Bro,

I hope Chloe is feeling better this morning. Emmy made lots of breakfast food. She wasn't sure what Chloe would like, so she went with your favorites. This should last for a few days. I will drop off lunch and dinner. I'll text beforehand in case Chloe doesn't want to see me.

I hope you found some peace last night.

I'm proud as hell to call you my brother.

Sabastian

Wow!

Being the youngest, Santino hadn't had a lot of personal interaction with his three older brothers growing up. Well, not until they started building the resort. He and Alessandro had always been close, though.

When he had realized they were all amazing men, he had wanted to be just like them when he grew up. For years, he had worshiped them. None of his friends even came close to how cool his brothers were. Their strength of character, fortitude, and resilience were enviable. When they had lost Marcello and their dad, he had also learned that his brothers were amazing in a crisis. However, in the last forty-eight hours, his admiration had grown.

"Santino? If you're having regrets about me being here, I can call an Uber," Chloe stated from the bedroom door, seeing his head hung low.

Shocked, he pulled himself together and lifted his face. "God, no. I was just thinking about how lucky I am to have such great brothers. Sabastian left food that Emmy made for us." Grinning, he said, "I don't know if you remember how good Emmy's breakfasts are, but damn, that girl can cook."

Without thinking, she mumbled, "Just like a good woman should."

"My brothers can cook amazingly too. They tease me unmercifully because I can't. But it doesn't make me less of a person. We all have things we can do and things we can't. If it bugs you that much, I could ask Emmy to give us cooking classes. She keeps telling me one day she's going to teach me how to cook. She says if I can read and follow instructions, she can teach me how to cook anything. I'll try, if you will." He didn't move from his spot. "Tea or coffee?"

Chloe hobbled slowly into the kitchen. "Tea, please. And I won't be here long enough to try. I'm leaving Pennsylvania today."

Santino tried not to overreact, collecting his thoughts as he moved to the table and pulled a chair out for her. Then he moved away to give her space, grabbing the food and some dishes. When he had everything set up, he told her, "I would really like you to reconsider. You have no car, no clothes, and you're hurt. Please stay with me for a while. You can have the guest room. We can start getting your life back on track by going back to your house and seeing if anything is salvageable. If not, we can buy what you need."

He blew out a breath. "Chloe, you're not safe to be on your own until Keith catches the people responsible for hurting you. I would go crazy if I thought they could get to you."

Sitting straighter, she said in a determined voice, "I can't let you help me. I'll figure something out."

Santino didn't show his aggravation as he opened the containers. Whenever Quinn talked to him in therapy sessions, he always used a soothing voice, telling him to think about the options available before coming to any conclusions. Chloe needed to be in control of what was left of her life, and he needed to be patient if he was going to help her.

"If you're convinced you have to leave, then let's come up with a plan B. I will drive you to the bank so you can get some money for clothes, and then we can find a place to fix your car. After you figure out where you want to go, we can search online for a place to rent. Is there any way you can transfer to another city with your job? Maybe that will make it easier to choose a location." He hoped against hope she wouldn't leave.

Chloe thought about how far she could stretch her money. She would have to leave her car behind and buy just enough second-hand clothes to get her through. She would have to live off Mr. Noodles for the first little while. The rest of the money would have to be enough for first and last month's rent. Without a job or a vehicle, she would have to move to a big city with public transportation. But that would mean the rent would be higher, and she didn't know if she could afford it. It all suddenly felt overwhelming.

She bit the inside of her bottom lip, trying to contain the tears threatening to fall.

He saw the minute neither option seemed to work for her. Her shoulders dropped, and her eyes spilled over with moisture as her breathing became erratic. The need to reach out was killing him.

"Stellina, you still have option A. Don't be too quick to dismiss it. Stay with me for a little while, regroup, heal, and get stronger. Then everything will come together. Besides, I really want you to talk to Quinn. I don't know if you remember meeting him last night. He was my therapist and wants to help."

"I can't afford a therapist," she said, knowing those types of luxuries were a thing of the past.

That was too much for Santino. Moving from his chair, he knelt on one knee in front of her but didn't touch her. "Quinn knows you don't have the money right now, but he wants to help you, so he is offering his services pro bono." Seeing her gear up to turn down the offer, he said, "Wait before rejecting his offer. Consider for one minute all you have been through—"

"I don't have to consider," she interrupted angrily. "I relive it every minute of the day." She brought her hands up, irritably swiping at the tears. "I'm such an idiot. Why did I ever think I deserved more than I got?"

For Santino, watching her beat herself up was like having a boa constrictor around his chest. With the small amount of air he was able to get into his lungs, he said, "Nobody deserved what happened to you. Only a coward would do what Jacob did. My famiglia is famous for saying, 'It's not your cross to bear,' and no truer words were ever spoken, especially in your situation. Jacob is a very sick, demented man."

"Your mom feels the same way. Does that make her sick and demented?" It was a low blow, but Chloe had to make him realize how impossible it was for her to stay here.

"I'll call it temporary insanity with Mamma. Once she gets past the initial shock, she'll see the light and feel terrible. But let me assure you that I don't condone what she said or did. She was wrong. This cabin is my home—no one can tell me whom I can or can't have here. Nothing would make me happier than if you would stay here for a little while and heal. If it makes you feel better, Mamma doesn't have to know you're here."

He winked as he stood. "Now we have spent so much time talking that the food is cold. It's time to put your skills to use and tell me how long to heat up our breakfast in the microwave." He then explained everything in the containers and convinced her to try the red velvet pancakes because those were his absolute favorite.

Chloe relished the taste and wished more than anything that she was capable of making such amazing food. She hadn't realized how hungry she was until she had devoured the pancakes and was reaching for a blueberry buttermilk scone.

Santino watched, thrilled at knowing sustenance would help give her a clearer mind and regain her strength. He was also starving and devoured half the food Emmy had sent.

When he was finally done, he leaned back and rubbed his belly. "That was delicious. I can't eat another bite."

Chloe's eyes were huge. Astonished, she commented, "You ate more in one sitting than I do in a week."

He smiled. "I'm bigger than you, and still a growing boy. I've also learned to eat as much as possible when other people cook. That way I have to make less paninis."

"What's a panini?" she asked, forgetting about her problems for a minute.

Santino picked up his fork and pointed it at her. "Oh, Chloe, you haven't lived until you've had one of my paninis. They're the other thing I'm really good at making. It's an Italian sandwich with crusty buns filled with prosciutto, soppressata, mortadella, capicolo, and salami topped with provolone cheese and olive spread. I'll have to make you one. I'm drooling just thinking about it."

She screwed up her bruised face. "I don't recognize any of the things you just named off. What's wrong with white bread, butter, and American cheese?"

Putting the fork back down, he gave a hearty laugh. "I'll let you be the judge. I'll make an Italian panini, and you make an American cheese sandwich, and we'll see whose is better."

Her inquisitive face fell, along with her eyes. "I'll lose. No two ways about it."

This time he did reach out to touch her, picking up her hand and holding tighter when she tried to pull back. "Chloe, I didn't mean to offend you. When I'm around you, I just want to share everything that I love. It wasn't a dig about the things you like." He released her hand before he scared her off, then started to pack up the leftovers.

They both froze when they heard a knock at the door.

Santino watched as Chloe went into complete panic mode, her eyes darting around, looking for another exit. Her hands also shook.

"I'll get rid of whoever is here." He stormed toward the door, nearly ripping it off the hinges when he opened it. "What?" he yelled.

Emmy jumped back, dropping the bag she was carrying. Little Shawn, who was in the baby carrier attached to her front, started to cry.

"Sorry, Emmy. I thought it was one of my brothers." Santino felt like an absolute coglione for scaring his sister-in-law and nephew.

"Sorry, I should have called first." She patted Shawn's back while bouncing, trying to calm the baby down. "I didn't mean to intrude, but Sabastian said Chloe didn't have any clothes, and I have a bagful I was getting rid of because I don't think my mommy body will ever fit into them again. They might be a little big, but I think she's about the size I was before I got pregnant. I'll just leave the bag here. Sorry again. I didn't mean to make you mad." She turned to rush away.

Santino stepped out to stop her, grabbing her retreating arm. "Emmy, I'm sorry. I didn't mean to scare you or Shawn. I guess I'm a little overprotective of Chloe. She's been through a lot and got scared when there was an unexpected knock at the door."

Disheartened, she continued to run her hands down the now-settling baby's back. "Sabastian told me that he would deliver the clothes later but, as usual, I didn't listen. I thought Chloe might want something clean to wear now. It was stupid to barrel right over here."

Santino wrapped his arms around his flustered sister-in-law, whispering, "Emmy, that was really sweet. I'm sure Chloe will be very thankful. Next time, if you don't mind, text before you come over. She's a little skittish after everything that happened."

She pulled back when Shawn started to squawk over being squished between his mommy and uncle.

"I should have known better." Emmy's eyes got glassy. "I want to help her, Santino. Sabastian told me everything, and my heart is breaking for her. She needs a friend, and I'm a really good friend."

Santino bent down, kissing her forehead. "I know, Emmy, and she could really use a good friend. But first, I have to convince her that she's safe and that she should stay. She is bound and determined to run, yet she has nothing left. Correction. Now she has some clothes. Thanks for that. I know she'll really appreciate it. And if I can get her to stay, I will let her know she has a friend in the wings, waiting to get to know her. By the way, I can't thank you enough for all the food you sent over."

Emmy gave him a little push. "I'd do anything for you. You know that." Barely audible, she said, "Tell her this is the last place they will look for her. I also know how to keep my mouth shut."

Santino knew she meant Mamma. That was huge because Emmy and Mamma were as close as any biological daughter and mamma. But what she said about no one looking for Chloe here was brilliant. In Jacob's twisted mind, he would never consider looking at the resort. He would assume it was the last place Chloe would hide.

"Emmy, you might have just given me the perfect argument to keep her here. I should have gone to my smart sister-in-law first, instead of racking my own brain for a solution. Thanks." He bent, kissing her forehead again before moving down to the baby and kissing the back of his head. "Love you guys."

Emmy had an all-encompassing smile when he pulled back. "We love you too, Uncle Santino." There was a bounce in her step that hadn't been there before as she walked down the stairs, heading toward the main lodge.

When Santino entered his cabin, he noticed that Chloe wasn't in the kitchen where he had left her. He called out to her. Still nothing. Then he moved to his bedroom. It was empty. The washroom door was open, but he didn't see her in there. An uneasy feeling crept into his bones.

"Chloe, where are you?"

Panicking, he rushed around the cabin, but she wasn't anywhere. He then rushed to the back door, but it was still locked. She couldn't have relocked it from the outside without a key. She had to be somewhere inside.

He frantically searched in the hall, the spare room's closet, and under the beds like he did when he was playing hide-and-seek with Eli. His last stop was his walk-in closet.

At first, he didn't see her. But just as he turned to search somewhere else, he saw the baseball bat lying on the floor.

He got down on his hands and knees and, sure enough, Chloe was tucked tightly behind his dress pants in the corner. He slowly separated them, finding her tucked up in a ball with her head down on her bent knees, rocking as she shook. She was terrified.

"Aw . . . Chloe, I didn't mean to scare you. It was Emmy. You remember Emmy, right? Come here, baby." Santino reached out for her, but Chloe squeaked in fear, so he yanked his hand back quickly, then sat down.

"I don't know how else to explain to you that you're safe here. I won't let anything happen to you. Emmy just wanted to drop some clothes off for you. She said they don't fit her anymore since she had the baby. Please talk to me. Tell me what frightened you, and I will make sure it doesn't happen again."

Chloe felt like an idiot for hiding in his closet like a three-year-old. But when she had heard the knock at the door, she had thought Jacob was coming to get her. Her fight-or-flight instinct had kicked in, just like when she was younger. If they couldn't find her, they couldn't hurt her.

After a few minutes of silence, she wondered if he had gotten tired of waiting for her to respond and had left. Cautiously, she lifted her head, seeing Santino sitting cross-legged, patiently waiting her out. Bewildered as to why he wasn't striking out at her for not answering or at least yelling, she gulped. Still, he said nothing. What kind of game was he playing? Men always struck out or screamed when she did something wrong.

Chloe couldn't take the tension another second. Truly baffled, she asked, "What are you going to do to me?"

"I'm going to wait here until you feel comfortable enough to tell me why you hid," Santino responded calmly. "I told you I won't hurt you, and I won't let anyone else hurt you either. I need to understand why you don't believe me. Help me understand, Chloe."

All her life, she had learned to tell people what they wanted to hear, not the truth. He was changing all the rules, which made her nervous. Chloe didn't know how to answer.

Santino tried another approach.

"I keep asking you questions and wanting answers, but maybe it's you who should be asking questions. Go ahead and ask me anything you want. I promise to give you honest answers."

She tilted her head, not believing him for a second. "Why are you trying to help the girl whose father murdered your family?"

Wow, she wasn't mincing words. "Because first and foremost, I don't blame you for something your dad did. Second, because it is the right thing to do. Third, because I felt a connection to you the minute I laid eyes on you, and nothing has changed."

Chloe scoffed.

"I said I would be honest, and I was. You might not like my answers, but they are the truth. It would have been easier for me not to admit the last part, but if I want you to be honest, then I have to be totally honest. Next question." He shifted to get more comfortable.

Chloe released her arms from around her knees, stretching out her throbbing leg. "How did you know where I lived? Did the sheriff give you my address?"

Now he had put himself in a pickle. "No, absolutely not. Promise not to freak out?"

That had her drawing her legs back up protectively.

"I got your address from Brooklyn and followed the deputy to the shelter. Keith told me that if he found me anywhere near you, he would arrest me for stalking. I told him he should do what he thought was right and so would I. I'm afraid he's a little pissed off with me right now. But I swear to God, I wasn't stalking you. I was just so worried about you. I had to make sure you were all right. Brooklyn told us you didn't have any family."

"Did you follow me from the shelter?"

"Yes, and I thank God every minute that I did. Chloe, if I hadn't been there, you would have died when you slipped." Santino wiggled again. He wasn't comfortable sitting cross-legged like that. "Do you mind if I move to the other side of the closet across from you? I'm not made to sit like this."

She looked at him closely. Santino was willing to sit in the closet all day if it made it easier for her. Maybe she had learned enough about him to trust him enough that she could sit in the living room, where they would both be comfortable.

Before he crawled to the other side of the closet, she asked, "Can you hand me the bat?"

He looked at her quizzically before he turned, crawled three steps, and then handed her the bat before retreating. As he settled, he watched as she made three attempts to stand, failing miserably each time.

Chloe finally gave up and asked, "Can you help me get to the living room?"

"Are you leaving?"

"Not yet. I need more answers, but neither of us are comfortable in here."

Santino tried not to beam and failed. It felt like they had just jumped over a huge hurdle.

"Can I carry you? It will speed things up, and you won't put any extra strain on your leg."

She bit her lip again in indecision. Finally, she nodded.

Santino didn't give her a chance to change her mind. He scooped her up and delivered her to the couch.

She watched as he propped her leg up on a pillow. Then he moved across from the couch and sat in a club chair.

"I'll ask you one last time. Why are you helping me?"

Santino really looked at her. Even bruised and slightly miffed, Chloe was still the most beautiful woman he had ever seen. Her quiet, soft voice made him long to listen to every word she had to say.

She sat quietly, nervously waiting for his answer.

"I want more than anything to do what is right by you. I want to teach you that not every man is harsh and cruel. I want to be the one person you turn to. I want you safe, and the safest place for you right now is here. Nobody will think to come to the place you were attacked to look for you. But more than anything else, I want a chance to get to know you."

Aggravated by his stupidity, she said, "Nobody willingly wants to know me. I'm the devil's spawn. In fact, I have nothing to offer. I have no home, no friends or family, and no job. I make really bad decisions, and I'm crippled. Tell me again you want to know me."

"I do," he said, realizing he had never met a lonelier person.

Chloe leaned forward, pleading, "Why?"

He lowered his head, yanking on his curls, trying to figure out how to express what he felt. "If I lost everything and everyone I cared for, I would be just like you, and it scares the shit out of me. I would like to think someone would help me."

That was the truth. She knew it.

"Thank you for your honesty."

They sat staring at one another for over five minutes.

Even though Santino was afraid to ask, he did. "Will you stay and let me help you?"

Chloe dropped her head to the side, exhausted from the emotional roller coaster. "I don't know. I can't make any promises. I can't even begin to think beyond the next hour."

He could work with that. "If you're only comfortable with one hour at a time, then that's what we'll do." Now came the question he knew was going to make or break this hour.

He got up, grabbed the bag Emmy brought, and carried it to Chloe. "Here, choose an outfit, and I'll put it in the master bathroom for you. There is a seat in the shower, which should make it easier for you to bathe. In the meantime, I'm going to call Quinn and invite him over so you can talk to him."

She balked, but Santino had anticipated it.

"Chloe, what happened to you is bigger than both of us. You might not feel it yet, but it will surface when you least expect it. I can't help you the way Quinn can—he's worked with people suffering from PTSD. Now that you're safe, the magnitude of everything might be more than you can bear. Your mind and body both need to heal. Just talk to him once, and if you never want to again, I won't push. Please."

It made sense. Sort of. But, regardless of whether she liked Quinn or not, Chloe knew she had to become less vulnerable. She couldn't lean on Santino forever, so she needed to accept whatever help they were offering, become stronger, and then rebuild her life.

"I'll talk to him, but no promises."

Chapter 7
"Broken Girl" by Matthew West

For five days, Chloe had been slowly healing at Santino's. However reluctant she was to speak to Quinn in the beginning, he had turned out to be a Godsend. He was extremely patient and never pushed when she said she didn't want to talk about her past. He didn't ask about the attack. Instead, they talked about her taking back control of her life.

Today they sat together at the table to make a list. Quinn ripped off a sheet for himself, then handed her the pad, suggesting she write a list of ten things she wished were her rights. Chloe struggled to understand what he was asking.

"I wish I had the right to be listened to without bias," he gave as an example, writing on his own paper. "What's important to you, Chloe? What do you wish for more than anything? When you're done, if you don't want to talk about your list, that is also your choice."

She gawked at him. "You mean, I can write my list and you're not going to demand to see it?" She rubbed her leg, the pain ever-present on her face.

"Chloe, I've watched you struggle with physical pain for the last five days. My son is a physiotherapist and has recently moved to Allentown. I didn't tell him your name or your circumstances, but I did explain that one of my patients had a re-injury and is in pain. I told him you weren't in a position to pay for physio at this moment, so he offered to come here and give you a few exercises to help."

She didn't respond, tormented at the thought of always being weak and dependent on others. She sat at the table, gnawing at the end of the pen. What did she want more than anything?

"I wish I had the right to be in a position where I'm not a pathetic charity case."

Quinn had known it was going to be a sensitive topic that might evoke this response.

"There is power in taking help when you need it. If it makes you stronger and better able to face challenges, use it as tool for becoming more independent. I can assure you that Owen and I don't see your situation as pathetic or charity. When you get to my age, you'll learn there are times in everyone's life when they need to accept help. It's not a case of weakness or financial circumstances; it's life. I'm trying to make you as strong as possible so you can make decisions for yourself without having to rely on other people. But if you aren't comfortable with Owen's help, I understand and won't mention it again. The choices we're exploring are always yours to make."

Now she felt stupid. He was right—it would make her stronger faster, so she could leave.

"If I accept, can it be with a condition that I pay you both back when I get on my feet? That's the only way I can accept the offer in good conscience. It won't be in the next six months, but eventually, I would like to pay back all my debts."

Quinn smiled. "Of course. Whatever you're comfortable with. I'll text him while you write your list." He got up and headed to the couch.

Now that it was settled, Chloe could think about what she wished for. She wrote the first one, and the rest followed.

I wish I had the right to be happy.

I wish I had the right to not be responsible for other people's actions.

I wish I had the right to be strong enough to make decisions for myself with no explanations or guilt.

I wish I had the right to say no or change my mind with no explanations or repercussions.

I wish I had the right to have a safe and happy environment to live and work.

I wish I had the right to my feelings (sad, mad, scared, frustrated, or happy).

I wish I had the right to have real friends of my choosing and keep them because they liked me.

I wish I had the right to see my own self-worth and to be treated with dignity.

I wish I had the right to have a future free of hatred!

The last line she wrote with apprehension and dread, fearing she was setting herself up for failure yet again. Those things weren't meant for the likes of her.

I wish I had the right to fall in love and trust a man so I can have lots of children to love unconditionally without passing my genes on to them.

When Quinn heard the pen hit the table with force, he got up and approached, choosing the farthest seat from her. "If you don't want me to see your answers, put it on your lap. Now, why do you think I asked you to do this exercise?"

Not knowing how to reply, she grabbed the paper and moved it down, embarrassed by what she had written. Keeping her eyes down, she answered, "I don't know what you mean."

"Don't look beyond the question. It's not a trick. Why do you think I would want you to write things you wish for yourself?"

Quinn tried to make everything easy, but it wasn't that simple for Chloe. How did he want her respond?

The list made her feel even worse about herself. She had realized she had always been trying to make everyone else happy and had sacrificed who she could have been.

She was shifting around so much that she hit the table leg with her sore knee. Flustered, Chloe cursed out in pain, moving her hand to rub another ache. "I don't know. I guess if I was someone else's daughter, these would be the things I would want. But the things I wrote aren't attainable for me."

Quinn comfortably clasped his hands on top of the table. "Somewhere along the way, you've been convinced you shouldn't have the same rights and freedom as everyone else who lives in this country.

"I want you to read the first sentence you wrote and change it from I wish I had the right to I have the right. If you feel comfortable, you can read it out loud, or if you prefer, silently to yourself. Go ahead and start."

There was no way she would let Quinn hear what she wrote.

She looked at the first line, reciting it in her head. It sounded totally different when she changed the beginning.

Without making a conscious decision to do so, she was suddenly rereading it out loud. "I have the right to be happy. I have the right to not be responsible for other people's actions." After three more sentences, a light went off in her head. For the first time, she realized these weren't wishes; these were her rights.

She continued to read a little louder and with righteousness. After the last one, she looked up at Quinn in awe.

He smiled from ear to ear. "Yes, Chloe, these are a few of your rights and freedoms. Consider it your very own Declaration of Independence. Today, I want you to think of the rest of the things that should be added to your list and add them. But instead of writing I wish, I want you to rewrite them all to say I have the right. Take the time to really understand and appreciate your rights. Respect them. From this moment on, anyone who has the pleasure of getting to know you has to respect your rights, or they forfeit the chance to be in your life. You are in control and hold all the power of whom you want in your life and whom you don't. In the future, it will be a privilege to get to know Chloe Marsh."

She was elated with the realization that she did indeed hold some power. Taking ownership meant that, from now on, it would be her fault if she chose to ignore it. Nobody had the right to take away her independence. She was an adult and would pick up the pieces of her life. It wouldn't come naturally, though; she would have to constantly remind herself.

Quinn was absorbed in watching the young woman gain a little bit of confidence when his cell phone beeped. Looking down, he saw Owen was in front of Santino's cabin. He must have been visiting Valentina.

"Chloe, Owen is outside. Can I let him in?"

Panic filled her face until she looked down at the paper with her rights written in her own handwriting. Quinn wouldn't let him in unless she welcomed it.

She nodded with self-assurance.

Quinn couldn't help feeling a certain amount of fatherly pride with her first big breakthrough. He opened the door and invited his son in.

They had a silent conversation with one look. Owen knew instinctively to be cautious with his dad's patient. He had been at the family lunch last week, the day after the attack, and knew some of the details.

Shaking his son's hand, Quinn said, "Thank you for coming. I would like to introduce you to my friend Chloe Marsh."

Owen stood beside his dad. "It's a pleasure to meet you, Chloe."

She tried to stand but faltered a bit with the title of friend. Finally getting her bearings, she responded, "Sorry, my leg is very weak. Hi,

Owen. I want to thank you for offering your services. I told your dad I could only accept your offer with the promise that I will pay you back when I get another job. It might be a while, but I promise to pay in full."

Chloe was a tiny, delicate woman with the softest voice he had ever heard. He couldn't help seeing the bruises that had turned yellowish, and hearing the honesty in her words. She had taken a real beating, but appeared to be fighting back. He admired her courage.

He smiled genuinely. "If those are your conditions, I will work hard to get you back on track as soon as I can."

Relieved, she responded, "Thank you."

Chloe couldn't get over how he acknowledged her request for dignity. Quinn was right; when she made her boundaries known immediately, it left no room for arguments. Owen either agreed or he left. There were no other options.

"We can start right now, if you're ready. The rehabilitation center I started working for is still finalizing my schedule, so I have more time available for now. Can you change into a pair of shorts? I need to access your range of motion."

There weren't any shorts in the bag of clothes Emmy had given her, but she could probably cut a pair of pants. "Give me five minutes?"

"No problem. Take your time. I'll walk Dad to his car."

Quinn saw the second she questioned if they would discuss her. "Actually, I have to make a call, so I'll catch up with you later. Son, do mind giving us a minute to finish up?"

"Certainly, I'll be outside. Chloe, just pop your head out when you're ready." He watched her nod before he walked outside to wait.

Quinn gathered his briefcase. "Chloe, I saw you when Owen said he would walk me out. I want to assure you that whatever is said between you and me will remain private. I would never break your confidence by discussing anything we talk about with anyone else."

Embarrassed that he had read her so easily, she picked up the pen and fiddled with it, stuttering, "I-I didn't mean to offend you—"

"You have the right to an explanation without guilt or repercussions. If you need reassurances every time we talk, ask for it. It's your right. Even though you set boundaries, there is no problem redefining them as many times as it takes before you believe them. You did an excellent job with Owen. I'm very proud of you."

Quinn saw the small smile lifting at the edges of her mouth. He also saw her begin to reach out to his hands, then pull back. He waited patiently for her to lift her eyes. "Is there something you want to ask me?"

She shook her head, but her eyes were pleading for the simple gesture of offering thanks through touch.

"When you're ready, all you have to do is ask." He turned, bidding her a good day as he left.

Chloe stood there for a minute, mad at herself for not reaching out. She wasn't even sure if she wanted to touch his hands. Then she leaned down and wrote, I have the right to have a hug or hold hands when I'm ready and not a minute before.

She was proud of herself for knowing she wanted something but also knowing she wasn't ready. And for setting boundaries for herself and not pushing too soon.

Ten minutes later, after creating some makeshift shorts with a pair of scissors, she popped her head outside to let Owen know she was ready.

When Owen came in again, Chloe stepped back and swallowed deeply. It took her breath away just how tall and fit he was. He could literally snap her in half without even trying.

Owen hated when his size intimidated women. He knew the drill: smile a lot and keep his body language open. First and foremost, he would give her a chance to get to know him.

"Let's talk for a few minutes. Are you more comfortable at the table or the couch?"

The table offered a barrier, so she chose that. She knew she was safe, sort of. Owen was Quinn's son after all.

Softening his voice, he asked, "Can you give me a little history about your previous injuries?" When panic raced across her face, he clarified, "Not how it happened, but what was the end result? Did you have breaks, torn muscles, or tissue damage?"

"I had a femoral neck fracture in my hip, two inches from where the bone meets the socket, and torn blood vessels. A piece of the broken bone embedded into the muscle. I also fractured my femur and broke my tibia in two places. I had a partial hip replacement, and I have plates and screws in my leg."

Goddamn, whatever had happened to Chloe, the recovery must have been long and painful. With the extent of the damage, Owen assumed it had to have been a car accident.

"Well, if you're walking after all those injuries, you know a lot about physiotherapy. Can I check the range of motion in your leg?"

She tensed. "Yes."

He bent down, manipulating her leg left and right, then up and down. There weren't only scars from surgeries; there were long gashes, like from a belt. His heart sank.

"Can you take your sock off? I'll need to check the ankle as well."

Instant panic filled Chloe as she slowly peeled her sock off, avoiding looking at Owen.

As much as the bruises had started to heal, the scabbing and developing scar tissue were not healing as fast. They were seeping and angry red.

Owen had a hard time trying to hide the shock from his face or voice. "Chloe, your ankle is infected. Does the other one look the same? Have you been airing the wounds?"

She nodded at first, then shook her head as the sting of fresh tears prickled at the back of her eyes. Chloe covered the wounds in the day so they weren't visible to Santino and Quinn. And at night, she kept them covered so she wouldn't ruin Santino's sheets.

Schooling his tone, he asked, "Chloe?" He waited for her to look at him. "You should know that I was here the day after the attack. I'm friends with the Savages, so I know a little bit of what happened. I didn't know it was you until this minute, so there's no need to explain. I won't ask any questions or judge. From this moment on, we need to manage the infection first. Will you come with me to a friend of mine, who is a doctor? She's a great person, and I think you'll really like her."

All the confidence she had gained with Quinn flew out the window, reverting her back to her old habits as she sat silently with tears in her eyes. It floored her that he knew, but that was one of those things Quinn said she couldn't change.

Right now, Chloe had to focus on the infection. She couldn't afford another doctor, and she wasn't even sure how the last visit had been paid.

At a loss on how to deal with her, he excused himself to call his dad. When Quinn answered on the first ring, Owen explained the situation. Quinn said he was still on the property and would be right there.

On the way back to the cabin, Owen then called Santino, explaining what he had discovered.

Quinn walked in, finding the strong, self-assured woman he had left was a mess. He moved quickly toward her and bent down, looking at the angry scabs.

At eye-level with her, he spoke in his ever-present calm voice. "Chloe? Please look at me." He patiently waited for the crying woman to pull herself together enough to remove her hands from her face. "Good. Thank you. It is your right to get medical care, no matter the cost. Do you understand?"

She was sniffling, looking totally baffled.

"Did you hide it because of money? Remember, you have the right to answer or not. I will respect your decision because, even though something went wrong, you still have boundaries and we'll work around them."

Santino flew in the door at that moment, scaring the crap out of her.

"Stellina, are you okay?" he asked, out of breath.

Chloe saw the sheer panic on his face and felt even worse. Biting her lip, she nodded, then dropped her face to hide her mortification.

Santino took his cue from her body language and the look Quinn gave him. He bent down beside Quinn, gently reaching out for her ankle. "Aw . . . Stellina, why didn't you tell me?"

Quinn's voice became threatening for the first time ever, stopping Santino's hand. "Santino, you need to ask permission before you enter her personal space. She has the right to refuse if she isn't ready."

Santino twisted his pissed-off face toward his mamma's boyfriend. How dare he tell him how to deal with Stellina? They had been slowly building a relationship on trust with quiet, non-intrusive conversations each day.

Quinn was not bending on this issue, though. Santino saw his hand poised, ready to strike if he touched Chloe without permission. His eyes were pleading with Santino not to cross this line.

He shifted back to Chloe, who was gnawing on her lip like it was a steak. The boa constrictor was tightly squeezing him again. "Sweetheart, would it be okay if I touched your ankle to look at it closer?"

Chloe looked from Santino to Quinn, trying to figure out how not to offend anyone."

"You have the right to refuse with no repercussions," Quinn coached her. "You don't owe Santino, me, or Owen anything. You have the right to ask questions if you aren't comfortable. You hold all the power, Chloe. Only you can choose who enters your comfort zone, and how they do it."

She nodded with tears streaming down her face. "I need a minute to think," she rushed out, looking at Quinn for reassurance.

"Good girl. We're going to back up and give you some space. Don't rush. We have all the time in the world. Do you need us to step outside?"

While she contemplated how to ask them to give her a minute to regroup, Santino caught sight of her list of rights. He didn't have time to read them all, but he did see the first three. They took his breath away, but the third one caused a switch to flip in his head.

I wish I had the right to be strong enough to make decisions for myself with no explanations or guilt.

Quinn was working to give her control back, and Santino might have just blown it for her. As bad as things had been in his life, he had always maintained control over his own decisions. He couldn't even imagine what it would be like to be stripped of that.

Chloe's voice shook him out of his thoughts. "I need a few minutes alone to think. If that's okay?"

"No need to apologize. The decision is yours alone. We'll be right outside, so call out when you're ready, and not a minute before," Quinn said with satisfaction, eyeing both younger men, who followed without argument.

Once outside, and before Santino could say a word, Owen jumped all over his dad, pacing like a wild man, but wise enough to speak in a low tone. "She needs to go to a doctor, Dad. Her ankles are infected."

"Chloe needs control over any decisions about herself more than she needs a doctor," Santino answered before Quinn had the chance, stretching the tight muscles in his neck from side to side.

"Her health has to come first!" Owen jammed his hands into his pockets to keep from shaking some sense into both men.

"Yes, son, her mental health. Even if you drag her somewhere, they won't touch her without her consent. It's her choice to make. You're going to accept any decision she comes up with and not say another word. If you can't abide by those rules, then I suggest you leave."

"Dad, you're not being reasonable." He fisted his hands in his pockets.

"I appreciate your help, but you need to leave."

"Dad?"

With a firm voice, Quinn said, "Now, Owen. Leave. When you calm down, I'll explain my reasons. But until then, I don't want you ruining the little bit of power she has gained."

"Fine. But it goes against my professional opinion. Remember, you brought me into this. Tell Valentina I'll talk to her later." He stormed off without another word.

Quinn turned, gearing up for the same fight from Santino. Instead, he saw the man lost in thought.

"Santino?"

"It wasn't just Jacob. This goes back years, doesn't it?" Santino had seen the scars and was grappling with an overwhelming sadness at the thought of what his Stellina might have gone through.

"Honestly, I can't answer that. And even if I could, I wouldn't. The first step is getting her to take back control. You have to let her make her own decisions, whether you agree with them or not. It's her right."

After having seen the list, he hoped the first ten were only the beginning. Intrinsically, he knew everyone should have more.

It took three tries to ask his next question, because every time he opened his mouth, the words got stuck in his throat. "How could anyone hurt her? What could an innocent child, or that small woman, have done to incite that much cruelty? Sometimes, I wonder if this is a world I want to bring children into."

Quinn couldn't forget this man had seen more than his fair share of the dark side of humanity. "She is stronger than you think. And given the proper tools, only God knows what she could do. Chloe has dreams. That's a start. I need you to be strong and pull from everything you've ever learned in therapy to help her succeed."

Santino was crippled by the thought of her unknown suffering, but he was willing to put everything on the line to help her achieve every dream she had.

Just then, the door opened, and Chloe came out a step with her sheet of paper folded in her hand. Both men advanced as she said, "I have the right to not see a doctor. I looked it up online, and if a scab gets infected, I can treat it by cleaning the area with soapy water and a clean towel and wrapping it with sterilized bandages. That is my decision." She looked straight at Santino, clutching the paper tighter in her hand.

"There's a first-aid kit in your bathroom. If you need help, just ask."

Surprised, she whipped her head over to Quinn. He grinned and nodded to her.

As she turned to walk inside, they all heard, "What is she doing here? How dare you bring her on my and Daddy's property?"

"Ma, this is my cabin. You have no say over who I invite into my home. You need to leave." He crossed his arms in a defensive pose.

Narrowing her eyes, her hands flailing, she screeched, "How dare I? Really, shamo? Get her off my property!"

"Valentina," Quinn commanded as she advanced on her son like the devil she was so famous for resembling.

She turned her fury on him. "Is this where you've been sneaking off to? You told me you had a patient. You lied to me!" she screamed, totally out of control.

"Valentina, is everything all right?" Raimer, the dance instructor, asked, running toward the group.

They ignored him as Quinn told her, "I did not lie to you."

The realization hit. He was helping her enemy.

Valentina stumbled, pointing at the terrified girl, who had pushed herself up against the doorjamb. "Her? The daughter of the man who murdered my husband and son!" She shook her head. "We're done. I don't want to ever lay eyes on you again. Leave, Quinn!"

"If Chloe leaves, then so do I." Santino stood his ground.

Seething out with more hatred than Santino had ever seen, she yelled, "Then pack your bags and get out! Did you honestly think I would ever allow that little bitch to stay here?"

Santino didn't dignify her slander with a response, because if he did, he might not be able to take it back.

He climbed the stairs to his cabin. "Chloe, we're leaving."

She shook her head with huge eyes. "No, please, you stay. I'll leave. Your mom needs you. Please don't destroy your family over me." This was her fault, and she had to own up to it. Santino had already lost his dad and brother; he couldn't afford to lose his mom too.

Turning toward the woman who hated her, she said, "Valentina, I'm sorry. I'll leave. Please don't punish Quinn or Santino for trying to help me. I swear I'll disappear."

"It's too late," Valentina spat out venomously. "What your father didn't destroy of my famiglia, you have."

"Ma!" Alessandro yelled, causing everyone to stop as he ran up beside his brother. "That was beyond cruel, even feeling the way you do. You're wrong. Just listen to yourself. Santino is your son. The one who hasn't left your side since Daddy died. The one who helped every single one of us. Chloe is a victim. If you can't see that, then you are blinded by hatred and selfishness. Daddy wouldn't approve of your behavior. None of us can accept this."

Valentina spun back around to face Chloe. "You've turned them all against me! Are you happy now? Did you get what you wanted? I've lost everyone because of you!" she screamed, then took off for the main resort.

"I'll deal with Mamma; you take care of Chloe," Alessandro told his brother before turning to Quinn. "I think it's best if you wait a couple of days until she calms down before you contact her. Unless you can't get past what she said." He then took off after his mamma.

Santino was furious. Quinn could feel it bleeding from his pores.

"Don't do anything rash, son."

"Too late. She laid the gauntlet down. I'm leaving."

"I just moved into a three-bedroom condo, and I have two spare rooms. You and Chloe can come stay at my place until things settle down." Everyone had forgotten that Raimer was still there.

"I would really appreciate it. I'll pay you, and we won't stay long. Just until I find something more permanent." Santino couldn't take them to her place, so he didn't have a lot of options at this minute.

Raimer flicked his hand. "Don't worry, gorgeous; we can work it out in trade." He winked cheekily. "Do you need me to haul any of your stuff?"

Santino was so relieved that he retorted in the same cheeky fashion, "Nah, I wouldn't trust you with my tighty-whities. One of my brothers can take care of my stuff. I'll pack enough to hold me off for a couple of days. And thanks, Raimer."

The hand was moving again. "Pft. I've been waiting a long time to get one of you Savage hotties into my bed. I was hoping it would be the master and not the spare room, but now that I have you, the possibilities are limitless." He rubbed his hands together.

Santino barked out a laugh as he walked up the steps. "Come on, Stellina; let's collect our things before Raimer becomes so eager we leave with nothing."

Stunned, she replied, "How can you joke at a time like this? You can't leave."

He bent down to look into her eyes. "Yes, Stellina, the choice is mine, and I made it. I'm leaving with or without you. I would prefer if you chose to go with me, but that's your choice. I'm moving into Raimer's until I can find a place of my own."

With her eyelashes covered in moisture, she blinked twice. "But your mom? Your job?"

"She made her choice, and I made mine. Nothing changes with my job. I'm part-owner."

Chapter 8
"Lullaby" by Dixie Chicks

The emotional upheaval of the move to Raimer's and the consequences of Valentina discovering her at Santino's cabin had taken its toll. Chloe had been sleeping now for a couple of hours.

The room she was staying in was beautiful. It had a big bed with a white upholstered headboard, silver studs framing it. The linens were elegant in white with blue accented pillows that matched the drapes. The sign over the bed read Be Your Own Kind of Beautiful. Raimer had placed an oversized reading chair in the corner that begged her to crawl into it and spend the afternoon. He really had a good eye for decorating.

When a knock at the door woke her, she heard hushed voices as she dragged herself out of the bed. She had no idea who had arrived, but she needed to find out if someone was here to change Santino's mind about leaving the resort. The guilt Chloe felt about it was overwhelming. Why had she let him talk her into staying at his cabin in the first place?

Santino wasn't only the most gorgeous man she had ever laid eyes on, he was also the sweetest. Slowly, day by day, he had broken down her resistance by sharing things about life at the resort. Stories about his nephews became the best part of her day. He never pushed about her own past.

He took care of her by buying her essential items like shampoo, a toothbrush, and toothpaste, as well as underwear and bras. She didn't know how he knew her size, and that made her nervous. Her subconscious continued to gnaw at the back of her mind, questioning: why was he doing all this? Then she would wonder how she could ever repay him for all he had given her. She decided she would deal with that later.

He had tried to explain on the way to Raimer's that the incident at his cabin with his mom had very little to do with her, and more to do with his mom's unresolved issues. Chloe didn't say a word as she listened, not believing it for a second. Again, she had to question what his motives were.

Just before she opened the door, she realized she was still wearing shorts, and her scars would be on display. She went through the bag of clothes, changing into a pair of yoga pants. The bandages she had put on were seeping again. She would have to clean and redress them at the first available opportunity.

She silently walked down the hall, hearing a baby. When she turned the corner, Emmy, the baby, and Sabastian were sitting on the couch with Santino. Chloe was transfixed, her eyes never leaving the baby.

"Hey there, Stellina. You're awake. How are you feeling?" Santino asked with concern as he stood, advancing toward her. He saw a flash of uncertainty when she realized everyone was staring at her. "I hope you don't mind, but Sabastian and Emmy stopped by to bring us some dinner. They figured we might not have eaten lunch."

Sabastian stood. "We can leave if you're not comfortable with us being here."

When the baby started to fuss, Chloe couldn't help herself. Peeking around Santino, her face lit up when she saw Emmy stand to jiggle the baby.

"Would you like to hold Shawn?" Emmy asked, seeing the

longing in her eyes.

Chloe's expression exuded jubilance. She loved children more than anything else in the world. Kids had an amazing ability to love and be loved without prejudice.

Without thought, she advanced toward Emmy and the baby. On second thought, she stopped dead in her tracks, letting her arms drop. Who would want a murderer's daughter to taint their innocent child?

As the longing was replaced by a dose of reality, she wrapped her arms around her waist. "No, that's okay."

"You'd actually be helping me," Emmy coaxed, knowing what Chloe was feeling by the look on her face. "My back is killing me. Shawn is like his papa; he eats nonstop and he's getting heavy. I could really use a few minutes to myself." Emmy extended her baby-filled arms toward Chloe.

The fractured girl looked at the sincerity on Emmy's face, then turned to look at Sabastian. When he gave her an encouraging chin lift, Chloe's eyes traveled back to Shawn. The yearning on her face was indescribable and affected each of them as they watched her internal battle. It was clear that with every fiber of her body, she wanted nothing more than to hold to him.

Santino moved beside her. "Shawn loves to be rocked and sung to. If you would like to hold him, the choice is yours."

Her eyes were brimming with unshed tears as she slowly reached out to let Emmy transfer the baby.

Shawn looked up at Chloe and broke out into a huge, toothless grin. She couldn't help choking on a sob as she smiled, a couple of tears escaping.

Chloe had once seen a quote on childinsider.com that she had never forgotten. The most beautiful thing in the world is a child's smile. The next best thing? Knowing you're the reason why. This was exactly what the person who wrote the quote meant. Shawn didn't understand that not very many people wanted to be in her presence, so his smile was a gift from the angels.

When Shawn tittered, she dropped her face closer, nuzzling her lips to his head for a quick kiss. He smelled like baby powder and sunshine all wrapped up in one adorable package.

"You are the most beautiful baby I've ever seen, and you smell like heaven."

The baby reached out, grabbing a lock of her hair and gurgling back to the softness of her voice. Even though she had never held such a young child before, she instinctively started to sway gently. Without thought, she started to sing "Lullaby" by Dixie Chicks.

The adults were as mesmerized as the baby, who closed his eyes and was asleep before the last verse ended.

Emmy was in awe as she said, "Wow, your voice is beautiful. I wish I had that ability to make him go back to sleep in the middle of night. Next to you, only his papa can do that. Thank you. Please sit down, so you're more comfortable."

Lifting her eyes from the baby to his mom, Chloe asked, "Do you want him back?" not really ready to relinquish him quite yet.

"Gosh, no. If you don't mind, he looks very cozy in your arms."

The smile on Chloe's face was enough to melt their hearts as she sat gingerly, cuddling the infant close. Santino had never seen the woman he was enamored with so happy. It did his heart good.

He knew she was self-conscious, so he directed the attention away from her, asking his brother, "After we check the guests out tomorrow morning, do you mind coming with me to look at a couple of places for me to rent?"

"You sure you're not moving too fast? Why not wait a few days until things calm down?"

Chloe popped her head up. "Please don't do this because of me. As soon as I'm able, I have to leave."

Santino didn't want her to leave, but he also understood the choice would be hers. He wanted to keep her safe, and to continue to get to know her. He needed to create a bond with her so she wouldn't leave, and he didn't have a lot of time to make that happen.

"Stellina, focus on getting healthy first, and then decide. I won't be going back, with or without you in my life. I love Mamma, but she overstepped and had no right. She needs to understand she can't threaten any of us with our homes."

Chloe knew none of it would have happened without her involvement. She also knew he would eventually move back to the resort, because that was where he belonged. Besides, if he rented another place, it would be such a waste of money.

"You can stay with Raimer until you're ready to move back home, and I'll move back to my house. Things should get better with your mom if I'm not around."

Santino moved from the chair to the coffee table in front of her, placing his hands on his thighs; otherwise, he might be tempted to touch her. "Chloe, they destroyed your place. It will take months to make it livable again. On top of that, I'd go crazy worrying about you living there alone."

She rubbed the baby's back while she thought about whether she should agree to stay at Raimer's until the insurance money came in. Maybe, by then, he would work things out with his mom. In the meantime, she could clean and do laundry to pull her weight. Once she had the money, then Chloe could pay Raimer back with the proceeds from the house. She could also pay everyone else who had helped her. It might not leave much for her in the end, but she could live with that.

"Fine. I'll stay here until my house is fixed and sold, if you will?"

Santino tilted his head. For the life of him he couldn't figure out why she was suddenly willing to stay and not follow through with the plan she had for running. But this was the time he desperately needed for her to get to know him.

"Okay, deal. We'll stay here until the house is fixed, and you decide what you're going to do. That way you can still see Quinn and Owen."

That agitated her, but she couldn't move with the baby sound asleep in her arms. The injustice of breaking up his family gave her the courage to counter his argument, speaking quietly but firmly. "I don't think I should see either one of them again. I didn't know Quinn was your mom's boyfriend. I thought he was your therapist. Had I known the truth, I would have never accepted his help."

"That's not fair to Santino. He wasn't lying," Sabastian answered before Santino could. "Quinn was our therapist, and he's damn good. In fact, he's the best. He helped all of us overcome and manage a lot of issues, as a famiglia and individually. There is no one else I would have recommended. Quinn knows how to separate his professional life from his personal one."

Santino saw her cringe and pull inward with Sabastian's blatant answer, so he spoke quickly, trying to soften the blow. "Besides, I've seen the change in you. Chloe, think about how much stronger you are since you have been working with Quinn. Don't discount the progress you've made. That strength will help you make your own choices for the future. All that being said, if you don't want to see him again, the choice is yours."

God, she was so confused. Everything they said only solidified what Quinn had been helping her realize. He was always telling her not to rush when considering things.

It had been so long since she had to make decisions for herself. Jacob had taken control of everything in her life and, somewhere along the way, she had become the same needy, helpless adolescent of her past.

"I can't make a decision right now. I need time to think."

"Fair enough—"

"Damn, hermosa." Santino was cut off by Raimer walking in. "If you living with me means I come home to find a happy meal of Savage men in my home, you and I can be roomies forever." Raimer walked straight to Chloe, bent down, and kissed her forehead, then the baby's. "Hey, pequeño rey. He gets more handsome every time I see him. Hermosa, you look like you were born to hold a babé." He lifted his eyes from the baby back to Chloe.

When she tilted her head, Santino translated. "Hermosa means beautiful in Spanish, and pequeño rey is little king. Raimer has a term of endearment for everyone he cares about. But sometimes he forgets he's in America, not Cuba."

Raimer barked out a laugh, dramatically saying, "Oh, that's rich. Savage men are notorious for terms of endearments. I could never come close."

The baby startled, crying out, and Chloe started to sing again, rocking him gently.

Always the drama queen, Raimer fell to his knees beside her. "Jesucristo, now I know what an angel sounds like. Hermosa, you should be singing professionally."

Chloe blushed but didn't stop singing because Shawn was quieting and started to close his eyes again.

"Wow, Chloe, you are amazing with him," Emmy gushed. "I wish you still lived at the resort. It's hard juggling the baby between the family while working. I could use a babysitter that I trust."

Chloe didn't answer until she was done with the song. With surprise written all over her face, she finally responded, "But you don't know me. Why would you trust me with little Shawn?"

Reaching over and touching her arm, Emmy clarified, "I'm a good judge of character. Besides, you haven't done anything wrong. We can't help who our parents are. Nobody can seriously blame you."

Chloe turned bright red. "Valentina does. Jacob and his friends do. Actually, a lot of people blame me. Valentina and Jacob aren't the first."

Santino touched her knee. "I will say it again. Mamma and Jacob have other issues that have nothing to do with you. If you continue to work with Quinn, he'll help you realize that sometimes we seek answers to questions that will never be answered. As a result, we blame others to help get some sort of closure to a senseless crime. Especially if the perpetrator goes unpunished and denies us justice.

"Alessandro talks about survivor's guilt all the time. I want him to tell you his story because, much like you, he blamed himself for our brother's death, and he was no more responsible than you. Chloe, I'm begging you, don't run. Stay and face the monsters in your closet, become stronger with our help, and Quinn's. Once you figure everything out, then decide how you want to move forward."

She looked at the eager faces around her. "Fine, but I hate being a charity case."

Sabastian stood. "I have a proposal for you. Evangeline and I have a standing date every Monday night, and we haven't been able to go since Shawn was born because the family already helps so much. Also, Thursdays, Evangeline has a full day because she teaches a cooking class. I have to do banking that day. Maybe on those days, I could bring Shawn to you to babysit for us. Evangeline could pump so you could feed Shawn. You would really be helping us out, and of course, we would pay you."

Chloe whipped her head to Emmy, then to Santino, who were both nodding and smiling. Looking back at Sabastian, she asked, "Really? My goodness, I would love to babysit, but you wouldn't have to pay me. I swear to all of you that I will watch him like a hawk. Actually, I might never let him out of my arms."

Emmy laughed. "Well, you can't go spoiling him, or you're going to have to move into our cabin and rock him all night." She saw Chloe's doubts surface again. "Relax, it was a joke. He would love the attention."

Chloe turned to Raimer, who was still kneeling beside her. "I didn't even ask your permission. This is your home, after all."

"Hermosa, the only rule is no one gets more sex in this house than me. Everything else is at your discretion, and you don't have to ask me for permission. This is your home for as long as you want it to be. Plus, if that's Emmy's cooking I smell, I'll be your roommate forever." He waggled his eyebrows as he got up and headed toward the kitchen to take a peek at what she had brought.

Chloe looked back to Sabastian. The stoic man still made her nervous. "Are you sure?"

"Yes. We would never leave our child with someone we didn't trust, and we do trust you, Chloe. We have to head out now, but we will drop Shawn off tomorrow night at five. If you're feeling up to it?"

"I'll be here to help if she needs anything," Santino offered.

Emmy proudly nodded at Santino as she took Shawn from Chloe's arms and placed him in the car seat. "I'm so excited. I've missed dancing with my husband. Thank you so much, Chloe."

Chloe instantly missed the baby in her arms. "It will be my pleasure. I can't wait. Thank you, both of you."

Sabastian and Emmy kissed both her cheeks before leaving, which was another thing she was getting used to—how much this family touched.

After Santino walked them to the door, he and Chloe joined Raimer in the kitchen. He had already started eating and made no bones about it. As far as roommates went, first come, first served.

Chloe relaxed that evening, enjoying the banter between Raimer and Santino, while consumed with thoughts of babysitting the next night. To her surprise, she slept like a rock.

***

Chloe had just finished rebandaging her wounds when a knock came to the door. Raimer answered it because he worked nights, preforming in the Poconos, and was home the days he wasn't teaching at the resort. Santino had left to grab some more stuff from his cabin.

"Mamácita and my main man." Raimer high-fived Eli. "Get your big butts in here."

Brooklyn rolled her eyes as she dragged Eli in. The little guy laughed his head off at Raimer saying big butts.

"You never visit me at my place. Oh . . . wait a minute. I get it. You didn't come to visit your best friend; you're here to visit Chloe. Well, I just might be keeping Stellina if this is the only way the Savages will come to my house."

Brooklyn shook her head as she kissed him, then walked into the kitchen. "He's such a drama queen," she told Chloe before turning back to Raimer. "I would come over more often if I was invited. Besides, we see each other at least three times a week, and you mooch at least one meal a week from me."

Raimer followed in, smirking. "Yeah, well, if you brought Luca, I would invite you more often. No eye candy, no invitation." He flicked her ass. "I see your cushy job is adding to the junk in your trunk and dimples to those babé legs." He blew on his hand like it had hurt.

"Raimer! Not appropriate." She eyed her son.

"Come on, Mommy; Waimer has been hitting your big butt forever." He laughed like she had said the stupidest thing ever.

Brooklyn glared at both of them, then gave up. Having Raimer and Eli in the same room was like having two five-year-olds.

"Chloe, I hope you don't mind me stopping by. I promised to introduce Eli, and I made pulled pork last night. It's one of Santino's favorites, and I thought you might like it. Actually, pulled pork is really best served the next day, with fresh buns." She placed the bag on the counter, then leaned in to hug her friend.

"Thank you, Brooklyn. That was very nice of you."

Holding his hand to his ear, Raimer asked, "Eli, did I hear wrong, or did my mamácita not mention my name in that equation?"

"Nope, she didn't. But I know she made wots, so you can have some too." He pointed at the big bag.

Brooklyn ignored the jab. "Chloe, this very diplomatic little man is my son, Eli."

She smiled at the adorable little boy. "Eli, nice to see you again."

Eli suddenly turned to Raimer, his hands balling into fists. "What'd you do to make Uncle Santino move here? I want him back, Waimer. I went to his cabin this morning, and he wasn't there. Daddy says he's staying with you. That's not fair. He's mine."

"Eli! Sometimes adults have to do things we don't understand, but we have to respect their decisions," Brooklyn reprimanded.

As Chloe's face fell, Raimer got down on his haunches. "Uncle Santino moved in with me so he could help a friend in the city, but he will still be at the resort every day working. He didn't abandon you, buddy. You don't mind sharing him for a little while, do you?"

Eli kicked the ground, trying not to cry. "No. But I usually have a sleepover once a week at his cabin, and we watch movies." He looked up hopefully. "Can I come here?"

"Eli—"

Raimer shook his head. "I got this, mamácita. You can come over whenever you want to see Uncle Santino. Think of the fun you'll have together in the city. You can go to McDonald's and the movies."

"Oookay, I forgive you for letting Uncle Santino move in without telling me."

"Cucciolo, I'm so sorry. You have every reason to be mad. I should have told you myself, or at least called. It's not Raimer's fault."

Nobody had heard Santino and Luca arrive.

Eli ran to Santino, throwing himself into his arms. He got very emotional. "I thought you weft like Uncle Weece and Uncle Al. Why'd you wun away?"

Every adult in the room choked up, having forgotten how important communication was, even with the youngest amongst them. And Santino was so close to tears that he couldn't answer as he wrapped the boy tightly in his arms and stood.

Eli's uncle Reece had been killed, and Alessandro had disappeared for months without a word. The kid had been through a lot of loss.

Chloe backed out of the kitchen, feeling sick to her stomach. This was all her fault. She quietly made her way to her room and closed the door. Then she sat on the bed and cried. She understood loss, and she would never have wanted to be the cause of anyone feeling that way, especially not a child.

She was blowing her nose when she heard a knock at her door. Clearing her throat, she called out, "Come in."

Brooklyn came in, teary-eyed. "Chloe, don't take this on too. He didn't mean to make you feel bad."

"It should be me apologizing. I caused Eli to think he lost him. Santino has to go back to the resort tonight. I won't be the cause of breaking up your family."

Brooklyn sat beside her. "I understand how you feel, but, believe me, this has nothing to do with you and everything to do with Valentina. I understand both sides because she didn't like me either at the beginning." She paused and gave a small smile. "I can see on your face that you don't believe me, but if you give me a few minutes, I will tell you my story. I think you might see some similarities.

"One thing you have to understand is Valentina raised her sons almost single-handedly. It wasn't easy, and she had to work hard to maintain control over five growing, strong-willed boys. Luca says she started trying to control them again when Shawn and Marcello died. It was the only thing she could control, and they let her, thinking it would help."

Chloe stood. "And that is also my fault. None of them would have had to suffer through that if it wasn't for my dad."

Brooklyn reached out for hand and guided her back to the bed. "You said it yourself, your dad, not you. Please hear me out. It might help." They sat for a couple of hours as Brooklyn spewed her not-so-pretty past.

Meanwhile, Santino finally found his voice and admitted he was wrong to the devastated little boy. Then he promised to never leave again without letting him know. Like children do, Eli forgave his uncle the minute he suggested the two of them go to McDonald's and then for ice cream.

Luca and Raimer were talking in the kitchen when another knock was heard.

"This place has turned into Grand Central Station. I bet it's Alessandro. He's the only one who hasn't shown up in the last twenty-four hours." Raimer opened the front door, finding Owen standing there.

"Hi, Raimer. I'm sorry to drop by unannounced, but I was hoping to see Chloe for a minute. I'm afraid I owe her an apology."

Clasping his hand to his heart, Raimer exclaimed, "Jesucristo, I'm never letting her leave! Chloe has brought more hot men to my door than Allentown's gay dating service." He sighed dramatically. "I don't know if my heart can take another gorgeous man in my home, but I'm willing to try if you are." He made a theatrical sweeping gesture with one hand for Owen to enter. "Head to the kitchen; Luca's in there."

Luca stood and shook Owen's hand. "Hey, Owen. What are you doing here?"

"Luca." He returned his handshake. "Sorry to interrupt. I just got off the phone with my dad, and he told me everything that happened with Valentina. I was at the resort yesterday and must have left right before the fireworks. Anyway, I told Dad I would help Chloe, then freaked out when he didn't insist she get the medical attention I thought she needed. I overstepped, and if Chloe will still allow me, I'd like to help her with physiotherapy."

Raimer's hand was at his heart again. "Gorgeous, humble, and kind. Could my day get any better? Tell me you're free for dinner!"

Owen blushed at the absurd comment but recovered quickly. "Is he always like this?"

"Yes, that's Raimer. You're only halfway safe, even if you're married. Sit down. Can I get you a coffee?"

"Sure, I'd love one. How's Valentina today?" He sat down at the seat that didn't have a mug. Raimer sat across from him, while Luca got the coffee.

"Not very good, unfortunately. She's not talking to us guys, but the girls are staying close. We don't know how to reach her. This isn't like our mamma. She can be pigheaded, but this is beyond anything we've ever seen." Placing a mug in front of Owen, he asked, "Has she taken any calls from your dad yet?"

Owen took a sip before he answered. "Dad said he's not calling for a couple of days. He feels like she needs time to process. On the way here, I thought, if it's okay with you guys, maybe I would call her today and see if I can help. Your mom and I have had many heart-to-heart talks over the years."

"If you can reach her, we'd sure appreciate it," Luca answered for all the brothers. "We're all at a loss as to how to help her. She's being completely unreasonable and cruel. Chloe is a victim, who continues to be victimized by her. That delicate little flower couldn't hurt a fly if she tried. Mamma would see that if she could only get past her own selfishness."

Owen stood. "It's hard for your mom. She needs someone to blame. We all know it isn't Chloe; it's the fact that she's his daughter." Owen had been friends with Valentina long before he had ever found out she was the woman his dad was dating. He had been assigned her deceased husband's phone number, and after multiple mistaken phone calls, he encouraged her to talk. From then on, they had formed a bond. He was very protective of his friend, who was like a mother figure to him. "But I saw Chloe's legs yesterday, and I'll tell you right now, that woman was beaten years before the attack. I know abuse marks when I see them."

They all had assumed the same thing, but to get clarification was disheartening.

Luca pulled his phone out, scrolling through his pictures. "Alessandro and I went to her house yesterday to see if we could salvage any clothes for her." He stopped to shake his head. "What Jacob and his friends did was beyond disturbing. There isn't one salvageable thing in that house." He handed the phone to Owen, letting him scroll through the pictures. Raimer leaned over to look, while Luca continued. "I came here today to convince Santino to do anything in his power to keep her close. I'm afraid they're not done with her. There was a hangman's noose in the garage. Sick fucks."

Owen's and Raimer's stomachs dropped at the sight of the carnage.

Owen swiped one picture too far and saw the photo of Chloe hanging upside down on the cross, covered in blood. "Jesus fucking Christ, how did she survive with her mind intact?" Owen spewed out, afraid his lunch was going to follow. "Did you show these to Valentina?"

Shocked, Luca responded with a whoosh, "God, no. I don't think she could handle it."

Owen continued to scroll as he spoke. "I'm not bound by the same ethical standards as my dad. Let me tell her the truth, and if words don't work, would you trust me enough to show these to Valentina? I think you're all trying to protect her because you're afraid she'll try to hurt herself, but I think she needs to see all of it. She's stronger than you think.

"Give me Chloe's address, and let me take her there. By protecting her and keeping Valentina in the dark, I think you're all perpetuating the situation and allowing her to foster hatred. This is the dose of reality she needs. I'll be gentle with her, I swear."

Luca scrubbed his hands down his face. "I don't know. I wish more than anything I could talk to your dad, but he's too close to the situation. Let me call Alessandro and see what he says."

Owen looked at Raimer, who was staring off into space. "Are you okay?"

For the very first time, Raimer didn't joke as he dipped a spoon into the sugar and swirled it around. "I can relate to Chloe about being ostracized and bullied. It wasn't easy growing up in a communist country as a gay teenager. I mean, look at me; it's not like I could hide it. I had to leave everything I loved when people started to take their prejudice out on my family. My papa disowned me, and my mama and brother paid dearly on my behalf."

Owen felt a certain amount of guilt after hearing Raimer's confession, knowing he was hiding his sexual orientation from his own dad, a man who wouldn't judge him in the least. He had been given every opportunity to be whomever he was, while Raimer had his choices taken away.

Chloe couldn't change who she was any more than Raimer or he could. If he was going to make Valentina see the truth, then he owed it to everyone to be truthful.

"Raimer, after I see Valentina, will you go to dinner with me to talk?"

Raimer snapped out of his dulled demeanor. "Sure. I'm warning you, though, I'm not a cheap date. But I am a good listener if you can ever get me to shut up." He winked with a chuckle as Luca walked in.

"Owen, Alessandro and I agree, with one stipulation. If things get out of hand, you call us to help. Thanks, man." They shook hands again.

"I'll call Valentina now. Send me all the pictures, and Chloe's address. Will you also tell Chloe that I was here today, and if she's up for it, I would love to stop by early tomorrow before work and start physiotherapy." He turned to face Raimer. "Give me your phone number, and I'll call when I'm done so we can decide on a place to meet."

Five minutes later, he was off. He wished he could have gotten Santino's consent, but sometimes it was better to ask for forgiveness than permission.

Chapter 9
"Head Above Water" by Avril Lavigne

"Where are we going?" They had been traveling for about twenty-five minutes before Valentina spoke. She had agreed to see Owen, only with the promise that they not discuss Chloe or his dad.

He glanced over at her from the driver's seat. "I want to show you something."

"Owen," she spat, "I know you're trying to help, but I don't want to ruin our relationship. There is nothing you can show me that will change my mind. Chloe is the devil's spawn and deserves everything she got. And I'll never forgive Santino and your dad for taking her side."

Owen cringed at the tone and ugliness of her words as he glanced back through the windshield. He couldn't believe this was the woman he had idolized for her compassion and wisdom. He knew better than anyone how hard she had struggled with her losses. He prayed it hadn't hardened her beyond what he was going to show her.

"There aren't any sides in this situation. Everyone involved is a victim of the fallout. Valentina, hate can do terrible things to good, generous people. I'm hoping against hope that it hasn't changed the woman who is like a mother to me."

When the GPS announced they had reached their destination, he pulled into the driveway and parked.

Valentina saw the vandalized car and whipped her head toward

Owen, narrowing her eyes. "How dare you bring me to her house! I don't want to see her. Take me home right now." She crossed her arms over her chest, furious that the only friend she had left was trying to manipulate her.

"She's not here. Nobody is or can be." He took his seat belt off and turned toward her. "If you insist on condemning Chloe, then I want you to see what it can lead to. If you truly believe what you're saying, then anything you see shouldn't bother you. Still, I want you to see the inside of that house because it's what your soul will turn into if you let your hate rule your heart. If you really intend to banish your son and the man you love, at least have the courage to face the malignant spirit that drove them to help her."

She clenched her jaw tightly, shaking her head in disgust. "Fine. But it won't change a thing for me, except to know that your little intervention cost us our friendship, because I can hear by your argument that you have also chosen Chloe's side over mine." She yanked open the door, then waited for him to get out. Owen watched as she tried to avoid looking at the car.

As they crunched over the glass from the broken window of the front door, he saw her look questioningly at the spray-painted door. "That's a pentagram with a circle around it. It's the sign of the devil."

She glared at him from over her shoulder. "I'm not stupid. I recognize the sign of the devil."

Owen was having second thoughts. Maybe she was too far gone, blinded by her anger, for this to work.

Even as distracted as he was, though, nothing could dull his senses enough from the punch to the gut when they walked over the threshold. It was ten times worse than the pictures. The whole environment seemed to be suffocating with more evilness than Owen had believed existed.

Valentina squeaked as her hand flew to her mouth.

Owen circled her shoulders with his arm, pulling her closer to him. "This is what Jacob and his friends did to her home. I know it's frightening, but this is only the tip of the iceberg. Come on."

Valentina was in a state of shock, questioning herself as her eyes moved from room to room with extreme horror.

The smell in the kitchen nearly made her double over. Owen didn't hide anything, telling her the smell was from animal remains in the fridge.

She stopped to pick up a broken spout that was surrounded by shattered pieces of a Royal Albert china teapot. It had to have been an heirloom, because she knew that design had been discontinued years ago. "Who owned this house?"

"Luca told me it was Chloe's maternal grandparents' farm that she inherited. Brooklyn said her mom and her identical twin died when she was young."

A lump formed in Valentina's throat as a rock settled in her stomach. Chloe had obviously lost a lot of people.

He led her to the bedroom and moved to the right to give her an unobstructed view. "Santino told Luca that Chloe said every item from her past was destroyed, but the thing that broke her was them burning every picture of her family. She has nothing left of the people she loved."

Valentina breathed deeply, choking each time she tried to get some air into her lungs. Owen was relieved when she finally coughed out a desperate, ravaged cry.

She brushed off his hands as she walked to the bed and saw the knives through the little girls' faces. She pulled out each one, only able to see the curly blonde locks of the young twins. She then lifted her eyes to the words: One down, one to go. You can run, but you can't hide. Die, whore! She turned around and slid down the wall, clutching the picture to her chest. What had she done?

Owen knew Valentina was in a state of aporia. Throughout his childhood, his dad had studied psychological theories and would teach his kids one theory that had caught his eye at dinner each night. Freudian was usually his favorite, but Owen had always remembered this ancient Greek term.

This was the moment Valentina was filled with all-consuming emptiness, realizing everything she had believed about Chloe wasn't true. She was at an impasse between logic and what she had convinced her heart were the facts. She was being bombarded with visual information overload that challenged all her opposing views.

Owen moved beside her and slid down the wall. "I'm sorry, Valentina, but that's not all."

She looked over at him, mentally defeated.

"You owe it to Chloe to hear the whole story."

When she nodded, he told her about the signs of abuse he saw on her body. He also told her how Brooklyn said she had gotten the worst of her injuries in the fire. Then he went on to describe everything Luca had told him that happened after Valentina had attacked her that night.

She dropped her head and silently cried as she listened.

Owen wasn't done. He took out his phone and opened the pictures, handing it to her and telling her to scroll through them all.

Valentina knew she had no option but to look, so she slowly scrolled through each picture, sobbing and having to wipe her running nose and eyes after each one.

She wasn't any better than the people who had committed these heinous crimes. When had she become so heartless? Being faced with the same ugly hatefulness she was consumed with had helped her understand why her sons were so furious with her.

Owen continued, "What they did to her wreaked havoc with her old injuries, but I haven't been able to assess them yet because the wounds she got from hanging upside down are infected. She can't afford medical attention and refuses to see a doctor.

"Dad and I got into a horrible fight about her right to choose. I didn't understand his protectiveness in giving her control over those decisions until I was faced with the whole story. Dad has no idea what really happened to her, but he still put himself in the line of fire with you and me because he knew it was right. I owe him an apology because, with no demands for the truth or questions, he helped a woman who, by all rights, should be in a mental institution after all she's had to deal with."

Valentina handed him back the phone. What could she say? He was right.

"There is one more thing we have to see." He stood, extending his hand.

With a hoarse voice, she responded, "No, please, I understand how wrong I was. I don't need to see anymore."

"Yes, Valentina, you do." He led her to the door Luca said was the garage. They saw the crates all crumbled around the noose. Somberly, he said, "When Santino found Chloe, she was standing on those crates with that noose around her neck. Jacob left it for her to commit suicide so his hands would remain clean. If Santino hadn't been here, she would have died, despondent, unloved, and all alone, paying for a crime she didn't even commit. Shawn and Marcello dealt with his terror for fifteen minutes, but I think Chloe dealt with it for years.

"Santino was attracted to her before any of this came to light. But I'm warning you, Valentina, the man you raised learned all your lessons about protectiveness and love; he isn't going to walk away from her. And I thank God every second for that. Chloe deserves someone like Santino."

Valentina dropped down to the step and sobbed her eyes out. She knew a thousand Hail Marys wouldn't absolve her transgressions. If their roles were reversed, Valentina would never forgive herself. Maybe some acts were truly unforgivable.

"I need your dad. Will you please call him and see if he would be willing to talk to me?" One thing she had learned when she had lost her husband and son had been to take everything one step at a time, and to ask for help.

Owen bent down and hugged her. "Of course, Valentina. He loves you. He'll come." He pulled back and cupped both sides of her jaw, forcing her head up. "I love you too, Valentina. Dad and your sons will forgive you." He kissed both her wet cheeks.

She took a deep breath and hiccupped, whispering out, "The problem is, I don't know if I can forgive myself. I was filled with as much contempt as the shooter. I accused Chloe of being the devil's spawn, but I'm no better than him. I was blinded beyond reason by hatred. How do you come back from that?"

"I have faith in you. You're not alone. Even if it takes everyone else a while, you'll always have me. You're mom squared to me."

Valentina screwed up her face. "Mom squared?"

He chuckled. "Yeah, a woman who is like a second mom or to the second power."

Valentina threw her arms around this young man who had been her voice of reason for a while. "Thank you."

Owen then excused himself to call his dad, knowing he would be furious at him for bringing Valentina to Chloe's without permission.

Valentina looked around the garage. Everything had been yanked off the shelves and thrown all over the place. She started to clean up, picking up a box and putting things back into it. When she was done, she lifted the box to the shelf and noticed a plastic container wedged between the shelf and the wall. She pulled it down and opened it.

The container was filled with pictures. There were a lot of old ones she assumed belonged to Chloe's grandmother. She dug down and saw some colored photos. She grabbed one of two little girls with blonde curls.

Her left hand flew to her mouth. Chloe's mamma must have sent pictures of her children to their grandmother. Chloe hadn't lost everything.

She looked heavenward. Thank you, Shawn, for allowing me to make something right.

Owen walked back into the garage and saw Valentina kneeling in front of a box, her head dropped to her chest. "Valentina, are you okay?"

She turned toward him with tears streaming down her face. "They didn't destroy everything. They missed a box filled with pictures that Chloe's grandmother must have kept. Owen, you have to help me. I want to go through these without anyone knowing and, hopefully, I'll find enough to make a book. If I can give Chloe something from her past, maybe she'll find it in her heart to forgive me."

He was proud of her. This was a big step, but he also knew his dad wouldn't approve of them taking anything from Chloe's house. "Dad is on his way. I know for a fact he won't agree. Let me put that box in my trunk, and I'll bring it to your place later."

She slowly stood, dusting off her knees. "There's something else I need help with. I know it sounds crazy, but much like Alessandro had to rebuild Marcello's cabin, I have to fix this house. I need to right some of the wrongs done to Chloe. I will pay for everything and hire people, but will you help me coordinate it?"

His face broke into a huge smile. "I'd be honored. Let's head outside so I can stash this box before Dad gets here. He's not very happy with me right now as it is." Bending over, he picked up the box.

Valentina closed the doors behind them as they made their way back through the house. "I'm sorry. I didn't mean to cause any problems between you and your dad." She stopped to grab a piece of the shattered teapot and pocketed it.

When they got to the car, Owen popped the trunk and placed the box inside. "This week, I've learned that we sometimes have to do things, even if it makes other people angry. The only regret I have is pushing Chloe into choices she wasn't comfortable with. It won't happen again."

They stood together, leaning against the car for fifteen minutes before Quinn pulled into the driveway. The minute he stepped out, Valentina ran to him, sobbing and begging for forgiveness. He hugged her tightly, looking at his son from over her head and nodding his thanks.

Quinn watched his son drive away, letting Valentina cry for about ten minutes before he lifted her face. "Let's go to my place." He led her around the car, opening the passenger door.

Before he could close it, she held her hand out. "Wait." She got back out and walked over to Chloe's car. She hadn't looked at it the first time, so now she took in the immensity of the damage. Valentina didn't have to be a mechanic to know it was a total write-off. She noted the model and stored it in the back of her mind.

***

Chloe relaxed marginally after hearing Brooklyn's story. It gave her a small amount of hope. Then Chloe and Brooklyn made tea and were talking lightheartedly about babies when Eli busted through the door.

"Mommy, we went to McDonald's and had ice cream in the park. Uncle Santino says I can stay over next week, if it's okay with you. Me, Chloe, and Uncle Santino are gonna go to a movie. Can I, please? Can I?"

Santino was thrilled by the comfortable scene in front of him. Chloe looked incredibly relaxed and content. He knew having his famiglia help would be instrumental in keeping her here.

"Did you hear me? I have a favor to ask you two," Brooklyn said again with uncertainty. He had missed what Brooklyn said while staring at Chloe, smiling with her eyes glued to Eli.

Chloe tensed but encouraged her to continue.

"I wanted to take Luca out for dinner tonight. I need to talk to him in private"—she eyed Eli—"but I don't have anyone to watch Eli. Alessandro and Ava are going to her parents', and Sabastian and Emmy have plans. Do you think you could watch him? I promise we won't be long."

Chloe unfolded her legs from the couch and winced in pain. With a soft, bubbly voice, she said, "We'd love to. We're also babysitting Shawn tonight, so the more, the merrier."

Brooklyn looked horrified. "Oh, gosh no, don't worry about it. I didn't know you were already babysitting. We'll do it another night."

Chloe remembered Brooklyn telling her that she was pregnant. She'd bet anything she was taking Luca out to tell him. "Please, nothing would make me happier or feel better than babysitting both of them. There are two of us, and Eli, you'll help with Shawn, right?"

Eli pumped his arm. "Yeah! Can we take him to McDonald's?"

Santino ruffled his hair. "Not a chance, but we could order pizza and watch Netflix."

Eli turned to his mommy and gave her puppy dog eyes.

Brooklyn raised her hands. "Okay, okay."

While her son screeched, she thanked the couple and told them she would drop Eli off around six. Eli complained about leaving, but Brooklyn told him he had to shower and grab his PJs before they came back. Chloe then hugged them both before Santino walked them to the door.

When he came back to the living room, he sat down on the other end of the couch and asked, "Are you sure you don't mind babysitting?"

"I love children more than anything, especially little ones." She beamed and shared without thinking, "When I was growing up, all I wanted to do was get my teaching degree and work at a Montessori school, but my social worker was afraid someone might find out who I was and it would create a scandal. In hindsight, I guess she was right."

"I'm sorry, Chloe," he replied genuinely. "You would have made a great teacher."

She tilted her head with a forced smile. "I've accepted it. It's okay. It's probably for the better."

Santino felt horrible for her. He knew realistically that, even if she got married and had a new name, people might still find out who she was. He hoped they could have children together in the future, but that was a long way off.

"One day, you can have lots of kids and home school them."

Right before his eyes, she withdrew inwardly.

"I always thought I would, but after this last incident, I realized it's a pipe dream," Chloe replied softly. "For the sake of the children I might have had, Jacob proved I can't protect them from my past. I don't want my babies to ever have to feel the hatred I felt."

Santino couldn't take it another minute. He shifted over, asking her if it was okay if he held her for a minute, then waited for a nod before he pulled her into his arms. He felt her go completely rigid, but it didn't deter him.

He kissed the top of her head. "Stellina, don't give up on your dreams. When one door closes, another one opens. Don't be afraid of what's behind that door. I'll be here to walk you through it."

She sniffled. "Honestly, I don't want to open any more doors. I just want to walk safely down the hallway forever."

"I'm trying not to push you, but I wish you would believe me when I tell you that you're not alone anymore. We won't abandon you. You have me, my brothers, their wives, and their children. You also seem to have inherited our famiglia mascot Raimer, but I'm not taking credit for that one. Oh, by the way, Luca texted me and said Owen stopped by today. He wants to know if he can stop by early tomorrow to start working on your physio."

Chloe didn't want to dig too deeply into his statement, so she changed the subject. "Why do you call me Stellina?"

Santino grinned charmingly. "It's a term of endearment in Italian. It means little star. The first time I saw you at the resort, you turned, and your eyes were like beautiful, twinkling stars. You truly have the most beautiful eyes I've ever seen. In fact, you are by far the most exquisite woman I have ever seen."

Chloe tensed and pulled back. She hated to offend him, but he had crossed a big line. Quinn said she should make people aware of her rights, so she told him, "You have been so nice to me, but when you talk like that, it makes me wary. I know I'm not beautiful by any stretch of the imagination, so when you say things that aren't true, it makes me question everything else you've said."

The look of shock on his face made her think she had just made a huge mistake. She dropped her eyes to the couch.

"Please forgive me. You have every right to be angry."

She couldn't believe she heard him apologize. Wow, Quinn was right; if people were in her space, they had to respect her limitations.

"Thank you for being honest and telling me I made you uncomfortable. I won't do it again. If I do anything that makes you feel awkward, always feel free to tell me. I want you to believe everything I say, and to feel safe in my presence." How could he have forgotten that she had just spent months being duped by a man who probably said those same things all the time? He was such an idiot. One day he would convince her she was the most beautiful woman on Earth, just not today, or any day soon. "Would it be okay if I still called you Stellina?"

She smiled proudly, and it reached her eyes. "Sure. I've never had a nickname. A lot of kids I knew did. I like it. It kinda makes me feel special."

He smiled back as he reminded himself that she would be creating and redefining her boundaries for some time to come. He moved to a safer subject. "Where's Raimer?"

"He said he had to buy a new shirt before he met a friend for dinner. I hope he isn't going out because of us."

Barking out a laugh, Santino said, "Not a chance. He really must be meeting someone special. Otherwise, he would have hung around to see which one of my brothers showed up tonight that he could harass. He lives for the shock factor. I hope when he finally meets the right guy that he tones it down, because if a woman I was in love flirted like that, it would be a deal breaker for me. There is nothing wrong with appreciating an attractive person, but it's disrespectful to say it out loud if you have a partner."

Chloe had to admit she was impressed with how all the Savage men treated women. His brothers obviously adored their wives. They were respectful to women in general. His dad must have been a good example.

That thought made her flinch.

Santino watched as she worked out something in her mind. "Can I ask what you were just thinking?"

She was taken aback. People didn't usually ask her that. Could she be honest about it? Better to see if he was truly sincere right now.

"I was thinking how respectful you and your brothers are toward women, and I wondered if it was because of your dad. Then I realized I'm the reason he isn't here."

He got up before answering and moved to the bar, reaching for a bottle of red wine. "I'm going to answer, but first, I would love a glass of wine while we talk about the greatest man who ever graced the earth. Would you like a glass?" He looked over his shoulder at her.

His actions instantly put her hackles up. Did he need the wine because he was mad about what she had said, or was it still too painful to talk about his dad? Maybe some liquid courage would help her too.

"I'm not a big drinker, but I'll have half a glass. I don't think we should have any more because I don't want Sabastian or Luca nervous about leaving the kids with us."

"Smart girl." He grabbed the corkscrew, two wineglasses, and a bottle, and brought them to the coffee table. He uncorked the wine. "My dad was the most amazing man. If I could be half the man he was, I would be happy." Once Santino poured them each half a glass, he handed one to Chloe. He then clinked his glass against hers and took a sip. Placing it down, he continued, "Shawn Savage was a legend, and he was passionate about three things in his life. His greatest love was my mamma, his sons were second, and music was third. He lived for his famiglia and respected all three of his loves.

"Believe it or not, my parents only knew each other for about eight weeks before they got married. My dad used to say that, when we met the right woman, we would know it. He was famous for saying, Treat the woman you love like a princess, and you'll live like a king."

Chloe's eyes were huge. "Wow."

"Every time he came home from being on a tour, he walked through the door and yelled, 'Where's my beautiful angel?' As excited as he was to see us, we always knew he couldn't give us his attention until he was welcomed home by his wife's arms. I think part of it was they were apart for a lot of their marriage, so they didn't have time to get on each other's nerves."

He picked up his glass and took another sip. "He always taught us to respect women—it was nonnegotiable. He thought women should be cherished and respected. He saw a lot on the road, especially with groupies, and that only reinforced that his sons would never treat women like a piece of meat.

"Dad used to say he worked with guys who entertained a different woman every night, and he had never met lonelier men. It was one thing to hear it, but it was another to see it. He didn't just preach a good talk, he walked the walk. Everyone he worked with had the utmost respect for him, and they always made a point of telling us. Even as a young boy, I knew I wanted people to remember me for being a good man like my dad. I learned from him that what you put out there, you get back. My brothers' marriages prove that tenfold. It's simple for me. I want to give and receive the same kind of love and respect from the woman I love. It's the only way I know."

Chloe was blown away by his admission. He wanted to be like his dad, and he was. Santino was a good man.

It was time she shared and gave back some honesty. She chose to trust him a little.

Santino watched as she worked out something important in her head. This beautiful, delicate little star was as easy to read as a children's book. Simple, animated, and beautiful.

Chloe took a huge gulp of wine, then spoke so softly that Santino had to strain to hear her. "I didn't grow up with a father like yours. My father couldn't stand me or my sister. Actually, he couldn't stand any woman. He hated our mom. He demanded we respect him, but never gave any in return. I don't think I ever knew for sure why he hated us, but I think it's because Harper and I were girls. Two babies and neither one a boy. Not once did he ever show us any affection. The only thing he was convinced of was that we would grow up to be as useless as our mother."

She wiggled her legs from underneath her and stood. After sitting for so long, her limp was more prominent. "If he was mad, he hit us for the smallest infraction. It drove him crazy when he took everything away from the two of us, yet we could still amuse ourselves and loved one another." Chloe wandered to the window to look at the city below. The wine in her glass sloshed around as she moved. "There are so many people out there"—she turned to look at her confessor—"but no matter where we lived, no one ever helped us. I know people had to have known, but it's strange that not once did someone try to help."

Santino sat there, imagining two little girls being hurt by a large adult male. It made him sick.

He also couldn't sit any longer, but he didn't want to move in case it frightened her, so he tapped his right fingers on his knee in increments of five repeatedly. It was a habit he had formed years ago, and right now, it was the only way to keep him in his seat.

Chloe took the last sip of her wine, then placed the empty glass on the window ledge. "When Harper died, I think part of me died too. My mother's spirit finally broke that day. She checked out and, eventually, her body followed her mind. I was left with no one to love or be loved by, and I think, because it had been so long since I felt real love, I was easily fooled by Jacob's act." Chloe cackled irritably. "I finally understand that what my father said is true. I am gullible and useless." She ruptured on the last word, bending forward and clenching her belly with a heaving sob.

Santino sprang up to catch his falling star. He cooed into her ear as he rocked her back and forth, soothing her, while desperately trying not to overwhelm her. "No, Stellina. Let me take over where Harper left off. I swear, not all men are like your father or Jacob. Deep down, you know my brothers, Quinn, Owen, Raimer, and I are all good men. Everyone should have the right to be loved and cared for unconditionally, especially you.

"Maybe people did try to help, but your mom refused it for whatever reason. I know it's scary, but if you choose to let me help, little by little, I'm going to prove it to you. The choice is yours."

Chapter 10
"Shadow Days" by John Mayer

Chloe finally accepted Santino's help after she had her meltdown. It was the turning point in their relationship. They spent the next month getting to know one another and building trust.

Santino had been avoiding his mamma at all costs, with the help of his brothers. Sabastian, Luca, and Alessandro still struggled to understand the scornful attitude Valentina had shown and didn't engage her any more than was necessary for the resort. The fact that she had become quiet and disappeared after work and on her days off proved that she hadn't seen the error of her ways. The three were at a loss because they had always relied on Santino to be the buffer when she acted unreasonably.

Ava had run into Quinn the day he had brought Valentina home after Owen called him. They all figured she had reconciled with Quinn and was spending her time with him or at the cemetery. Quinn was trained to deal with anger issues, unlike the rest of them, so they prayed he could reach her where they couldn't.

Emmy reported that Valentina was always tired and looked like she hadn't slept in months. Emmy had also gotten into the habit of taking Shawn to Chloe when she needed a babysitter because of Valentina's absence. Eli had become a permanent fixture at Chloe's side Fridays after school and Saturday and Monday evenings. Santino continued to encourage his brothers' wives to let her babysit as much as possible. She was at her happiest when she was busy with the kids. The children were making strides with her in areas he couldn't. Santino's beautiful Stellina was beginning to shine.

Owen came over every morning during the week to work on physio, and Quinn came at lunch to help work with the trauma of her past and present with cognitive behavioral therapy. After Chloe finally accepted that she had rights, they worked on reliving traumatic events that had led to the one event she avoided like the plague. Quinn knew he couldn't change her hyperarousal of constantly looking for danger, or her natural need to detach from adults until they dealt with the catalyst of the most severe abuse.

It was a Monday, and Santino was home when Quinn knocked at the door. The two men had a silent understanding not to discuss Valentina when they ran into each other. When Quinn was at Raimer's, it was all about Chloe.

Santino had been feeling Chloe's stress all morning, and when she burst into tears at hearing Quinn's knock, he asked what was wrong. Then he yelled to Quinn that he would be there in a minute as Chloe blurted out that they were dealing with a terrifying subject today and she was beyond frightened.

He cradled her face, wiping the tears off her cheeks with his thumbs. "Stellina, if you want me to stay to support you, all you have to do is ask."

She bit her lip so hard that he thought she had broken the skin.

He changed his wording to make it easier for her to answer. "Would you like me to stay?"

She nodded as big fat tears rolled down and snagged her lip again.

Santino gently tugged it out from between her teeth before he kissed her forehead. "I would gladly do anything for you. I'll let Quinn in and tell him I'm staying. You go wash your face."

Santino was thrilled. He had been waiting patiently for her to rely on him on her own accord. On the flip side, it was going to be hard to hear, because this was obviously bigger than he thought he might be capable of handling.

He knew she had been abused, but the idea of hearing the details was daunting. Maybe Quinn was pushing too hard.

He guided her toward the washroom before opening the door and stepping out into the hall to speak to Quinn privately.

"Chloe wants me to stay for this session. Honestly, I don't think she's ready. She's petrified."

As calmly as ever, Quinn answered, "I understand your concern, but she can't take the next step in healing until she faces the biggest stumbling block. So many of her triggers are tied to this one event."

Santino blew out a frustrated breath, yanking at the strands of his hair. Then he turned his tortured expression to Quinn. "What if I can't handle what she says? What if I panic and fail her?" Mortified, he turned away, dropping his forehead against the wall.

Quinn patted his shoulder, then squeezed his tense muscles. "You're human, Santino. If you need to express emotion, do it. It isn't a failure if she sees it affect you. It means you care. I have total faith in you."

He took a deep breath and gathered his courage. That was exactly what he had needed to hear. Quinn was right; he could do this for Stellina.

He opened the door, welcoming Quinn in. Chloe was just walking down the hall and stopped on a dime.

Quinn took over. "I understand you have invited Santino to stay. That's a big step, Chloe. I'm proud you're putting safeguards in place for yourself. Santino explained you're extremely nervous. Is there anything that would help?"

She looked bewildered, until Santino said, "Go get Lambie. He represents Harper, and you need her with you as well."

Relieved and thankful he thought of it, Chloe nodded, then rushed away to get her solace.

"Good thinking, son. Let's get comfortable in the living room. Is Raimer home?" Quinn asked, not wanting any interruptions.

"He's out, but I'll text him and ask him to hold off from coming home for a couple of hours." Santino plucked his phone from his pocket, sending off a quick text. Raimer responded instantly, telling him to give Chloe a kiss from him and wish her luck.

He heard the shuffle of her feet slowing with dread the closer she got to the living room.

"Stellina, if you're not ready, all you have to do is tell Quinn and he'll reschedule. I can be here anytime you need me."

She was relieved, but when she looked at Lambie, she knew that if she didn't face the skeleton in her closet, she would never move on. Having the option of canceling, though, gave her the courage to follow through.

"Thank you, but everyone's already here."

He walked up to her, gently taking the lamb from her hands to check to see if his miserable stitching was still holding the toy's stuffing in. Satisfied, he handed it back. "Do it because you're ready, not to accommodate our schedules. I want you to get better for you, not for us."

Chloe lifted her eyes, looking up through her eyelashes. When Santino saw her expression, it took his breath away. He saw adoration and a more in-depth trust that burst from those stunning eyes. With a shit-eating grin, he lifted his hand to one of hers and weaved his fingers through them before leading them to the couch.

Quinn sat in the chair beside them and extended her phone that had been on the end table. "I don't want you to focus on us, so I'm going to ask you to put your music on low and lie back with your eyes closed."

Nervously, her eyes skipped over to Santino. He calmed her by telling her to put Harper's playlist on.

Over the last few weeks, he had noticed she'd put on that particular playlist to calm herself when she became stressed out.

When she was ready, he took one finger and guided her chin toward him. With every ounce of his faith, he said, "I'm going to hold your hand so you'll remember I'm right beside you. If at any time you need a break or want to stop, just say so and everything stops. I promise."

Quinn had watched Santino heal and grow over the last couple of years, but this man in front of him impressed him beyond words.

"Chloe, I think Santino is vying for my job." He relished in her giggles. This was exactly the state he wanted her in to deal with this part of her recovery. "All joking aside, you hold all the power here. By offering his hand, what Santino did, without even knowing it, was give you a concrete connection to the present, to know that you are safe and well looked after.

"Nothing you talk about has the power to hurt you anymore. You have already experienced the physical and emotional pain of the experience. This session is about extracting the potency of the negative memories. I may stop you from time to time to help you understand the capacity of your reaction or response as a child to the trauma. You might not have been allowed to voice your feelings then, but you are now. If you need to ask questions, by all means, there are no rules on how we proceed. When you're ready, start with whatever part of the day you're comfortable with."

It only took the power of the first memory and the sound of her music to transport her back in time.

Chloe dropped her knapsack on her bed. She was relieved to be home from school because she never fit in there, but she also knew home wasn't any safer.

Her anxiety had skyrocketed when she had walked into their apartment and found her mom zoned out on her bed. She hadn't started dinner, and nothing had been taken out of the freezer. Her father was going to blow his top if he came home and didn't have supper waiting for him. She had half an hour before that happened.

She didn't want a repeat of last week, when the neighbors had called the police after he lost it on her mom for the same thing. The police officers had escorted all of them down the three flights of winding stairs to the front lawn of the six-plex they lived in to discuss the altercation.

Chloe had been coached her whole life never to tell anyone what went on in their house, so she had stayed silent when the officers questioned her. With mother and daughter not talking, the police only had her father's side to go by, and they gave him the usual lecture on keeping his temper in check, then added that if they had to come back, they would charge him with disturbing the peace.

Out of the corner of her eye, she had seen a boy from school watching. The kids were still tormenting her because of it.

The eleven-year-old knew that, in order to prevent the same thing from happening again, she would have to make his dinner. However, Chloe had no idea how to cook, and if her father was right, neither did her mother.

She moved a chair to the pantry, stood on it, and moved things around until she found an old jar of spaghetti sauce. If she read the instructions, she could surely do it. She also grabbed a bag of elbow noodles. Then, sitting at the table, she read the instructions. It didn't seem that hard.

She couldn't have been more wrong.

Chloe put a pot of water on the stove, lit the gas burner, and then tried to take the lid off the sauce, but it was too tight. She tapped it with a spoon like her mother always did, and still it wouldn't come off.

She ran it under water like she had seen, but that wasn't any more effective. Then she grabbed the funny hammer her mother used to hit the meat. After a couple of taps, she wound up hitting the lid too hard, and the jar shattered.

Chloe started chanting, "Oh God, oh God, he's going to be so mad." Her hand started to twitch, but her eyes remained closed.

Santino squeezed her hand to reinforce to her that he was still there. When it didn't help, he ran his other hand down her arm. Then he looked at Quinn for help.

Quinn nodded his approval.

Desperate to calm her, he pulled her closer and wrapped his arm around her shoulders. That seemed to work, and she started to recount the story from where she had left off.

She put the jar down and ran for another pot and a spoon. Chloe poured the remainder of the sauce in and tried to scoop up as much sauce as she could from the floor. Leaving the pot on the floor, she picked up a big shard of glass, cutting her finger. That was the least of her worries.

By that time, the water was boiling, so she put the whole bag of noodles into the boiling water before she went back to cleaning up. She painstakingly picked up each piece of glass and cut two more fingers. Before she could wipe up the sauce, the water boiled over, putting out the flame.

Santino watched as two lines formed between her eyes. He moved his fingers to soothe the desperation in her face. Chloe didn't respond. It was like she was lost in a hypnotic trance.

Quinn didn't stop her to ask questions, letting it play out.

Panicking, she turned on the burner beside the one she was using and dragged the pot over, sloshing boiling water over the edges. When she went back to cleaning up the sauce, the noodles absorbed all the water and started to burn.

She had just carried the broken jar to the garbage can when the door slammed shut, scaring the life out of her. Her father stood there, looking madder than she had ever seen.

"What the fuck are you doing?" he yelled.

Chloe gulped. "Making dinner."

"Where the hell is that useless piece of shit mother of yours?"

Her eyes filled with tears. She was in more trouble now than if she had just left things alone.

"Answer me, girl!" he roared.

With a shaking hand, she pointed toward her parents' bedroom.

He walked into the kitchen, looking at the pot of sauce on the floor with pieces of glass in it. "Are you trying to kill me, brat?" He kicked the pot at her as she shook her head as fast as she could. It hit her arm with a painful thud and covered her with tomato sauce.

She wiped her face to keep the acidic sting from burning her eyes as he stomped away, crashing through the bedroom door.

"Wake up, you lazy bitch!" He dragged her mother, kicking and screaming, into the kitchen by her hair.

In the meantime, Chloe tried to pull the hot pot off the stove and accidentally lit the tea towel on fire. She dropped the flaming towel on the counter as he became enraged, letting go of her mother and stalking toward her.

"You're just as stupid and useless as that cow."

Chloe's whole body started to shake as she began to cry. Santino dragged her closer, cuddling her and mumbling that she was all right.

She continued talking as if she was reliving every painful minute.

His face was red, and the veins in his neck were bulging out. "I work hard to put food on this table, and this is how I'm rewarded? This whole country has gone to shit, allowing immigrants and women freedom to do what they want. Why couldn't you have died the day the other brat did?"

Chloe lost her mind, attacking him when he got close. "I hate you! Don't you say anything about my sister. Harper was the only good thing about this family. I wish I had died!" Not only was she mouthing off to him, she was fighting like the Tasmanian devil.

"You want to die, that can be arranged. It would be one less mouth for me to feed." He slapped her across the face.

The impact resonated through her head, jarring her thoughts and striking her dumb for a moment. In the span of that time, he grabbed the little girl by her long hair and dragged her toward the door.

Chloe could hear her mother screaming as he opened the door. She thought he was going to lock her out, but then he picked her up, lifted her over his head, and tossed her over the banister.

Santino's heart shattered into a million pieces. He couldn't believe the man had thrown his defenseless, little daughter down three flights of stairs. He couldn't stop himself from imagining the sound of her tiny body hitting the bottom and breaking into pieces. By all rights, she should be dead. He wanted to vomit more than breathe.

Chloe jackknifed up, banging her forehead on his chin and shrieking with an ear-piercing sound. When she stopped howling, she started to hyperventilate.

Quinn knelt beside her. "Chloe, listen to my voice. You're safe. You're with Santino and me." Lifting his distraught expression to Santino, he asked, "Where are the paper bags?"

"I'm not sure. Check the drawers beside the stove," he answered, while doing everything he could think of to bring her back, running his hands over her trembling body. Her teeth were even chattering. If Santino didn't know better, he would swear she was choking on a chicken bone—she couldn't seem to get enough air in.

Quinn came back, opening a bag. Then, shifting her upright, he instructed, "Take deep breaths into the bag, Chloe. That's it. In and out. Now try to slow it down. Good girl. Keep doing it."

Santino held his breath as he waited for her to regulate hers. He smoothed the damp strands of hair away from her face so she could see them.

After ten minutes, she calmed. Santino finally took his first deep breath as he crushed her to his chest. In a strangled, overly emotional voice, he said, "As God is my witness, I will never let another living soul hurt you. Do you understand me, Stellina? No. One."

Chloe could feel the thumping of his heart and was comforted by his touch.

Quinn gave the couple a minute before he spoke. "Sweetheart, you did very well. I know that was hard to relive, but it's done now. The worst is over, and he can't hurt you anymore. He's gone, Chloe. You're safe."

Anguish pinched her face when he said safe. She would never be safe when there was a world full of people like her father and Jacob. It was only a matter of time before someone else found her.

As if Santino had read her thoughts, he told her, "No one will touch you again. Do you know why? Because they'd have to go through me first, and if by the slightest chance they succeed, then they would have to go through Luca, Alessandro, Sabastian, Emmy, Brooklyn, Ava, Quinn, Owen, and Raimer. And God forbid we release Eli on them."

Even as horrible as she felt, she couldn't help giggling.

Santino cupped her face, tilting it up. "Just like the song 'Shadow Days' by John Mayer, your shadow days are behind you. It's only sunshine and rainbows from here on out." He lowered his head and ever so gently kissed her lips. When he pulled back, her eyes were fluttering open, and he saw hope sparkling in them for the first time. Damn, what he wouldn't do to keep that look in her eyes. "Tell me you're okay."

Chloe laid her head against his chest, breathing in his unique scent, and closed her eyes. Even more softly than normal, she said, "I'm getting there because of you and everyone else. I know I don't say it enough, but thank you."

He held her tighter. "You never have to thank me. I'm honored that you've allowed me to get to know you and help you. This is only the beginning for us." He released her after a few minutes and helped her sit up.

"Let me start by saying, I'm sorry for what you experienced," Quinn told her. "As a child, you had the right to no-risk dependency from your parents. Children have no choice but to rely on adults for their absolute survival. It goes without saying a child should have food, shelter, and protection from any threats. And above all, love. But sadly, not all do, as you know. That is why you have trouble trusting or believing in yourself. Things that should be intrinsically part of your makeup haven't been taught. Those are skills I can help you learn, like your rights and freedoms. We can't change your past, but, together, we can change your future.

"Things that shaped you as a child don't have to define you as an adult. You created a protective mechanism to disassociate and accept blame for things you didn't do in order to survive. Together, we're going to work on strengthening your self-worth, independence, and self-confidence.

"Chloe, you have a lot to offer, and I hold you in high esteem. Not many could survive what you did and not become angry and bitter. That being said, there are times when you will be angry and bitter; that is also part of the healing process. Embrace it and allow yourself to feel all the things you have been denied."

She yawned.

"I think you have dealt with more than enough for today. Tomorrow, we will analyze anything you're comfortable with. Now rest. You relived a trauma today, and that was strenuous on your mind and body. I'll leave you in Santino's capable hands."

The couple got up and walked him to the door.

Before leaving, Quinn asked, "Would it be okay if I hugged you? I have never hugged a patient before, but I have also never been this proud of one. You did amazing."

She tucked a piece of hair behind her ear as she smiled. Then she hugged the man who was helping her regain her life. "Thank you, Quinn. I wish you had been my father."

The man held the young woman, feeling humbled beyond anything he had ever felt before. He wasn't a man who cried, but there were a few people who deserved to have a tear shed for them, and this little girl definitely did. "I do too, sweetheart." One more small squeeze, and he was on his way.

Santino led Chloe into the kitchen. "Can I make you tea or coffee?"

She wrapped her arms around herself. "No, I didn't sleep very well last night, so if it's okay, I'm going to grab a drink of water and lie down for a while. But wake me in enough time to get ready for the boys."

"Are you sure you still want to babysit? I could call and cancel," he asked with concern. If she slept, he hated the thought of waking her.

That frightened her. "Please, I really need to hold the boys. They always make me feel so much better about myself."

He softened. "Then, baby, they'll be here. You sleep, and I'll be in the living room if you need me." He kissed the top of her head, got her a glass of water, and then led her to her bedroom, where he covered her with the soft throw blanket from the end of the bed. He took one last look at her before he closed the door and snapped, his chest expanding in and out as he fought for control.

When his phone rang, he rushed to the living room to answer so it didn't disturb Chloe. The display screen read Alessandro. He placed it to his ear, whimpering out, "Hello?"

"Santino, what's wrong?" Alessandro demanded. When his brother didn't answer, he yelled, "What the fuck, coglione?"

Santino cleared his throat as best he could. "I'm okay."

"Like hell you are. Where is Chloe? Is she okay? What's going on?"

The sound of concern in his brother's voice and his questions were Santino's undoing. His voice cracked as he rubbed his forehead. "Her father tried to kill her, Alessandro. How the fuck do I help her with that on top of everything else? I don't know . . ." He started to sob.

"We're on our way. I'll get Albert to watch the kids for a little while."

"No!" Santino cleared his throat again and wiped his nose. "She needs the boys. Please let me at least give her them."

"We'll be there before you know it. Hold tight, bro. We got you."

Santino lowered his phone, knowing they were the only ones who could help him. Then he reached over, turning up Chloe's playlist, listening with more understanding to the songs she clung to like a lifeline.

He was filled with so much sorrow and blind rage. How was that sweet woman still walking? She had survived it all, only to be tortured by Jacob. He never wished a person dead as much as he did Jacob at this minute. He had used and abused a girl who had already been put through the wringer.

Santino didn't know how long he had been sitting there when the key in the door brought him out of his thoughts and Alessandro came in with the rest of his brothers and sisters-in-law.

Panicking, he asked, "Where are the kids?"

"We ran into Raimer downstairs. He offered to take them to the park for a little while," Sabastian answered. "Alessandro didn't think

Eli should see you yet."

Santino blew out a relieved breath. He hadn't thought of that. "Thanks." He pursed his lips tightly, his chin quivering.

"Where's Chloe?" Luca asked, knowing his little brother was hanging by a thread.

He lifted his chin toward the bedroom. "Sleeping."

Alessandro didn't wait another second before enveloping his brother in a huge hug, slapping his back. "Let it out, bro. It's okay."

His face was marred with so much pain that the others got teary-eyed.

He hugged Alessandro as if his life depended on it. The sadness and despair he experienced for Chloe spilled out in gut-wrenching, almost silent sobs.

It took ten minutes to eradicate the visions of her tiny body flying over the railing. He couldn't get past the thought of her knowing she was going to die. Was she scared? Was she relieved?

After letting it all out, he led the group into the living room and retold parts of her story and asked them the same questions that had been haunting him. No one had the answers that he couldn't answer himself. It didn't make any sense.

He told them that Chloe wanted the kids here tonight, and how he wanted to give that to her. He became fierce when he said, "The minute I put a ring on her finger, I'm putting a baby in her belly. I don't give a shit if she waddles up the aisle nine months pregnant. She'll have everything she ever wanted."

"Good plan," Sabastian said. "How about, instead of us going out tonight, we have a big famiglia dinner here? Let's get her used to all of us together. The kids will make it easier for her."

Santino brightened up. "I would love that. I want to show her that she has friends and famiglia. I'm not kidding. You understand she is going to be a permanent fixture in my life, right?"

Ava laughed. "Your dad already predicted that. Do you remember the day I gave you a reading and your dad's message?"

Santino was still so out of sorts that he couldn't remember anything.

She continued, "Shawn gave his consent when he said, and I quote, 'He wants you to trust in yourself and what's in your heart, because it's right. He wants you to always fight for what's right, even if it hurts others.' Then he mentioned the number eight. You met Chloe in August, the eighth month. This is hurting Valentina, but it's still right, and she'll accept it when the time is right."

Everyone's mouths gaped open.

Suddenly, Santino tackled Ava. "Goddammit, gypsy, you're right. Dad gave me his blessing to be with Chloe."

Alessandro peeled his brother off his wife. "You have your own now; leave my strega alone." He then dragged Ava into his lap.

They all relaxed after hearing Ava's word-for-word recollection. Then Emmy and Brooklyn decided to go shopping and fix a feast the famiglia could enjoy together, while Ava went to the liquor store to grab some wine.

The guys grabbed a beer out of the fridge, except for Alessandro, whom they began ribbing about being their DD.

He retorted, "If you're not careful, I might dump your sorry drunk asses into the deepest ditch."

Sabastian looked at their youngest brother and decided to broach a subject he knew they were going to lock horns over. "Santino, it's time to come home."

"Not a chance in hell," he snidely snapped back. "Stellina needs a place she can flourish, not hide in fear."

It was obviously something his brothers had taken time to think about and talked over, because Luca jumped right in. "We understand your protective response, but hear us out. We're all there, and the kids will be at your Stellina's disposal whenever she wants. She needs friends and famiglia, and we have everything in one place. You'll never have to worry about her being alone or not protected. We've talked, and if Mamma can't accept your relationship and stay, then we're going to buy her out. Between the four of us, we can afford it. Besides, Chloe is going to want to work, and we need a full-time babysitter at the resort. Especially now that there's going to be two more."

Santino was still trying to wrap his head around his brothers and him buying their mamma out before it hit him like a two-by-four. He looked at Luca, then Alessandro.

Alessandro waved his hands. "No, not us. I need my strega all to myself for a little while longer."

Santino whipped his head toward Sabastian, horrified. "Again? Emmy's going to string you up by the nuts after the last delivery."

Sabastian laughed. "Nope, not yet. Although we're working on it. Won't be long now."

Santino tilted his head, deep lines of confusion prominent between his eyes. If there were two babies coming, he figured one was Luca's, but if the other one wasn't Alessandro's or Sabastian's . . . He paled. "Fanculo, Mamma!"

They all started gagging. "No, fucker. Brooklyn's having twins!" Alessandro spat out.

The relief that swept over him was tangible. He jumped up to shake his brother's hand. "Congratulations! Wow, when you do it, you do it in a big way. Twins! That's so cool."

"Twins?" Chloe asked at the entrance of the room, wiping the sleep out of her eyes.

Santino beamed at his beautiful Stellina. "Brooklyn and Luca are having twins."

She smiled. "Yeah, I've known since Brooklyn found—" She

covered her mouth in horror as they all laughed at her.

Chapter 11
"Speak to a Girl" by Faith Hill & Tim McGraw

Santino looked at the clock. It was two thirty-two in the morning. He had been tossing and turning for hours, trying to fall asleep.

His brothers wanted to buy out Mamma. The resort had been her dream, yet they were going to force her out. Even with what she had done, he couldn't get past how wrong it was. He understood that they had young families to think about, but his dad would never rest peacefully knowing his beloved angel was forced from her business.

He shucked off the covers, getting out of bed and heading right to the liquor cabinet for a shot of Sambuca. He hoped the potency of the black licorice-flavored liqueur would help put his mind at rest.

He poured a shot and downed it. The burn of the alcohol traveled down, warming his stomach, while the vapors cleared his sinuses. Mamma would flip if she knew he drank her favorite Italian liqueur without the customary three espresso beans floating on top, representing health, happiness, and prosperity.

Even with the liqueur, he knew he could never force Valentina Savage from Savage's Buck & Doe. It was as much a child to her as her five boys had been. His parents had dreamed, planned, and built that resort. She might not have actually lifted a hammer, but every nail and board were in place because of her. It was the last tangible gift she had received from their dad. He could never take that away from her.

What she had done to Chloe was irrefutably wrong, but deep

down, he understood what drove her to do it, because he felt that same protectiveness over Chloe, especially after today. If Jacob came within ten feet of her, Santino wasn't sure he could be held responsible for his actions.

If Mamma lost the resort and her purpose in life, along with having her famiglia steps away on a daily basis, it would kill her. The resort had survived the loss of Alessandro all those months. The only answer was for Santino to sell his shares and leave with Chloe.

He reached for the bottle and poured another shot.

"It won't help you find the answers you seek," Raimer said, scaring the shit out of him and making him spill some of the clear liquid over the rim of the shot glass and onto the carpet.

His heart still pounding from fright, he asked, "What the hell are you doing sitting in the dark?"

Raimer lifted a bottle of Grand Marnier liqueur. "Realizing the answers aren't in the bottom of this bottle either." He placed it down.

Santino looked at Raimer, seeing he wasn't his funny, put-together self. In fact, the buttons on his shirt were in the wrong holes, and his normally perfectly styled hair was mussed.

"If alcohol isn't helping, maybe you need to talk," he said as he took the chair across from his friend. "What's got your panties in a twist? I hope Stellina and I aren't cramping your style by being here."

Raimer waved his hand before lifting his hips slightly, pulling the waistband of his jeans out and looking in. "If my panties are in a twist, it's because they're still under my lover's bed." Satisfied he was correct, he let go of the material and shifted his hips back down.

Santino laughed quietly. "You really are fucked up."

Chloe woke up. It was very dark, but she heard two low voices, so she got out of bed and crept down the hall in her bare feet just in time to hear Raimer's retort.

"Ah, says the sexy, Italian stallion in his brand-name boxers, who's also looking for answers in the bottom of a bottle."

Santino arched a brow that Raimer barely caught with the light of the moon. "I guess you have a point. So, why are you sitting here, drowning your sorrows?"

Raimer thought for a moment, then gazed over to see if his friend sincerely wanted to hear his problems. "I met the man of my dreams."

That caught Santino by surprise. "Congratulations. But if you found him, why are you sitting here and not chaining him to his bed so he can't get away?"

He chortled. "Because I can't get him out of the closet long enough to chain him to the bed. I wonder if it's because of me, or if he's stressing because it's all new to him."

Santino shifted to the edge of his seat and leaned forward with his forearms resting on his knees. "Do you know if he's new to the lifestyle? Or has he always known he was gay? Because I'm telling you right now, it's not you. My famiglia and I think the world of you. Any man who gets your love and attention would be the luckiest guy out there."

Raimer lifted his sad eyes. "Thanks." Then he responded like the character Santino knew and loved. "Are you sure you want Chloe? Because I still think we would make an awesome couple, and instead of drowning our sorrows, you could untwist my panties when I find them."

Looking like a love-sick puppy, Santino answered truthfully, "That ship sailed the day I laid eyes on Chloe. She is the woman my dad promised me I would find. She's everything I ever wanted and more. Stellina is sweet, gorgeous, and generous to a fault. But she has to discover who she is before I can have her completely. I fall more and more in love with her each day. She is my future, and I want to give her all the things she's always dreamed about.

"I have dreams too. I go out of my mind thinking of her ripe with one of my children. I'd give her a soccer team of kids if that's what she wants. Have you seen her with my nephews? She's going to be a great mom."

His words heated her skin and caused tingling in her lower belly as she listened. She couldn't imagine loving a more incredible man.

Santino had truly become her lifeline since the attack. She was afraid to admit to herself that she had been falling for him, convinced it was just hero worship. But maybe she was wrong.

Raimer's voice brought her back as she continued to eavesdrop.

"Wow. I'm jealous. I want all of that too. Minus seeing my man's stomach ripe, because that would mean I was feeding him too many fatty dinners." Raimer laughed at his own joke before he got a longing look. "One day, though, I'd love to adopt children with him." Shaking his head, he was still confused about what Santino had said. "So, if you're that sure about Chloe, why are you up in the middle of the night drinking?"

Santino told Raimer all about his brothers' plan and the conclusion he had come up with to not only move out completely but to find another job. He admitted for the first time he couldn't change the relationship between him and Mamma, but he would be damned if he took the rest of her famiglia away. He would much rather leave the resort than take it from Valentina. He would never give up Chloe or the relationship they both had with his brothers' famiglia, but it would have to be cultivated away from the resort.

Talking it out with Raimer made him understand the choice wasn't a choice at all; it was just how it had to be. With that realization, a thought occurred to Santino.

"Your boyfriend is a lot like Chloe. They're trying to find their rightful place in the world. Just because you're ready, doesn't mean he shouldn't have the right to take his time. If you push too hard, you're going to shut him down. Don't force him out of the closet. Be patient and understanding. Gently open the door and lead him out."

Raimer contemplated quietly for a minute, then bounced up. "You're right. I wasted a quarter of a bottle when I should have just gone to your room and stared at your Emporio Armani skivvies while you worked out all my problems. Chloe's a lucky woman." He became serious. "I know you both came here under the worst circumstances, but it has been my absolute pleasure to share my space and spend this time with the two of you."

Santino stood, extending his hand. "Thank you, Raimer. You've been like a brother to me, and I hope more than anything that your man realizes he'll never get anyone better than you."

Raimer pushed away his hand and gave him a bro-hug. "The day I stepped foot on Savage's Buck & Doe, I found a family. Thanks, man."

The conversation was over, and Chloe didn't want to get caught, so she snuck back to her room. Moving as quietly as possible, she closed the door and crawled back into bed. She couldn't sleep either, feeling bad for Santino.

She sat up, put her headphones in, and turned on random play. The first song to come on was "Speak to a Girl" by Faith Hill & Tim McGraw. The song made her think of Valentina.

She felt horrible for the woman who was going to lose another cherished son because she couldn't get past Chloe's lineage. If she hadn't grown up with different parents, it might have bothered her more that Valentina hated her, but she was accustomed to the feeling.

Valentina had raised her sons well, and it showed. Santino's love was so strong and respectful for his mamma that he would walk away from everything just so his mamma didn't have to. Chloe couldn't let that happen, but she knew if she ran, he would only follow, and with more anger directed at his mom than before. No, she had to try to come to some sort of resolution with Valentina. That scared the crap of her, but Santino had fought so hard for her, so it was time she did the same.

A plan began to form in her head. She would need help, and she knew just who to ask.

***

Alessandro couldn't stop thinking about the conclusion they had all come to, and decided to give it one last chance with Mamma. He was chopping wood when he saw her rushing out of the resort at seven o'clock on Tuesday morning.

She disappeared every Sunday afternoon and Monday and Tuesday. If she was going to Quinn's, why didn't she just stay over at his place? She hadn't been home when they arrived late last night, and now she was heading out just after dawn. Things weren't adding up.

His brothers had all agreed to meet in the conference room at ten a.m. to discuss the buy-out before they approached her. This was his last chance.

"Mamma?" he called out to her.

She turned just as he saw Luca and Sabastian also heading her way.

"Where are you going?" Sabastian asked as they all converged on her.

Looking guilty as hell, she answered with contempt, "Out."

"No shit, but where?" Alessandro snarked with the same attitude.

Valentina stepped closer, cuffing the side of his head. "Language, shamo. I'm an adult. I don't have to tell you where I'm going." She folded her arms over her chest.

This was the wrong way to start this conversation off, so Luca tried to smooth the waters. "You're right, Mamma; you don't. We aren't asking because we're being nosy. We're asking because we love you. You look tired all time, and you're constantly running away from the resort. It's time we talk about it."

Valentina had the decency to look chagrined. "I know, bambino, and I love all of you, but I'm not ready to talk. There is something I have to finish first."

"Time is running out, Mamma. We can't keep living like this. You have to let the hatred go. It's not only eating away at you; it's gnawing at all of us. Santino has fallen in love with Chloe, and she is going to be a part of our lives. You have to accept it," Alessandro said with sadness plaguing his heart.

As if she were protecting secrets, Valentina clutched her purse closer to her chest. "I'm not ready. I have to do it my own way and in my own time. I have to go."

Frustrated beyond belief, Sabastian begged, "If you wait too long, you might find everything has changed and can't go back. Please, Mamma, we don't want our children growing up without all of their famiglia here." Luca and Brooklyn hadn't shared her pregnancy with Mamma yet.

Giving one last look to each of them, she turned and walked away. Valentina understood, but didn't need Sabastian to guilt her. She was working as fast as she could and was nearly done. She wouldn't let them force her until it was ready.

The exasperation they all felt at watching her walk away made Alessandro long for something. "I'd kill for a drink or a line to take the edge off," he said, licking his lips.

Luca and Sabastian stared at him in horror.

Sabastian was the oldest by default and made the decision. "That's it. We finish this today. We can't let her hatred destroy everyone in the process. Alessandro, shower and meet us in the conference room."

***

Chloe snuck into Raimer's room before dawn, waking him and asking if he could help her today but not tell Santino. At first, his heart had sunk, thinking she was running, until she explained what she needed. Then Raimer was on board, knowing Valentina had been going somewhere on the days the resort was closed and left early in the morning, and nobody had a clue where she went. He knew she wasn't with Quinn, because he worked Monday to Friday, so they would have to follow her.

Chloe texted both Quinn and Owen and left a message saying she was taking a day off from therapy and told them Raimer was taking her to the mountains. Then she left Santino a note.

Santino,

I remember you said you were going to meet your brothers today. Raimer was up early, so I asked him if he didn't mind taking me up to the mountains to think.

I promise I'm fine. I just need to be outside today to clear my head. I hope you don't mind. Call me when you get this note so I can assure you I'm not running away, because I know that's what you're thinking. I swear I won't go anywhere without talking to you.

Thank you for yesterday.

Stellina

They snuck out of the condo as quietly as they could, then sat up the road from the resort at an intersection, waiting for Valentina's car to pass just after sunrise.

Raimer watched as Chloe fidgeted. "Are you sure you're ready to confront Valentina?"

"No, but I don't have a choice." She stopped wringing her hands. Peering over, she decided to confess, "I heard you and Santino talking last night. I didn't mean to eavesdrop, but I'm also not sorry I heard what I did. He's going to walk away from the resort and his mom because of me. I need to at least try to beg Valentina to forgive me for his sake."

Raimer reached for her hand. "He loves you, chiquita, and if things don't work out with Valentina, I want you to know he's okay with it. I've been friends with these guys for years, before any of them had wives, so I can tell you, when one of those Savage hotties falls in love, it's forever."

She looked even more worried.

"Relax, he isn't going to rush you, but it is a gift you should treasure. I can only hope the guy I'm seeing will feel the same way about me."

She squeezed his hand. "I believe he already does, because you're a very special man. Do you think I'm good enough for Santino? Be honest."

Raimer looked left, out the driver's side window, looking for cars, before turning back. "Chiquita, you're more than good enough for him. He thinks you were made especially for him. The guy was ready to fight your ex-fiancé for a chance to protect you and get to know you. I've never seen him like this before. Just promise me one thing."

She tilted her head sideways and nodded.

"Promise me you'll never hurt him. I've watched him fight tooth and nail for every one of his family members. He's everyone's champion. Nobody deserves to be loved or happy more than Santino."

Wow, that was quite the endorsement, though she had already known that in her heart.

"That's why I have to take this chance with Valentina. I want to give him everything he wants, the same as he gives to me.

"Raimer, I think—no, I know I'm falling in love with Santino. I don't know when it happened, but day by day, I have fallen for an honorable man who has stood by my side, nurturing and caring for me when the rest of the world wanted to fry me."

Raimer saw a car coming up the road and started his car, edging up to the stop sign until after she passed. Then he followed at a safe distance.

Agitated, he said, "Chiquita, you're not wrong about Santino caring, but you are wrong about everyone wanting to fry you. I grew up in a country that wasn't very accepting of different people, so I'm accustomed to the bias of others. The conclusion I came up with is people who choose to judge without knowing aren't people you want in your life.

"I love Valentina, but I admit I have lost a lot of respect for her. You and I can't help who we are and shouldn't be condemned for it. Hold your head up high when you talk to her. Represent not only you, but everyone who is judged unfairly. From what I have seen, you would jump in and fight if you thought a child was being bullied. Do the same thing for the child who lives inside both of us."

That hit the mark and gave her the courage to face one of the people who frightened her. She would hold her head high with no tears and fight for Santino, Raimer, but mostly for herself, because she had the right not to be blamed for the actions of her father.

They were about half a mile from their destination when Chloe yelled out, "Pull over!"

Raimer yanked the car off the road, scared half to death, amazed that soft voice could get so loud. "What the hell, chiquita? Are you trying to give me a heart attack?"

She turned her whole body toward him, pointing toward the house. "Valentina! She's in my house. Why would she be in there? There's nothing else she can ruin since Jacob destroyed everything. The insurance adjuster said I didn't have contents insurance, so they're only fixing the structural issues. They haven't started yet because I have to pay to have a bin and clean it out, and I have to get a job before I can afford it."

Raimer didn't answer as he saw a familiar car coming up the road from the rearview mirror. He grabbed Chloe's head and pushed her down, placing himself on top of her.

She started freaking out, afraid he had lost his mind.

"Relax, Owen is pulling up. What the hell is he doing here?" When the car passed, Raimer lifted his head and watched him pull in behind Valentina's car. "Something very weird is going on. Come on. Let's get out and see what the hell they're up to."

Chloe and Raimer exited the car and walked up the road toward the driveway.

Owen was lifting a box out of the trunk and nearly dropped it when Raimer said, "Fancy meeting you here, guapola."

Owen looked like he got caught with his pants down. "Raimer? Um . . . Chloe?"

She couldn't help the hurt that swept across her face. Another person she had trusted had fooled her.

Overly emotional, Chloe squeaked out, "Why would you pretend to be my friend? What did I ever do to you?" She choked out, "Raimer, please take me back to your condo. I'm not sure who I can trust anymore."

Owen rushed to put the box back in the trunk, then extended his hands toward her. "Chloe, I swear, it isn't what you think. I didn't betray you, I promise. What are you two doing here, anyway?"

Raimer knocked his hands away, then placed his on his hips. He was furious. Chloe wasn't the only one feeling betrayed. "Guapola, you have the nerve to ask what we're doing here? You are obviously not the man I thought you were. I made a mistake trying to bring her here to find Valentina."

Dismissing Owen, he shifted to look at Chloe. "You tried to do the right thing by putting yourself out there to fix things for Santino, but it doesn't look like it was worth—"

"Stop and look at me." Owen stepped closer to the angry man and grabbed his shoulders. "Please, Raimer, let me explain."

He twisted to look at Chloe. "And while I chat with him, you can take this box in to Valentina and have your talk. I swear on my mom's soul that you won't regret it. You know in your heart I'm your friend, and as your friend, I'm begging you to go talk to her."

Chloe looked unsure as she bit her lip, looking at the house. It looked different. She tilted her head, trying to figure it out. Then she moved two steps to the left so she could see past Owen's open trunk.

The graffiti was gone on the door. In fact, there was a brand-new door and flower planters under the windows. The house actually looked amazing on the outside.

She whipped her head toward Owen.

"Go see. I think you'll be happy you did." He let go of Raimer and handed her the box, directing her toward the front door.

Owen turned back to Raimer and pleaded, "I'm sorry I didn't tell you that I was helping Valentina, but she begged me not to tell a soul. She made a mistake, but she's trying to make up for it. She was hoping that, if she was able to give Chloe her house back, she would forgive her. I've been helping when I have time. Can you forgive me for not telling you?"

Raimer smiled before he reached out, dragging the man he was falling in love with into his arms and answering with a sensual kiss.

A phone ringing broke the couple apart. They both looked down. Chloe must have dropped her phone. When Raimer picked it up, he saw Santino's name on the display.

"Hello?"

Santino became alarmed. "Raimer, why are you answering Chloe's phone? Is she okay?"

"Relax, she's fine. I need you to do me a favor. We're at Chloe's house—"

Raimer held the phone back as Santino screamed, "What the fuck is she doing there?"

He put it back to his ear when Santino stopped yelling. "Calm down and just come here. I promise you'll want to see this."

Santino didn't answer before he hung up, pissed to the hilt. He then told his brothers that he had to leave and get to Chloe's house. When Luca said he wasn't going alone, they all followed him out and piled into his car. He took off like a bat out of hell.

Meanwhile, Chloe walked into the house, floored by what she was seeing. The house looked amazing from where she stood. The walls in the living room were fixed, painted, and brand-new furnishings filled the room.

"Owen, I'm in the kitchen. Thanks for grabbing the parcel yesterday from the post office. The appliances were due to arrive, and I didn't want to miss the delivery. Owen?" Valentina stepped from the kitchen and proceeded down the hall, not yet able to see that it was Chloe standing there, since the box was blocking her face. For the life of her, Valentina couldn't understand why he was standing at the entrance. "Owen, why are—"

Chloe lowered the box.

Valentina was so shocked that her hand jumped to her throat. "Chloe? I-I thought you were Owen."

Chloe's hands were trembling as she gestured to the living room, softly asking, "Why?"

Valentina walked toward her, and Chloe instinctively stepped back.

"I won't hurt you. I promise," the older woman tried to reassure her. "You have no reason to believe me. I just don't want you to drop the box. It's breakable, and I've been waiting for it for three weeks. It came from England."

Chloe thrust the box toward her, happy to do it if it meant she would back up.

"Thank you." Valentina stepped back a couple of paces, looking at the frightened girl. She couldn't help feeling even more remorse. "I know I don't deserve it, but I would really like it if I could talk to you.

Please come into the kitchen. I need to apologize." Not waiting for Chloe to answer, she turned and walked away.

Chloe stood there and really looked around. The house looked beautiful, even nicer than when her grandparents had owned it.

She moved into the living room. The hardwood floors had all been refinished to a dark, rich walnut brown, and the room was decorated country chic like that show Fixer Upper. The couch was oversized with pretty decorative pillows organized like in the magazines, and there were also two beautiful, wingback chairs and a wooden coffee table.

After leaving the living room, she moved trance-like down the hall, looking at the tasteful artwork. Her breath hitched when she walked into a beautiful kitchen. It was airy and bright, yet still felt country and warm.

Valentina was drying a teapot when she walked in. She stopped mid-step when she saw it was the teapot her nana had used her whole life.

"How did you get my nana's teapot? Jacob smashed it into a million pieces."

Valentina smiled. "Your nana had an original Royal Albert, 1962, Old Country Rose tea set. It has been out of circulation since 1973. I found a woman in England who was selling her mother's complete set and bought it to replace the one that was smashed. I know it isn't your nana's, but it's identical. I hope it makes you feel like you still have a little bit of her here."

Chloe's legs were shaking so badly that she had to sit down. As she made her way to the table, she couldn't believe it when she saw two teacups with saucers set up with the matching creamer and sugar.

When the whistle of the kettle startled her, she screamed.

Valentina rushed to take the kettle off the burner. "Sorry, carina. I hope you don't mind, but I thought I'd make some tea to share while we talk. Please, sit down." She gestured toward the table.

Chloe, still feeling overwhelmed, sat and looked around while Valentina made the tea. When she placed the lid on it, she brought the pot to the table and set it down, saying, "Honestly, I've never had tea before."

At that moment, Chloe decided it was her right to accept the woman who was trying to make things okay. If the two of them could mend fences, the rest of the family could continue as they always had.

With the courage Quinn had taught her, she said, "Well, Nana always said tea tastes better in Royal Albert, so this will be as good as it gets. Can I pour?"

"I would like that." Valentina relaxed and smiled. It was apparent Chloe was going to give her a chance to say her piece. "Carina, I owe you an apology and so much more. I don't even know how to start. I thought I would have another week to figure it all out."

After pouring them each a cup of the steeped tea, Chloe lifted the creamer. "Would you like milk or sugar?"

Chagrined, Valentina lifted her hands and shoulders. "I'll have it the same way you do, because I'm not sure how to drink it."

A small giggle escaped Chloe's throat. "Okay. I just have milk. I don't like it sweet. That's what cookies are for." She added milk, then stirred them both. Then, without looking up, she said, "I can't believe you fixed up my house. It looks beautiful. But you didn't need to do that. You aren't the one who destroyed it."

"Yes, I did. I might not have wrecked your home personally, but what I did was just as bad. I was so blinded by unresolved anger that I did some terrible things to you. I can never take back what I did and said, but I can give you back some of your past. I did a lot of the work myself, and what I couldn't do, I hired other people to help."

Chloe's eyes expanded. "I can't pay you back until I sell the house. But I promise, the minute I get the money from the sale, you will get back every dime you put into it."

Valentina placed her hand on the distraught young woman's hand. "Please, carina, stop. I don't want any money. I did this for you because I'm so sorry. Honestly, I'm not trying to buy your forgiveness. It just made me feel better about myself to do something nice after the way I treated you."

Chloe put her other hand on top of Valentina's. "I forgive you, and I'm so sorry for what my father did. Can you forgive me?"

Valentina choked on a sob as she moved her chair out and bent forward to bring the younger woman into her arms. "Thank you, carina, but you never have to apologize for the actions of another person. I know that now. Do you think we could start over and be tea-toting friends?"

Pulling back, Chloe grinned from ear to ear. "I would like that."

She reached for her cup, then waited for Valentina to do the same. They clicked cups then each took a sip.

Just as they placed their cups down, they heard Santino bust in, screaming, "Chloe! Mamma, I swear, if you hurt her in any way, I will never forgive—"

He came barreling into the kitchen and stopped. His three brothers were so close behind him that they all banged into one another in succession.

"What the hell is going on here?" he screeched.

Chloe raised her teacup. "Your mom made tea. We have enough cups for all of you. Would you like some?"

Valentina burst out laughing at the stunned faces of her four sons.

Chapter 12
"My Life, My Love" by ABBA

Santino's heart was thumping so loudly that he wasn't sure he had heard Stellina correctly. With his face screwed up in confusion, he asked, "You want us to have tea?"

Both women laughed at his expression.

"Yes, shamo. Chloe is introducing me to the traditions she shared with her nana. Now sit down if you're going stay, and I'll get more cups." Valentina got up to bustle around the kitchen.

The men all moved around the table, Santino choosing the chair beside Chloe.

She demurely tucked her chin in when he shifted his chair as close as he could and placed his hand on her thigh. "What does shamo mean?" she whispered.

Alessandro, who was on the other side of her, laughed. "Ma called Santino stupid."

She lifted her head with new resolve and bravely said, "Valentina, if our friendship is starting fresh, I have to ask you not to call my boyfriend stupid. He is the kindest, most intelligent man I have ever met. Can you do that for me?"

Valentina glanced at where Santino sat there, mouth wide open, with a look of goofy astonishment still on his face. "Carina, look at him and tell me I'm wrong."

Chloe looked, then pushed his chin up. "Yes, you're wrong. Quinn helped me to recognize the true traits in people. I'm still learning, and I've made a lot of mistakes, but falling in love with your son wasn't one of them."

Santino didn't let anyone else speak before he grabbed her hand and dragged her into the living room. There, he swung her around, then cupped both sides of her beautiful face. He brought his face so close to hers that they shared the same air. "Did you mean that?" He let his fingers roam over the soft skin of her face. "You're falling in love with me?"

"Yes. I love you as a friend, but it's more than that."

Faster than the blink of an eye, he descended on her lips. Chloe's lips tingled as he deepened the kiss.

Thrilled that she had accepted his invitation, he licked the seam of the fleshy skin he had watched her bite a hundred times over the past months.

She opened and relished the feel of his tongue gently swooping in, tasting every inch of her. Santino moaned as his dick stiffened to the point of pain. Holding her, tasting her was better than he ever thought it could be. As lost as he was in this dream come true, though, a nagging at the back of his mind wouldn't let him continue until he got some answers. He hated to break the precious connection, yet he regrettably pulled back to get some answers.

"How did this happen?"

She reluctantly opened her eyes. "Honestly, I'm not sure. We had only just started to talk when you came in. Did you see what she did?" Chloe stepped back, expanding her hands to encompass the room they were in.

Santino pulled her hips back. "I may have postponed our kiss, but I'm not ready to let you go. I want you to know it's your right to get used to me touching you, because I don't intend to ever stop."

He wrapped himself around her back, resting his chin on her shoulder and looking at his surroundings for the first time. "Holy shit, she renovated the whole house. I was so focused on getting to you that I didn't see anything. Fanculo, it looks magnificent. How did she accomplish it all in such a short amount of time?"

Chloe tilted her head, lifting her chin to peck his lips, then said, "I think we need to ask her." She turned in his arms and grabbed his hand as his groaned out in disappointment at having to release her. "Come on." She tugged him back toward the kitchen.

Before they made it to the table, Santino waved his hand around and asked, "Ma, you did all this? How did you even know about the damage?"

She nodded sheepishly. "The day after I freaked out at the resort, Owen called and asked me to go somewhere with him. He put everything on the line. He risked destroying our friendship and dealing with all of your wrath, as well as putting a wedge between him and his father, so he could show me what would happen if I didn't let go of the unhealthy grudge I was harboring and put the blame where it belonged. I was turning into my own worst nightmare. I was attacking innocent people, just like Chloe's father did. My selfishness was destroying everyone I loved, and a girl who needed my love."

Valentina got up and tried to collect Chloe's hands but gave up when Santino wouldn't budge on both, accepting the one he did release. "I also concluded that it must have been horrible for you growing up with that kind of malice. Nobody should have to grow up like that.

"As I told you before, I can never tell you how sorry I am, but I had to make up for some of my sins. Each thing I fixed in this house allowed me some small amount of absolution."

She took a deep breath. "What happened to my husband and son wasn't your fault. It took seeing this house for me to realize that."

Chloe's eyes were filled to the brim, but she had promised herself she wouldn't cry. Assuredly, she responded, "I gave you my forgiveness because those you hold so dear to your heart have taught me there is a lot of good people I can love and depend on. It takes a lot of courage to admit you're wrong. Thank you. Now, will you show me the rest of the house?"

Valentina smiled with relief. "I would love to show it to you. If there is anything you don't like, you can change it. I tried to decorate it from little things I found in each room." Valentina guided them from room to room, steering clear from Chloe's room, because she wanted to leave that until the end.

When Chloe stumbled back into Santino as his mom opened the door to the garage, he whispered in her ear, "Trust me; it will be okay. I'll always catch you, like I did the first time."

The fear in her eyes disappeared. She believed Santino and had faith that Valentina had truly changed.

The garage looked as different as the rest of the house, but what caught everyone's eye was the car nestled in one of the parking spots. It was a brand-new Fiat 500, bi-colored with black on the bottom and red on top, and had funky, black hash marks on the red to look like the two colors had been sewn together. It instantly reminded Chloe of Santino's stitching.

"No, no, no. I can't accept a car."

Valentina proudly dragged them down for a closer look. "Non-negotiable, carina. Your car was ruined beyond repair." She opened the door and encouraged Chloe into the driver's seat. "I wrote down the make and model of your car, but when I went to purchase it, I decided I preferred you in a piece of my Italian heritage. It's adorable and suits you to a tee." Valentina walked to the wall and plucked the keys from a hook beside the button for the garage door she had installed. She had to pry Chloe's hand open to place them in it.

Chloe shook her head. "I can't accept it. You already spent a fortune on the house."

Valentina pushed Santino out of the way, telling him to get in the passenger side so Chloe could take them for a spin. Then she bent down, looking right into the young woman's eyes. "As I said before, I'm not trying to buy you. But you deserve to have a few luxuries after all you have been through. I've been working for years with nothing to spend my money on, except my grandchildren. Sabastian and Luca keep threatening to buy bigger houses off the resort if I don't stop spoiling their children so badly. If you accept this gift, I get to keep my famiglia together in one place. Not only that, but Santino has had a very rough five years dealing with one crisis after another. He deserves some happiness. Look at him. He's radiating with love and bliss. For the first time in a long time, I put that smile there. Please, Chloe, let me do this. If not for you, then for me."

It went against the grain of everything she believed in to accept, but Valentina was right. Maybe this would go a long way in healing the family.

"Okay, I'll accept the car, but I have to explain to you that I'm saying yes because, when Santino found me here, he also found my twin's stuffed animal that I treasured. It had been completely destroyed. The first night at his cabin, he sewed it back together, returning the only thing I had left of her." This time, the tears couldn't be held at bay. One by one, they trailed down her face.

Although Valentina wanted her to test drive the car, she said, "I have one more thing to show you. Please come with me." She walked back up the steps to the house.

Santino got out of the car as his brothers followed their mamma. When he got to Chloe's side, he wiped her face, then helped her out. They didn't speak, each anticipating what was coming next.

The group stood by the closed bedroom door. When they arrived, Valentina opened it, and Chloe walked through with Santino hot on her heels.

Her legs weakened, and Santino caught her like he had promised. Chloe leaned back against him and started to mewl uncontrollably like a tiny kitten, overcome with astonishment. She couldn't believe she was seeing something she thought had been gone forever.

Over her bed was a huge, framed picture of her and Harper. On the dresser and nightstands were dozens of other pictures of the two of them. There was even one of her grandparents, her mom, and the two of them. It was too much after yesterday, and she wailed out a desperate cry that had even the tough men crying like babies.

Valentina stepped into the room, choking out through her own tears, "Your nana had a box in the garage that Jacob missed. I wanted you to have Harper back, and the famiglia you loved."

Chloe let go of Santino's comforting hold long enough to throw herself into Valentina's arms. "I would go through it all again for these invaluable gifts. What Jacob took from me, you gave me back tenfold. I will treasure these most of all." She looked back at the large photo of her sister and her. "I've never seen that picture before. It's beautiful." Then she picked up a frame of the picture Jacob had put the knife through. "I never thought I would see this one again."

"I was going to place these pictures all around the house so every room would feel like home. I found more and made this for you." Valentina held out a book. "Alessandro, Sabastian, Luca, let's give her a moment to share some of her past with Santino. We'll make a fresh pot of tea and meet you in the kitchen when you're ready." She then quietly led her three older boys out and closed the door.

Chloe cradled the book close to heart as she sat down. With pride that blissfully tore out of her, she patted the spot beside her. "Come and meet my twin." She opened the book and laughed. "We weren't the cutest babies ever born."

Santino sat, looking over her shoulder. He was still overwhelmed with all the things his mamma had done to make amends. The woman who had helped Chloe was the woman he had held in such high regard his whole life.

While he had been healing her body and heart, Mamma had been working to heal her soul. How did he ever think she had turned into a monster?

He also had much to atone for.

"That's not true. You both were adorable. I don't know how your mom could tell you apart."

She pointed to the slightly bigger one. "That's Harper. She was half a pound bigger. She was also the brave one, and the smarter and more friendly of the two of us. She was my first hero." She looked at him. "You are my second."

He tilted her head. "And you're mine."

She turned page after page, explaining each picture. Year by year, he started to recognize her shy look. Halfway through, he started pointing her out, and she smiled with pride.

"I'd know my Stellina anywhere. You have a sparkle in your eyes that has called out to me from day one. You two are the most adorable girls I have ever seen."

After they finished, she closed the book. "Let's go have some tea, so I can thank your mom again. Tonight, I want to spend hours looking through it." Again, she cuddled the book close to her chest.

"As long as I get to look at it with you," Santino said, opening the door.

The couple were surprised when they walked into the kitchen and found Owen, Raimer, and Quinn had joined the Savages.

Quinn stepped forward. "How are you, Chloe? I understand you've had an eventful day."

She handed the album to Santino, then rushed into Quinn's arms, hugging him like she had wanted to so many times. Then she pulled back abruptly, dropping her eyes. "Sorry. I shouldn't have entered your personal space without your permission."

He tilted her chin up. "You have my permission to enter my personal space anytime you want. I'm happy for you, sweetheart. Now I know where Valentina has been spending all her time. She said she needed to work on something to make herself better. I think she did an amazing job, and I'm thinking of hiring her to do my place. What do you think?"

Chloe grinned. "I think we're both lucky to have her in our lives. Can I show you around? I really want you to see a picture of Harper."

"It would be my absolute pleasure. Lead the way."

She tucked her arm around his waist and led him to her bedroom.

Santino walked to his mamma, lifted her out of her seat, and swung her around. "Grazie, Mamma. Ti amo. I'm sorry I lost faith in you."

When he put her down, she looked at him, and then at each man around the room. "I'm embarrassed by my actions. I made a lot of horrible decisions and let you all down. But I'm thankful I'm surrounded by men strong enough to stand up to me for what was right and kick my butt."

"Screw kicking your ass. I want just one shot to the head." Alessandro laughed, raising a hand.

"You touch her and you answer to me," Santino puffed out.

"And me." Owen stepped up on Valentina's other side.

Facing Owen, Santino cut off Alessandro's retort. "My brothers have walked me down many rough roads, but you took brotherhood to a whole new level. Mamma told us what you did, and I'm stumped on how to thank you. If you ever need anything, you come to me, because I'll gladly repay the favor. Thank you, Owen." He engulfed the man in his arms.

Quinn and Chloe walked back into the room, quietly watching the moment play out.

When Santino released him, Owen said, "Actually, I could use some advice." He looked from Santino to Valentina, then back. "I've met the most incredible person, and I've been afraid to tell my dad because I'm afraid he'll be disappointed. Not because this person isn't amazing but because of the dreams he had for me."

It was like a shot to the heart for Raimer, who lowered his head in shame.

Chloe caught Raimer's look, and all the pieces fell into place at the exact same time it did for Santino.

Chloe cleared her throat. "Owen, you must have been away from home too long. Somewhere along the road, you must have changed in your mind as to who your dad is. The man you created out of fear is not the man standing here. He isn't prejudiced in any way and would accept anyone you loved if that person makes you happy.

"If I learned anything from this man, it's that we can't always expect bad reactions; we have to have faith in the good ones."

Santino expanded on her thoughts as he walked to Chloe, looking into those stunning eyes. "Love is a rare and beautiful thing. Once you find the person you're meant to be with, everyone else becomes secondary. Don't let fear of disappointing or hurting anyone get in the way. Be proud of who you are and the love you share." He dropped a kiss onto Chloe's head.

Quinn was stunned speechless for one of the first times ever.

Shifting from side to side like a ten-year-old and tucking his hands into his pockets, Owen started, "Dad—"

"Wait, son, before you start. If I ever gave you the impression that I had expectations of you, other than finding someone to share your life with, I'm sorry. I've suspected since you were young that you were gay. I've been waiting for you to come to me, wanting you to choose the time you revealed that part of yourself, but I was wrong. After all, it's not like heterosexual kids have to declare to their parents their sexual orientation. I should have told you years ago and taken the pressure off you. I'm sorry."

There was a whoosh of breath from the four guys sitting at the table.

Quinn spied Raimer's surprised eyes. "The two of you might have been hiding behind everything going on in the Savage family, but I saw the instant attraction. I've watched it grow and was happy two people I love deeply found each other. The one thing I'm not happy about is—"

"Quinn?" Valentina advanced, afraid things were about to go sour. "Maybe you should take them into the other room and talk privately."

"No, sweetheart, I need witnesses."

He turned toward Raimer. "If you think you can date my son and flirt like you're single, well, that isn't going to sit well with me. You're either in or you're out. My son deserves your undivided attention."

Alessandro burst out in laughter. "I have waited for this day for five long years." He smacked Raimer's head. "Shamo, I agree with Quinn." He got up and saddled himself behind Owen, running his hands over his muscular shoulders, taunting the Cuban. "You've got yourself some hot tamale grande here, Raimer. If he feels neglected, I might have to introduce him to a few of my friends, or get Ava to agree to a threesome, because this man is sizzling hot." He licked his fingertip and placed it on Owen's bicep, making a sizzling sound.

Raimer stood, pushing his chair out of the way before stomping over. "Get your greasy, dago hands off my man. Nobody touches him but me." He pushed Alessandro a little harder than necessary, then placed his arm possessively around his man's hips, pulling him tightly against his side.

"Oh, I don't know," Luca said as he got up and ran his hand along Owen's face as he walked by. "His babé face is tempting me too. Not to mention his tight ass."

Raimer swatted Luca's hand before it landed on Owen's ass. "Stop it! I get it, okay? I shouldn't have teased you guys for all these years."

Sabastian got up, walked straight over to cup Owen's face, and kissed him smack-dab on the lips.

Raimer growled as Sabastian said, "Oh, but now I see how much fun it was."

They all burst out laughing, each wishing they had had the forethought to video everything to show the girls. No one who hadn't seen it for themselves would ever believe the stuffy, stoic Sabastian had kissed Owen on the lips.

Quinn held his hand up when he regained his breath from laughing. "Oh, Owen, somehow, I think they're going to be mauling you for years to come. It sucks when you have to reap what you sow, eh, Raimer?"

With a flick of his hand that Raimer was famous for, he snapped back, "Payback is a bitch, and this bitch is ready to protect his man, so bring it on, boys. But I swear, Valentina, I won't be responsible for what I do to your sons. I've waited a long time to find the man of my dreams."

Valentina redirected the taunting. "Owen, could you please formally introduce your boyfriend to your dad and me?"

He smiled. "Mom squared, Dad, I'd like to officially introduce you to the man who captured my heart, my boyfriend, Raimer."

Chloe couldn't wait another second, excusing herself to the washroom.

Valentina threw her arms around both men and squeezed tightly before pulling back. "I'm taking credit for this match, like with Alessandro and Ava, because I brought Owen home so Raimer could find him."

"Come on, Ma, Raimer's been vying to be a part of this famiglia from day one. This has to be divine intervention," Alessandro said.

Valentina swung around and cuffed him in the head. "It. Was. Me. Va bene. Now, how about we all go out to dinner to celebrate?"

"Ma, why don't the four of you go out together, and we'll join next time?" Santino suggested.

Owen threw him a thankful look. He still had a couple of apologies to hand out.

A few minutes later, the group heard a musical instrumental intro they recognized. They followed the sound and found Chloe standing on the bed with her phone, looking at her sister as she started singing the most beautifully haunting version of "My Love, My Life" by ABBA. Every single one of them had chills covering their bodies.

On the second verse, Valentina moved beside the bed and joined Chloe in singing, just like Meryl Streep had with Amanda Seyfried in Mamma Mia! Here We Go Again. On the last verse, Valentina then got on the bed and swayed with Chloe, locked arm in arm. They hugged at the end. No words were spoken, but many were silently exchanged.

Afterward, they all got ready to leave, except for Chloe and Santino. The brothers were taking Valentina's car so she could go with Quinn. Raimer said he was going with Owen and leaving his car for Santino, until Chloe reminded everyone that she had a new car. Owen then decided he would follow Raimer so he could drop off his car.

Santino pulled Raimer aside after hearing that, to tell him that he could have his condo back to himself so he could share his space with Owen. He told him they would pick up their stuff this afternoon. Raimer shook his hand, thanking him for everything he had done. Santino returned the sentiment.

Before the three brothers left, Luca declared a famiglia breakfast at his cabin in the morning and included Owen and Raimer. He still had to tell the rest of them about the babies.

Valentina talked to Owen, telling him how proud she was of him, giving him her blessing again. She then thanked him for making her see the light, and for helping her get her famiglia back. He thanked her for keeping his secret for so long, and admitted she had been right about his dad all along.

Quinn and Chloe had their minute to tell each other that they might not be father and daughter by blood, but the feelings couldn't have been any more real if they were.

Finally, they all left, and Chloe and Santino decided to go to the condo and collect their stuff first, then pick up some take-out food to bring back.

Chloe went into her bedroom, kissed her fingers, and placed it to Harper's cheek. "I'll see you later, sis."

In her haste to get to the car, Chloe forgot her phone, but Santino had seen it and grabbed it, hooking it up to the Bluetooth.

He looked at Chloe. "Do I need to ask, or should I just play Harper's playlist?"

When she smiled, that was the only confirmation he needed.

Chloe shook her head and opened the door.

"Where are you going?" Santino asked.

"I have to open the garage door."

He pushed the button on the visor and it started to rise.

"Wow, Valentina thought of everything," she said, pulling out of the garage, then pushing the button to shut the door.

"When she puts her mind to something, there's no stopping her. It was very generous of you to forgive her. I know how deeply she hurt you."

She moved her hands around the new steering wheel, trying to find the best position. "Everybody was hurt. I'm no different than your mom. I didn't think of the spiderweb effect from that one night. It impacted hundreds, if not thousands. Years later, the effect is still being felt by people just like us. Do you think he knew that?"

Santino shook his head. "Further along in your therapy, Quinn will teach you not to dwell on things we'll never know the answers to. Besides, we have so many other things to talk about, like how you ended up at your house with Raimer and Owen."

He liked the smallness of this vehicle. It allowed him to have his hand on her shoulders. He would never get tired of touching her. He had patiently waited for weeks, and now the thought of not touching her was stifling.

Chloe took comfort in his continuous touches as she recounted the whole story.

After they loaded the car, they decided on picking up some Chinese food. Once back at Chloe's, they set all the food out.

"I can't believe this is my house." Chloe loved the dishes Valentina had picked out. They were pretty and feminine, and the colors matched the Royal Albert tea set.

Santino had been pondering how to approach the next subject. He figured he might as well rip the Band-Aid off, because it didn't matter what she chose, he would follow her anywhere. "Stellina, your house is beautiful, but I don't want you living here alone. Jacob and his crew are still out there, and I don't think they're going to let sleeping dogs lie."

Chloe hadn't thought of that.

"We need to decide where we are going to live."

"We?" she squeaked out, afraid to believe what he was saying.

Santino reached for her hand. "Yes, we. Baby, you're it for me, the woman I want to spend my life with. I'm not trying to rush you, but I won't be leaving you alone. It's not safe. Besides, after living with you for over a month, I can't stand the thought of being separated from you. I'm giving you the option to stay here or my cabin. I'll be happy anywhere, as long as we are together."

Chloe could have melted onto the floor in a puddle with his declaration.

He wasn't looking at her as he loaded his plate with food. She knew he was giving her a moment to absorb all that he had said. That was one of the things she absolutely adored about him—he never rushed her and always gave her options, unlike Jacob. Ultimately, he was giving her the final decision and that was huge.

On one hand, she loved what Valentina had done to her house. She felt close to Harper here. For the first time, she had a beautiful space, surrounded with memories. On the other hand, Santino had a beautiful home and was surrounded with family, and his job was there. She was so confused, wanting to make herself happy but also wanting him happy.

"Stellina, you had a long day. Don't stress. It's not something that has to be decided tonight. We'll stay here until you've had time to really think about what you want. Let's give both places a try and see what best suits us. I don't want you to make this decision for me, because wherever you are is home to me."

She smiled up at him and started to add food to her plate.

Another thing occurred to Santino. "Oh, by the way, my brothers have a proposal for you. But I want to make it clear right off the bat that this is also something you don't have to decide right now. I also don't want you saying yes out of obligation to me. If you accept, it needs to be because you really want to. Do you understand?"

Chloe nodded as she took a mouthful of chow mein.

"My brothers want to hire you as a full-time daycare worker."

Chloe choked on the mouthful.

Santino got up to pat her back. After she took a sip of water and he was convinced she could breathe properly, he sat back down.

"Really? They want me to look after their kids?"

Santino ripped off the top of his egg roll and doused it with plum sauce. When he was convinced that he couldn't fit any more in, he licked his fingers.

Chloe watched as he dragged his tongue along his index finger. It felt like her stomach had a nest of angry hornets all buzzing around.

He caught her expression and watched as she unconsciously licked that fat bottom lip. He groaned, then saw her turn five different shades of pink, so he redirected both their thoughts away from something she wasn't ready for.

"The guys and I talked, and we're thinking of building a little place to put in a daycare. It would be like your very own Montessori school. At the beginning, it would only be you, but after Brooklyn has the twins, we'll hire more people. We are thinking of offering it to the employees. The resort would pay your wages, because it would allow the rest of us to do our jobs easier, knowing the kids were all being taken care of properly.

"Don't give me your answer now. I want you to think about it." He looked down and took another big bite of egg roll.

Chloe couldn't believe her ears. Happier than she had ever been, she launched herself at an unsuspecting Santino, smashing the egg roll between their chests. "Yes! I don't need to think about it. I would love to!" She waited for him to swallow, then initiated a very sensual kiss.

Chapter 13
"Heaven" by Kane Brown

They cleaned up the kitchen, then spent hours side by side on the couch with the album as Chloe recounted story after story of Harper. Santino asked all kinds of questions about being a twin, and she told him that, when she had been a teenager, she had researched about identical twins just to feel closer to Harper.

"Can a boy and a girl be identical?" Santino was so intrigued by the whole concept, especially now that Brooklyn and Luca were having twins.

Chuckling, Chloe answered, "Uh, no. Boy parts are not identical to girl parts. Identical twins are one egg, fertilized by one sperm that splits into two."

Santino felt stupid. "Duh, I can't believe I asked that. So, because you are an identical twin, does that mean you have a higher chance of having them?" He could envision her belly big, filled with two children.

She opened the book to their newborn pictures. "Sadly, no. If twins ran in my family and I was a fraternal twin, I would have a higher chance. Scientists haven't figured out yet why the egg splits. But one odd fact I remember is that tall women are more likely to have twins. It makes sense that Brooklyn is having twins."

That was totally bizarre. "What other cool facts did you learn?"

This was a subject she loved to talk about, which could explain why she was so animated, constantly flipping her hair over her shoulders and gushing while she talked.

"You know how you said you couldn't tell us apart? That's because sometimes identical twins are mirror images of one another."

He tilted his head in confusion, trying to work it out before he blurted another stupid question. Finally giving up, he asked, "Shouldn't all identical twins be mirror images?"

She smiled proudly for knowing the answer. "Actually, there are a few reasons they might not be the mirror images. There are three types of identical twins. First, a single egg is fertilized and splits before being implanted into the woman's womb, so there are two placentas and two birth sacs. Second, the egg implants then splits, so one placenta but two birth sacs. Third, the egg implants and splits later, so one placenta and one sac. Whenever a placenta is shared, it means the twins share the same blood supply, so one could get more nutrients, and that affects every part of development. The ones that share a sac also have a risk of the umbilical cord getting tangled, which could also cause lack of blood flow at times."

Running his hands through his curly locks, Santino blew out some air. "Damn, that's some scary shit. I'm definitely not sharing that info with Luca. He's already had one bleeding ulcer. It really is a miracle when a woman gives birth to identical twins." That explanation also had him changing his mind about seeing Chloe pregnant with twins.

She moved the photo album to the coffee table then shifted closer to him, bumping his shoulder. "Sorry. Maybe I shouldn't have told you that. But remember, with ultrasounds, Brooklyn and the babies can be monitored closely. Plus, they'll know right off the bat how many sacs and placentas she has."

He twisted his head with his hands still woven through his hair. "Tell me something else not so scary."

"Identical twins don't have identical fingerprints. But some of us have telepathic abilities, and I can tell you for certain that Harper and I did. We never needed to speak to know what the other one was thinking. And a lot of times, we finished each other's sentences. We also had our own language until we were three and a half. My mom thought she was going to have to keep us back a year from starting school because we didn't speak English." Chloe giggled an adorable sound, then yawned.

It was getting late, and Santino still had to broach another touchy subject.

"Stellina, don't take this the wrong way, but I think we should share the same bed." He saw her shocked look, so he rushed out, "The reason I say that is because I still don't trust Jacob or his friends. They know which room you sleep in. Not only that, I'm worried you might have nightmares—this being the first night you've slept here since the attack. I promise not to touch you because I know you're not ready."

There he was, taking care of her again, and it made her fall a little more in love with him. Up until now, they had thought they were in love. But, without a sexual relationship, how could they really know? What if she repulsed him like she had Jacob? Chloe couldn't honestly see herself ever having the confidence to enjoy sex again. Was that fair to Santino?

A lot of good things had happened in the last twenty-four hours, but she was still so screwed up.

He saw the wheels turning. "Please stop. Don't overthink everything. I promised not to push you. You'll have your pajamas on, and I'll have my sleep pants. Let's just get through this first night without stressing about it, okay?" Santino stood, reached for her hand, and helped her up. "You take the washroom first. Get ready, and then I'll take my turn. Trust me, baby; it will all be fine."

Twenty minutes later, Santino walked around the bed and crawled in beside Chloe before turning off the light. There was still some light filtering in from the streetlamp at the end of the driveway.

They lay on their backs, side by side, each conscious of the other's breathing.

As Santino lifted his left arm to tuck behind his head, he felt Lambie pushed behind the pillows. Chloe must have hidden it there, embarrassed to admit she still slept with the toy cuddled tightly in her arms. Santino had already known, though, because he had checked on her every night at Raimer's. A few times, he had found the pathetic little guy on the floor, so he had picked it up and placed it back into her arms. Chloe deserved to have something to keep the nightmares at bay.

He glanced over and saw Chloe had her eyes tightly closed, obviously nowhere near falling asleep, so he gently pulled Lambie out, rolled onto his side, and smooshed the nose of the lamb into her neck. "Aren't you she-ep-ee, Stellina?" he said in a goofy, high-pitched voice.

Opening her eyes, she giggled. "Give him to me." She attempted to snatch it back.

Lifting it out of her reach, he moved the lamb's head from side to side, saying in the same annoying voice, "Come on, tell me. Are you she-ep-ee?"

She sat up, lurching forward for the stuffed animal. "You sound like a goof. Besides, it's a lamb, not a sheep."

Squeakily, he placed it beside his mouth, pretending to reply for the toy. "No, lambs are baby she-e-ep. I'm older than a year, so I'm a she-e-ep."

Crossing her arms over her chest, she retorted, "Lamb!"

He quickly shoved it in her face. "She-e-ep!" Then he pulled it away quickly so she couldn't grab it.

She pursed her lips, fighting not to laugh.

He lifted his arm up, arcing it high over her. In his goofy voice, he started, "One she-e-ep"—arcing it again—"two she-e-ep"—flying it over her and back after each count—"three she-ep-ee, four she-e-ep. Are you getting she-ep-ee yet?"

Chloe waited until it was up high before pouncing, tickling his stomach. He barked out a laugh, lowering his arm, and she reached out again but was a second too late. Frustrated, she threw her leg over his toned abs and straddled him, trying to reach higher.

"Your arms are too long. That's not fair."

He continued to taunt her by bringing it closer, then snatching it away.

Chloe's wiggling made him hard as a rock. He had to make her stop before she saw his boner and kicked him out.

In his own voice, he said, "I'll give him back if you answer this joke."

In an exaggerated motion, she sat down on his belly, lifting a brow. "Fine."

"What do you call a she-e-ep covered in chocolate?"

Chloe rolled her eyes. "What?"

"A candy b-a-a." He laughed at her pinched face. "Okay, okay. What do you call a she-e-ep with no legs?"

When she couldn't think of anything, she pouted. Santino couldn't help touching the puffy, plump skin that drove him to distraction.

With a throatier sound, he said, "A cloud."

She giggled at that.

"This is the last one. If you don't get this joke, you have to kiss me, and then I'll give you Lambie. If you win, I get to kiss you, and then you'll get Lambie."

She giggled even harder. "Has anyone ever told you you're a b-a-a, b-a-a boy?"

The look on his face was priceless before he broke out into laughter.

Chloe couldn't help laughing with him, because he was laughing so hard. His contracting abdominal muscles were making the wasps go crazy in her tummy again.

Santino had tears streaming down his face he was laughing so hard, which only made her laugh harder. It really wasn't that funny, but the silliness of the whole conversation had them howling.

Even through the uncontrollable laughter, Santino couldn't help thinking this was the moment he had been waiting for. Stellina was belly-laughing uncontrollably, and she had never looked more enchanting.

Suddenly, he jackknifed up, causing her to fall back on his knees. He raised them quickly, then bent at the waist to capture that delectable mouth. He framed her face, deepening the kiss. God, she was perfect and so receptive.

As he dug his fingers deeper into her scalp, the pinch of pain caused Chloe to moan. He was thrilled by it.

For Chloe, it brought Jacob's word back with a vengeance.

It sickened me to touch her, so I punished her during sex, my hand burning from the spankings I gave her. She thought I liked rough sex, while the joke was on her because, every time I wrapped my hands around her neck, I had to stop myself from snuffing her out like her father did to Nicole.

Santino felt her go from relaxed to rigid. "Stellina, talk to me. What just happened?"

She scrambled off his lap, grabbed Lambie, and held him tightly to her belly, while pushing up against the headboard.

"Chloe, please don't do that. If I did something that freaked you out, tell me." He crawled up beside her and carefully pried one of her hands from the stuffed toy. Interlacing their fingers, he brought her knuckles up to his mouth, brushing a kiss to them. "Be honest, amore. There isn't anything you can say that I'd judge. Did I do something?"

"No, it wasn't you; it was all me." It was still natural for Chloe to think he was going to be mad like Jacob used to react. "Please don't make me say it. You were there. You heard what he said."

Santino sat patiently, giving her all the time in the world to decide if she trusted him enough to talk about intimacy.

How did Quinn wait for his clients to talk when all he wanted to do was extract the words from her?

Finally, she blurted out, "I liked it rough. How perverted is that? Jacob did it because he hated me, while I got off on some of it. Not all of it. Some of it really hurt, but sometimes he did things that made me . . . I don't know."

The rage building in him to kill the bastard was overwhelming, but he had to tamp it down to get to the root of the issue. Santino knew this was a topic she would never discuss with Quinn, so, by default, that left him. He would have to be the calm, mature, methodical man she needed.

"There is nothing perverted about having sexual desires that lean to the darker side. I do."

She swung her face toward his with surprise, and then it changed. "You're just saying that to make me feel less like a sexual deviant." Her eyes fell with understanding.

"Look at me," he commanded intensely.

Those beautiful, expressive eyes lifted immediately. He was pleased with her reaction.

"Why would I lie? If you called me on it, I would have to prove it, right?" He waited for a response, and when she didn't answer quickly enough, he spoke sharply, "Right?"

"Yes," she panted out.

God, the sound of her soft voice, with a touch of pleading, had his dick coming back to life. He lifted a pillow and placed it over his lap. Then, thinking better of it, he took it off.

"Look." He pointed at his erection. "Does it look like I'm turned off?"

Her cheeks turned pink when she saw his pants tenting.

"Eyes back on mine. Tell me what turns you on and what doesn't. Then I'll tell you what turns my crank. That way, we can eliminate any fears." He waited a few seconds, then used that voice again. "Stellina, when I ask you a question, I want an answer right away. I don't want you to overthink or try to decide how to soften it for me. I want honest answers; the same as I will give you."

Flustered, she blurted, "I don't want to make any decisions. All my life, I had to make all the decisions for myself. I hate it because, half the time, I make the wrong choices. I want someone to take all my power away. I don't want to be responsible for making sex good."

He smiled. "That works out perfectly for me, because I like control in the bedroom. As the fifth son, I never had a say in anything. I was bossed around by everyone. The only place I have ever had any say was in the bedroom. I like being dominant."

That word freaked her the hell out. Shoving back, she told him, "I don't want to be a sex slave. I like some unconventional things, but I hate real pain. I've had too much physical pain in my life. The word dominant scares me."

Santino scooped her up before she got away. "Relax, baby, I don't want a sex slave. Maybe after the Fifty Shades phenomenon that was the wrong word. I don't like beating women black and blue because I have deep-seated anger issues. I just like control." She relaxed as he continued, "I do like a playful spanking just to add a little sting, and I love tying a woman up. But definitely no whips, floggers, or any other implement."

Chloe felt a flush crawl up her neck and face. That was exactly what she liked, but she needed him to understand. "Jacob used to hit my backside so bad that I couldn't walk without a severe limp. But the thought of you correcting me for being intentionally naughty makes the wasps go crazy."

That was a two-fold statement. The initial one caused him to scowl, yet the other had him drawing his eyebrows together.

"What Jacob did was depraved, plain and simple. He labeled it as dominance, but that was a cop-out. The man needs help. He is a deeply disturbed abuser. We have to remove him from our conversation about exploring our sexuality, because everything he did was vengeful. Let's try to figure out what we like and want to explore. Now . . . explain about the wasps?"

Chloe let her hair drape over her face before answering, but Santino immediately caught on.

"Nice try, Stellina." He tucked the fallen pieces behind her warm ears, then lifted her chin. "I want to see your face."

She answered without overthinking like he asked. "Whenever I see you or you touch me, I feel like I have a wasp hive in my lower tummy, and they're mad, flying around like crazy, stinging me. Sometimes, it actually feels painful. Dumb, huh?"

He preened as he dragged her closer, sensually kissing the question of her intelligence right off her tongue.

It hit him then that she wasn't ever going to be any more ready than she was right now. In fact, she would overthink it to death and drive herself to the brink. This sweet woman was the whole damn insecure package, and waiting wasn't an option anymore. He needed to prove to her that sex could be magical for them.

He moved his hands up to her hair and gently tugged. The shiver he felt race up her body was all the confirmation he needed.

Fisting her hair, he pulled back, causing a pop from the suction of their mouths breaking apart. "Stellina, I want you. Can you trust me to make it good for both of us?"

She blinked her big, wide eyes twice as she processed the depth of the question.

He would allow this extra time to consider the ramifications, because she had to trust him for it to work.

He felt the minute she tried to nod and shook his head. "I want all your answers to be verbal as we go along, so I need your acknowledgment that this is something you want to pursue."

She ever so softly answered with conviction, "Yes."

An afterthought occurred to her. It was still early in their relationship, so if the sex wasn't going to work out, she could still walk away with a fraction of her heart intact.

Santino saw the hint of sadness flash in her eyes. He would use his cock to pound that last thought right out of her head.

"Your safe word is Lambie. There is no chance in hell you would scream that out in passion. And trust me, Stellina; I will make you scream."

Well, hot damn, her panties went from damp to soaked. He took this shit seriously.

This must have been what skydiving felt like—once you jump, there was no turning back. Free-falling into sex with Santino was like learning the difference between pulling the right cord or not.

He placed her beside him and got out of bed. Then, in the deep, commanding voice, he ordered, "Take my pants off."

She reached out, then hesitated.

"I don't like repeating myself. You know your word if you need to use it."

This time, she didn't stop to think. Moving to the edge of the bed and stepping down, she bent at the waist to lower his pants.

Holy crap, he didn't have underwear on, and the elastic waistband got caught on his impressive length. She licked her lips in concentration, pulling the elastic out farther as her knuckles brushed along his length, making them both jump.

"Sorry," she mumbled.

He grunted, doing everything in his power not to blow his load. Thankfully, she managed to get his pants to his ankles, and he stepped out.

Back in control, he commanded, "Va bene, good girl. Now, without thinking or stalling, strip."

She brought her hands to the hem of her flowy camisole and lifted it. She kept reminding herself that she couldn't be held accountable if Santino didn't like what he saw or if the sex was lousy, because she didn't have any control over it. He did.

When she was standing straight, Santino's toes curled into the carpet as he got his first glimpse of her bare breasts. The fleshy mounds looked almost too big for her tiny build. Her tits were more than a mouthful, and that made him want to weep along with his cock. Her nipples were tight, the color of a ripened peach where the hues blended toward the pit into a glorious peachy-pink color.

He stopped himself in the nick of time before he smacked his own head. Fanculo!

Her eyes only skimmed his longing look for a second before focusing on the task of removing her pajama bottoms. Her fingers shook as she hooked them under the fabric of her bottoms and panties, dragging them both down. She stepped out of them and raised nervously for his assessment. Chloe knew her scars were like a beacon.

Scars? What scars? All Santino saw were those tits and the prettiest pussy he had ever seen. If her pubic hair matched the blonde on her head, he would never know, because there wasn't a hair to be seen. He thought her lips that surrounded her mouth were plump and delectable, but they had nothing on her feminine lips. Saliva pooled heavily in his mouth, needing to taste her right the fuck now.

In the gruffest voice so far, he ordered, "On the bed, on your back, now!"

She jumped, then rushed to get into place.

She wasn't sure why he wanted her on the bed. Jacob always made her give him a blowjob first. Maybe he didn't like foreplay and just wanted to get to the main event.

Santino fell to his knees, inhaling her scent, her excitement. She smelled like honey. Bending forward to find out if she tasted the same way, he glanced up, seeing Chloe's eyes were squeezed tightly shut. He had become so enthralled with her body that he had forgotten to walk Chloe through her insecurities.

He placed his hands on either side of her knees, pushing himself up and placing a kiss on her tummy. Then he rested his chin in the valley of her luscious tits. "Bella Stellina, you are the most spectacular woman I have ever laid eyes on. To me, you are perfect in every sense of the word. I'm not going to ask if I can taste you, because I don't think an army could drag me away."

Chloe had never had a man do that, which made her doubly nervous. The only reason she was bare was because Jacob had wanted to make her feel exposed. What if she didn't react appropriately?

"I'm not going to ask you again. Look at me." He pinched her left nipple, hard.

With a yelp, Chloe's eyes sprang open.

"Is that what I have to do to keep you out of your own head? I want you to see and feel how privileged I am to share this with you, because this is the closest that I'm going to get to heaven before my time. I love you, Stellina."

After he kissed her face, he drifted downward, and she jumped when he nipped the inside of her thigh, then licked the sting. Next, he nuzzled her nether lips, dragging his tongue all around. Her eyes fought to stay open as she twisted her head from side to side.

He growled out, causing an awesome vibration that made her eyes open completely. Even though she had been unsure and self-conscious, the wasps had gone into full assault mode. It felt unbelievable.

Santino moved his forearms to split her legs wider, resting them on her thighs and lifting his hands up to capture her nipples. He gave a sharp tug, causing her to yelp, then dipped both index fingers into her open mouth, wetting them on her tongue. Chloe tried to suck on them, but they disappeared as quickly as they had appeared.

He moved the wet fingertips to her nipples, running them ever so softly just on the tips. At the exact same time, he latched on to her swollen nub and sucked hard.

Aaaggghhh, yes! Her hips flew up as an orgasm ripped through her unexpectedly.

He didn't stop feasting, and every nerve ending felt exposed and sensitive, causing her to wiggle and fight. It was sensory overload.

When she eventually relaxed, Santino moved up between her thighs. She looked sated and past the point of overthinking. He couldn't be more pleased.

He moved stray strands of damp hair from her face and kissed her. Chloe instantly tasted herself on him and turned away in aversion.

"No, Stellina, I want you to taste the most amazing flavor I ever have."

She wondered if he would be so eager to taste his own climax off her tongue.

It hit Chloe that she was being selfish, so she broke the kiss, knowing her job was to get on her knees now.

He pressed down as she tried to lift.

"Santino, let me up so I can pay you back."

Nuzzling her neck, he said, "No. Sex between us isn't about payback. I went down on you because I wanted to and I love it. Get used to me feasting between those creamy thighs. Besides, tonight is all about you. There will be plenty of time for me to take that mouth the way I want." He kissed her one more time before he instructed her to roll over and get on her hands and knees.

Santino had dreamed a lot about making love to Chloe, but he had expected a skittish woman whom he was going to have to treat with kid gloves. Instead, Stellina was the woman who had walked right out of his fantasies

"If I don't get my cock in you in the next minute, I'm going to explode all over the bed. I'm going to take you hard and fast, and you're going to love it. Right, baby?" When she didn't respond, he swatted her ass. "Answer me," he said, soothing the sting, then slapping her again on the other cheek just because he loved seeing his handprint on her pure white skin.

"Oooh!" she purred, arching her spine and pushing into the hand rubbing the dull ache. This kind of mindless abandonment was exactly what she had always wanted.

Santino reached for his pants on the chair, took a condom out of his wallet, and then slid it on faster than he ever had before. Even the feel of the latex rolling on his painfully erect cock caused it to pulse. Then he shifted over and angled her hips perfectly before grabbing himself at the base and lining up to her core. They both groaned out in ecstasy as he pushed in slowly and didn't stop until his thighs met her perfect ass.

"I'm going to hold you so tight you won't be able to move. I'll control how fast and hard your body accepts me. Get ready, baby." He wound one arm around her waist, yanking her backward so his body was covering her smaller one. With his other hand, he held himself up as he lifted one knee slightly so he could move his hips without losing their full-on connection. Santino pulled back then let loose, thrusting hard in and out.

He nudged her hair with his chin and nipped the shell of her ear, groaning into it, "You're so fucking sexy, Stellina. Everything about you makes me want to pound you into next week. You're a good girl taking all of me so well. Let me hear you."

With his permission, she screamed, loving the force and the feeling of being guilt-free. She had absolutely no control, which elevated the encounter off the charts.

He listened to make sure she was okay. Her panting and moaning were verbal enough to know she was into it. She was close, but she wouldn't get there as fast as his orgasm was coming, so he moved the hand that was splayed across her belly down until he was circling her clit. He pushed harder when he felt the inevitable blasting from his tight balls. "Fanculo!"

Chloe screamed his name as her walls steamrolled over his cock, extracting every last swimmer from him.

He fell to his side, dragging her with him. They were both breathing heavily, exhausted and extremely satisfied. It was an epic encounter that neither would soon forget. There was something surreal about finding your soulmate, especially when they matched you in intelligence, courage, and sexual prowess.

When Santino was able, he pulled himself out of his beautiful Stellina's body, then moved to the washroom to clean up. He was so lost in the afterglow of the experience that he neglected to hear her come in. Startled, he asked, "What are you doing?"

She moved back, stunned by his question. "I have to pee and clean up."

He dumped the condom in the trash can. "Why are your pajamas back on?"

She tilted her head to the left. "Because we're going to she-e-ep."

Santino laughed.

Moving closer, he started to pull her top up, but she batted his hands away.

He stood back, leaning against the counter, crossing his hands over his chest. "Who's in control in the bedroom?"

Chloe froze. "Thankfully, you are, because that was off the charts." The blush traveled up her chest and over her face.

He preened again. "That's right, so lose the pajamas. It's bad enough we had to have a rubber between us. I won't let another thing stop me from touching every part of you whenever I want. Drop them!"

Goodness gracious, this man was finer than a frog hair!

Chloe did as he had firmly suggested and, as a reward, he left another handprint on her bottom before walking out to give her some privacy.

Chloe was still luminous when she crept back into the bedroom.

Her knee had just hit the mattress when he dragged her over, placing her in the crux of his arm, her head resting on his chest.

Content, Santino was almost at the fall-off point of sleep and consciousness when her voice brought him back.

"Are you she-e-eping?"

He tightened his hold with a small chuckle. "What's up?"

She kissed his chest. "I just wanted to thank you. I didn't think I would ever be able to have sex again. I certainly didn't think I would enjoy it."

"Enjoy?" Santino sleepily yanked on one of her curls. "It was fucking amazing, not enjoyable."

She giggled. "You're right. I didn't enjoy it . . . I loved it. I didn't know it could be like—"

"Like what?"

"How come it's so easy with you? Never any pressure. And if I'm not crying because you said something sweet, I'm laughing because you're goofy." She lifted up to look at his face. "Santino, I have lost a lot of things in my life, but I won't survive losing you. Please don't leave me."

This sweet, beautiful woman who had been through so much

smashed his heart into smithereens.

He cupped her face, dragging her lips to his, and kissed her senseless. "Stellina, you are mine, and I'm never letting you go. I've never loved another woman, because I was waiting for you. I love you, and I need you to believe in us. It only gets better from here." He reached back, then smushed Lambie in her face before tucking it under her arm. "Now go to she-e-ep."

Chapter 14
"She's Stronger Than Me" by Garth Brooks

It had been five months since the couple moved back to Santino's cabin to be closer to both their jobs and his famiglia. Once immersed in the resort, Chloe began to consider the Savages as her family. The tension was long gone, and the peace she had made with Valentina blossomed into a true friendship, giving her a mother figure, something she hadn't had since before Harper had died and left her mother a shell of a woman.

Santino and Chloe continued to talk about everything, from their childhoods to their dreams. At night, they explored her sexual liberation, except the one time he tried to tie her up and she had a panic attack. Santino assured her that he could live without that element of his desire.

Deep down, it bothered Chloe that Jacob still held her hostage, leaving her unable to give Santino something he craved. She trusted him with every fiber of her being, yet the minute the rope touched her skin, she had freaked.

Santino had tried to move her past the incident, but what she perceived as inadequacy stayed locked in the recesses of her mind like a hidden virus in a computer, just waiting to destroy their sexual contentment.

It had been a big step when Santino and Luca moved all the things she wanted to keep into the cabin. It became her home, with all her pictures, the Royal Albert tea set, and a few other awesome pieces.

Chloe didn't want to sell the farmhouse because it was one of the few good links to her past, but she also didn't want renters trashing the beautiful space Valentina had created.

As it turned out, Owen and Raimer approached her and asked if they could rent it. Owen wanted a real home and all the domestic things that came along with it. Raimer wasn't convinced, though, so it would give them the chance to try it out without buying something they might have to sell.

Chloe insisted she didn't want their money after all they had done for her and Santino. If they covered the expenses, it would give her a chance to decide what she wanted to do with the house.

Chloe had experienced so many things at the resort. Because of her hip injury, she couldn't go horseback riding, though, so Santino had taken her on horse-drawn sleigh rides throughout the winter, snuggled under a warm blanket with a thermos of spiked hot cider. He also made accommodations so she could enjoy all the other toys on the property.

He bought a side-by-side two-seater ATV so they could tear up the mountains. Santino had even hooked up a two-seater tube so Ava could drag them behind her on the snowmobile. Alessandro swore Santino was pazzo for getting behind his speed demon wife. However, Santino had faith in his best friend. In fact, at one point, he encouraged Ava to speed up so they didn't fall asleep. Alessandro couldn't watch, deciding chopping wood would be better for his heart than watching Ava in control of the couple's lives.

The absolute best things to date had been Thanksgiving and Christmas. Chloe had been so nervous about Thanksgiving and how to fit in, especially because the extent of her cooking still only involved burnt toast and steeping tea. Valentina had known she was freaking out, so she had given her the job of decorating for the celebration.

The days before the big day, Eli had joined her in the little daycare after school to make pumpkins out of folded paper, and they had made garland out of the leaves they had pressed between wax paper. Also, everyone got turkey hats with the tail feather cut out of Eli's and Shawn's handprints in colorful paper.

One day, Chloe had solicited Emmy to make them Rice Krispies treats so they could attach pretzels and mini marshmallows dipped in white chocolate. Then they had shaped the treats into tasty little turkey legs. Eli had chatted her head off, talking about all the food and fun they would have. She had then sent Eli around with a piece of paper for everyone to fill out what they were thankful for.

The famiglia had been blown away with how awesome everything looked, and that she had involved the children in every project.

After dinner, Sabastian had read all the pieces of paper, and everyone sat speechless when he read, "I'm thankful for Jacob Moore, because he didn't just bring me the moon, he brought me my Stellina." Everyone sat stupefied, until Valentina had raised her glass and hollered, "To Jacob!"

Although shocking, it was the bare-naked truth, and Chloe had kissed Santino for the understanding. It was probably one of the most profound things she had ever mulled over, and was the last piece needed to close the door to a past foregone.

Christmas had been something right out of a Hallmark movie. The Christmas trees, presents, foods, and of course, the sleigh ride that the whole famiglia had taken on Christmas Eve. Everyone couldn't believe the sight when they had pulled up to a clearing covered in twinkling lights that had a table set up with hot cider. They were all trying to figure out who had done it when Santino took his guitar from the driver. He had then placed Chloe in a specific spot in the snow, where a string of lights lit up in the shape of a heart around her feet before he began to sing Garth Brooks's "She's Stronger Than Me." Chloe had wept through the entire thing. At the end, he had handed his guitar to Eli and dropped to one knee.

The famiglia backed up to watch and give them some privacy.

"Wishing on a falling star has come to mean so much more to me. When you fell, I had no idea that, when I caught my girl, not only would I get the wish I had always hoped for, but every wish I could ever dream of.

"I thought I knew the meaning of strength, but you taught me differently. You are the strongest person I know, and when I wake up every morning, I know I can't live a day without you." He pulled a black velvet box out of his coat pocket. "Can we make a date? Let's meet here in twenty years and tell our children about this proposal."

Santino opened the box. "It will never shine as brightly as my Stellina, but will you marry me anyway?"

Chloe stood there, her bottom lip quivering in and out of her mouth, while teardrops as big as the teardrop diamond in her ring spilled down her cheeks. "Are you sure?" she choked out on a whisper.

He grinned, whispering back, "As sure as tomorrow will follow tonight. As sure as my next breath. As sure as taxes and death. As sure as shit. And definitely as sure as the punishment I'll be giving you tonight for making me wait for your answer. As sure—"

"Okay!" she cried out softly as she blushed from head to toe.

Chuckling, he shook his head. "I recite a speech good enough for TMZ and the best answer you can come up with is okay?"

Bending forward, she whispered just for his ears, "Maybe I want to marry you and receive the outcome of being bad all in one unforgettable night."

He jumped to his feet, picked her up, and swung her around. "Okay it is! God, you're perfect for me." He leaned close to her ear. "We aren't telling our kids that part of the proposal."

Yup, over the last five months, Santino had given her enough memories to replace all the bad. And today, another memory was in the making, because it was the day Brooklyn was scheduled for the cesarean birth of the twins.

They had grown healthy, but because of her history with Eli's fast delivery, the doctors had decided the safest course was to schedule their births.

Poor Luca was a nervous wreck, swearing he was getting himself snipped, because three kids would be enough, and his stomach couldn't handle going through it again.

Chloe and Santino had kept Eli overnight and had ended up spending most of the night eating microwave popcorn and watching movies. The little guy was so excited about his siblings coming into the world that he couldn't sleep. Now they all sat in the waiting room, nervously awaiting news.

They were all surprised when the sheriff walked through the door, taking off his hat and running his hands through his hair as he stomped toward Valentina.

"Is Brooklyn okay? Are the babies here?"

Valentina got up and hugged the distraught man. Everyone but Chloe knew he was like a father to Brooklyn.

"Relax, Papa Keith. She'll be fine. We haven't heard anything yet. Sit down and wait with us."

He blew out an upset breath. "I didn't sleep a wink last night. I haven't been this nervous since Marybeth gave birth to my kids, and that was only one at a time. Sorry, I didn't even say hi to everyone." He turned and stumbled when he saw Chloe sitting there, holding Santino's hand.

"What in damnation is this? I've been looking for you for months."

Santino stood, pulling Chloe up with him. "She's been with me this whole time. Chloe and I are engaged." He lifted her hand.

Keith's eyebrows shot skyward. "You're what? I thought I told you I'd charge you with stalking if you ever contacted her." Pissed, he turned and glared at everyone. "And not one of you thought to tell me?"

Quinn moved behind Chloe, placing his hands on her shoulders as she answered, "I thank God every day that Santino ignored you, because he saved my life in more ways than one."

Quinn moved in front of the couple. "I have been there every step and can assure you that Santino was her saving grace. He asked for my help the day after the attack, and I have been counseling Chloe ever since. She had to work through a lot of issues and is flourishing with her new family."

Astonished, Keith whirled around to face Valentina. "You mean to tell me you've accepted Chloe into your family?"

Valentina walked over to Chloe, placing her arm around the young woman's waist. "I'm not proud of the depths I sank to, but my carina found it in her heart to forgive me. It wasn't easy, but she also helped me heal, and I'm proud to call her my new daughter."

Keith was sure he was in a dream. "I can't believe Brooklyn didn't tell me, or I didn't run into you at the resort. We have dinner together every other Monday."

Sabastian said, "Chloe babysits for us on Monday nights. That's probably why you never ran in to her at dinner."

Raimer stepped forward, hand in hand with Owen. "Besides, it wasn't mamácita's story to tell. And if I've learned anything from our surrogate Italian famiglia, it's I panni sporchi si lavano in famiglia. For those not in the know, it translates to: Dirty clothes should be washed inside the family! We are famiglia, and famiglia looks after famiglia."

Keith looked at the two men holding hands. With a slow, irregular shake of his head, he responded, "Apparently, mamácita left out more than a few developments. Congratulations to all the new couples."

Running his hand over his overwhelmed face, Keith continued,

"Actually, I was going to stop by next week, so I might as well address it with all of you together. The Moore's high-priced lawyer has finally run out of postponements, so the trial for Jacob and his tribe is scheduled for a month from now."

The news took all of their breaths away. Chloe got weak in the knees, and if it weren't for Valentina and Santino, she would have slipped down.

Santino got her into a chair, telling her, "It's okay, amore. We'll get through this like everything else."

Chloe looked into his worried eyes and remembered her favorite Italian quote.

Not too long ago, after one Sunday lunch, Valentina was arguing with Emmy's granddad, Albert, about the best phrases. The two of them cornered Owen, Raimer, and Chloe to settle their argument. Valentina had recited her favorites from her youth, like the one Raimer had just used. The one that had stuck in Chloe's head was, "Quando arrivano i problemi, è la tua famiglia che ti sostiene."

Santino smiled like all the world's problems had just been solved. Chloe was going to be perfectly fine, because she had just told him, "When trouble comes, it's your family that supports you."

None of them had another chance to say anything before Luca came busting through the door. "Where is my cucciolo?"

Eli jumped up from his seat, where he had been playing on Alessandro's phone. "I'm here, Daddy!" Eli handed off the phone and ran as fast as he could to jump into his daddy's arms.

With a big smile on his face, Luca announced, "Eli, my only son, you have two beautiful, healthy baby sisters." They hugged as Luca got emotional and Eli screamed, "Woohoo!" Then Luca lifted his head to kiss his son and said to everyone else, "Our daughters were just born. The doctor is allowing Eli to come and meet them. I'll come and get you all when they're ready to meet their extended famiglia." He gave Keith a quick chin lift, including him, before running off with his cucciolo.

The whole group hugged and congratulated each other.

Chloe noticed Keith had pulled back from everyone, facing the windows, his shoulders heaving. She walked to him and placed her hand on his back, rubbing circles. "Congratulations, Grandpa."

He turned, swiping at the embarrassing tears. "I wish."

A smile radiated from Chloe. "Brooklyn is a lucky woman to have a stand-in dad who loves her and her family as much as you do. Quinn has earned the same title with me. Even without a blood connection, some men are just meant to nurture and protect young people they didn't create. To be a chosen daughter means it's not out of obligation but honest to God love. I'll say it again, congratulations, Grandpa."

Keith crushed the young woman to his chest. "Thank you, darlin'." He pulled back to look at her. "You've been haunting me for months. You were one of the girls I was driven to reach out to, especially after I couldn't find you. I have been so worried those animals had gotten the best of you. I never stopped looking. Each day, I dedicated a personal hour to search for you." When she dropped her gaze, Keith called her name and waited until she lifted her eyes. "Because I knew in my heart you needed a man to replace the man who never deserved the title of father. A girl doesn't have to have just one, you know. I'd sure like a chance to be part of your life."

She was charmed by the big, burly man who proved to her that Quinn wasn't an anomaly, that maybe her father had been the anomaly.

She crushed him back, speaking into his chest, "I would like that. Do you think I could take you to dinner one night? Just the two of us?"

"Nothing would make me happier. I have a lot of things to discuss with you, but not at dinner—that's personal. I want to get to know who the adorable, strong Chloe Marsh is."

Santino approached. "She's my fiancée. And as you get to know her, you'll see she was worth any jail time you would've given me." He stuck his hand out. "Sorry, Keith, I didn't mean to disrespect you or your authority."

He reverently took Santino's hand in the gesture it was offered. "Thank you, son. And congratulations. You got a hell of a fighter here."

Luca came in and gathered all of the famiglia, including Keith, leading them to meet his daughters.

Luca placed his daughter who was named after Brooklyn's brother, Reece, in his mamma's arms, and then he placed Marcella, named after his oldest brother, Marcello, in Alessandro's arms. The two cried, unlike the infants in their arms.

Santino saw Chloe fidgeting and forfeited his chance to hold one of the girls first so Chloe and Keith could have a chance. They smiled at one another, holding the precious bundles, knowing they were part of the Savages one hundred percent.

When the twins started to get really cranky, everyone said their goodbyes. Santino was the last, unable to drag his girl away from them. The two little babies reminded Chloe of Harper and her.

Before she left, she suggested placing the twins in one bassinet. The twins instantly stopped fussing.

"How did you know?" Luca asked.

She smiled sadly. "Twins aren't meant to be separated."

Santino framed Chloe's shoulders, kissing her head. "You're right, Stellina. It's just not natural."

At that moment, he got the chills. He knew they would never have twins, but it was time to give her a baby.

When the couple walked outside, they saw a bunch of photographers standing outside the hospital and wondered what had happened to have a horde of media there. They then saw Keith screech up to the entrance with his lights on. They both balked, knowing this wasn't his jurisdiction.

The reporters started yelling both their names.

One said, "Is it true you're getting married?"

"Santino, your father must be rolling in his grave knowing you're engaged to his murderer's daughter," another reporter yelled.

"Antagonists make strange bedfellows," one man piped up.

Santino lost his shit, charging full-out at the belligerent assholes. Thank goodness Keith intercepted before he made contact.

Frozen to her spot, Chloe screamed, "Please don't!"

Yanking him back, Keith said, "Don't be stupid, son." Seething out between clenched teeth, he said, "Don't give them what they're looking for. They're baiting you. Get Chloe into my car."

He had been so blinded by rage that he had been temporarily sidetracked from his first priority.

He pivoted, his heart sinking as he saw the woman who had come so far shatter into a million pieces. "Stellina!" he snapped, going with a firm voice as he stalked toward her. He was not letting her slide backward.

Her fearful, pale face popped up at hearing the authority in his voice.

"You will not take this on. They don't know anything. I love you, and that's all that matters."

By the time he reached her, Chloe was shaking like a leaf. He pushed her head into his chest and led her toward the cruiser.

Meanwhile, a female reporter, whom Keith had gone to school with, pulled him aside, whispering, "Jacob Moore's cousin is a nurse here and tipped him off after seeing the ring and Santino. They know the Savage family from when the eldest one's wife had her accident."

Keith shook his head, disgusted in not only Jacob but the news executives who had allowed this mockery. It was such an abuse of power.

"Thanks for the heads-up, Deb. But you have to know this whole display is revolting. That little girl has paid a thousand different ways for something she didn't do."

"I'm only here because I was ordered to report the story," she tried to pacify him. "All of us are just doing our job, the same as you."

Loudly, so more than a few of the reporters could hear, Keith said, "Maybe you could remind those two vipers they hit below the belt. The difference is, I live by the ethics of my job. This so-called story is yellow journalism, not responsible journalism." He walked away without another word.

Chloe was pulling inward. Santino couldn't allow it, but he also couldn't say what he needed to and how she needed it said until they were alone.

Keith jumped into the car. "It was that prick Jacob. Excuse my language, darlin'."

"Fanculo!" Santino spat. "Is that bastard ever going to give up?"

Chloe shivered, frightened, knowing Jacob would now find out she was at the resort and hadn't left town. This nightmare was never going to end.

Keith looked into the rearview mirror. "Darlin', I know what they said hurt, but the people who know the truth are the only ones who matter. You are loved. And between the Savages and my department, we're going to make sure you're safe until this is all over. Please believe me. I want you to remember you have family now. You don't only belong to the Savages, but to me as well, and I protect what's mine."

While Keith talked to Chloe, Santino sent a famiglia text to let them all know what had happened. The phone vibrated nonstop, everyone telling him that they would be waiting for them. He wanted time alone with her, but he knew the famiglia would show her that they were supporting her, that she would never again have to face her problems alone, and she needed that confirmation first and foremost.

When they arrived at the resort, Chloe had just stepped out of the cruiser when Sabastian pulled her into his arms. "You've come a long way. Don't you let them get to you. They don't know shit. None of us have to justify a thing to those bloodsuckers."

When he finally released her, each of the famiglia took her into their arms with reassuring words. But when she got to Valentina, Chloe exploded into sobs.

The woman coddled her as she walked her into the main lodge. She sat her on a stool, then sat in the one beside her, taking her hands. "Carina, it was bound to come out sooner or later. Instead of letting them win, I think we should confront it head-on."

"What do you mean?" Quinn asked from behind them.

Valentina twisted to look at her boyfriend, and then at the rest of the famiglia. "It occurred to me a while ago, after something Chloe said about her history always catching up to her and losing her job. I think she should tell her story to the reporters."

"That's not anyone's business, Ma!" Alessandro snarled.

Pushing her chair out so she could get down and move, she explained, "I know, shamo, but hear me out. We need to show them the injustice of blaming Chloe. It has to end here and now. She had a terrible life, and if people knew, they'd think differently. We have to change that mob mentality, not just for Chloe, but for anyone else carrying the same weight." She twirled around toward the young woman. "Carina, if you tell as much of your story as you are comfortable with, maybe it will be the deciding factor in Jacob's case."

"Nope, I wouldn't advise that," Keith said. "It could alter Jacob getting a fair trial; therefore, it could be thrown out of court. Besides, you can't be sure they won't twist her words. I don't trust a soul with her story but Chloe herself. Let the hysteria die down. Something else will replace it in a few days."

"I have a suggestion," Ava announced, moving onto the stool Valentina had abandoned. "I learned at my brother's trial that victims are given an opportunity to give a victim impact statement before sentencing. It was the only time I was able to tell the police that, if they had just listened to me, my brother would still be alive. It was powerful to finally have my feelings be known, and for the people who had killed him to hear how losing my brother affected me. The press is obviously going to be there to hear Jacob's side at the trial, and you can have your say with the press there as well."

Owen cleared his throat. He wanted to speak but wasn't sure if it was his place.

Santino nudged his chin up for him to say his piece.

"But once the verdict is read, what guarantee is there that the press will remain for that part?"

Keith shifted the utility belt resting on his hip. "I can assure it. The reporter who told me where the information came from is an old friend from high school. She'll start a frenzy about Chloe's statement.

"The choice is yours, and not one you have to make today. I want you to think long and hard about what we have all said and decide what works for you. No one will push you, darlin'."

Chloe looked at everyone, still amazed by how united they stood.

She got up and stood beside Santino, clasping his hand. "Thank you, Keith." She looked around. "I know this is as hard on all of you as it is me. I'm not sure what I want to do yet, except for one thing . . ." She repositioned herself in front of Santino, resting her hands on his hips. "The only thing I know for sure is I want to marry you. I don't care about anything else."

Santino yanked her closer. "How about tomorrow?"

"Tomorrow!" Valentina screeched. "I've pulled it off once, but that was a miracle. Can you at least give me a week?"

Feeling Chloe flinch, Santino yelled, "Ma! It's not your wedding to plan. We might elope, just the two of us." Even more firmly, he said, "The decision is ours to make."

Valentina took a step back at the finality in his voice.

Chloe saw the devastation on Valentina's face. Then she looked back up at Santino's angry face. She smoothed the frown lines on his forehead. "I want them with us. I also want Brooklyn, Luca, and the twins there. But . . ." She looked over to Valentina. "I only want our immediate family, and that includes Owen, Raimer, Quinn's daughter, Keith, and his wife. But that's it. I'm sorry. I wouldn't be comfortable with anyone else. How about in three weeks?"

Santino smiled from ear to ear. "Three weeks it is. And because you conceded, we will go on our honeymoon the minute the trial is over. Where have you always dreamt of going?"

Chloe's face flamed red. "I've never dreamed of going anywhere. I stopped dreaming years ago."

That hit everyone in the gut.

Sabastian looked at Alessandro, and they both nodded.

"Santino was instrumental in going beyond the call of duty for all of us, and I know you've heard how," Sabastian told her. "It's very important for the six of us to do something special for him. We have also fallen as much in love with you as he has."

Santino snorted through his nose—Humph!

Sabastian chuckled. "Okay, maybe not as much as the coglione. Do you trust us?"

Chloe squished her face together. "Yes, without a doubt."

Alessandro stepped forward. "Then let us plan your honeymoon. All you have to do is have your passport ready. I swear it will be the most romantic place on Earth. The trip of a lifetime. We want it to be perfect. A special thank you for completing our famiglia and the brother who held us all together."

Chloe was at a loss for words. Her mind was working overtime, trying to imagine just getting married, let alone traveling on a plane to an exotic location for her honeymoon. The first wasn't scary, but the second was. "I've never been on a plane or left the States. I don't have a passport."

"You have six weeks," Raimer told her. "You can apply in person today, and that will speed it up, and then you should have it in four weeks. And when you're done, I'm sure Valentina can swing a special appointment at her favorite bridal shop."

Emmy clapped her hands. "Can I come? Please? Sabastian, can you look after Shawn?"

"I'll phone right now." Valentina excitedly ran for her phone.

"Wait!" Chloe called out, causing everyone to stop.

"Stellina, speak your mind," Santino told her, drawing her chin toward his face. "Are we moving too fast?"

She shook her head, her long curls bouncing from side to side, her big blue eyes glazing over.

"Tell me."

"The only person I want to love my dress the day we get married is you. I don't care what I wear. Will you come with us and choose the dress that you'd like me in?"

He couldn't have been any prouder of his girl. "I would be honored. And, Mamma, if you say one word, you're not coming."

Valentina wanted to scream from the rooftop that it wasn't proper for the groom to see the bride in her dress before the wedding, but she wisely shut up. "Scustumad, I had no intention of saying anything."

Alessandro coughed into his hand, "Bullshit," and everyone burst out laughing at the absurdity of her statement.

Ava cuffed his head. "Do you have a death wish or something?"

Chloe had to wait to stop laughing before saying, "As long as the only one with a say is Santino, I don't care if everyone comes. Quinn—."

He lifted his hands, waving them. "No, sweetheart. Thanks for the offer, but I'm not any good at that stuff."

Chloe walked up to him. "That's not what I wanted to ask you. Will you give me away? And—" She couldn't finish her question, because he had pressed her face into his chest.

"I'd be honored. Thank you, sweetheart." He kissed her head.

She smiled at his fatherly response and squeezed him one last time. "I also want you to stand up for me."

His eyebrows hit the sky. Tilting his head, he asked, "You mean, be your maid of honor?"

Alessandro laughed the hardest. "Quinn, you're showing your age. Evidently, you haven't attended that many Savage weddings. Now that you're the maid of honor, you'll have to go with them to pick your dress."

"I guess that means Ava's in a tux. Gypsy, will you be my best wo . . . man?"

Ava, who hadn't had a large group of friends until this famiglia, beamed. "I would be honored, bestie. Quinn, I'll tell you what, I'll get a dress as best man, and you get a tux as maid of honor." She stuck her hand out. "Deal?"

With much relief, Quinn shook her hand. "Deal."

Santino marveled over the fact his famiglia had made a brutal situation into something amazing. He would have to remember to thank them all individually.

However, he was having second thoughts about letting Mamma come, because his Stellina would be getting the sexiest dress he could find so she would outshine any star.

Chapter 15
"One Man Band" by Old Dominion

Dress shopping had gone way better than any of them had expected.

Raimer, who wouldn't miss it for the world, had pulled Valentina aside to remind her that the couple had just had a traumatic day and to allow them to do it their way. Her first reaction was to spout off at him and give him a hard smack to his head, except she remembered Owen whispering to him before they had left. Apparently, the message was from him, so she accepted it with the goodwill it was offered.

Santino looked at the rack of last year's samples, but nothing caught his eye, so he went to the area of the sample dresses that the salesgirl said they couldn't sell, and that took six months to order a new one.

Valentina asked the sales clerk if she could have a moment with the owner alone. Before Valentina went into the office, she fired a quick text to Brooklyn. When she got her reply, she confidently went in to make a deal.

Valentina offered the owner a fashion shoot with Brooklyn at the resort to showcase next year's line of dresses if she allowed Santino to pick any dress in the store and have it altered in less than three weeks. Valentina told the woman that she was paying for the dress and any accessories.

The woman was thrilled with the offer and gave them carte

blanche. Then the owner pulled the salesgirl aside and told her. The girl couldn't believe it, and happily recanted her statement to Santino.

He walked into another room, and there on the mannequin was the elusive dress he didn't know he had been looking for. It was a princess style, with a sweetheart neckline that flared out to a full tulle bottom. Clear crystal gems encrusted the bodice and sparkled, cascading down the tulle like falling stars.

"This is the one," he said confidently. "Stellina, I want to see you in this."

Chloe was in awe as she moved forward, looking for the price tag, then asking the saleswoman how much.

Before the woman could answer, Valentina spoke from behind them, "It doesn't matter. If that is the dress, it is my gift to my new daughter." She raised her hands, seeing Chloe was going to argue. "I bought all the other girls' dresses. If you care to fight it out, I'm more than happy to oblige. But I guarantee you will not win this one.

"I didn't get to have my own daughters, but God has graced me with beautiful, adult women to replace the mix-up He made. So it is my honor and duty as your new mamma. Do you care to take that privilege from me?" She crossed her arms over her chest.

"Uh, no," Chloe responded quietly, knowing her future mother-in-law had a bite.

"Excellent. Then head to the dressing room, and this young woman will bring the dress for you to try on."

Chloe followed one woman, while two other women rushed in to take the dress off the mannequin. A short time later, Chloe beamed as she cautiously floated into the room, her limp not visible. She only had eyes for one person.

Santino's heart nearly stopped when he saw her. She radiated.

He slowly stood, walking around her as they guided her up onto the pedestal. He didn't say a word for two full rotations, making her nervous.

Chloe gnawed on her lip. She absolutely loved it and prayed he felt the same way. She couldn't imagine trying on another.

"So, does that mean you like it?"

Finally, he met her eyes. "No, baby." He clasped her waist. "I love you in it. You make the dress stunning. In my wildest fantasies, I never thought I would pick a dress like this, but baby, it was made for you. How can I possibly wait three weeks to see you in it again?"

Chloe smiled triumphantly as everyone joined in, gushing about how great she looked.

The saleswoman brought in a pair of high heels. "These will complement the dress perfectly." She showed them the gorgeous gem-encrusted shoes.

Santino saw the longing in her eyes, and the disappointment.

"Actually, I would prefer my girl in ballet shoes."

The woman looked aghast, but caught herself and left to retrieve delicate, little white satin ballet shoes with satin ribbons to tie up her legs.

Chloe giggled as she looked closer. On one shoe was written I and the other Do. That giggle alone told Santino all he needed to know.

Another woman came forward with veils and headpieces. They gathered her long locks to pin them up.

"Sorry, ladies, but her beautiful hair stays down." He then watched as they put headpiece after headpiece on her.

He remembered a picture his buddy's girlfriend had gone ga-ga over. "Do you have a headband similar to but not as overpowering as the one Kim Kardashian wore at her wedding?"

The owner grinned. "Coming right up. Chloe, follow me, please."

They took Chloe into the hallway, attached a similar yet less flamboyant headband and a veil, and then walked her back out.

"You look bellissima! I would marry you this second if I could."

Santino got up and captured her face, bending in to kiss her.

Valentina lurched up to stop them, thinking it was bad luck, but Raimer was quicker, grabbing her arm and shaking his head. She crossed her arms, changing her approach.

"Okay, we'll take everything. Measure the dress for alterations, and we'll be on our way."

By the pitch of her voice, Santino knew he had pushed his mamma as far as he could. He pulled back from Chloe's lips so they could finish.

When the dress was pinned for alterations, she changed, and then they left, picking up some take-out for everyone before heading home.

Santino didn't think the smile left Chloe's face once since they had left the store. She even fell asleep with one on her face after they made passionate love later that night. An hour later, her murmuring woke him up. The smile was gone, replaced by terror as Chloe started talking in her sleep.

"I didn't do anything! You're going to kill me, aren't you?" Her arms flailed like she was trying to get away, her head thrashing from side to side, and her fists were clenched tightly.

Santino was attempting to wake her when he realized she had switched to internalized thoughts.

"They're going to nail me to the cross to pay for what my father did, but they're afraid someone will hear the hammering. Why doesn't anyone understand that Harper and I were the first ones he hurt? No child should know the difference between the feel of a one-prong belt buckle from two." She took deep, excruciating breaths, whimpering, "Jacob saw the scars. How could he not wonder?"

It was too much for Santino. He gently pulled Chloe into his warm arms, petting her head and back. "I'm here, baby. You're safe. It's over. No one will ever hurt you again, I swear," he whispered as he ran his hand down her body, stopping at the familiar scars that brought new meaning to the different feel of the puckered skin.

Chloe had settled without waking, but he was left feeling hollow and utterly destroyed. How could anyone intentionally hurt the little girl she had been or this woman so profoundly?

Quinn had been working with Santino to become a better sounding board for her, but actively listening wasn't the problem. The problem was it took all his strength to hear about her suffering. He knew intrinsically that Chloe felt his tension and sugarcoated most of it for his benefit. He only heard the truth when she talked at night.

Maybe Ava was right and they needed to rip off the Band-Aid all in one fell swoop. He would convince her to get it all out in a victim impact statement so she could cleanse her soul. It occurred to him that he should also write and read one, explaining how her agony affected him. He knew from therapy that you could be right as rain all day, yet the minute you shut your eyes, the evilness that hid from the conscious mind would come out to play. He wondered when the last time was that she was able to have a night free of bad dreams. He knew she hadn't since they had been together.

***

The next morning, Santino covered her up before heading to the main resort to grab something for their breakfast. He knew Emmy would be up, but he hadn't expected his mamma to be there.

She frowned when she saw him. "What's wrong? I thought you would be walking on cloud nine."

Santino pulled up a stool and told them what he had heard last night, and how he was struggling right alongside Chloe. He also shared about the impact statement he was going to write.

Valentina knew in an instant she had to do the same thing. "I will also tell the courts what I did and why. I want anyone who will listen to understand what vigilante persecution can do to a normal person. It is the worst form of bullying, and we would never tolerate it from children, yet we justify it as adults. I understand now how dangerous it is, and that it needs to be stopped."

Santino looked at her in amazement. "I'm proud of you, Mamma. It takes a lot of courage to admit your wrongdoing and take accountability for it. I truly believe, with this closure, Dad and Marcello will finally rest in peace."

Valentina added six pancakes to the platter she was making for them. The bacon, hash browns, and scrambled eggs completed it.

She thought back to her biggest worries before the shooting and said, "I'd like some peace. These last five years have taken their toll on all of us. How nice would it be if our biggest complaint was that tomatoes were tasteless in the winter? Or how about complaining about the weather for a change? It's been too long. Life shouldn't be this hard."

Emmy listened as she took a fresh batch of tea biscuits out of the oven. She added four to a small plate for Santino to bring back to his cabin for a snack later. She couldn't allow them to wallow in all the bad.

"I agree. It has been hard for the last five years, but we can't forget how many good things have happened. Mamma, you have four healthy grandchildren, and a much larger extended family. Santino, you found the love of your life. If we didn't experience the bad, we might not be as thankful for all the good we have experienced."

Both softened at the truth.

"Thanks, Emmy. You're right. In less than a month, I'm going to be Chloe's husband and couldn't be happier. Hopefully, by this time next year, we'll be able to add to the grandchildren count." Santino took the last sip of his coffee, then covered the platter of food his mamma had made for them and placed the small plate on top. "Last night was hard on Chloe, so I'm going to join her in the daycare to plan the wedding."

***

Alessandro started playing the guitar as Chloe stepped into the room on Quinn's arm, shaking like a leaf. Santino stood by the fireplace in the resort's bar, his heart skipping a beat for the second time at seeing her in that dress, not believing this beautiful creature was his. They were getting married at eleven a.m., because Santino knew his bride would overthink all day if she had to wait.

Chloe started to walk as he sang "One Man Band" by Old Dominion. He was beginning to think he had regained control of his knees, until her eyes lit up and her giggling at the song he had chosen had them buckling again.

It wasn't a traditional love song, but the lyrics spoke volumes to Chloe. It was Santino's way of telling her, you could have words, but without all the components, it wasn't a song. They could survive without each other, but they wouldn't be making beautiful music. It was simply awe-inspiring that she understood it like he did, sending shivers up his spine.

At the end of the song, Chloe was beside him. The minister asked who gives this woman away and, proudly clearing his voice of emotion, Quinn said, "I do." Then he kissed her trembling cheek as any father would before guiding her hand to join with Santino's. Quinn then moved to the side so he could stand as her witness, while Ava moved to stand beside Santino.

The minister was talking about the virtues of marriage when Chloe yawned loudly. She covered her mouth to try to stifle the sound, but everyone started to giggle. Santino knew she hadn't slept much in the past four nights as her anxiety grew.

"I'm sorry." Chloe blushed, mortified that she had ruined the ceremony, begging the minister to continue.

The minister looked to Santino as he chuckled.

Turning to face his bride, Santino cupped her clammy jaw with his free hand. "Don't be sorry, Stellina. I know you haven't slept. The only thing I ask is that you stay awake long enough to say your vows and sign the papers."

She started to sway as she tried to get air into her strangled lungs. "I'm so embarrassed. I can't believe I did that." Black dots started to float in front of her eyes as her stress level increased.

Santino had just moved his hand to her back when her muscles relaxed completely and her eyes rolled back. He caught her as everyone around them gasped, and then he scooped under the layers of tulle, placing his arm under her knees and carrying her to a chair that Quinn pulled out.

When Chloe started to come around, Santino reassured everyone that she was fine, asking them to step out and give them a few minutes so she wouldn't be embarrassed further.

Chloe blinked her eyes open in confusion. "What happened?"

He smiled down. "You fainted."

Tears welled up in her eyes. "I've wrecked everything. I knew I would."

Santino's heart hurt for her as he rubbed his fingers through the long strands of hair hanging over his hand. "You wrecked absolutely nothing. And it was a miracle I didn't pass out first when I heard you giggle. Thank you for that beautiful gift."

She lowered her lashes. "I was really nervous, and I panicked, thinking how you give me so much while I'm coming into this marriage with nothing but a lot of baggage. Santino, are you sure you want to marry me? I wouldn't blame you for backing out. Nothing is ever easy for me, as you just experienced. It's a curse that isn't going away. Are you sure you can live with that?"

Lifting the elbow that her head was nestled in, Santino kissed her forehead. Then he slowly lowered it so he could look at her. "Stellina, you're not cursed. We all have baggage, but today is a new start for both of us. We'll still have baggage, but now we have each other to help carry it."

She swiped away a rogue tear. "But I ruined the wedding for everyone."

He shifted her up so she was sitting. "Chloe, I wanted this wedding for you, not anyone else. I want you to feel like a princess for one incredible day. I want to remember this day because it's the first time you feel free from your past. The vows you make today mean I get to have you for the rest of my life. We become partners in everything. The good, the bad, the ugly, and the beautiful. I know you think I'm sacrificing myself by marrying you, but you couldn't be more wrong."

Chloe's eyes grew wide. "How did you know?"

With his forefinger and thumb, he captured her chin to keep her looking at him. "You talk a lot in your sleep."

She tried to close her eyes, but he gave her a little shake.

"I don't know how to reassure you that I feel as lucky as you. I have met hundreds, if not thousands, of women, but the instant I laid eyes on you, I felt like I had found my balance for the first time. You are the only person I have ever had this connection with. I think my soul knew instantly you were the one person meant just for me.

"If I give you everything I have for the rest of my life, it will never be enough to return what I get from you. Sometimes my heart hurts so much I think I'm having a heart attack, but it's just bursting with the love I have for you."

Those big, beautiful cornflower blue eyes shimmered with unshed tears. With her soft, velvet voice, she caressed his soul when she said, "I love you too. You're the only person besides Harper that I felt I couldn't live without."

He couldn't help hugging her tightly to him. "Then I want you to savor this day and let everything else go. Today is the day we legally, and in the eyes of God, become one. I want you to smile knowing that." He set Chloe on her feet, but not before he gave her a swift, sharp swat under her dress to her ass. "It's you and me against the world, bellissima."

Chloe jumped with a squeak, quickly looking around the room to make sure it was empty. Then she gave him a stern look.

Santino got up and stood at his full height over her delicate frame, leaning down and clearly stating, "You'll pay for that defiant look later. Your little tushie is going to be as hot and pink as your face." He kissed behind her ear, where the skin was flaming hot.

A moan escaped from Chloe's throat with the thought of consummating their marriage with a sting of heat that he had placed so lovingly. He loved the sound she made.

"You couldn't be any more perfect for me, and one day soon you're going to trust me enough to let me tie you up and know you are safe to completely let go. But for now, let's get this show on the road. Your white, little tushie has a date later with my itchy palms."

Alessandro had caught a glimpse of the smack and heard his younger brother's directive after Mamma had ordered him to make sure they were okay. He'd had no idea his brother was dominant in the bedroom. By the look of Chloe, he had found exactly what he needed, in and out of the sheets. Alessandro assumed she would be resistant to being tied up because of the attack, but he was sure there were ways around that. Another thing he was going to have to research for the honeymoon.

Santino caught a glimpse of his brother near the doorway. "Alessandro, perfect timing. Can you call everyone in? Chloe's doing much better, and we're ready."

When his brother smirked, Santino had no doubt he had caught part of their conversation. Oh well, it was what it was. He wasn't embarrassed. He was sure all his brothers had some kinks of their own.

He took Chloe's hand, led her under the draped fabric beside the fireplace, and then waited for everyone to join them.

The wedding went off without another hitch as they exchanged the vows that they had written for each other. Santino patted his breast pocket where the marriage license was safely tucked away, breathing easier knowing Stellina was his wife, signed, sealed, and delivered.

Mamma and Emmy had made a beautiful brunch for the reception, and Chloe devoured her meal now that her nerves had settled and she was finally Mrs. Chloe Savage.

The cake was spectacular. Emmy had outdone herself, creating a three-tier wedding cake, knowing Chloe's favorite dessert. The bride squealed at the discovery of layers of Rice Krispies treats when they cut the gorgeous cake that had a cake topper in script that said Mr. & Mrs. and icing that sparkled like freshly fallen snow.

Eli ran up with Shawn wobbling behind him to see why his favorite people seemed to be so delighted with the cake.

Chloe cut three big pieces and guided the boys to her seat. Eli sat in Santino's chair beside her, and Shawn on her lap as they gorged on Rice Krispies cake until they couldn't stuff another piece in.

In the meantime, Santino went to Emmy, filled with so much gratitude for all she had done for them. As a matter of fact, his whole famiglia had made it the most amazing day, and he thanked them all accordingly.

When it was time to start the dancing, some of the men cleared the tables in the dining room as Luca set up the karaoke machine. Sabastian dimmed all the lights except the chandelier that they would dance under and started the smoke machine. Swirling clouds billowed around their feet as the two joined each other in the center of the room for their first dance as husband and wife.

The two little boys squealed, running around and through the whimsical smoke. Their parents tried to corral them, but Chloe stopped them, insisting it was fitting to have two little angels in the clouds with them.

The couple sang "The Prayer" by Celine Dion and Andrea Bocelli to each other as they glided around the floor. Chloe had never danced, so Santino convinced her to place her tiny feet on his. It was a breathtaking scene that Chloe would watch for years to come from the video and photos Valentina had insisted they have. She would even laugh at herself for passing out in Santino's arms and remember the words he had said to her when the cameras were turned off.

Chloe had taken heed to his words—letting go completely for the first time—and had a blast. They had only expected the reception to last until dinner, but Chloe and everyone else was having so much fun that they kept celebrating. Mamma brought out all kinds of antipastos for everyone to munch on throughout the night.

It was ten o'clock when Santino finally took the microphone from his wife before she could start singing another duet with Sabastian, announcing they were leaving. Even though Chloe was having fun, he knew she was exhausted, and he had waited long enough to get his wife all to himself.

Alessandro boldly asked if he and Ava should stay in the main resort, seeing as they were their closest neighbors, or if they were going to keep it down.

Chloe dropped her face into her husband's chest as he suggested all their neighbors should take rooms in the main lodge.

Eli was fascinated by the conversation and looked at his uncle. "If you and Aunt Chloe are hammering and making lots of noise, I want to come with you."

Everyone exploded into fits of laughter at the innocence of the child's misunderstanding.

Santino knelt so he could look into his eyes. "Sorry, cucciolo, I would invite you, but this is adult-only hammering. It can be dangerous if not done correctly. But tomorrow, we can hammer some stuff."

Chloe nudged Santino's back with her knee, dying a thousand deaths as Ava choked.

Valentina was getting ready to cuff him one. Would her sons ever stop to think before blabbering off in front of the kids?

Luca came up with one of his daughters in his arms. "Actually, cucciolo, I need to fix one of the tables before we leave. Why don't you help me, and we'll see if we can't make more noise than them? Nonna, can you take Reece?"

A little disappointed, the boy answered, "Okay, Daddy, but it sounds like they're going to have fun."

Alessandro, being Alessandro, couldn't resist. "Eli, they are going to have fun, and before you know it, you'll find a girl you'll want to hammer with."

"Or a boy," Raimer threw out there.

Properly chastised, Alessandro repeated, "Or a boy."

Eli looked at Raimer with his arm around Owen. "Do you hammer loudly with Owen?"

Brooklyn placed the hand that wasn't holding Marcella over Raimer's mouth as Santino stood up and grabbed Chloe's hand. "O . . . kay. On that note, I think we should be leaving. Thank you all for making this day so special for the both of us." He turned to face his bride. "You ready, Mrs. Savage?"

She smiled proudly from ear to ear. "Ready, Mr. Savage."

He grabbed her hand and proceeded out of the main lodge. They ran as quickly as her dress would allow due to the cold. Chloe's laugh was like twinkling bells when it was from the belly. Santino loved to hear it.

He was so horny by the time he closed the door, he demanded she take the dress off right where they stood.

Chloe bit her lip. "Make me," she answered coyly.

Santino made an animalistic sound that had her nipples pulling into tight buds and created a quivering in her womb. "You already have a spanking coming; don't make it worse on yourself, wife."

With bravado she didn't know she possessed, she shook her head.

A sinfully wicked grin appeared on his face. She had laid the challenge down, and now he had to figure out how far to take it.

"Oh, wife, you've made my cock go from rock-hard to diamond status," Santino said as he stalked toward her, grabbing her hair close to the roots and angling her head so she couldn't help seeing the dilated pupils of the alpha male she had unhinged.

Chloe's breath hitched at the slight sting. Her body was on fire with excitement and trepidation. The submissive in her wanted to antagonize the boss in him.

Not giving her a chance to overanalyze, he pushed her down to her knees as he undid his belt. Her eyes enlarged, igniting with a spark of lust. She might think he was in control, but that couldn't be farther from the truth. Chloe held all the power.

With a deep baritone voice, Santino barked, "Hands behind your back, clasp your fingers, and don't release them until I tell you otherwise." Arching his brow, he said, "Not a word."

She swallowed saliva down her suddenly dry throat as she followed his instructions to the letter.

Santino allowed his pants to fall to his ankles as he yanked his cock out of his Armani's and stroked himself from root to tip in front of her face. Pre-come covered his fingers, and he lifted them to her lips. "You caused this, so clean them."

Chloe slid her tongue out of her mouth and swirled it around his fingers, laving the clear fluid.

Santino totally lost his shit at the interactive show in front of him. Chloe looked like an innocent angel kneeling in that dress as she prodded the devil.

He snatched his fingers away and grabbed both sides of her head. "Open." Santino lost all control, jamming in as much of his cock as he could before hitting the back of her throat, causing her to gag and her eyes to water. He immediately pulled out, afraid he had hurt her. "Sorry, baby, are you okay?"

Chloe blinked, clearing her throat. "More." She licked her pink lips.

His knees buckled as he grabbed the root of his cock and squeezed hard to stop himself from coming on that one word. Releasing himself, he then grabbed her head tighter as he mastered his urge to plow back in.

She leaned in and sealed her mouth around his hard, sensitive length, sucking every inch enthusiastically.

All semblance of control vanished as he vigorously pumped in and out of her mouth. It took a mere two minutes before he coated her mouth, roaring with his climax. Then he pulled himself from between her lips, seeing her triumphant smile. Reaching around, he grabbed her elbow, guided her to the bench, and upended her onto his lap. She screeched, moving her hands to the floor, afraid she was going to faceplant.

Santino secured her legs between his as he tossed all the fabric up, slapping the right cheek of her ass. "What you just did was topping, wife." He slapped her other cheek, pleased with both handprints. "You controlled that whole scene." Smack! After each slap, he rubbed the sting away. "Who's in charge here?" Smack!

Chloe yelped. "You are." Then she moaned from the comfort of the soothing light brush of his hand. The spanking stopped her mind from going beyond the here and now. It allowed her to concentrate on the pain, not the slutty way she was acting.

"That's right." Smack! After rubbing the spot, he grabbed her thong and dragged it off. It was saturated with her excitement. He brought it closer to his nose and relished in her scent. "You like this, don't you?"

She squirmed with the embarrassing question.

Smack!

"Yes!" she screamed.

He moved his hand between her legs. "You're so wet for me that it's dripping down your legs. That's my perfect girl. I love that you weep for me." He flipped her up. "Can you straddle me?"

Chloe shook her head, disappointment filling her eyes.

It vanished the minute she felt the sting in exactly the same spot of the last slap.

In the blink of an eye, Santino hoisted her up against the door as she curled her good leg around his hip. He held up her bad hip and used his upper body to pin her in place against the door. Not giving her chance to second-guess, he rammed in fast and furiously.

Chloe cried out his name as she dug her nails into his shoulders.

"My fucking hot wife," he chanted. "You're so goddamn perfect."

It didn't take long for Chloe to reach her pinnacle. She yelled his name, then slumped, figuring he would be right behind her.

"Not even close to being done, wife," he grunted out. "I'm gonna keep going, and you're gonna keep coming. Next time, you'll think twice about topping me."

He was true to his word. Only after she came two more times did he finally relent and let himself come. Then Santino carried his exhausted wife into their bedroom, stripped her bare, and followed her into bed.

As he snuggled her into his chest, he couldn't help looking heavenward. "You were right, Dad. She was worth fighting everyone for."

Chapter 16
"Concrete Angel" by Martina McBride

On the first day of court, the charges against Jacob were read. First-degree kidnapping, unlawful confinement, aggravated assault, and cruelty to animals. His pricey lawyer's defense was guilty by reason of temporary insanity, the repercussions of PTSD following a mass shooting. It was the first time that culpability and competency were being justified and tested after homegrown terrorism.

Less than one percent of cases heard in the courts pleaded insanity, and only a quarter of them were successful. It was a risky defense for Jacob because, if he were to lose, there would be no cases to cite in appellate court.

The first week of marriage had flown by before Santino knew it, and now he sat in the courtroom with Keith, listening to testimony.

Jacob's merry band of idiots, or not such idiots, all took lesser charges, agreeing to testify against him. So much for honor among thieves, or idiots.

Santino was one of the first to testify, along with his brothers, so he was free to listen to the rest of the court proceedings. The prosecutor assumed the trial would only last a week because the evidence was stacked against Jacob. The fact that he lived a very normal life with no other signs of insanity throughout the years before he set up Chloe, very much worked against his defense.

Chloe opted not to attend the trial, and didn't testify. She was still writing her impact statement, even though she thought it was premature. She had asked Santino not to tell her about the trial, hoping not to relive it each night. However, her happiness had been short-lived, and now she was back to having nonstop nightmares. Also, phantom pains made her hip and leg ache more than usual, and her limp was more prominent.

She thanked the powers above every day for having the children to look after. No matter how shitty she felt, their innocent happiness was infectious.

During the day, when Sabastian or Emmy took Shawn, and Eli wasn't home from school or was at an afterschool activity, she would spend her time helping Brooklyn with the twins. Sabastian purposely didn't bring Shawn to the little daycare as early as usual, allowing her to help Brooklyn feed and bathe the babies at the beginning of the day.

When Santino came home from court, he spent every minute with Chloe, no matter where she was. It was as much for his comfort as for hers after hearing the horrific facts of Jacob's plan and execution of each shocking detail that he arranged to eliminate Chloe.

They spent a lot of time at night in their different roles of submissive and dominant to help them both through the stress. But since the trial had started, Santino couldn't spank Chloe, which left her frustrated and doing naughty things, desperately needing the separation from her mind and the release it gave her.

Today, Alessandro found her behind the shed, tears silently falling down her face. "Chloe, what's wrong?" Lost in her thoughts, she hadn't seen him approach and yelped with fright before embarrassment took over. "Nothing."

He sat on a log beside her and placed an arm over her shoulder. "I know the trial is hard on you. What can I do or say to make it better?"

She hiccupped after pulling herself together. "The only one who can help me is Santino." She swiped the tears away, glancing up at him through wet eyelashes, wondering how much she could tell him. "And he's . . . afraid I'm too fragile; that I'll break. He's handling me with kid gloves. I've tried everything. I don't know . . . Oh, forget it. Please, can we talk about something else?"

Guessing what her self-consciousness was about but knowing he wasn't the person she needed to talk to, he changed the subject, asking if she was excited about the honeymoon. Chloe begged him to tell her something about the location so she could pack accordingly.

"You don't have to pack anything. Santino bought you everything you need for your trip. He wanted you to have a fresh start after the trial."

A little surprised, she looked at the time on her phone, then stood to get back to work. "I have to get back to Shawn. Does Santino know where we're going?"

"No, but I did tell him the climate." He got up and started escorting her to the daycare, seeing her limp was more prominent. "Did you hurt your leg or hip?" When Chloe tried to correct her limp, he nudged her arm before threading his arm through hers. "Don't do that. If your hip hurts, don't try to overcompensate so people won't notice. Walk whichever way you're comfortable."

"Yeah." She rubbed the ache. "I don't know why. I haven't done anything to aggravate it."

"Why don't you go to the spa and get one of the girls to give you a massage? You're strung tighter than a guitar string."

That caused Chloe's face to turn beet-red. She tucked her hands into her pockets. "No, thanks."

Alessandro changed their direction, heading toward the main lodge. "Yes, Chloe. Do it for Santino. He's struggling—so worried about you." Alessandro knew the only way she would do it was if he guilted her. "If you're more relaxed, he will be too. He's trying to carry the weight of the world on his shoulders. Give him this little concession."

Her shoulders slumped. "I don't have time now. I have to pick up Shawn. Maybe tomorrow."

"Let me take care of Shawn. Come on." He wasn't letting her get out of this.

Alessandro brought her into the main lodge and went straight into the spa. The woman in reception told him that she thought one of the registered masseuses was free and went to get her.

Chloe whirled around. "I don't have any money."

Alessandro's face screwed up. "You don't need money. You're a Savage. They work for you."

Aghast, she twisted her fingers in dismay. "No, I'm not part of the business."

He gently untangled her fingers, quietly asking, "What is your last name?"

"Savage, but—"

"No buts about it." He cut her off with a swipe of his hand. "Santino must have forgotten to tell you with the trial going on, but the minute you became legally one of us, you became a full partner. If you want to tip the masseuse, I'll give you some cash, and you can pay me back."

Overwhelmed, she grabbed the counter, swaying. "No, that's not right." She whispered even quieter, "You guys already pay me to look after my nieces and nephews, which is insane. I'm not a partner. I can't be. Nobody has ever trusted me that much." Most of what she said was really meant to be an inside thought, so she jumped when he replied.

"I can't punish you for such a degrading statement," he snapped back, angry at everyone who had ever made her feel like that. "But I can assure you my brother will when I tell him." He then lightened up at the look on her face.

Chloe was baffled, trying to figure out how much he knew. Or was he just assuming? Did Alessandro and Ava have the same relationship as her and Santino? She couldn't imagine Ava submitting to anyone.

She shook her head at the absurdity of her thoughts and was saved from answering when the masseuse came through the door.

"Mrs. Savage has a prior injury that is bothering her. Please see what you can do. She also wanted to make sure you got your tip." Alessandro pulled a twenty from his pocket and handed it to the masseuse.

The woman beamed at Chloe. "Thank you, Mrs. Savage. I'm sure I can help. Come this way."

Chloe swallowed uneasily, not wanting to offend the woman, but why the freak was Alessandro calling her Mrs. Savage? They never used formalities at the resort. "Please, call me Chloe," she said, following the woman through the door.

Alessandro texted Santino, telling him that he wanted to talk in private when he got back. Santino responded, telling him that he was just pulling in, and Alessandro met him in the parking lot as he was getting out of his car.

"Got a minute, bro?"

Shutting the door, Santino said, "Yeah. Is everything okay? Where's Chloe?" The panic was instant when he saw his brother struggling to tell him something.

Alessandro leaned his back against the car. "I just made her go for a massage. Her leg and hip are really bothering her. I found her behind the shed, crying."

Santino tensed, getting ready to go to her, not caring where she was, until Alessandro grabbed his forearm.

"She's fine. We talked. But now I have to address something with you that might be crossing the line. However, Chloe's mental health has to come first."

Santino didn't know how much more he could take today after hearing Jacob's testimony that made him want to kill someone. He stretched his neck muscles, moving his head from side to side. He needed a massage as desperately as his wife.

He leaned back against the car, smirking as he asked, "I guess this is payback for the shit I pulled with Ava?"

His playful comment gave Alessandro the confidence to continue. "You're right. Fanculo! Okay, coglione, here goes. But remember, ask questions first before you start hitting." He paused. "I know you're a Dominant and Chloe is a submissive, and whatever you usually do, you aren't, and she's feeling lost and insecure."

Santino wasn't embarrassed about who he was and could discuss it with Alessandro with no problem, but he would never have suspected Chloe would have. With the realization, his eyebrows hit the sky as he asked, "Stellina talked to you about it?"

Alessandro shook his head.

"Ah, then you saw a little more than you should have the day of the wedding, right?"

Alessandro nodded.

"Come on, bro; you must have felt the same things growing up—being bossed around and having no authority with three older brothers and a controlling mamma. Chloe allows me to make all the decisions in the bedroom. After the life she's had, she doesn't want to be responsible for not being a good girl to get what she needs. I take all the worry away and make sure she can only concentrate on us."

Alessandro crossed his arms over his chest, shaking his head. "Damn, if I tried that shit with Ava, she'd have my balls in her purse."

"That's because Ava isn't submissive. Jacob taught Chloe to associate love with pain. Don't get me wrong; I don't beat her with whips or chains—the sting of my hand does the job. It's not sick, and neither one of us is a masochist or sadist."

Hands raised, Alessandro said defensively, "I never assumed either one of you were. But whatever you usually do has changed, and she doesn't know how to deal with it."

Now it was Santino's turn to get defensive. "I haven't been able to spank her since the trial started. Hearing and seeing evidence of the abuse she went through makes me sick. I'm starting to question if I'm doing the same thing. But she isn't getting off. Chloe actually faked climaxing last night. My girl is as easy to read as a book. I don't know what to do."

Alessandro clapped his shoulder. "Stop making it about you, coglione. You might need tender right now, but she needs to know nothing has changed because of what you're hearing. Stop changing the rules on her without discussing it. You're not helping Chloe; you're confusing her." He looked at his watch. "I told her I would look after Shawn for her. Take the rest of the day off and give her a solid hammering."

Santino burst out in laughter. Then he hugged his brother, slapping his back. "Thanks, man. And if you ever decide to walk on the wild side, send Ava to me for training."

Alessandro gave his brother a well-deserved punch in the gut. "Fanculo, I don't need a dominatrix. She already carries one of my balls around in her purse."

Santino walked away, still laughing as he went to the spa to wait for his wife.

Chloe stumbled when she saw Santino sitting there. "Um . . . I got a massage. I hope that's okay?"

Extending his hand, he pulled her closer and kissed the side of her head. "Did it help?"

Chloe grinned. "Yes. I didn't think it would, but it was amazing. Franny said the muscles were so tight that it was making it hard for the bones to move properly."

She stopped when he did, as Santino turned to the receptionist.

"What day does Franny work late?"

"Thursdays," the woman responded.

"Perfect. Can you book a weekly appointment for my wife at seven?"

"Yes, I'll enter it into the computer. Shall I send Chloe a text at six each week to remind her?"

"Actually, send it to me. I'll make sure she gets here. Thank you." Santino held the door open, gesturing to get her moving.

Chloe put the brakes on after they cleared the door and it closed. "You can't make appointments or talk about me like I'm not there. What if I don't want a massage every week?"

He lowered his voice a few octaves as he bent to her ear. "You already have twenty swats coming." He pulled back a bit and narrowed his eyes at her. "Do you want to continue to add to the number? Because if you do, I'm happy to oblige. I'll use my left hand, because my right will already be stinging from the ones you've already earned."

Chloe didn't say a word as her pupils dilated and she shivered.

"That's what I thought. I don't like that you have been topping me all week and provoking me. I think that deserves another ten. That's thirty, Chloe. And after each one, you will thank me. If you forget, we start at one again. Do you understand?"

She nodded.

"You know I need a verbal response. That's thirty-one."

"Yes, Sir."

He chuckled. "That's husband, not Sir." She had never called him Sir, and he didn't want her to. "I'll forgive this one transgression because we've never discussed it, but it will cost you next time. Do you understand, Stellina?"

Mesmerized, she blinked ever so slowly, replying, "Yes, husband."

"Are you hungry? Because you have a long night ahead of you, and you'll need all your energy."

"Yes, husband."

"Good girl. Let's grab some food, and when we get back to our place, you will strip the instant we walk through the door, while I serve dinner. You will be naked, kneeling beside me as I feed you, and you will not utter a word until you are fed and properly punished."

Her eyes glazed over with relief. "Yes, Husband." Shivering again, she whispered softly, "Thank you, husband."

Chloe didn't utter another word, except for counting and calling out Santino's name in completion until he had her in the bath, soothing her stinging ass. Then he comforted her as she told him how sorry she was for not asking him for what she needed. They both slept a lot better that night.

***

After seven days of evidence, the verdict had been reached and read the day before. Jacob Moore was found guilty, and the temporary insanity plea denied. Today, all the famiglia was at the sentencing to support those reading their victim impact statements.

Chloe was a nervous wreck, but Santino reassured her that, if she didn't want to or couldn't read her statement, he would do it for her.

The courtroom was packed as the judge invited Chloe up to read her statement. It was the first time any of the reporters or the court personnel had seen her, other than in the horrific pictures that had been entered into evidence.

Santino wrapped his arm around her waist as she shook at the podium. Keith had requested a microphone be set up because Chloe's voice was soft.

She looked at Santino, and he nodded. Then Chloe took a deep breath, looked down at her paper, and started.

"I would like to thank the judge and the court for allowing me to be heard. My name is Chloe Marsh Savage, and I am the daughter of the Las Vegas shooter and married into the family of two of his victims.

"Jacob Moore tried to make me accountable for my father's actions, but what he failed to understand was my twin sister, Harper, and I were his first victims.

"Life wasn't easy growing up with that man. I can't tell you why he hated us or what we did to evoke those feelings. He demeaned us every chance he got, and would fly into fits of rage for the smallest infractions, like reading or playing too loud. We were beaten with belts, tree branches, or pieces of broken chairs, and locked in our room to heal for days."

Santino shuddered at the image of the cute little girls being beaten with a broken chair. He had never felt so helpless in his life.

With his fingers around her waist, he tapped her side in intervals of five. He then shifted on his feet, trying to stop himself from bolting and not having to hear the rest. Before he could, though, Chloe continued.

"For a short time, we lived on a farm. Twice, when we were outside playing too loudly, he came out, pointed a gun at us, and shot the ground close to our feet, threatening to kill us if we didn't shut up. He laughed when we peed ourselves as we silently stood there, crying, too terrified to move an inch. We were seven years old.

"A few times, he dumped us on an abandoned road, telling us that we wouldn't be found before the elements or animals killed us. Once, we spent all night huddled together in a cold ditch before he came back."

Santino tried to wipe the tears before they fell, as did everyone who sat there, listening. He could hear his mamma, Emmy, Brooklyn, and Ava all sobbing. But what really broke him was hearing the stoic Sebastian breathe in a heaving sob while holding his sleeping son. He also heard Alessandro curse quietly and Raimer, just as quietly, swear in Spanish.

God help him, he had to get his shit together to stand strong beside his wife.

"He was a man who knew how to act normal in front of most people and coworkers, but I always thought someone had to have heard or seen something that made them think twice, yet no one ever helped us. There was no escape. We were left to wonder every day if that day would be our last.

"When we were ten, our parents got into an argument, and our mom finally decided to leave him. We stood near the car, shocked that she was abandoning us to that monster. We stared at each other, frozen in fear, as the car backed up and crushed my sister."

Chloe stopped and bit her lip, breathing deeply, trying to maintain her composure. She had promised Harper that she wouldn't cry. She would deliver her statement with the dignity that they had both deserved.

"The day Harper died, I wished I had died too, because it had to be easier than being left behind, alone, with no one to protect or love me.

"The day he threw me over the banister, down the center corridor of three flights of stairs, I was surprised no one questioned it. I spent a year recovering, with everyone believing he had saved my life from a fire.

"One day, while I was still recovering, he disappeared. I never saw him again. I don't know why he left, but I always slept with one eye open, waiting for him to come back and finish the job.

"My mom died, consumed with guilt. I was eighteen and all alone, but determined to make the best of my life by helping others. I worked with veterans who were trying to assimilate back into society. I could have grown bitter, and should have, but I owed it to Harper to only see the good in the world because she hadn't seen much of any. Harper taught me how to love and be loved. So, when a shy, young, damaged loner was swept off her feet by a handsome young man in college, I clung to him like a lifeline. I believed him when he promised me a life filled with happiness and love. But it was all a lie.

"I didn't know anyone could hurt me as much as my father had, but Jacob Moore proved me wrong. He destroyed what I had managed to rebuild in Harper's honor. He accused me of being Satan's spawn, but he was the evil one.

"After attacking and injuring me, he destroyed the only possessions I had left of the family that I loved, as well as made sure I lost my job. In four days, he succeeded in what took my father twelve years to do. I lost everything, and was back to wishing for death. And he even gave me the means in which to achieve it.

"I hadn't felt that alone since the day I heard my father was responsible for the deaths of fifty-eight people.

"I'm so sorry for the families of the victims, because I know how it feels to lose someone you love to him. I understand the gut-wrenching feeling of having your world turned upside down from a senseless act. But I didn't kill those people, and I didn't know he would kill them, any more than Jacob or any of you did. I hadn't seen or heard from the man in years. Would I have stopped it if I could? The answer is yes, because I wouldn't want anyone to suffer like I did.

"Judge, when you sentence Jacob, I hope you make him pay for his crimes, but also show him some leniency. Maybe if someone had taught my father the difference between right and wrong, he could have been helped before he snapped. Maybe if he was a better person, those people wouldn't have been killed and thousands of lives shattered.

"Jacob, I hope you learn to control your temper, and that you regret the decisions you made, because Harper taught me love is stronger than hate.

"Thank you, Judge, for your consideration."

Chloe folded her paper and moved aside so Santino could give his statement. She still hadn't looked over at him, afraid she would crumble if her eyes met his. But when he didn't move, she did glance over just as the judge asked him if he needed a recess.

Santino nodded silently, sobbing beside her.

As the judge suggested a fifteen-minute break, people got up to clear the courtroom, and Chloe turned, tucking herself into his arms. "I'm okay," was all she could get out.

His chest convulsed as he asked, "How, Stellina? How are you so strong and loving?"

"By the grace of God, Harper's spirit, and you."

They stayed like that until the court reconvened. Then Santino drew his strength from the strongest person he knew—his wife. He unfolded his paper, but instead of reading from it, he looked at the judge, and then at Jacob.

"I would like to thank the court for giving me the chance to tell the judge how this experience affected me and the one I love. I had a statement written, but I would like to speak freely." He glanced back over at the judge.

"I'm sorry, Mr. Savage, but your statement has been entered and recorded. You must read what is written. I don't want my sentencing tainted by legalities."

Santino nodded, then began.

"I would like to thank the court and the judge for considering my impact statement. My name is Santino Savage, and the victim in this case is Chloe Savage, my wife." He reached for her hand and squeezed.

"I understand Jacob Moore better than most. My dad and oldest brother were killed in the Las Vegas massacre. I understand the feelings of helplessness, anger, and even vengefulness. But after meeting Chloe, I don't understand how Jacob couldn't see she was also her father's victim.

"Chloe is the bravest, most loving person I know. I don't know how she is so good after learning all the things she suffered as a child, but she is. I watched this woman come to our resort, a happy bride-to-be, willing to give Jacob everything. Then I watched him abuse, degrade, and hurt her, leaving her broken and shattered to the point of lifting a noose around her neck that Jacob had left for her, to end her misery. His ultimate goal was to drive her to commit suicide, thereby keeping his own hands clean.

"I will never have the words to tell you how it felt seeing her strung upside down on a wooden cross, tortured, covered in blood, terrified, and whimpering. Even after losing my dad and brother, I honestly didn't know humans could be that cruel. But after witnessing all of that, nothing could have prepared me for watching her clutch the picture of her beloved twin that had been destroyed beyond recognition. Every picture she had left of the people she loved had been burnt to a crisp on her bed."

Santino stopped, choking on a cry, and then he tried to continue between deep breaths. "It was the first time I watched the lifeline of a person bleed out in sorrow, the same way blood would from a gunshot wound. Jacob had maimed her soul.

"I can't imagine how she felt, but I can tell you that I hold her each and every night when she relives those horrors. Chloe wakes up screaming for help, terrified they're going to kill her. I can wipe away the tears, but I can't wipe away the memories."

Santino choked again on the truth of his words. He wondered how either of them would ever sleep soundly again.

When he couldn't seem to catch his breath, Alessandro asked the judge if he could read the rest of his statement, and told Santino to sit with his wife.

Valentina was a mess by the time it was her turn. Quinn, in his infinite wisdom, helped her up and read her statement for her.

It was a humbling experience for Chloe to hear. She wished she could have told everyone what Valentina did to make up for it. She had forgiven her, but Valentina obviously hadn't forgiven herself.

When all was said and done, and after a lunch break, the judge called the court in session and read Jacob's sentence.

After making him stand, he talked about some of the same things Valentina had—about vigilantism and the dangers of it. Then he apologized to Chloe for the system failing her continuously. He preached about social responsibility and not being afraid to get involved. He told Jacob that, even after all she had been through, Chloe had still asked for leniency on his behalf. The judge honored Chloe's request and made psychiatric treatment mandatory as part of his sentence. In the end, he gave him seven years in a federal penitentiary. Then he asked Jacob if there was anything he wanted to say to the court.

Jacob declined, and then it was over.

After getting through the hordes of reporters, the family went home, where a bunch of their friends from the community had dinner waiting for them.

Before they sat down, someone knocked on the door.

Keith said he would get it. He was at his limit with the press, ready to charge whomever was on the other side of the door with trespassing.

He yanked the door open, snapping, "What can I do for you?"

Taken aback, the man stepped back a few steps. "I'm sorry to bother you. I'm looking for Chloe Savage."

Puffing himself up and shifting his belt where his gun rested, the sheriff asked, "Who the hell are you, and what do you want?"

The man cleared his throat. "I'm Reverend Patrick O'Connor. I was friends with Mrs. Savage's parents."

Keith had been so angry that he had neglected to see the collar the man wore. "Sorry, Reverend." He was unsettled at swearing in front of man of God. "You're a friend of Chloe's father?" the lawman within him asked protectively, narrowing his eyes and looking for an ulterior motive. "What's your business with Chloe? Does she know you?"

Reverend O'Connor shook his head. "No, sir, she doesn't know me. I haven't seen any of the family since we parted ways about a year after college. I've been following the case and thought I could offer some help to Mrs. Savage. I was neighbors with Lori. More of a friend to her than the father, and I felt the need to reach out to her daughter now that she's alone."

"I'm sure she'd appreciate the offer of spiritual guidance, but that young lady isn't alone anymore. She has a big family who loves her."

Keith stepped outside and closed the door behind him. "Listen, I'm not trying to be rude, but Chloe has been through a lot, and we're very protective of her. If you are who you say you are, then allow me to do a background check. If everything comes back clean, I'll ask Chloe if she wants to meet you." He took his little pad out and flipped open to a blank page. "I'll need your driver's license."

The reverend pulled his wallet out and handed his license to Keith. "I mean her no harm. I heard the stories of the type of mother Lori was in the papers. That's not the girl I grew up with. I want Mrs. Savage to have some good memories of her mom."

Keith softened a bit as he handed back the license once he had written down the information, tucking his notepad back into place. "If everything checks out, I'll talk to Chloe. Although, I warn you now, it won't be alone. I know for sure her husband will want to be present, and truthfully, I will also be there."

The reverend smiled. "I understand. I'll be waiting to hear from you. Thank you, Sheriff."

Chapter 17
"Con Te Partiro" by Andrea Bocelli

Chloe stood at the open window of their room, breathing in the distinct salty air as she gazed at the Grand Canal. Never in the far reaches of her imagination had she ever considered she would be in one of the most romantic cities in the world. She couldn't conceive of a city with no cars and canals for roads. This was the perfect place for a woman who loved to explore.

As she had walked the island, looking across the other side at the charming buildings that emerged from the water had fascinated her. The gentleman who had welcomed them to the hotel had told her that most of the stilted buildings had been built eight hundred years ago. Chloe questioned how something so beautiful could be strong enough to withstand so many years in water.

Santino walked out of the washroom after his shower with a towel wrapped around his waist, using another one to dry his hair.

Chloe was already dressed, the breeze lifting some of her long ringlets off her bare shoulders. She was stunning in a white, strapless maxi dress that fell to her ankles. Her little feet were lifted onto her toes, hands braced on the window ledge as she leaned over, watching a boat that had caught her eye moving down the waterway. He knew the smile he could scarcely see from her profile would melt his heart.

It brought him back to the airport, when their famiglia had come to see them off. Chloe had been speechless when Sabastian had presented her with the tickets to Venice for a week, and then to a private villa in Tuscany for another week. After Alessandro had told her about clothes for a specific climate, she had assumed they were going to the Caribbean.

Luca and Brooklyn had loaded every chick flick that took place in Venice or Tuscany onto Santino's tablet. On the flight, Chloe had watched The Tourist, Under the Tuscan Sun, and had fallen asleep after Letters to Juliet.

Santino had woken up a few times after her eyes had finally closed and checked on his wife. Her head had been tucked into his arm, softly blowing out little puffs of air. He couldn't have been happier they were going to Italy so he could share some of his heritage with her.

Even a week after the sentencing, Santino was still struggling with everything he had heard. He hadn't passed a ditch since without stopping and imagining Chloe and Harper as tiny girls, huddling together, shivering, terrified of the dark. Now it made so much sense why she had to have the bathroom light on to sleep.

He couldn't stand it when she was out of his sight for any length of time. Every minute they were together, he felt the need to touch her. Somehow, feeling the warmth of her hand or her body calmed his nerves. He knew a few times she was feeling claustrophobic, but one look into his eyes and she relented. Santino hoped, with only the two of them on their honeymoon, he would settle down.

"You take my breath away, Stellina," he told her, tossing the towel he was drying himself with onto a chair.

Chloe turned with a stunning smile. "I can't believe we're in Venice. I feel like I'm dreaming.

"I saw a gondola. Can you believe it? It was so beautiful, and I could hear the man singing to the tourists. There are also boats that are like buses or subways. They pull up to the station, and people get on and off, carrying groceries and baby strollers."

The animated way she talked and her smile were infectious. He grinned back. "Would you like to go on one?"

She looked back out when she heard the boat pulling up to the station across the canal. "I would love to." Chloe giggled with glee. "I can pretend I'm a real Italian. I'll carry a bag with bottled waters like I just went grocery shopping and I'm carrying fresh ingredients home to make pasta with a fresh sauce made from Italian tomatoes. Let's go and blend in with the locals."

He laughed. He couldn't deny this woman anything. "I meant a gondola." He dropped the towel around his waist, facing her buck naked.

She screeched, closing the curtained window. "Santino! They can see you from the boats."

He grabbed a pair of Armani boxer briefs out of his luggage, slipping them on. "So what? They'll never see us again. Open the window back up; I'm covered."

Chloe waited until he slipped on his pants, then opened the window. She was torn between looking at the gorgeous scenery outside or her gorgeous husband.

He yanked on a funky T-shirt to complement his ripped jeans. On any other guy, the outfit would look grubby, but her man looked like a model for those European cologne ads.

Santino grabbed his silver necklace from off the desk, putting it on. He was trying to latch a leather bracelet when he felt her staring.

Not lifting his head, he shifted his eyes over. "Stellina, if you keep looking at me like that, the only part of Venice you're going to see is out that window from the bed."

Shifting lightly from foot to foot, she contemplated her options. "That's a difficult choice."

He barked out a laugh. "I think I've created a monster. Come on, wife; gondola ride, early dinner, and then you can watch the sunset from bed. Tomorrow, Sabastian booked us a private tour in Murano at a glass factory, so we'll be taking your"—he made air quotes—"'subway' for that."

"What's Murano?" she asked, collecting her purse and making sure her phone was inside.

Santino placed their passports in the safe, responding, "It's not a what but a where. Murano is an island where Venetian glass is made. Mamma wants us to pick a glass necklace for each of her daughters-in-law, and she listed the colors she wants. After the tour is done, we'll wander around all the shops until you find four necklaces you love."

"Really?" Her eyes lit up. "I'm going to have a necklace from Venice? That's so nice of Valentina. I'll have to find her one from us."

Santino softened again for a second time in less than an hour as he led them out of the hotel. Chloe's charitable personality still boggled his mind. His mamma had been as vicious as he had ever seen, and although she had made amends, if the roles were reversed, Santino didn't think he could have been completely forgiving.

"Mamma would love that. I guess that's the difference between having a lot of sons instead of daughters, because I would never have thought of that."

She reached for his hand and swung them back and forth, responding saucily, "That's why we make such an awesome team. You think like a man, and I think like a woman."

He gave her a quick swat to the ass. "That attitude is gonna cost you, Stellina."

Responding a couple of steps later, she asked, "Promises—"

Chloe stumbled and would have fallen if not for holding his hand. "Oops."

"Is your leg bothering you?" He placed her hand in the crux of his arm so she could lean on him.

"It's just a little stiff after being in the same position for so many hours on the plane. I'm fine."

He looked down at her to make sure she wasn't fibbing just so she could explore. "Maybe we should see if the hotel has a masseuse?"

She scrunched up her face. "No, I don't want a massage. I can't stand the thought of missing an hour of this place. Please, the walk will help, I promise."

"Okay, but if it starts to bother you and you don't say anything, it's going to cost you."

The cheeky little imp had the gall to roll her eyes and answer with a sarcastic, "Yes, husband."

"Ah, that's eleven. Ten for not telling me your leg was stiff and one for that smart mouth." He expected her to argue; instead, she smiled slyly. "Fifteen for topping again."

Chloe didn't hear the number he fired off because a gondola tied up to a pole beside the walkway had caught her attention. "Oh my goodness, look at how beautiful that gondola is."

Santino saw the gondolier having a cigarette and walked up to him. In Italian, he asked the man if he was available for a tour. The gondolier said he was and told him the price for the standard forty minutes, or if they wanted an hour, the extra cost. When Santino asked if he sang and if he could bring a bottle of Prosecco, the man declined, but he did give him instructions on how to get to one of the older gondoliers who would accommodate the singing request, and even offered to call him to see if he was free. Santino asked him to request a two-hour ride, and if he could grab a couple of other things, saying he would pay extra because it had to be perfect for his wife. The man smiled, looking at the gorgeous blonde, and said if he had a bella wife like Chloe, he would do the same thing.

Chloe was disappointed when they walked away without a ride, assuming it must have been too expensive. She wouldn't push the issue. It was still amazing to just see them.

They meandered their way along the pathways and over the Rialto Bridge when Chloe asked, "Why are there masks everywhere?"

"Carnevale is a two-week celebration before the forty days of lent. You'll have to ask Mamma about the time she came to Venice for it."

"I don't understand. You have a party before lent?"

Santino could see her limp was a little more prominent, so he suggested they stop for a coffee. He guided Chloe to a chair, then ordered a latté and an espresso.

"During lent, Roman Catholics sacrifice things they indulge in throughout the year, like rich foods, alcohol, and celebrating for forty days. Lent is to honor the sacrifice Christ made for us, so we indulge, having a big party the days before lent. The name came from the Latin words carne and vale, which means farewell to meat in Medieval times. The masks came about because it was the one time of the year the peasants and upper class celebrated together. They lived out their fantasies and kept their identities secret."

Chloe put her coffee down. "Wow, that's so cool. So, if we lived in Medieval times, I could celebrate with you because of you being upper crust and, with how I was raised, I would be a peasant."

Santino stiffened, his jaw grinding tight. "That just earned you ten more. Stellina, in any time period, you would be a princess." He lifted a challenging brow. "Not a word or you'll be adding to the count." He looked down at his phone to check the time. "Come on." He placed some euros on the table, then helped her up.

Feeling his anger simmering just below the surface, Chloe knew she was in deep shit. She had only been kidding. He had to know that sometimes the truth hurt.

Santino felt bad for being pissy, but it killed him that Chloe still didn't see what was so clear to everyone else.

They walked through winding pathways and over beautiful bridges as Chloe wondered how they would ever find their way back.

In one pathway, there was a cool outdoor restaurant that looked Medieval, with old stone arches between columns overlooking a canal.

"This place is so cool. Do you think we could have dinner here?"

He walked over to the waiter standing outside and requested a reservation in two hours, asking for a back table beside the canal. He slipped the man a bill when he shook his hand.

"Done. We'll come back in two hours."

"But, what if we can't find our way back? Why don't we just eat now?"

"Can't. We have something to do first." He urged her to get moving.

Instead of going over the bridge, he led her down a walkway beside the canal.

"Lorenzo?" he asked a man.

"Si. Welcome to Venice. Please, let me assist you in, signorina," the older gondolier said in a heavy Italian accent, reaching out to take her hand to help her into the flat-bottom boat.

Chloe flipped her face over to her husband, smiling from ear to ear. "We're going on a gondola ride? Really?"

"Yes, amore," he answered smugly.

"But why didn't we go on the other one?" she asked, stepping onto the stunning gondola that had a red interior as magnificent as the intricate carvings in the wooden structure.

"You'll see why soon enough," Santino answered, settling in beside Chloe and placing his arm over her shoulders, pulling her close.

Santino and the man spoke in Italian as the gondolier grabbed a bottle and two glasses. After placing the glasses on a small table, he popped the cork.

"Oh my, we're having champagne?" She couldn't help but be impressed.

"No, no, no, signorina. My name is Lorenzo, and Lorenzo would never serve you anything but the finest sparkling wine in the world—prosecco." He poured them each a glass. "Saluti." Then he removed the ropes from the boat.

Santino tipped his glass toward Chloe's. "Saluti, wife. I hope this adventure is better than your dreams."

"Saluti, husband. I can't believe you did this." They clinked, and after her sip, she bent to kiss him. "I love you."

"Ti amo, Stellina."

The gondolier heard the exchange and started to row as he sang a song he was sure she would be familiar with: "That's Amore" by Dean Martin. He was so enamored with Chloe's reaction that he continued with "Con Te Partiro" by Andrea Bocelli. Santino joined in.

Listening to the gondolier was one thing, but hearing her husband accompany him was unbelievable. Other gondolas were pulling closer to listen and watch the performance as people on the pathways cheered them on.

Chloe nearly fainted when Santino dropped to a knee at the end of the song and presented her with a single red rose.

"One rose means I fell in love at first sight." He pulled another from beside him. "Two means I'm deeply in love. And three"—he reached for the last one—"means I love you."

Chloe started to tear up as the people watching from the edge of the pathway clapped. It was the perfect afternoon.

Chloe recorded everything on her phone. Surprisingly, she even got a weird angle of the rose exchange from her lap, which she showed him over dinner.

Santino ordered them a Pinot Grigio, a white wine that was particular to this region of Italy, to complement the spaghetti alle vongole.

"I've never had clams and pasta before. It's really good."

"It was one of my dad's favorites, so Mamma doesn't make it

anymore. Don't be sad. My parents had almost thirty years of love. That's a gift not many people get. Now she has Quinn, and his favorite is spaghetti Bolognese."

She smiled with the thought of the man who had become so much like a father figure to her. "I love Quinn, but I can't imagine living one day without you. I hope God takes me first."

He grabbed her hand and kissed her knuckles. "I feel the same way. Ti amo, bellissima."

The waiter took away their plates, but before he left, Santino ordered his mamma's favorite dessert and coffees as Chloe yawned.

"Dessert, then back to the hotel, because someone has a punishment coming up." He rubbed his hands together with an evil grin.

Chloe blushed, seeing the man beside them looking at her. She leaned over the table. "Shh! I think that man heard you." She shifted her eyes to the side.

"I don't care who hears. Stellina, nobody knows us here, and we'll never see them again. I want you to stop worrying about what people think. Let loose." Just as he said that, a streak of lightning lit the sky. They hadn't noticed the clouds rolling in.

"Could it get any more magical here? But I hope we get back to the hotel before the rain comes," Chloe worried.

Santino moved back so the waiter could put the dessert and coffee down. "And if we don't, so what? We won't melt in the rain."

"It's not the rain I worry about. It's falling. I've fallen on slick sidewalks before."

"I would never let you fall. Trust me. Now, this is panna cotta with a caramel sauce. Try it so when we phone home tomorrow, you can tell Mamma you had panna cotta in Venice."

Santino hadn't known what he was asking for when she took a bite and hummed in delight, closing her eyes at the exquisite taste. He actually growled at her reaction.

Chloe's eyes flew open, seeing lust written all over his face.

"Mmmm . . . This is so good." She took another bite and made the same sound.

In a strained voice, he said, "You have exactly three minutes to finish your dessert and latte."

She giggled and stuffed each mouthful in as quickly as possible, relishing the taste despite the rush.

They were just getting up when a loud crack of thunder scared the life out of Chloe.

Santino held her hand that wasn't holding her roses and started to lead her back to the hotel just as the first drops of rain began to fall. "The disadvantage to no cars is you can't jump in a cab when it starts to rain."

They were only five minutes into their twenty-minute walk when the skies opened up and it started to pour. Santino didn't rush her, though, knowing she was nervous about her stability on the wet cobblestone.

When they stopped to rest for a second, Santino got silly, running to a light pole and swinging around it, singing "Singin' in the Rain" by Gene Kelly.

Chloe, soaked to the bone, laughed as she placed a hand on the wall and took her sandals off. "I couldn't ask for a better way to end the perfect day," she told him when he was done.

A loud clap of thunder and a bright streak of lightning hit, making Chloe scream.

Worried about the lightning, Santino pulled Chloe into a little niche with a statue just off the pathway. To distract his wife, Santino pulled her into his arms and gently kissed her wet lips. She moaned just like she had while she ate the dessert. The sound was like an aphrodisiac.

Without warning, he spun her around. "Hands above your head on the wall. Ass out."

She dropped her shoes and roses, grappling to tell him she was afraid of getting caught. However, Chloe found that all the people had scattered as fast as the rain fell, and there wasn't a soul around.

"Don't fight me or I will spank you right here in front of whomever walks by, and then fuck you. Do you understand me, wife?"

Chloe moaned, "Yes." Her panties were already wet from the rain, and now they were wet for a whole other reason.

Santino bent toward her ear. "I've wanted to fuck you all goddamn day." He skimmed his hand down her body, yanking the hem of her dress up and over her hips. Then he pulled her panties completely off. "So fucking bellissima, and all mine. Do you know how many men were staring at you today? I could have poked out hundreds of eyes. The only thing that stopped me was knowing this"—he cupped her pussy—"belongs to me. Remind me, wife, who does this belong to?" He dragged his fingers through her glossy lips

With a whoosh of breath, she said, "You!"

"That's right. And I want what's mine now. Do you have a problem with that, wife?"

She shook her head as a fast, wet slap landed on her ass. "Argh . . . No! I want you right here, please!"

He nipped her earlobe, chuckling. "That's my good girl." He then pushed his knees into her thighs with just enough pressure to keep her pinned and hold her dress up without hurting her, while he released his cock. As if orchestrated by a conductor, the second a loud clap of thunder exploded around them, with one hand on her hip and the other guiding his cock into her sleek warmness, it covered the passionate scream that ripped from her throat.

Her unleashed passion urged him on as he grabbed the top of her soaked dress, jerking it down to her waist. "These beauties should never be covered up," Santino said, groping her breasts. He found her tightly budded nipples and pulled with the motion of his hips. The action was bringing her to completion too quickly, so he slowed it down. "Does it feel different being fucked against an eight-hundred-year-old wall? How many other women have been screwed right here over time?"

"Your tits are freezing but, Dio mio, your pussy is so hot."

It didn't matter if he went slow or fast, he couldn't stop the inevitable crest that Chloe was experiencing. He could feel her walls begin to squeeze.

"Don't you dare come until I tell you, or you'll add fifty to your count."

Chloe cried out, struggling, clenching every muscle in her body to try to stop the inevitable. "Please, husband, please. I need to come so bad!"

Her begging was his undoing. "Come, Stellina!"

They both screeched into the raging storm that made the climax that much more intense.

When Santino felt all her muscles relax, he helped her slide down the wall so he could put his softening member back into his pants.

A light came on in the apartment overlooking the nook they were in, and then the window was opened. Chloe yelped as an old Italian woman started yelling in her language, and Santino laughed. She whipped her top back up and pulled her soaked dress down as quickly as possible.

Proud as a peacock, he apologized to the woman, telling her that his wife was frightened by the storm.

Chloe jumped when Santino bellowed out in laughter, answering, "Si, scusa, signora!" He then handed Chloe her shoes, roses, and panties before scooping her up into his arms and taking off.

He was still smiling from ear to ear when she wiped the rain from her face and asked what had happened.

"The old lady told me to take our activities inside. I told her that you were scared by the storm, and that's why you screamed. The old grandmother responded that she wasn't born yesterday and that we both must have been really scared to yell so loud. Then she reminded me to not forget your panties." He barked out another laugh when Chloe groaned, pushing her face into his chest in shame. "I can't wait to tell Alessandro that one."

Chloe slapped his chest. "You'll do no such thing. What happens in Italy stays in Italy. Promise, husband. Now put me down. I'm okay to walk."

"I promise." Santino kissed the top of her wet head, then gently placed her down, holding her arm tightly. It was a slow, careful walk, since the little pathways had become raging rivers as the heavy rainfall rushed toward the canals.

When they finally made it back to the hotel, the doorman rushed to open the door. They then hurried through the lobby, where people stared, watching them run up the stairs to the third floor. Chloe said they must look like drowned rats for people to stare so much.

Santino dragged Chloe to the floor-length mirror, and her mouth dropped open when she saw her wet dress had become totally transparent. Her breasts and tight nipples stood out like beacons, and her nether lips were plastered to the wet fabric. Chloe dropped her head in disgust.

Santino lifted her chin so they could see each other in the mirror. "I'm the luckiest bastard in the world. Didn't you think it was strange that the doorman didn't say good evening? That was because your beauty tongue-tied him. I'll say it again, luckiest bastard in the world. Come on; let's warm up with a shower."

Chloe let it go after he washed her hair and she washed his in the tiniest shower she had ever been in. When they were both clean, he dirtied her up again from behind.

It had been the best day of Chloe's life. She actually fell asleep sitting up while Santino insisted on drying her long hair, afraid she would get sick because of the air-conditioning in the room after being chilled to the bone in the rain.

***

Chloe woke up the next morning to feeling Santino's chest bumping back and forth against her back. She stretched her neck over to see him desperately trying to contain his mirth, and doing a shitty job at it.

Lifting herself up, she questioned in a raspy voice, "What are you laughing at?"

Santino rolled onto his back, laughing until he was clutching his abdomen. When he regained his senses, he explained, "The old woman last night. Oh my God, she was so witty. I still can't believe what she said. If we have as much fun every day as the first, we may never want to go home."

Even mortified, Chloe couldn't help giggling along with him. "As much as I know I'm going to love everything about Italy and being here with you, I'll be excited to go home. I've never had a real home filled with happiness and love. The months we have been together have been like a dream I never want to end."

He stopped chuckling and pulled her into his arms. "Home is where you are. You're my happy place, my only place. It's only the beginning, amore."

Santino made passionate love to his wife with just enough sting to make it good for the both of them.

After they got dressed, they headed to Murano on the subway boat. There, Chloe watched in awe as the glass blower created a horse and a delicate wineglass, adding different beautiful streaks of colors.

After they toured the plant, their guide took them into the

showroom. Chloe saw a set of four wineglasses like the one the man had made in front of them. She looked at the tag, seeing they were one hundred euros, so instead of buying them, she took a picture.

Seeing the whole display of emotions cross her face, from elation at seeing the glasses to disappointment in the price, Santino called the guide over. "Can you ship to the US?"

"Si, we can have anything delivered to your home in a week."

"Excellent. I would like five sets of these glasses delivered, but only if you can include the one the man just made in front of us. I want that set marked differently, since it's for my wife. The rest are gifts for our famiglia."

Santino grabbed for Chloe as she wobbled. "You okay?"

The man walked away to talk to the glassblower as Chloe asked nervously, "Do you know the price of those glasses?"

"I can read."

"But they are twenty-five euros each! Plus shipping. That's a lot of money."

He smoothed her hair from her face. "Did you fall in love with them?"

Chloe nodded.

"Then I want you to have something special to pass down to one of our children from our honeymoon. Actually, maybe we should keep them all. I don't know how many kids we're going to have, and they'll each need a set."

When Chloe's face went white as a sheet, he led her to a chair, afraid she was going to pass out.

"Are you not feeling well?" He felt her forehead for a temperature.

She quirked her head to the side after brushing his hand away. "Do you mean what you said?"

He moved the hand she had swatted away to pet the back of her head. "What? That I wanted five sets of glasses?"

"No." Chloe tightened her hands into fists. "You would let me have that many children?"

He cupped her jaw. "Chloe, I will have as many children as you want. I love our nieces and nephews, but I can't wait to have our own."

As Chloe burst into tears, the salesman walked back into the room and rushed over to make sure everything was all right. Santino reassured him that they were happy tears.

After she calmed down, they spent the day shopping, then dropped off all the parcels and changed for dinner.

Chloe came out of the bathroom. "Santino, I can't find my birth control pills. I swear they were on the counter before we left. Did you pick them up by accident?"

Santino was lying on the bed, dressed for dinner with his arm behind his head, propped up on all the pillows. "Yeah, babe, I threw them out. They're in the garbage can."

"What? Why would you throw my pills out?" she asked, annoyed.

He jackknifed up to a sitting position. "Because I have a feeling that we're going to have a lot of bambini, and I'm not getting any younger, so I thought we should go ahead and start trying to have a made-in-Italy bambino."

Chloe's face was comical. It went from totally pissed to disbelief to elation all in the span of three seconds. When her mind caught up to her expressions, she launched herself at him.

He laughed as she tackled him, kissing him everywhere skin was exposed. "I'll take that to mean you want to start a famiglia like right now."

They never made it out to dinner that night. Instead, the restaurant had to send the food up when they finally came up for air.

Day two had been even better than day one.

Chapter 18
"Some Of It" by Eric Church

Chloe took one last look of the canals from the boat terminal as they drove away after renting a car. She'd had so much fun and was sad to leave, yet equally excited to head to Tuscany.

She reached over the back seat, opening her carry-on to check one more time that she had packed the stunning necklaces they had bought. Smiling when she saw them, she remembered her conversation with Valentina about necklaces and loving panna cotta. Valentina had actually shrieked over the phone. She had never imagined her mother-in-law could make such a sound.

Chloe had eaten panna cotta every day, knowing she would never experience the taste again. She had made the mistake of ordering one with a raspberry sauce. Turning her nose up, she had made Santino eat it and ordered another one with caramel sauce for herself. He had teased her after she refused to eat in a restaurant that didn't have the caramel treat on the menu.

After driving an hour and a half, Santino pulled into a city and parked.

"Where are we?" Chloe knew they weren't in Tuscany yet, because the drive was supposed to be much longer.

Undoing his seatbelt, Santino answered, "Verona. I saw you watching Letters to Juliet on the plane, so I thought you might like to see Juliet's balcony."

She shrieked, sounding just like Valentina. "Really?"

Santino didn't respond until he went around, opening her door and helping her out. Her leg was really stiff after all the excessive walking they had done in Venice. "Yes, really. I'm curious to see things that excite you. If there is anything else that interests you or grabs your attention, tell me, and we'll stop to check it out."

The pressure on her heart made her stop walking. With awe, Chloe said, "Nobody has ever cared what I wanted. I have spent my life internalizing my thoughts after being ignored or told to shut up time and time again. Thank you for that priceless gift."

He cupped her face and tilted it up. She looked ready to cry. "Baby, from here on out, I don't want you keeping anything to yourself because, if I can make it happen, I will move heaven and earth to see you happy every day for the rest of our lives." He gently touched his lips to hers, then said, "First, we have to stop at a café so you can write a letter to Juliet." He led her to a café, then gave her a piece of paper and a pen he had snatched from their hotel.

Santino thought Chloe would need to give it some thought, but the words flew onto the paper.

Dear Juliet,

I found a man I love as much as you loved Romeo. I couldn't live one day without Santino.

I finally understand you. The true tragedy would have been if you never felt that kind of love. Love like that doesn't ever die.

I know you're happy together in heaven!

Love,

Chloe Savage

After they finished their coffees, they went to the balcony, where she left her letter folded against the wall. Then Santino asked a man to take their picture with the balcony above them.

Santino shook his head as Chloe looked back at the balcony one last time, and then at her letter. He smiled because the smallest act of kindness made his wife so happy. She would be ecstatic with their next stop.

The drive from Verona to Collodi took longer than the three hours it should have, because Chloe had seen a castle off the highway, and Santino had to backtrack when she'd asked if they could see it up close.

Chloe was like a child in Disney World for the first time. He got so much fulfillment from learning her cheeks hurt from smiling so much. But then she would scare the crap out of him every time she squealed at the endless fields of sunflowers. Finally, he stopped on a road after leaving the castle and paid the farmer ten euros so he could pick one flower for his wife while the farmer took a picture of them standing in the fields.

"Where are we?" Chloe asked when he came to her side of the car.

He tucked his hand into hers. "We're in Collodi. This is the town of the famous Carlo Collodi."

She racked her brain, trying to remember him mentioning the name. "Sorry, I don't remember you telling me about him."

He jostled her. "That's because I didn't. But you asked why there were so many Pinocchio puppets in Venice. I told you the story took place in Italy, but I didn't tell you Pinocchio was created in Tuscany. The author's name was actually Carlo Lorenzini. He took the name of his mamma's hometown for his pseudonym. I wanted to show you the park and town dedicated to the story and the character you seemed so intrigued with."

Chloe looked around at the adorable little town, explaining, "Harper and I had no choice except to tell our father a lot of lies so he wouldn't hit us. Secretly, we were terrified our noses would grow after seeing the movie, and that it would get us in more trouble. We felt sorry for Pinocchio, but we were glad it was him and not us."

How sad that a story meant to teach children morals had turned into the girls feeling guilty for the puppet that couldn't lie.

In Pinocchio's park, Santino allowed the child in himself to emerge, playing with Stellina as they raced through the ivy maze and crouched down to climb through the teeth of the whale in a pond, pretending to be caught in the belly. They then bought five Pinocchio marionettes for their nieces and nephews, and one for Chloe in memory of Harper.

It was five o'clock before they met Monica, the woman who owned the private villa that his brothers had rented for them in the town of Greve in Chianti. They followed her car up the mountain and were both blown away when they entered the modern yet rustic, Italian-style villa overlooking the town.

It had a beautiful, big kitchen that looked out onto the patio and private swimming pool. Neither one of them had ever seen a walk-in pool before. The concrete of the patio gradually sloped into the water and leveled off before the deeper end. They would be able to place lounge chairs in the pool and gaze at the vineyards in the distance, while sipping on the wines of the region.

Santino pointed out an old olive tree shading the pool.

Monica gave them the menus of three good restaurants in town and suggested they pick their favorite for tonight, because Ettore had plans for them for the next seven days.

Chloe looked at Santino, curious about who Ettore was.

He lifted both shoulders, not knowing who she was talking about either. When he questioned Monica, she said to ask Valentina, who had organized it.

When they FaceTimed home, Chloe told everyone about the perfect, most romantic place in all of Tuscany. The famiglia watched as she gushed about Juliet's balcony, her letter, seeing a real live castle, and Pinocchio's village.

Feeling bad that she was monopolizing the conversation, she told Santino to say hello.

"Ciao, everyone."

"Santino, it sounds like you two are having a lot of fun," Valentina said when the phone moved to her face.

Looking at her smiling face, he said, "Mamma, it's truly been magical. The perfect honeymoon. But listen, Monica said to ask you about Ettore. Who is he?"

Her face changed. He could tell she was nervous. "Well . . . uh . . . Ettore De Benedetto is a very renowned chef in Tuscany."

Santino smiled at Chloe. "You guys hired a famous chef to cook for us? That's so unbelievable."

When his brothers all laughed harder than they should have, Chloe and Santino looked at each other in confusion.

Alessandro grabbed the phone, looking at them with a cocky expression. "No, coglione, we hired Executive Chef Ettore De Benedetto to teach you two how to cook. For the next week, he will be meeting you at eleven a.m. for a food tour, lunch, and then you're going to cook your dinner with his guidance and expertise."

"What?" they screeched together.

Sabastian took the phone, looking serious. "Santino, you've been telling all of us that you're going to give Chloe her own soccer team of kids. One or both of you has to learn how to cook. That's a lot of mouths to feed."

Chloe looked as ill as Santino. The perfect honeymoon had just become a nightmare.

Uncomfortable with their silence, Emmy took the phone. "Santino, look at it as an adventure. Have fun with it, and when you get back, Valentina and I will help you both expand on what you learn."

Luca jumped on the screen behind Emmy. "Chloe, get Ettore to teach you how to make the panna cotta we've heard so much about. Think about it. You'll be able to cook something Mamma and Emmy can't. Besides, not even you two can live off of just love."

Santino saw her go paler. Annoyed, he fired back, "That's a lot of pressure to put on her. I don't care if we can cook. We'll survive just fine."

Valentina took the phone back. "We didn't do it because we think either of you are lacking. When Chloe came to the resort the first time, she begged me to teach her to cook, because it was one of the things missing from her childhood. I suggested it for your honeymoon because I want her to have everything her heart desires, and to share it with you. Put Chloe on." When Valentina saw her face, she said, "Carina, I want you to feel confident, and I know in my heart being a mamma and not cooking will eat away at you. Am I right?"

Chloe nodded. "Yes. I hate that I can't cook like the rest of the girls. Even my brothers-in-law can cook. Sometimes I feel like a failure as a woman."

Cooking had never troubled Santino one way or another, but he had no idea it bothered Stellina. He never wanted her to feel less than any other woman.

He took the phone. "Okay, tell those cogliones that the first Sunday we're back, Chloe and I are making lunch for everyone. And you better be prepared to have your socks blown off."

Alessandro laughed, taking the phone from Mamma. "I'll be happy if it doesn't taste like your nasty socks." The phone jarred. "Ouch! Dammit, Mamma, that hurt."

Chloe and Santino burst out laughing at seeing the pain on his face as he got a good cuff to the head.

"I'm sure it will be perfect," Valentina said, now back in possession of the phone. "Relax tonight and have fun with Ettore tomorrow. He is the best chef in Tuscany. We had to work miracles to hire him. I wanted only the best to teach you both. Love you two. Bye."

They both said goodbye then hung up.

"Let's go eat dinner, then come back and have some fun in that pool." He waggled his brows.

Chloe had no doubt what he had in mind. She might as well enjoy tonight, because tomorrow was going to be horrible.

***

The couple were enjoying their second cup of coffee after breakfast and sliced fruit on the patio when a gentleman walked around the side of the villa and came through the backyard. "Ciao! Are you the Savages?"

Santino and Chloe both got to their feet, and Santino extended his hand. "Chef Ettore, it's a pleasure to meet you. Please call me Santino, and this is my wife, Chloe."

"The pleasure is mine. Please sit, and let's talk for a few minutes."

"Can I get you an espresso?" Chloe offered.

"Si, grazie. I would enjoy to share an espresso with you. English is my second language, so forgive me if I say something wrong."

"Chloe doesn't speak Italian, so we appreciate the effort." Santino watched as his wife went into the kitchen, then launched into Italian. "I have to warn you; we were both surprised by your classes. My wife is very intimidated. She has had a very difficult life and is very shy and nervous about your classes."

"I understand," Ettore answered in Italian in case Chloe came back. "Valentina told me a little bit of history. A saying I know applies perfectly. 'Let food be the medicine and the medicine be the food.' My goal for both of you, is to fall in love with the art of creating simple but delicious food and letting go of all your inhibitions."

"Grazie, Ettore." Santino was very impressed. Maybe this wasn't going to be bad as they thought.

After their coffee and a little bit of conversation, they started out on their first tour.

They arrived at a farm not too far away and met the chef's friend Salvatore.

"The secret to good food is good ingredients. To allow the simplicity of each ingredient to excite the taste buds," Ettore said to the couple. "This morning, we will taste different olive oils, olives, wines, and make pecorino and ricotta cheese. When you see the love put into the end product, you'll appreciate the purest of ingredients."

They watched and participated in milking the sheep, boiling the milk, forming the cheese, and then pressing them into the round forms. After storing the hard cheeses, they boiled the whey a second time to make fresh, soft ricotta.

When they picked herbs from the garden, Ettore encouraged them to smell, taste, and then rub them together, breaking the fibers before tasting them again. The herbs became more robust, with a stronger, more pungent taste. Ettore wanted to teach them that they could control the flavors by the quality and how they extracted the flavor from whatever they cooked. To Chloe, the science made sense.

Excitedly, Chloe associated the oregano with pizza and the basil with Valentina's sauce. Meanwhile, Santino couldn't get over the fact that the four-foot-high hedge surrounding the garden was rosemary.

When they were done, Salvatore's wife made a lunch of antipastos with all the cheeses, olives, and salami. To wash it down, they sampled his wine.

Chloe was blown away at the sharpness of the hard-cured pecorino versus the light, subtle taste of the ricotta. It amazed her how the same milk tasted so different when treated differently.

Ettore encouraged them to explain what flavors they could detect. They were surprised when they separated and defined different herbs and the difference between extra virgin olive oil versus regular olive oil.

Chloe got excited. This wasn't cooking; it was science, and science had been her best subject in high school.

They stopped at a market and picked up more ingredients. The minute Chloe got into the kitchen, though, she started to panic. When Ettore asked why, she answered, "I can't even make toast."

"Si, you can. You said you like science. It's chemistry and passion, like love."

He heated the oven. "I want three types of toasted bread for the antipasto. One light brown, one brown, and one dark brown.

"You tell me you love music, si?" Very smartly, the chef had been asking questions all day about the things they liked to do in order to figure out how to take the apprehension out of the equation.

Chloe nodded.

"Play me a beautiful, soft song from your phone."

Chloe did. Halfway through, he stopped her.

"That was bella. Now I want a song that is the perfect mix of soft and hard music."

She obliged again, and then he again stopped her halfway through.

"Third, pick me a song that is heavy but not too dark. Now make the first piece of bread light like the first song. When you think it is light like the song, take it out."

Chloe did as instructed. The bread toasted to match the music. The second was the same, but she had left the last one in a little too long.

When she took it out, Ettore laughed at her discouraged face. "Ah, you like heavy metal rock! No problem. We scrape a little of the dark off to make it just rock music."

Wiping her sweating hands on her apron, she said, "See? I messed up already. I told you I couldn't do it."

Ettore grabbed Santino's shoulder. "Chloe, you love your husband?"

Still disheartened, she said, "More than I can tell you."

He smiled at the sweet woman. "Was he your first boyfriend?"

She quirked her head to the side, not understanding what he was getting at. "No."

"You had to kiss a lot of toads before you found your prince. Cooking is like love. It doesn't always work, but we keep trying until we get the right combination. Then we create the perfect dish, like a marriage. But not everyone loves the same way. It's your preference. You have to understand the foundation, work at it, and learn what works for you."

Elated, Chloe smiled with understanding. "You're right. You're a very smart man."

Now that she was back on track, he gave them each tasks, demonstrated when necessary, and guided them when they didn't understand. Ettore was so passionate about everything as they worked hand in hand.

Santino watched his girl get excited, asking all kinds of questions. He also got caught up in the enthusiasm.

They started off simply by taking the ricotta that had a very simple taste and adding a bit of extra virgin olive oil, salt, pepper, freshly cut basil, and a bit of pecorino, mixing it together, and putting it on toast. The flavors exploded in Chloe's mouth, each combination subtly different because of the level the bread was toasted and the amount of herbs. Different but good. Next, they made fresh pasta, and instead of measuring the ingredients, Ettore had them weigh them. Science again; Chloe liked that.

Together, the three of them created a succulent dinner.

Santino took pictures of everything, knowing Chloe would want to show everyone.

"I can't believe we did this." He proudly looked at the meal fit for a king that was laid out on the patio table.

"One hand washes the other, and together, they wash the face," Ettore answered.

"What do you mean?" Santino asked as he put down the phone and poured the wine, while they all settled in at the table.

"It is like singing a song. You can't have a good song without a musical instrument, a beautiful voice, and heartfelt words. We all worked together, and because of it, we have a delectable meal and excellent wine with very good music. Eh?" Ettore spoke a language Santino understood.

Chloe had brought her phone out that was still playing music, which made his analogy even better.

She tasted the ricotta-filled raviolis that had chives and basil embedded into the pasta dough. "Mmm . . . This is delicious. I would never have thought of a white meat sauce served under the raviolis. I still can't believe we made this." After another heartfelt sound, she asked how Ettore had become a chef.

He helped himself to the rabbit and said, "My nonna raised me and taught me all she knew. She equated food with love. Her way of giving me as much love as possible was to allow me to learn at her side. Some of my best boyhood memories were spent in the kitchen with her. Today, when I feel the dough in my hands, I think of her. Almost like when you listen to music and it reminds you of someone or some place."

They both nodded in understanding. When Santino thought of music, his mind always wandered to his dad and everything he had taught him. When he thought of food, it always went to his mamma. Chloe was learning to equate food with love, like scones, butter tarts, and Rice Krispies treats to her sister-in-law Emmy, and panna cotta to Valentina. Her music would always remind her of Harper and Santino.

Ettore went on, "I like to cook with my daughter. It's a gift we can share. And by doing so, I pass down a legacy of sorts. Although she has never met some of my famiglia, she knows them through the recipes that were handed down to me. I keep the originals, but I also love to change them, mix the old with the new. That is the beauty of culinary arts; you can make it your own."

The man was like a poet when it came to his passions in life. Santino was again reminded of his dad.

"You make me want to learn everything I can about cooking," he said after tasting the rabbit and rolling his eyes in delight at the flavor. He handed the plate to Chloe, who took it and placed it down. Ettore noticed.

"Chloe, you have to try the rabbit."

She scrunched her face up. "I can't stand the thought of eating Bugs Bunny."

Santino laughed, but Ettore was confused.

"Why?"

"Bunnies are cute. It seems cruel." Her face turned red, not wanting to offend the man she was growing to respect and care for.

Ettore refilled everyone's wineglass, then took a sip. "Ah, well, my daughter was not happy when she learned her favorite meat was a little lamb. But in the old days, to survive, they ate what they could to stay strong. By making it taste wonderful, we are respecting its beauty and nourishing our bodies. There is beauty in all animals we eat.

"Try a little for me, because I picked those olives myself in the wine sauce we made. If you don't like it, I will respect your opinion. Everything we make is not palatable to everyone, like certain types of music don't agree with everyone."

Chloe took the smallest piece, dragging it through a lot of sauce before placing it in her mouth. As much as she wanted to hate it, she couldn't. It was amazing. She dug around the platter for the biggest piece she could find.

The men looked at each other and secretly smiled.

After her second mouthful, she said with the same distressed face, "Sadly, Bugs Bunny tastes delicious, and it was the easiest thing we made."

The chef laughed as he helped himself to more of the tasty dish. "Always reserve judgment for your taste buds. You truly can't say if it is to your liking without sampling."

After the meal was completed, the trio cleared the table, then brought out the tiramisu they had made. Groans of delight followed each bite.

"Stellina, do you have a new favorite dessert?" Santino was waiting for his wife to ask about the panna cotta.

Realizing she was scarfing it down like she had never seen food before, she gently placed her spoon down to wait for them to catch up. "Nope." She shook her head, then shyly turned to face Ettore. "Would you mind teaching us how to make caramel panna cotta? It's always been my mother-in-law's favorite, and recently became mine as well. I would like to make it for her when we get home."

"No . . ."

Her heart sank.

"I would be honored to teach you."

Chloe glowed like he had just given her a pot of gold. Jumping up, she went around the table and gave the man a quick little hug. "Ettore, you are such a gentleman. I have learned more today than I have my whole life. Thank you. I can't believe I had so much fun."

He stood, ready to go clean the kitchen. "That gives me much pride to hear such praise from il mio nurmero uno studente."

Chloe instantly looked at Santino for translation.

"He called you his number one student."

The words tickled her pink.

Santino looked at the man with a world of gratitude. Ettore had been equally impressed throughout the day with their musical talents, so Santino figured out a way to give back to this humble man.

"How about we start early on the last day of class and you invite your wife, daughter, and a few friends. We'll cook, have an early dinner with everyone, and then we'll have an American sing-along by the fire. Do you know anyone with a guitar?"

"Yes," he said instantly, his face lighting up. "That would be fantastico. We love American music. My daughter will be so happy. Thank you, my friends. Now I will clean up and be on my way. I want to be home to spend some time with my daughter before she goes to sleep."

Chloe grabbed his hand and started dragging him through the villa. "Absolutely not. We'll clean. You go home to your family, and thank them for sharing you with us this week."

The chef laughed at the tiny woman dragging him and looked to Santino. "She has strength as well as courage. You're a lucky man."

Santino waved. "You have no idea, but you're right. I am a very lucky man. Ciao! See you tomorrow."

Santino started to fill the sink, thinking about what they had accomplished over the course of the day. Never in his wildest dreams had he thought learning to cook with Chloe would be so freeing and fun. Damn, he owed his mamma. She had been right. The change in Chloe in one day was incredible, and he had to admit he might just learn to love cooking, as long as Stellina was at his side.

Chloe came up behind him and wrapped her arms around his waist, leaning her head onto his back. "I really enjoyed the day, and learned so much. How can every day get better than the last? I feel like Sleeping Beauty awakening since Harper left me. My life is beyond anything I could have dreamt."

When she moved her hands down to his belt and undid it, she heard his hitch of breath. She lowered his zipper, then pulled his pants down enough to release his suddenly hard length. Then she dropped to the ground and shifted his legs apart. Pushing his hips back, she crawled between them, then knelt up and turned around. Looking up, she said, "Keep working. If you stop, I stop."

Santino hissed when she ran her tongue down from the tip to the root. Then Chloe pulled back when he stopped. He growled and started washing the dishes again.

She went back to her task, and Santino nearly dropped a wineglass when she took him as deeply as she could. He placed the glass down with one hand and gripped the farm sink, swishing the soapy water around with his other hand like he was working, when there was no way in hell he could concentrate as she polished his dick. Soon, his hips were moving in time with her up-and-down motion.

The day couldn't get any better. Well, actually, Chloe had a spanking coming her way for torturing him like this, so they still had endless hours to make it even better.

Santino moved to his toes as her suction picked up, and then he finally bellowed out when he couldn't take it another second. When he was spent, Chloe fell to her bottom, proud of herself in more ways than one with this glorious day.

He snatched her up and carried her to the couch, kissing her lips madly, while undoing her pants. Whipping them off, he sat down and flipped her over his lap. The first slap caused her to groan sensually, and by ten, she was ready to go off like a firework.

He flipped her up onto his lap, facing away from him, and let her slide down his hard cock. Holding her hips, he guided her up and down.

"Look at the mess we still have to clean up before we take this to the bedroom. Brace your hands on my thighs, and ride me hard and fast." He grabbed the hem of her shirt and pulled it up and off. Next, her bra was flying across the room. "Thanks for teaching me that cleaning is as fun as cooking together in the kitchen." He cupped her breasts, massaging the pliable flesh and tweaking her nipples every so often. It didn't take long for Chloe to clamp down and scream.

When she started to melt with completion, he tugged harder on her nipples. "This isn't over until you give me one more climax." He swatted her left ass cheek when she moved up. Chloe yelped and moved faster. "That's it, baby. Work me."

He could feel his climax approaching and moved one hand down to her clit. Gathering some of her juices, he swirled his fingertips faster over her sensitive nub. Before long, she was chanting to God and every other power above.

"San . . . tino!" She came again, half a second before he was howling her name in ecstasy.

They collapsed back on the couch and stayed there, recovering for fifteen minutes before either could move. Finally, they cleaned the kitchen as naked as the day they were born, then went to bed to commence with round two.

***

The rest of the trip flew by as fast as the first part. Ettore took them shopping at an open-air market, to a fish monger who taught them how to fillet fish, a butcher to learn how to choose the best cuts of meat and to make cured meats, and to wineries.

Every day, their knowledge and confidence grew. They learned to trust their taste buds, and that exact measurements were meant for baking, not creating savory delights. When he gave them recipes, he included variations to create different meals. But mostly, he taught them not to be intimidated, to have fun, and to experiment with food. The sky was the limit.

They had their sing-along the last day of class and met the people who made Ettore's world important.

The last day, before they went home, Ettore invited them to the restaurant, where he was executive chef at Ristoro di Lamole. The restaurant looked over the hills of Tuscany, and he reserved the best outdoor table for them. He treated them like royalty and introduced them to the owners. Chloe gushed over Ettore's talents, the ambiance of the restaurant, as well as the spectacular art incorporated around the premises.

Ettore graciously decided their appetizer for them, which was a true work of art. The trio of treats exploded in their mouths, but finding out one was steak tartare, with egg yolk, delicately ceviche with sugar and salt, topped with threads of saffron was the highlight.

Chloe asked to take pictures of everything, and Ettore encouraged her, telling her there was no greater honor for a chef than to make something that looked as beautiful as it tasted. Of course, Chloe finished her meal with caramel panna cotta that was equally as good as her own. Then they hugged and took their last pictures together.

Although miles would separate them, the friends had formed a bond with great wine, excellent food, and lots of laughter. As sad as Chloe was to leave, the thought of beginning their future together filled her with excitement.

Chapter 19
"Miracle" by Foo Fighters

Santino brought the empty plate from their appetizers back into the kitchen. They had nailed it. Ettore would have been proud. They had made a chicken liver crostini and bruschetta with white beans and kale, and Chloe was just shaving the truffles on top of their homemade tagliatelle pasta.

Finding truffles hadn't been easy or cheap. They were subterranean fungi imported from Italy, but there was no flavor in the world like it, and this dinner was important to Chloe. The flavors were as unique as her experience, and she wanted to share it.

Santino had to slice the huge, grilled veal chops they were serving with green beans that had lemon and capers, complemented with fennel and arugula salad.

Not only had they already blown the socks off Alessandro, but soon they would have him begging for not just a second helping but a third.

Chloe did one final wipe of the dish so the presentation was as beautiful as the flavor. Then they carried out the meal and were rewarded by oohs and aahs, but it was the satisfaction of the groans when the famiglia tasted the meal that made the last five hours worth all the work.

The highlight was when Valentina begged Chloe to teach her how to make caramel panna cotta. Everyone loved it and totally understood her fascination with the delicate Italian custard topped with rich caramel sauce. Chloe had truly never been as proud of herself as she was hearing all their praises. Imagine her mother-in-law, the woman who cooked the best food she had ever tasted—aside from Ettore, who was a master—asking her to teach her something.

"It would be my honor. But if you want, I can make it anytime you have a craving."

As much as Valentina would have loved to learn to make the dessert to this quality, she wouldn't because Chloe was so proud to make it for her. "That's a great idea, because you have perfected it. The panna cotta tastes just like my nonna's. It was also her specialty. That reminds me, I have an old recipe book of hers. Maybe you would like to have it."

Chloe was floored. "Really? You would allow me to have it? But it's part of your history."

"And now it is part of yours, carina. Nothing would make me happier than tasting the flavors of some of my nonna's recipes that I haven't had in many years."

"Ettore said we get to know the family we never met through recipes passed down. I would love to have that connection to your grandmother." This was a side no one had seen of Chloe, the final crack in the protective shell she had created throughout her childhood.

Valentina placed her napkin down and eagerly pushed her chair back. "I'll go get it now and see if you can read any of it."

Wiggling with excitement in her chair, Chloe said, "If I can't, I'll Google translate. Thanks, Valentina."

Santino sat back, proudly watching the interaction, until Keith caught his eye, signaling to him.

"I have some paperwork I need your signature on before I close all the files. Do you mind giving me a few minutes?"

To keep everyone in the dark, he played along. "Yeah, sorry, I know you wanted it before I left. I forgot. Let's go into the conference room."

The famiglia seemed to accept the discussion for what it was presented as and carried on with their individual conversations.

Santino led Keith to the conference room and shut the door behind them, hesitant to hear what the man had to say when things were finally so good.

"What's up?"

Keith didn't mince words as he told him about Reverend Patrick O'Connor showing up at the resort and how he turned him away until he had a chance to do a background check. "He checks out, Santino. The man was neighbors with Chloe's grandparents and went to school with Chloe's mom. The reverend also knew her father. He would like to shed some light on the woman he knew, in order to give Chloe some positive memories of her mother. What do you want me to do? He asked if he could visit her today."

Santino got up from his chair and paced the room. "I don't know. She's finally happy and moving on. You saw her today, Keith, and tasted her food. This is a whole new Chloe. I don't want to make her sad again."

"There's one other thing." The lawman's voice turned cautious and awkward.

Santino watched as the man dragged his hand through his thinning hair. "Spit it out."

"His eyes, Santino. There's something about them that reminds me of Chloe. I've never really seen silver eyes like hers before, and while the reverend doesn't have the same color, the shape and brows are remarkably close to hers."

Santino narrowed his eyes at the sheriff. "What are you inferring?"

The man, who was always as cool a cucumber, was suddenly fidgety as hell. He stuck his hands in his pockets, jiggling some loose change. "It could be a coincidence, but I don't believe in coincidences."

Santino flopped into a chair. "Are you telling me that the reverend could be her father?"

"Honestly, my gut is telling me they have a connection. I researched the man who is supposedly Chloe's father, and the twins look nothing like him. I even tried to see if maybe there was a biological connection between the two men. There isn't. Invite him here today, introduce him to Chloe, and see if she picks up on anything, or if you do."

Santino couldn't help thinking they might be opening a can of worms. "If he's a priest, isn't he supposed to be celibate? Could this hurt his position and cause another scandal? I won't allow anyone to put Chloe back in the limelight."

Keith sat down, swinging the chair from side to side. "No, Roman Catholic priests aren't allowed to marry, but Protestant pastors are, even before they're ordained."

All the Savage sons had been raised in a strict Roman Catholic upbringing and never really gave thought to how different religions worked. "Can they have children?"

"Yes, families are encouraged."

Santino stood. "Okay, ask him if he would like to come to our cabin at seven this evening. That will allow Chloe a chance to get settled, and for me to tell her about him. I'm not going to tell her about your assumptions for now. But I'm warning you now, if she decides she doesn't want to meet anyone from her parents' past, I won't force her."

His relief was evident. "That's all I'm asking. If by some miracle I'm right, think of how it could change everything for her. It can't undo her past, but it would eliminate biological ties to that animal."

"It doesn't matter to me one way or another if she has his DNA or not. My wife is a gentle, beautiful soul. I just don't want her to ever feel lost or confused again."

"I understand, son. And if I didn't love that little darlin' so much, I'd tell the reverend to hit the road. I'll give him a call now and see if that time works for him."

The two men walked back into the dining room and enjoyed the rest of the afternoon. Keith had excused himself at one point to make the call, and when he got back, he subtly nodded at Santino.

At six o'clock, the couple was settled back in their cabin.

Chloe cuddled up to Santino on the couch and turned on the TV.

"Stellina, we have a visitor coming. He'll be here in an hour."

Chloe pushed up and twisted toward her husband. "Who's coming over?"

"His name is Reverend Patrick O'Connor. He was a neighbor of your grandparents and friends with your mom. He wants to meet you and share what he remembers of her."

Her mouth dropped open and her eyes widened. When she recovered from her shock, she said, "You know what? I remember the O'Connor family from when I would visit my grandparents. My nana and Mrs. O'Connor were best friends. They had tea together every day from what I remember. How did you find him, and why didn't you tell me?"

When he told her most of what Keith had told him, Chloe was touched by the fatherly protectiveness of the sheriff.

Santino couldn't help chuckling when she popped up from the couch, claiming she wanted to freshen up before the reverend showed up. But first, she was going to call Emmy and see if she could grab some baked goods from the main resort to offer their guest. He smiled at how domesticated she had become.

Chloe had just finished making a plate of treats and put hot water on for tea, readying the coffeepot in case he wanted coffee instead, when she heard the knock and Santino saying he would get it. Two minutes later, she walked out and there stood Reverend Patrick O'Connor.

He immediately smiled at her. "You're beautiful, just like your mom when she was your age. Chloe, my name is Patrick, and it is indeed a pleasure to finally meet you."

Chloe walked farther toward him to shake the man's hand. "Hi. It's nice to meet you. This is my husband, Santino Savage."

"He just introduced himself." He nodded at Santino before turning back to Chloe. "I would like to thank you both for agreeing to see me. The sheriff said you just got back from your honeymoon. Congratulations on your marriage. I have to tell you, my favorite part of my job is joining two people in love in the eyes of the Lord."

Chloe beamed. "Being married is my favorite part of my life. My husband saved my life in more ways than one. Oh my goodness, here I am rambling on, and I haven't invited you in. Please follow us to the kitchen. Can I make you a tea or coffee? We also have espresso or lattés, if you prefer."

"Ah, now you're talking my language. I've developed quite the addiction to lattés, thanks to Starbucks. But if you meet my wife, don't tell her. She doesn't like me having a lot of caffeine."

His good nature instantly put Santino at ease. However, Keith had been right; there was something about him.

"Stellina, I'll make the espresso. You heat the milk."

Patrick sat at the island at Chloe's insistence, watching the couple work in perfect unison.

"Is Stellina your middle name? I've never heard it before. It's quite beautiful and suits you."

Chloe blushed as Santino explained, "No, it's a term of endearment I gave her the second I saw her eyes. It means little star in Italian."

"That makes it even more beautiful." Patrick could see the love the young man had for Chloe, and for some reason, it gave him comfort after he had followed her history in the newspapers.

He felt a bit of tension in the lull of conversation, so he got right to it. "I asked to meet you, Chloe, because I was a good friend of your mom's. She was a lovely girl. I read some of the stories about her in the paper and wanted you to know that the things that were said didn't sound like the girl I knew. Lori was like the sunshine on a summer day—bright and warm."

Chloe look at the reverend with mixed emotions as she placed the mugs on the counter. His compliment drew out some unresolved anger at the woman who had abandoned her and Harper, if not in body than definitely in mind. She wanted to believe the man, especially because he was a man of God, but the woman she had known could never have been compared to sunshine.

She chose her words carefully, not wanting to offend Patrick. "I'm glad that's what you remember, but I never saw that side of my mom. I know I might sound harsh, but my mom gave up on life and forgot about us years before she died." Chloe took the lid off the sugar when the coffee was ready. "Would you like any sugar?"

"Yes, two teaspoons, please," he answered. Shaking his head, he added, "That saddens my heart, because the girl I knew laughed loudly, sang merrily, and was kind to everyone she met. I had a crush on her for years, and we even dated during our last two years of college. I planned to ask her to be my wife, but then she met your father."

The spoon fell from Chloe's hand. "Pardon me?" She couldn't help being angry. If her mother had made better choices, they would have been Patrick's children, and Harper would be alive.

Santino picked up on her vibe and moved closer, placing his hand at the small of her back.

Patrick picked up the spoon and handed it back to her. "Lori was beautiful, inside and out. Regrettably, I was angry at her for a long time.

"Not too long ago, her best friend from childhood, Evelyn, joined my congregation, and I learned the truth. Your dad was not a good man, even back then. He had caught her alone, walking home from the library one evening, and took advantage of her. When she threatened to go to the police, he threatened to tell everyone in our community that they were having an affair. He gave her a choice: break up with me and belong to him or he'd ruin her reputation and bring her parents down in the process."

Chloe's hand flew to her mouth as she gasped. Her father had been abusive even as a young man. He must have always been evil.

"She should have told someone," Santino said, furious on Chloe's behalf. "Certainly, she could have gone to her parents or an adult she trusted."

The reverend's expression softened. "The fault may lie with me. Evelyn said he knew your mother wasn't untouched and threatened to expose me and ruin my chances with the seminary application process. Now that I know the truth, I believe she sacrificed herself for me." The man's eyes dropped as they filled with moisture.

Chloe reached out and patted his hand. "Patrick, if Mom did, then it means she wasn't always the weak, withdrawn woman I knew. I remember her trying to protect us when we were little, but after Harper was killed, she became more and more of a coward. It's unimaginable to me that any mother would allow her child to suffer his wrath alone. He tried to kill me, and she didn't even report it."

Taking a sip of his latté, he took a minute to contemplate Chloe's angry response. Gently putting his cup down, he said, "That doesn't make sense to me." He shook his head and got a faraway look. "My dear, your father must have broken her, because the Lori I knew advocated for anyone in need. She would have been the perfect pastor's wife. It's distressing to think he destroyed her to a point of not even protecting her own children.

"Over the years, I have counseled many women suffering from domestic violence. I've taken courses that taught me that constant abuse can actually change the brain's chemistry badly enough that a person can't think for themselves anymore. I have to believe that happened to your mother, because the woman I knew would have fought tooth and nail for her children."

Santino had continued to rub circles over his wife's back until a thought occurred to him. He removed his hand, bringing it to his goatee and stroking it in deep thought. "Chloe, you said he disappeared during your recovery. Could it be possible she finally did something? You said he left and you never heard from him again. A man that people were saying was a hero for rescuing his daughter suddenly vanishes? It doesn't fit. Don't you think he would have stayed and fed his narcissistic personality?"

Chloe's jaw dropped. "Oh my God, you're right." She turned toward the reverend, realizing she had misused the Lord's name. Blushing, she said, "Sorry, Reverend."

He smiled at the adorable, little creature in front of him. "I'm sure He'll forgive your little transgression. But I think Santino is right. It's the only thing that makes sense."

Chloe picked up a butter tart and placed it on her dessert plate, lost in thought. The men watched as she plucked at the pastry shell until the golden filling started to flow out of the broken crust. "I do remember her telling me that he wouldn't be coming back. I didn't believe her. But, come to think of it, she said it with absolute certainty." She licked the sweet filling from her fingers, then looked at Santino. "It's the only answer. My mom must have threatened to tell someone, or maybe she did tell someone." A look of guilt covered her face. "All these years, and I never thanked her."

Patrick got up and approached Chloe, clasping her hands. "Trust me, child, she just heard you."

She blinked up through grateful eyes. "I'm just sorry it took me so long. For almost twenty-four years, I believed she didn't do anything to protect me. I guess I was wrong."

The man in front of her paled, and his hands began to shake.

"Patrick, are you all right?"

"I thought you were younger." He threw them for a loop when he continued, "When is your birthday?"

She quickly glanced at her husband in confusion, then back to the pastor. "I'll be twenty-four next month, on the fourth. Why? You don't look so good."

Patrick let go of her hands, placing his on the counter to stabilize himself. "I'm not thinking clearly. Hold on. I'm trying to do some math."

Santino already knew where his mind had gone. "She was conceived in October," he said as he encased his wife in his arms from behind.

"By all saints." He breathed in deeply. "Could it be true? I need to sit down."

They watched as he literally dragged himself back to his seat, shifting his hands along the counter.

"Patrick, could what be true?"

Now it was Patrick's turn to blush. "Your mother was attacked Thanksgiving weekend. That's the end of November. In October, your mom and I were still together."

Chloe tilted her head. "So, you think he attacked her earlier than you thought."

Santino twisted her in his arms. He wanted to cup her beautiful face but was afraid of her body's reaction once he said what he was thinking, so he held on tightly to her waist. "Stellina, Patrick thinks you might be his daughter."

Chloe didn't move or blink. She didn't react at all. Then she tilted her head the other way.

He was waiting for her to fall down when the realization finally hit. He placed a hand under her knees and back, scooping her up and walking to the couch. It took a minute or two for Patrick to follow them into the living room, where Santino sat with her on his lap.

She innocently looked at the man she trusted above anyone else. "I don't understand." She blinked, and a big fat tear fell.

It broke Santino's heart. She was terrified to let her mind even consider the possibility, and he didn't want to set her up for yet another disappointment if he could help it.

Cupping her face the way he wanted to before, he said, "Stellina, there might be the slightest chance Patrick is your father. I don't want you to overthink anything right now. There are numerous tests you can take to find out the truth, one way or the other. But it won't change the past or who you are, which is the most beautiful, sweetest woman I have ever met. Remember, I'll be with you every step of the way. I want you to talk to me about it, and promise you won't bottle anything up."

Patrick was a mess. "Chloe, I'm sorry. That was totally insensitive of me. I didn't mean to hurt you or cause you any pain. Never in a million years did I believe our conversation would turn out this way. I loved your mother and thought you should know the woman I knew. How can I make it up to you?"

She repositioned herself on the seat beside Santino, feeling inappropriate sitting on her husband's lap in front of a pastor. "Are you married?"

Both men were a little baffled by her question.

Patrick answered, "Yes, and I have two sons and a daughter." He wasn't sure why he had blurted all that out. Then it hit him like a freight train. "I would like to have the test if you would be willing. I don't want to get my hopes up, but if you are my daughter, I won't hide it from anyone. I would proudly scream it from the pulpit of my church if it's true."

Santino couldn't help thinking Patrick was the type of man Chloe should have been raised by.

They continued to make plans to have the DNA testing and agreed not to tell anyone except Patrick's wife, who had the right to know what was going on. By the time he was ready to leave, they had found a place online in Allentown to get the DNA test done and booked an appointment for the next day.

Chloe gave him a hug before he left. Even if it turned out he wasn't her father, he had given her the information she needed to help her forgive her mother.

A peace she hadn't felt since her mother passed engulfed her. Santino kept her close and encouraged her to tell Quinn the following morning before they left for the test. She was going to have to deal with a lot in the upcoming weeks, and he wanted to make sure all her supporters were in place.

***

Three weeks later, Patrick and his wife were sitting in Chloe and Santino's cabin, waiting for the results via internet.

The couple had met Elenore three days after Patrick had dropped the bomb. The woman was a saint. Instead of feeling threatened by the possibility of Chloe being Patrick's biological child, she had embraced the young woman with open arms. She knew about Lori and had followed the massacre, and then Jacob's trial right along with her husband. The woman was a Christian in every sense of the word and had convinced Chloe that they would like to be a part of her life, regardless of the outcome. The young woman and her husband had been humbled beyond words.

Chloe was dying to ask about their children and had confessed that to Santino. He had finally told her that Keith had questioned her paternity first. That made it even more real.

The prospect of maybe having siblings was overwhelming for her. The closest she had to a relative was Santino, his family, and Quinn. She didn't realize how much she had missed being a sister. No one could ever replace Harper, but it would be mind-blowing to have a blood-related father, half-brothers, and a half-sister.

The famiglia had all picked up on the fact that something was going on, but they didn't push the issue when Santino asked them to just be patient and told them that they would explain everything when the time was right.

Valentina was busy whispering to all her other children that she thought Chloe was pregnant. She also knew Quinn knew what was going on and was pissed that he wouldn't breach his ethics and give her a hint. She tried to convince him that if he didn't actually say the words but nodded his head, that wouldn't be breaking the rules. He disagreed.

Santino had called Patrick two days ago and asked if they minded if Quinn and Keith joined them to hear the results. He wanted the men who had stepped up to the plate and assumed a father-like relationship with her to support her despite the results.

The ding from the computer with a new email silenced the room.

"Let me get the results," Santino offered, opening the email and making a funny face.

"Come on! You're killing me. What does it say?" Chloe asked, shaking like a leaf.

His expression turned from confused to perturbed. "It says to phone for results. That's weird, because they said definitively that we could get the results online. It's one of the reasons I chose this lab."

Quinn moved in front of Chloe as he saw her face fall. "That doesn't mean bad news. If Patrick isn't your father, nothing has changed. You are a strong young woman who will carry on. Except, now you have another man and woman who want to be part of your life."

She wiped a tear. "You're right. Let's call."

Santino called, gave their case number, and then a doctor came on the line.

"Hello?"

"Hi, I'm Santino Savage. My wife is waiting for her paternity test, and we were informed to call. Is there a problem?"

"I'm sorry, Mr. Savage, but I can't give you any information. I have to speak to Mrs. Savage directly," the doctor replied.

Santino explained to Chloe that she was the only person who could get the information.

She took the phone. "Hello?"

"Mrs. Savage, my name is Dr. Thomas. I understand that you had a swab and blood test to determine paternity. I have the results of the test, and after I give you the results, I have some other information that we became aware of, so don't hang up."

The doctor sounded so mysterious, making Chloe apprehensive. "O—kay."

He continued, "The genetic results read as follows, based on our analysis: the probability of Patrick O'Connor being the biological father of the child, Chloe Savage, is ninety-nine point nine, nine, nine percent."

Chloe's heart thundered in her chest. Patrick was her father.

Flabbergasted, she came back to reality when the doctor asked, "Are you still there, Mrs. Savage?"

She cleared her throat. "Um . . . yes."

"Mrs. Savage, the bloodwork also determined that you are

pregnant. At the time of the test, you were four weeks along. That would make you seven weeks pregnant now."

She dropped the phone.

Santino freaked out, seeing the blood drain from her face as she grabbed her abdomen. He tried to get her to talk as Keith grabbed the fallen phone, asking the doctor what he said. The doctor refused to give him any information and ended the conversation.

Patrick's heart sank. He knew by Chloe's reaction that he wasn't her father. This poor young girl had not had it easy, and he had just set her up for another huge disappointment.

With a husky voice filled with emotion, he placed a hand on her leg. "I'm so sorry. Nothing would have made me prouder than to call you daughter. It doesn't change that I want to be a big part of your life. I might not be your biological father, but I've fallen in love with you. That won't change."

All the loud buzzing in her head started to subside as she heard the last two sentences. She removed one of her hands from Santino's grip, holding both their hands as she looked at Patrick. "You are my father." She then twisted toward Santino. "And my dad is going to be a grandpa."

All four of the people surrounding Chloe stared in silence.

She counted to five before Santino screeched, "WHAT!"

Smiling from ear to ear through her tears, she told him, "You're going to be a papa. I'm pregnant. And you just inherited a whole new family."

Thrilled, he picked her up and twirled her around. "I'm going to be a papa, and you're going to be a mommy!"

Patrick cleared his throat. "Um . . . you might want to be careful with my daughter and first grandchild."

Santino instantly stopped and looked over at Patrick. He saw the older man was grinning like the cat that swallowed the canary and burst out laughing. "Yes, sir." He could also see the man was itching to get his hands on his daughter. "Stellina, I think your dad needs a hug."

Chloe suddenly became shy. Then she heard a huge gasp of breath from Elenore, who was smiling through her sobs of happiness. Sniffling, she asked, "Can I have a hug from grandma and grandpa?"

The two opened their arms, and Chloe flew into them.

The scene made the men watching a daughter being welcomed into her parents' fold for the first time cry. Quinn wiped his eyes, and then asked Santino if he could call the rest of the family. Santino waited until Chloe pulled back before asking her, not sure if she wanted more time alone with the O'Connors to absorb everything. Of course, Chloe wanted everyone to celebrate with them, but she made the others there promise to let her tell them.

The famiglia all rushed over to find out what had been going on. Then, when the large group was assembled, Santino told them that Chloe wanted to introduce the people sitting in their living room.

Chloe began by introducing each of the Savages to the O'Connors.

Alessandro, being Alessandro, piped up, "Nice to meet you both, but why the big fuss?"

Valentina cuffed him. "Stupido, show some intelligence and patience, and she'll explain."

Smiling until her cheeks hurt, Chloe said, "Patrick O'Connor is my biological father, and Elenore is my stepmom."

"What!" everyone screamed loud enough to scare the twins, who started to cry.

After Luca and Brooklyn settled the babies, Santino retold the story, except for one detail.

With his fists mushed against his face, Eli, who was a little confused by the story, dejectedly said, "You were wrong, Nonna.

Auntie Chloe isn't giving me a new cousin."

Alessandro knelt down to look at his little nephew. "Cucciolo, you are getting another cousin. It just isn't Uncle Santino and Auntie Chloe giving you one. Auntie Ava has a baby in her tummy, and your cousin will be here in six months."

The group went wild, congratulating each other. Then, when things died down, Sabastian and Emmy announced they were also pregnant again.

Valentina was beyond herself. "Wow, our family just grew by leaps and bounds. I might as well tell you all that Quinn is moving in. And just in the nick of time, because I'm going to need help with all our grandchildren."

Elenore couldn't help saying, "You're a very blessed woman. I understand those feelings."

Santino, Chloe, and the O'Connors all looked at each other and smiled. Then Santino nodded his head toward Elenore, who smiled proudly as she said, "I'd like to offer you my assistance, Valentina, but I'll only have one arm to help, because my other will be filled with my own new grandchild."

Valentina shifted her head. "I'm sorry. I thought you said your children were a little younger and not married."

"They're not, but my new daughter is."

Valentina stared blankly at the woman.

Alessandro came up behind her and cuffed her gently on the head. "Come on, Ma! Maybe I got my intelligence from you. Chloe and Santino are having a baby too!"

Everyone laughed as she whipped around and pinched him good, one he would feel for a few days. Then she stopped, stood stock-still, and finally whirled around to look at Chloe, who nodded as Valentina hugged her.

"Miracles do happen." Valentina looked up. "I knew it. Thank you, Shawn."

Chapter 20
"Happiness" by NEEDTOBREATHE

Chloe went for a walk to the main lodge. It was getting closer to the end of her pregnancy, and she couldn't wait for it to be over. She was as big as a house.

She had sent Santino to help Sabastian because he was driving her crazy. He wouldn't stop hovering.

They had already welcomed Ava and Alessandro's daughter, Alianna, last month. And a week later, Sabastian and Emmy had their second son, John. Now they were all waiting on Chloe.

She smiled as she passed some guests on her way into the kitchen, where Valentina was instructing the new staff they had hired to fill in for Emmy. They had also hired a couple of nannies to help with all the new kids.

"Good morning, carina. How are you feeling?" Valentina asked, pulling out a stool for her.

"I didn't sleep again last night. I was a little grumpy with Santino," she huffed out, resting her big body. "I feel like I should be sleeping more because I won't get the chance in a couple of weeks."

Valentina smiled as she moved to ladle a bowl of soup she had just made. "You look like you have dropped. Do you feel any different?"

"Yeah, the pressure sometimes is unbelievable," Chloe complained, slumping over and holding her head up with one hand, elbow resting on the counter. "I just wish I wasn't so mean to my husband."

Valentina couldn't help chuckling at the woeful girl. "Your body is going through a lot of changes. Don't worry about Santino; he understands. He watched his brothers go through the same thing. Pregnancy is hell on our bodies. Every time I hear one of you girls, it brings back all my memories like it was yesterday." Valentina placed the bowl, spoon, and napkin in front of Chloe. "Here. Maybe this will help. It's Sicilian meatball soup. I'd like your opinion since it's a new recipe."

Chloe blew on a spoonful of the hot soup then tried a mouthful. "Mmm . . . This is delicious. Definitely a keeper."

Santino walked in, carrying an envelope. "Stellina, I could have brought you some soup. Are you feeling better?"

Chloe lifted her spoon for him to try after he kissed the side of her head. "Sorry I snapped." She felt bad for ordering him out of the cabin. No matter how grumpy she was, he took it all in stride.

Out of the corner of her eye, she saw her name handwritten on the envelope. "Is that for me?"

He moved the envelope out of her sight. "Yes, but before I give it to you, I have to warn you that it's from Jacob Moore. If you want, I can throw it out, or I can read it first to make sure it won't upset you."

Her heart sped up. On one hand, she was a little frightened to read it. On the other hand, she couldn't adore her husband any more if she tried.

A lot of husbands would have taken the choice away. In fact, she knew without a doubt that Sabastian would have opened it before giving it to Emmy.

"You know I love you, right? Thank you for wanting to protect me and still giving me options. My first instinct is to throw it away, but there isn't anything Jacob can say that can hurt me now. I have you, so I can handle anything he throws at me." She patted the stool beside her. "Sit. Let's read it together."

Santino sat, opening the letter and pulling it out. Then he handed it over.

Dear Chloe,

It has taken me a long time to find the right words to say to you. First, let me thank you for reading this letter. If I were in your shoes, I probably wouldn't. But then, you have always been a better person than me.

Believe it or not, I have learned a lot in prison. I'm getting help, and one of the men counseling me has taught me a lot about asking for forgiveness.

I made some terrible mistakes in my life, but what I did to you was inexcusable. My counselor suggested, if I was truly remorseful, that I should give it a shot by writing to you and telling you how sorry I am. I don't expect you to forgive me, but I still need to tell you how very sorry I am for everything I put you through.

I claimed temporary insanity, but honestly, I was very sick and cruel, and I wasn't raised to be that way. I'm embarrassed to tell you that I was raised in a storybook life compared to your history. I had two parents who worshiped the ground I walked on. I also had an extended family who cared and loved me. I guess, along the way, I became self-centered and believed the world revolved around me.

When I lost Nicole, I lost my mind. I wanted someone to pay. At school, I heard some grumblings about you being the shooter's daughter. I was furious that Nicole didn't get to live the life we had planned, yet there you were, going to college. I never once stopped to think about your life and all the suffering you endured at the hands of a madman. I never asked you questions about your past, and I realize now that was because, deep down, I knew your life couldn't have been easy, so I didn't want clarification. I wanted revenge any way I could get it.

I have watched my parents suffer for my actions. They have been ostracized from their community and a lot of our family. It's terrible to watch people you love being punished for something they didn't do. Essentially, they're paying the same way you did, and it makes me feel even worse for what I did, because you had to face it alone.

I have so much to apologize for, but even if I wrote a hundred letters, it would never be enough. One of my biggest regrets is damaging all your photos. Not a night goes by when I don't relive hearing about your twin sister's death, and knowing that I took the last thing you had left of her. Destroying those pictures and your childhood faces haunt me. I'm so sorry, Chloe.

I thank God every day that the Savage family found you both times before you were seriously hurt. What am I saying? You were seriously hurt. Please forgive me!

The only solace I have is that I heard you married Santino and that you are expecting. I'm happy that all your dreams are coming true, and with a man who deserves all the love you have to offer.

I'm sure you're wondering how I found out all about you in jail. The man I told you about who has been counseling me is your biological father, Reverend Patrick O'Connor.

The minute the pastor found out he was your dad, he contacted me and asked if I would like some spiritual help. At the time, I was confused about why this pastor was reaching out to me, but I accepted his help, believing my parents sent him, and I owe them so much.

Your dad is an incredibly forgiving man. I see a lot of your nature in him.

I ended up spending a month in solitary confinement after he told me the shooter wasn't your dad. I was so mad at myself that I tore my cell apart. I even stopped eating, not believing I had the right to live after what I did to you. If I could have found a way to take my life at the time, I would have. I tortured an innocent woman who was victimized from day one by the man who took Nicole from me. I'm so sorry!

They allowed him to visit me, even though I was secluded. Your dad saved my life. How ironic is that? There truly are angels on earth. I know because I've met two.

Anyway, I wanted you to know I'm truly sorry for everything. I wish you all the happiness in the world.

Love that child you're carrying with all your heart. I don't know why I said that, because I know you only have the capacity to love.

Have a great life.

When I get out of here, I'm going to turn my life around and spend the rest of it trying to give back. I hope I'm lucky enough to find a woman who can look past my record and love me the way you love Santino.

Sincerely,

Jacob Moore

Chloe wiped the tears falling down her face, then looked at her husband. He wasn't crying, but she could tell he was touched by the sincerity of the letter. She didn't think he would ever truly forgive Jacob, and she could live with that.

"I can't believe my dad has been helping Jacob all this time."

Santino brought his wife's head to his chest. "I'm not at all surprised. Jacob was right; your dad has a good nature, just like his daughter. Although, I believe he probably did it for you. He wanted you to have closure and to not have to worry about Jacob coming after you when he finally gets parole."

Chloe lifted her head but left her chin on his chest. "Santino, I need a favor."

"You know you never have to ask. I would do anything for you."

"I need you to take me to the prison today. I need to give Jacob my forgiveness before I deliver." She saw he was gearing up for a fight so, dropping her face back to chest, she said, "I know it isn't proper to take an extremely pregnant woman into a prison, but this is something I need to do for me. The minute it's done, I can finally close the door to one of the most painful times of my life. I want to start fresh. Please."

His mamma snorted. He knew she didn't like the idea, but this was something his wife needed, and she came first.

"You go get your purse, and I'll call your dad and see if he can get us in to see Jacob this afternoon. Stellina, look me in the eyes and promise me you're up for this."

Chloe climbed off the stool with his help and looked up into his eyes. Hugging her husband had become tricky with her big belly. "I swear I'm fine, and I'll be even better when I give Jacob my forgiveness."

He gave her a little swat on the behind. "Okay, amore, then grab your stuff and I'll meet you at the car." He watched her walk away. Her limp had become very prominent over the last two months due to the extra weight and pressure on her leg. However, her doctor had assured him that she was fine.

Two hours later, they met Patrick in the visitors holding room, where her dad rushed to her with open arms.

"I hope you can forgive me, sweetheart. I didn't mean to hurt you. I just wanted you to be assured he wouldn't hurt you after he was released."

She hugged the man she had truly grown to adore. "I know, Daddy. That's why I want to forgive Jacob in person. It will be a fresh start for our growing family." She rubbed her large belly to emphasize her words.

A few months ago, Chloe had called him daddy jokingly, yet his eyes had lit up. Therefore, she couldn't help continuing to do it, even though she was a grown woman, nine months pregnant, and already scheduled for a C-section.

"The prison's warden suggested we use the attorney's room instead of behind glass on those concrete stools because of your condition," Patrick explained. "Jacob will be tethered to the table with two guards in the room."

The pressure on the nerve on her bad leg caused her to flounder a bit. Santino took one arm and her dad took the other.

Smiling up at the two men she loved, she said, "I'm not scared, Daddy. I promise."

Santino looked at Patrick. "That's my crazy, beautiful, brave wife."

Her proud dad patted her hand.

They left their belongings in a locker, then went through security. They patted Chloe down because she didn't want to go through the X-ray machine.

Before she knew it, they were walking into a room, and Jacob was sitting there.

His eyes grew as big as possible. "Chloe? What are you doing here?"

Her two protectors helped her into a chair, then sat on either side of her. Poor Santino was jiggling his legs like mad and tapping her hand.

"Hello, Jacob. I got your letter today and wanted to come here personally to thank you. I also wanted to tell you that I forgive you."

Jacob sat there, stunned, before dropping his head and shaking it from side to side. He tried to talk but was too overcome with joy and lingering guilt. He started to weep. "I'm sorry, Chloe, so sorry."

The pressure in her womb made it hard to sit still. A couple of tears fell as she said, "It's over, Jacob. I forgive you. And now it's time for you to forgive yourself. Don't let your past influence your future."

He couldn't believe this woman. Still sobbing like a baby, with his nose running and no way to wipe it, he said, "I caused you so much heartache. I physically hurt you, and yet, here you sit, telling me to forgive myself."

"You did, but if it wasn't for you, I wouldn't have met my husband or my dad. I believe everything happens for a reason." She sat a little taller to ease the pressure. "Jacob, if you really want to do something for me, then forgive yourself, serve your time, and then live a good life."

"I will. Thank you. I also wish you and your family continued happiness." He turned first to her father, then her husband. "Take care of her, and love her like she deserves."

Santino and Patrick both nodded.

There was nothing else to say, so the three of them got up to go.

Suddenly, Chloe screeched and grabbed the table. As she doubled over, her water broke, and all five men froze. She screeched again when another burst of pain seized her.

The reverend yelled at one of the guards to call 9-1-1. The guard yelled, "Code green," into his walkie-talkie and, two minutes later, all hell broke loose as twelve men came charging into the room, guns drawn and pointed at Jacob.

Chloe screamed in fear this time, and Santino yelled to back off, that his wife was in labor, and to get an ambulance as soon as possible.

They all watched as Patrick and Santino moved her back to the chair. She couldn't sit, though, so she slumped down, wiggling to alleviate the pain. Chloe didn't seem to get a minute between contractions. It seemed like forever before help finally arrived.

In the meantime, six guards managed to get Jacob unhooked and out of the room.

There was yelling in the hallway as a stretcher came flying in, pushed by medical personnel. A male nurse started to talk to Chloe, but she didn't answer many questions because the contractions were nonstop.

Santino was frantic, kneeling beside his wife and holding her hand.

The medical personnel waited for a strong contraction to pass, then assisted her onto the stretcher before rushing her to the infirmary.

Chloe looked at the ceiling, in the worst pain imaginable, not believing she was in labor in a prison.

Santino kept pace, never letting go of her hand as he repeated, "I won't leave your side. I love you, Stellina."

By the time they got to the infirmary, the paramedics were just rushing in. Everyone else stayed outside the examination room except the paramedics, nurses, and Santino.

After a quick check of her vitals, they helped Santino strip her of her pants and underwear. After placing a sheet partially over her lower body, the paramedic tried to confirm how far she was dilated. He didn't get very far because a visual check of her progress had him declaring she was already crowning. They couldn't transport her. Chloe was going to have to deliver at the prison infirmary.

Santino was thankful it happened here with help, because if this had happened on their way home, he would have been alone, not knowing what to do.

Everyone was bustling around, trying to prepare for the birth, as Santino took the cloth the nurse offered him and wiped his wife's sweaty face.

"You're doing great, baby. Breathe like they taught us in class. You can do this."

She cried out after the next pain, "I'm sorry. I screwed up again." Huffing in as much air as she could, she then said, "I should have waited to see Jacob. Santino, I'm sorry I'm going to deliver in a prison. I didn't have any of the warning signs—" She stopped to scream, squeezing his hand.

He tried to reassure her between screams, but there wasn't a lot of time. "It doesn't matter where you deliver. It's just another story to tell our kids when they're older. Think—"

"Ma'am," the paramedic cut in, "on your next contraction, I want you to bear down. This baby is coming right now."

Chloe's scream should have lifted the roof off the prison.

Outside the door, more prison officials congregated with Patrick. He told them all about his daughter.

"The head is out," the paramedic yelled. "One more big push and your baby will be here."

Santino moved behind her and helped lift her up to bear down. She screamed one more time as the baby slid out.

"It's a boy!" the paramedic exclaimed. "You have a son, the first baby I have ever delivered. Congratulations. Let me cut the cord, and you can hold him."

"There's another one!" Santino yelled.

If they were in any other circumstance, they might have laughed at the paramedic as all the blood drained from his face. "What?"

Santino wrapped his arms around her shoulders, letting her relax against him. "Twins. My wife is having identical twins."

"Jesus Christ, I'm a paramedic, not an obstetrician. Okay, ma'am, I'm going to have check the position of baby B. Sometimes, the second one can be breech. This might hurt. Are you experiencing any more contractions?"

"No, the doctor told us, if I had a vaginal birth, the first would pave the way. I was scheduled for a C-section in two weeks. I'm thirty-five weeks. The second baby is smaller by about a pound. Please tell me everything is okay."

Santino was freaking the hell out. He knew the paramedic was scared, which frightened the hell out of him.

Before he yelled at the guy for scaring Chloe, a man burst through the door.

"I'm Dr. Fields. Oh, I see you have everything under control."

The relief on the paramedic's face was tangible. "Wrong! She's having twins. Baby A was born a couple of minutes ago. We have to check baby B's position."

The doctor took the gloves the nurse handed him, snapping them on. "What's your name?"

"Her name is Chloe, and I'm Santino."

The doctor was all business. "You know they're identical, so do we know if there was one placenta and how many sacs?"

Santino knew all the answers because he had flipped out when he had found out Chloe was carrying twins and made sure the doctor had explained everything. "Yes, two sacs, one placenta."

"Okay, that's good," the doctor said.

With tears streaming down her face, Chloe begged, "Check our son, Santino."

The doctor looked toward the nurse. "Bring baby A to the parents, while I check the position of baby B." He needed the parents to focus on baby A and not what he was doing.

One of the paramedics pulled a chair out for the nurse holding baby boy A. He opened the blanket and showed them the little guy's fingers and toes.

Chloe yelped and jumped from the examination. It hurt.

Santino's eyes flew to the doctor.

"Good news, folks. The baby is in the proper position and already making his way down. The next delivery should be easier. Chloe, I'm going to ask the nurse to back away with baby A so we can help this other little guy into the world. I know you're tired, but it won't be long now. Dad, help her lift up so she can push."

Santino was feeling a great amount of relief having a doctor here.

Now he could focus totally on his wife.

"How are you doing, Mommy?"

At the excitement in his voice, Chloe twisted her head, her hair plastered to her face. Her smile was the best gift he had ever received. She was by far the strongest woman he had ever met.

He had never been as scared as he was the last hour and a half. He understood now why Luca fixed himself after Brooklyn had their twins. He was struggling with his promise to give Chloe any number of children she wanted or getting a vasectomy. He never wanted to feel this helpless again, or see Chloe in this kind of pain.

Her face transformed with the pressure of the baby moving down the birth canal. He had seen her gorgeous, silvery eyes in pain too many times. He had to keep reminding himself that this was what she wanted.

When Baby A cried out, his first protective instinct as a papa kicked in. "Everything okay with our son?"

The nurse looked at him. "Yup. I think he's calling out to his brother to hurry up." The man smiled reassuringly.

Chloe lifted herself off the stretcher, snapping him back to reality. He helped her hold the position, not wanting her to have to work any harder than she already was.

"He's crowning," the doctor called out. "Okay, Chloe, I'm going to ask you to give me two good pushes, then stop. Now push! Good job. One more, and we'll have his shoulders out. Again." The doctor shifted baby B's shoulders side to side, easing his way out. "Okay, Mom, one more push and baby B will be here."

Chloe squeezed her eyes shut and pushed with all her might. She heard her son cry out.

"He's out, Stellina. You did great. You never stop amazing me."

"Check him," she rushed out as he lowered her back down and kissed her sweat-moist lips.

Santino got up, and the doctor offered to let him cut the cord as he approached.

Santino quickly counted all his toes and fingers. The little guy was still wailing. "He's perfect, Stellina. Although a lot smaller than our firstborn."

Chloe lifted her head to catch a glimpse of baby B. She was overwhelmed with guilt for mentally calling her son baby B, but she had refused to talk about names until she knew they were born healthy. "We have to name them. I don't want people calling them baby A and B."

Santino laughed as the doctor wrapped his son in a blanket and passed the baby to him. "He's so tiny. Thank goodness, because they look like the same kid." The nurse placed baby A in the crux of Chloe's arm, while Santino brought baby B to meet his mommy.

"Son, this is your beautiful mamma. Mommy, this is son number two."

Chloe cried when she saw with her own eyes that both her children were perfect. "Hi, sweetheart. Mommy loves you." Kissing his head, she looked at baby A. "I love both of you. We're going to make sure you boys have a good life, filled with love."

The doctor was dealing with the third stage of the births—delivering the placenta.

The paramedics came to admire the twins, and the one who delivered baby A said, "Sorry I lost it. I've never lost my cool in nine years, but I've never delivered a baby, and then the second took me for a loop. Please forgive me."

Chloe gave him a beautiful smile. "You never have to apologize. I don't know what I would have done without you guys. What's your name?"

"Connor, ma'am."

"Connor, thank you. And please don't call me ma'am. I'm

younger than you. I'm Chloe." She whipped her head to Santino. "Connor, I like that name. Our first son should be named after the man who delivered him. And my dad would love that because it's part of his last name."

Santino grinned. "Connor Savage. I love it." He turned to the doctor. "What's your name?"

The man chuckled. "Oh no, I don't like my name, and I would never saddle a boy with Diego, but I like my middle name—Gabriel."

Santino's grin grew into a huge smile. "That was my grandfather's name. Mamma's papa."

"Gabriel. It suits him. Our second son will be Gabriel. One Italian and one Irish, like us."

Santino proudly looked at Connor in Chloe's arms and Gabriel in his. "Thank you, Doctor."

The man chuckled. "It was my honor. I can honestly tell you that I never thought I would ever deliver a baby because of where I work. My wife won't believe me."

"I think we need some pictures." Santino turned to the nurse who wasn't assisting the doctor. "Can you take some pictures of my famiglia with the paramedics, and then with the doctor when he's done?"

"The stitches are done and will need to be checked when you get to the hospital," the doctor replied as soon as he finished safely wrapping up the placenta for transportation to the hospital. "Now let's take some pictures, because I need proof of this blessed event. This is a lot different than the usual things we deal with in here."

Suddenly, it hit Chloe that her dad didn't know yet. "When we're done, can my dad come in?"

The doctor stood, covering her with a blanket. "By all means, let me go get him." He peeled the gloves off and tossed them away before walking to the door and opening it.

Patrick jumped forward. "How's my daughter?"

"Come and see for yourself, Grandpa. You have two healthy, beautiful grandsons."

Patrick started to bawl as he shook the doctor's hand. "Thank you."

The sight in front of him would forever be ingrained in his mind. The daughter he had only known for months but loved like crazy had a little baby in her arms, and the husband Patrick couldn't have done a better job of picking for her was holding the other little babe.

He didn't move until Chloe said, "Come in, Daddy, and meet Connor and Gabriel."

Her father stumbled in. "Connor and Gabriel?"

Santino laughed. "Yes, partly for you and partly for the paramedic who delivered him. Our youngest son was named for the doctor and my grandfather."

Poor Patrick sobbed harder, kissing his daughter and then the little boys. Life couldn't get any better as he hugged his son-in-law.

The doctor stepped closer. "Okay, folks, as soon as we're done, I think it's time we got this little family to the hospital. I'm going to travel with them in the ambulance. Warden, call in a replacement. I have to look after our newest visitors to the prison," he said with so much pride. "Pictures first, though. Warden, come on and join us. When are we ever going to be able to say our population grew by two without a paddy wagon?"

They all chuckled at his sense of humor.

When all the pictures were taken, the couple were wheeled down the hallways as guards clapped like crazy, yelling congratulations.

By the time they reached the hospital, all the Savages and O'Connors were waiting for them in the triage area.

As the paramedic stopped the stretcher in front of the crowd, Santino pointed to his sons. "Famiglia, I'd like you to meet our sons.

Connor is the bigger one on Chloe's left side, and Gabriel is the smaller one on her right."

The famiglia went crazy, hugging and congratulating them.

Alessandro slapped his brother's shoulder. "Only you two would give birth in a prison."

"Yup, and damn proud of it. My wife is a rock star. The most courageous person to grace our planet. I was a nervous wreck, but at least I didn't pass out like you did on Ava." He gave his brother a friendly slap on the back.

Mamma grabbed Santino from Alessandro and hugged her son, whispering in his ear, "My baby is a daddy. If you look after those boys half as well as you have always looked after me, they're going to be very lucky. You saved my carina's life and gave her everything she ever wanted. I'm so proud of you, Santino. You're the mirror image of your dad."

Valentina couldn't help letting the tears fall. Five years ago, her world had fallen apart, and she hadn't believed she could live another second with all the loss and pain. She certainly hadn't thought she would ever be happy again. But standing here, looking at her famiglia, she got the chills.

Her sons had sacrificed so much for her and Shawn's dream, and the guilt had weighed heavily on her for so long. But now each one of them had found happiness and the same love she had shared with their dad. She had also found a new love with Quinn. Her famiglia had grown and extended, and she loved them all with every ounce of her heart.

It hadn't been an easy road, but when was life ever easy? There were regrets, as well as milestones. Lessons taught and learned. It had taken her a lot of tears, pain, and growth to realize that sometimes just surviving took courage. The courage that rewarded her with this beautiful picture in front of her.

It was a very good day to be a Savage.

Epilogue
"Blessed" by Elton John
Ten years later . . .

Santino never imagined being in this position and was freaking out. After three sets of twins and a vasectomy, he hadn't thought he would ever see the inside of a delivery room again.

He shook his head. Things never turned out like he expected, so really, he shouldn't have been surprised. But after this set of twins was delivered, he was either getting Chloe fixed or getting it in writing that she was never giving birth to another child.

After their first set of twins, the doctor had said the likelihood of Chloe having twins again were slim to none. By the third set, the doctor had conceded it had to be divine intervention and was beyond explanation.

Stellina always wanted a lot of kids, but after six in eight years, Santino had finally put his foot down. They didn't have the starting line for a soccer team, but they had the first line of a hockey team.

Enough was enough!

"You're doing great, Chloe," the doctor told her. "The first one is crowning. You know the drill. Two big pushes, then stop."

Answering so unlike herself, she snapped, "You try stopping a freight train on command!" Chloe was in excruciating pain.

The doctor had the audacity to chuckle. "I know it's hard—"

"No! You don't and never will," Chloe gritted out through clenched teeth.

"Mrs. Savage, you're being a little . . . savage."

The doctor, nurses, Santino, and Chloe all whipped their heads towards Raimer as Owen tried to cover his mouth.

Pushing Owen's hand away, he said, "What? I've never heard her be so rude before. I don't want our babies to get the wrong impression of their mamácita incubator."

Taking three deep breaths, she then fired off, "Until you can push a watermelon through your penis, you don't get to have an opinion." Chloe then screamed at the next contraction.

Santino barked out a laugh at Raimer's insulted face, then issued a final warning. "Dude, you're lucky she can't get up right now or those balls you're so proud of would be resting in the tray beside the doctor, waiting to be reattached."

The doctor and nurse looked at each other, unable to contain their laughter. This unusual group was by far the weirdest delivery either had ever experienced.

Gaining his composure, the doctor said, "Chloe, push now."

When Raimer and Owen shifted down to the end of the bed so they could see better, Santino growled, but no one heard since Chloe was screaming, her whole body pulling tight. Hands around her knees, she pushed hard twice on the fierce contraction.

Not thrilled that both men were looking at his wife's coochie, when it was quiet, Santino said, "This side of the blanket, guys." He swung his head over toward Chloe's upper body.

Raimer blew him off. "It's not like we were interested before. And let me assure you, we are even less now."

Owen totally ignored Raimer's comment, hand over his mouth, mumbling out, "Look, the baby's shoulders. Oh my God, what a miracle."

Raimer grabbed his hand as they watched their child coming out of Chloe.

Once the shoulders were delivered, the rest of the baby slid right out.

"It's a boy. We have a son!" Raimer screamed almost as loud as Chloe, jumping up and down. The two men quickly hugged. "Mamácita, you gave us a son. We're papàs. Owen, can you believe it?"

"You're papa. I'm daddy," Owen returned with pride, grinning like a fool.

Santino looked at his wife, who couldn't smile any bigger if she tried. It was humbling to be in the presence of such an incredibly giving woman.

One night, about a year ago, he came home to no kids in the cabin and his favorite meal cooking with the best bottle of wine they had. Chloe stood there, looking like every grown man's fantasy. His wife was like fine wine—she got better with each year. However, he knew this wasn't just a regular seduction when he spied the truffle and panna cotta on the counter.

She glided over in her fine, little dress, wrapping her arms around his shoulders and raising to her toes to kiss him senseless.

When she finally released his lips, he mumbled against her neck, "What are you up to, Stellina?"

Chloe smiled alluringly, and those beautiful eyes twinkled. That was all it took.

Santino knew he would give her anything she wanted when she looked at him like that. He lived for that look.

He'd had a vasectomy, so he knew it couldn't be more children. Chloe had said she was happy with six kids and teaching at their still-growing daycare.

They gave their children everything. They were surrounded with an abundance of love, and had as many playmates as any kid could handle. They traveled every year; two weeks with the kids and two alone. So, what was her game? His beautiful wife never wanted material things.

"Spill. What do you want? You wasted your time cooking all my favorites when all you had to do was look at me like that. But you already knew that, didn't you?" He emphasized the statement with a quick, sharp slap to her luscious ass. There was no way he could wait until she plied him with alcohol and great food to agree to whatever she wanted.

Chloe jumped from the sting, then purred. Santino was so screwed.

"I need to talk to you about something very important to me. I don't want you to say no until you promise to hear everything I have to say. Will you promise to hear me out?"

Santino wrapped one arm around her delicate shoulders and led her to the bottle of wine on the table. He didn't respond right away, mulling over her words. He had never denied her anything, so what could be so bad? Suddenly, Santino was nervous.

He poured the wine that had been breathing, then placed a glass in her hand before lifting his own. Then he moved to the stove to turn off the boiling water before leading her to the couch.

"Talk to me, amore."

She clinked her glass with her husband's, then took a big sip. Chloe would take whatever courage she could get, even the liquid form. "I talked to Quinn today. He broke my heart. The woman who was going to surrogate for Raimer and Owen pulled out when she found out they were a gay couple. I know how they feel, because when Jacob finally showed his true colors, I thought my dream of having a child was gone. Owen and Raimer want a child so badly, and they shouldn't be denied any more than I should have."

It didn't take a rocket scientist to figure out where she was going. "Stellina, I thought we agreed after the girls were born that you shouldn't have any more children because of your leg. Do you remember how you had to be on bed rest for the last two months of the pregnancy?"

Torn between knowing her husband was right and her desire to help her friends, she said, "I know, but Santino, they want a baby, and I might be their only chance. I've had three years to strengthen my muscles, and I have been extremely diligent. It was also because I didn't lose the weight from the pregnancy before. I'm back to my original weight now." Chloe had to convince him. Raimer and Owen had been instrumental in helping her when she had been at her lowest.

Cupping her jaw, he brought her mouth closer and kissed her. Would this woman ever stop amazing him? Her pregnancies had been brutal. The fact that she was even considering it was mind-boggling.

"I get that, I really do, but I don't want a child that will be half yours fathered by another man."

Her face lit up as she grabbed his hands and shifted up to her knees. If this was his only concern, then she had it in the bag.

"But it won't be. They will select donor eggs that will be fertilized with Owen and Raimer's sperm. Then they'll inseminate the viable eggs into my womb, and we'll hope one takes."

"How many? And what if they're all viable? You could have five or six. Face it, baby, you're as fertile as a rabbit. You're a tiny woman; your body couldn't sustain that many children safely and still be able to walk."

Her mind was working a hundred miles a minute. "Okay, so we'll make sure they only inseminate three at a time. Please, Santino, I really want to do this. I know it's a lot to ask my husband, and I know it will be hard on both of us, but remember everything they did for us. I know if the roles were reversed, either one would do it for us without a second thought."

Santino scrubbed his hands down his face. Mamma had just told him that Quinn was trying to convince them to start the adoption process again after waiting three years and being second from the top when China had closed their program down. They had both been devastated. Then he thought about how much happiness his six children had brought them. "Okay."

"Pardon me?" Chloe didn't think she had heard him right.

"I said okay. How can I deny them the happiness our kids have brought us?"

Chloe squealed and jumped off the couch. "I have to call them right now." She ran for her phone on the counter and started dialing, but then she pushed the end button before it connected and turned back to Santino. "Would you mind if I invited them over for dinner? I know it was supposed to be our special night, but I want to see their faces in person."

Chuckling from the couch, he told her, "I guess I should have held off giving you my answer until I got you in bed."

Now she felt bad. Walking over to him, she put her phone on the coffee table. "If you want me to wait, I'll invite them tomorrow."

He shook his head, picking up the phone and handing it to her. "No, baby, I want your total attention later tonight. Besides, you have a spanking coming for trying to seduce me into getting your way."

Chloe blushed as she picked up the phone. "I'm not sure I want them to come for dinner now." When she placed the phone to her ear, she heard laughing. Scrunching her face up, she said, "Uh . . . hello?"

"I have to tell you, Chloe, I usually like gay BDSM, but I think I just got a boner from that threat of a spanking!" Raimer howled.

"Oh, my freaking God, please tell me you did not hear our conversation." Her left hand flew to her forehead, not believing she hadn't ended the call.

She had to hold the phone back because Raimer was laughing so hard. Then she heard Owen's voice saying hello.

"Owen?"

"Yeah, the jackass is still laughing. What the hell did he hear?"

Mortified, she replied, "You don't want to know, and I don't want to tell you. I was going to invite you guys for dinner. I have something important to talk to you about. But now I'm not sure I can face Raimer."

"We accept," Owen was quick to say. "We came to the resort to scrounge a meal from Valentina and Dad, but we didn't know they were watching all your troublemakers. I love them all to death, but I don't know how you do it. In less than half an hour, I felt like I've been to war and back."

All she could think was, You better change your tune, because you're about to find out just how tiring it is. "Perfect. Come over. I'll put the water on for the pasta."

Not ten minutes later, the men walked in.

Raimer, being the absolute ass that he was, came in on Owen's arm, covering his eyes and asking if Chloe had clothes on or if she was tied up.

She walked up and gave him a smack on the head that Valentina would have been proud of. "Scustumad!"

Blindsided, Raimer rubbed his head, yelling, "Are you sure you're not the one giving the spankings? Because that hurt."

Chloe stomped her foot, blushing from head to toe.

Santino came over to shake the men's hands, then directed his words to Raimer, "If I were you, I wouldn't piss her off. Soon, you're going to be kissing her feet. And guarantee, I'm videotaping it."

Owen looked at the romantic setting. "Are you sure you want us here? I'm starting to think we're going to be the third and fourth wheel."

"Nope, we really want you guys here. Can you grab a couple more plates and set the table while I put the pasta in?" Chloe was so excited she was bouncing around like crazy.

"Sure, but I really do feel like we're intruding." Owen walked to the cupboard, grabbing two more plates and the cutlery. "What's the occasion?"

Dumping the box of linguine in the water and stirring to make sure all the long pasta was covered in water, she answered, "We're celebrating, but we can't tell you about it until after dinner."

Santino was busy pouring his special wine into two more glasses.

Accepting a glass, Raimer said, "That's kind of cruel to make us wait."

She placed her hands on her hips. "Well, if you worked for five hours on a special meal with six kids running around, you'd want people to eat it too." Chloe stirred the pasta again.

Raimer swished the wine in his mouth before swallowing. It was probably the best wine he had ever tasted. "This doesn't make sense. You obviously went to a lot of trouble to make a romantic dinner for your hubby, and now you want to share it with us? Did you suddenly get your period and the night was ruined, so you needed comic relief?"

"Oh my God, is there anything off limits to you?" Chloe snapped.

Owen extended his hand to her. "Hi, Chloe. I'm Owen. Have you met my husband, Raimer?"

"Very funny—"

"Dudes," Santino refereed again, "seriously, keep going and she won't tell you her news until after dessert. It would be a crime for you to wait that long." He saw her trying to lift the big pot with hot water to drain the pasta. "Here, Stellina, let me do that."

Raimer kneaded Owen's shoulder. "Why can't you be as considerate as Santino?"

"If you were a foot shorter and a hundred pounds lighter, I might consider it," Owen fired back at his husband.

Chloe looked over from the stove. "Owen, can you pass me the truffle and the grater?"

He picked up the ugly thing that looked like an old potato and a black mushroom had babies. "Truffles! Holy crap, this is a special night." He never forgot the first night he had tasted the delicacy and heard the price. "At this time of year, that must have cost you anywhere from two hundred and fifty to five hundred a pound. I'm thinking that little beauty cost you about three hundred and fifty bucks. Damn, girl, now I'm super curious."

Santino laughed. "Yup, my wife spared no expense at trying to get her way." He grabbed the osso buco out of the oven and placed it on the table.

When everything was on the table, the four sat down.

Chloe raised her glass. "To famiglia."

"To famiglia," the other three said, clinking glasses with her.

They enjoyed the meal immensely.

Owen rubbed his belly at the end. "Chloe, that was spectacular. I don't care what you have to tell us, the food made it worth the wait. Thank you so much."

Chloe couldn't sit still.

"Just tell them, Stellina. That way, you can enjoy your panna cotta."

She giggled with excitement. "Okay. But we need the Prosecco I put in the fridge."

Santino cleared the table, then retrieved four champagne flutes and the bottle. When he sat back down, Chloe started.

"I had an epiphany today, but I had to make sure Santino was okay with it first before I could share it with you guys."

"You want us to film you in a BDSM scene?" She had hesitated a minute too long for Raimer.

Since he was trying to embarrass her again, she blurted it out without thinking. "No, smartass. I want to give you guys a child."

Both balked, but Owen recovered first, his eyebrows in his hairline. "You want to give us one of your kids, and Santino agreed?"

"NO! Scustumad. I want to be your surrogate. You would have to get donor eggs, but I want you two to have the family you have always dreamed of."

Neither man reacted as her words sank in. Chloe was afraid she had made a mistake until she saw the tears shimmering in both their eyes. Owen grabbed his husband's hand.

Quietly, Raimer asked, "You won't change your mind?" He was as serious as she had ever seen or heard.

At that second, Santino knew one thousand percent what Chloe had proposed was the right thing to do. How had he missed how much these men wanted children of their own? They had babysat more times than he could count. With each set of twins, these two guys had spent hours rocking the new infants to give them a break, or spent time with their other kids.

"Once Stellina makes a decision, it's done," Santino told them. "I promise you, if she's able to carry a child for you, she will. I support her completely. Although, in the later months of her pregnancy when she is on bed rest, I might need a little more help with our kids."

Raimer bent forward, covering his face with his hands and making a wounded sound that broke all their hearts. Owen rubbed his back and consoled him.

"We're going to have a baby of our own. A child that no one can take from us."

They all started to tear up when Raimer wept harder.

Santino had never been more aware of how much he had taken for granted being able to have children. He got up and went to Raimer's other side. "You're going to be a great daddy. Although, I hope the baby is more like Owen, because I don't know if the world can handle a little version of you."

Raimer bellowed out a half-laugh, half-sob as he threw his arms around Santino. "Thank you, brother." He kept pounding his back while he cried.

Owen got up and went to Chloe. He opened his arms to take the crying woman in. "How can I thank you? I've wanted a child so badly. I was terrified it would never happen. God, Chloe, this is the kindest gesture I have ever heard of. I love you so much."

Raimer suddenly wrapped his arms around his sweet girl and the man he loved more than life itself. "My little mamácita incubator, there is nothing I can say to thank you. As long as we live, we will never be able to repay you for your kindness. You truly are an angel sent from God."

Three months later, the four of them sat in the living room, looking at the results of the pregnancy test. The stick said she was six weeks pregnant.

Owen and Raimer jumped up and down, screaming like her kids. When they finally calmed down, they all agreed not to tell a soul until they had the first ultrasound, because there was a bigger chance of complications with in vitro fertilization with donor eggs and sperm. Thank goodness Chloe could wear sweaters and hide her tummy.

At three months along, the four of them all squeezed into the ultrasound room.

The woman moved the wand around, and then bent her head in confusion. She looked at the requisition again, then moved the wand again. Suddenly, she stood. "I have to get the doctor. I'll be right back."

Everyone's hearts sank. Something was wrong with the baby.

Nobody said a word, each holding their partner's hand for comfort and praying for a miracle.

Because it was a fertility clinic, their doctor was on the premises. She walked into the somber room. "Hello, folks, the technician wants to show me something." The woman followed behind the table so she could see the screen.

The technician pointed at the screen, then punched in a few of the keys on the keyboard then pointed again.

"Get a close-up of the chambers and give me a count of the beats."

Both Chloe and Santino had been through this so many times that they knew she was talking about the four chambers of the heart. The baby's heart must be malformed or undeveloped.

At that moment, Chloe vowed she would get pregnant again if the pregnancy had to be terminated or if the baby died.

"Okay, folks, I'm sure you're all wondering what's going on. I have some news. The baby is growing beautifully, but—"

"No, please, don't say but," Raimer blurted out. "We're already head over heels in love with our baby."

The doctor smiled. "Well, I hope you have enough love for two, because you're having twins!"

"What!" all four of them screamed.

Chloe recovered first. "But you only heard one heartbeat."

"True, but that was because they are in perfect sync, and one baby is a bit bigger with a stronger heartbeat than the other. But they are both healthy and have all their limbs. We can tell the sex. Do you want to know?"

"NO!" Owen and Raimer screamed together.

"Okay, then, we'll let it be a surprise. But everything checks out. Your kids are growing exactly as they should. Mary will give you some pictures."

That night, Raimer and Owen invited the whole famiglia to their house for dinner. Everyone was speculating on the occasion, but the four remained tight-lipped all night until after coffee was served and the couple presented Valentina and Quinn with two boxes to open simultaneously.

When they opened the boxes, yellow and green balloons floated out, to the delight of all the children.

Valentina looked at Owen. "Please tell me this means what I think it means."

He beamed as he handed Valentina an envelope, and Raimer gave Quinn one. "Open it up and see."

Valentina opened the envelope and saw the sonogram picture at the same time Quinn did.

"I'm going to be a grandpa again?" Quinn said excitedly. "That's fantastic. Congratulations!" He jumped up to hug Raimer and Owen. "How many months before I get to meet my new grandchild?"

"Grandchildren," Raimer corrected. "Can't let the Savages outdo us. We're having twins."

The group all cheered with elation.

Sabastian, who was holding his newest baby, asked, "You guys found a new surrogate?"

Raimer looked at Owen before answering. "Actually, the surrogate found us."

Valentina was only half-listening, admiring both the pictures. "Hey, why do these pictures say Savage A and Savage B?"

Santino stood. "Because my unbelievable wife wanted to gift Owen and Raimer with a family of their own."

Everyone gasped as Quinn pushed his way through the crowd to get to Chloe, who was just starting to stand. He clasped her by the shoulders, tears overflowing from his eyes, and glanced down at her sweater.

She lifted the hem enough to see her baby bump, then picked up his hand and placed it on her belly. "You told me your greatest wish was for Raimer and Owen to have a family. I could never thank you enough for all you did for me." She looked at all of them individually.

"You all gave me a family, so it was my turn to give you one."

Quinn couldn't talk as he hugged Chloe, blown away by her generosity. In Quinn's line of work, he heard a lot of bad of what the world had to offer, but standing here today, he could only see the good. "I love you, daughter of my heart."

***

They watched as the nurse gathered their son up and took him to the side to clean and weigh him. Meanwhile, the doctor encouraged Chloe to take a quick rest because, if this birth was anything like the last one, he knew it wouldn't be long before the next one came.

Owen excitedly wandered over to watch the nurse take care of their son. When he heard Chloe say she felt like she had to push, the doctor got ready and, sure enough, the second baby was crowning. With less effort than the first one, Chloe delivered the second baby only two minutes after the first.

Raimer squealed, "Jesucristo, it's a girl! Owen, we have the all-American family."

Owen rushed over to look at his daughter. "Look how beautiful and tiny she is. She is the most beautiful girl I have ever seen."

The nurse came over and offered their son to them. Raimer reached out and scooped him up, while Owen followed the other nurse to watch her with their daughter. In less than three minutes, the nurse handed the little girl to Owen.

He cuddled her against the nape of his neck, breathing in her heavenly scent. "Come, angel, and meet your papá." Owen walked cautiously with his precious bundle. "Papá, look at our angel. Isn't she stunning?"

Raimer looked up, tears streaming down his face as he shook his head. "Oh my, she is magnificent. And so is our son. They're perfect." It was obvious the girl was all Owen and the boy was the spitting image of Raimer.

They heard Chloe sniffling behind them as Santino cooed to her and turned with a sense of gratitude that could never be put into words. The woman who made all their dreams come true was sobbing with happiness as hard as they were.

Owen nudged Raimer toward the bed.

"Mamácita, Santino, I'd like to do the honor of presenting Santiago, named after you Santino, and Stellina for you, mamácita." His voice cracked. "Thank you."

Owen leaned over so Chloe could kiss her namesake. "Hello, sweet Stellina. I'm so happy I had a part in bringing you into the world. You're going to have such a blessed life. I'm always here if you ever need me." She ran her hand over the child's baby-fine, fair hair.

Owen pulled back, then Raimer leaned over to show off their handsome son. "Mamácita, I bless the day I met you. Who knew the beaten little waif would give me my heart's desire? Thank you. I love you, mamácita."

Chloe kissed the dark hair of the little boy and touched his tiny fingers. "Welcome, Santiago. By the way you kicked me, I have a feeling you're going to make your dads proud and be a fine soccer player. Always trust your dads; they went through a lot to have you. Remember, I will always be here for you too."

Santino congratulated each man and thanked them for his namesake.

The men asked if the couple would also be the children's godparents. Without a thought, the couple agreed and said they would be honored.

Once they moved the group into a recovery room, the famiglia was invited in to meet the two newest members, while Owen fed Santiago and Raimer fed Stellina.

Valentina and Quinn cried, going back and forth between the children. The rest of the famiglia also wanted a chance to meet the new additions, so Quinn moved out of the way, maneuvering himself close to Santino and Chloe. He asked them to really look at the scene in front of them.

"It's almost like you both were able to be God. It truly is a miracle to gift parents with children. How does it feel to have gone through the whole process, then hand them over?"

Chloe smiled. "Like it was always meant to be. I love those babies, but it's different because I know they aren't ours. It really does feel just like meeting all the rest of my nieces and nephews. We love them with all our hearts, but they were always meant to be Owen's and Raimer's. Congratulations, Grandpa."

Chloe could have taken credit for the new lives in front of them, but they really didn't feel like they belonged to them. There was a special bond, that was for sure, but not like their own children.

All of a sudden, their six children rushed in with friends. They jumped onto Chloe's bed, and Santino got emotional. Life was full of surprises, some bad and some good.

He couldn't help looking up and thanking his dad for everything he had taught him. Without his love and guidance, he might not have been able to handle his wife carrying other men's children.

Many times over the last sixteen years, he had asked for his dad's advice. He might not have heard the actual words but he knew instinctively what his answer would have been.

His large, happy famiglia was a result of the massacre. He had questioned God's plan many times throughout the years, and it had taken him this long to come to terms with his losses, but maybe God had made up for needing his dad and brother in heaven.

Ava walked over to him. "Your dad says, Savages strong and proud!" She tapped his hand five times.

Santino looked at Ava. "My dad and brother may not be here, but they also never left. Savages strong and proud!"

The End

Thank you for reading my book!

If you enjoyed it, please take the time to review or rate this book at your purchaser and or Goodreads.com.

It's the only way independent authors like me get recognized.

Check out my website: annemariecitro.com

After the acknowledgments, take a sneak peek at my new series, Sins of Our Fathers, *There Is No Truth*.

Other books by Anne Marie Citro

Sista Series:
Under Her Wings
Lyrics Heart & Soul
Thicker Than Blood
Breaking Down My Walls
My Beloved Past
Consequences of Being JoJo

Savage's Buck & Doe Series:
Savory Sabastian
Lascivious Luca
Addictive Alessandro
Seductive Santino

Acknowledgments

To my husband, Tony. You have always been my savior and protector, and nothing has changed through all these years later. The scene about the she-ee-py sheep came about because we bought our granddaughter a puppet sheep in South Dakota, and it traveled with us through Wyoming. He turned to me after I made a snarky comment, picked up the sheep, stuffed it in my face, and asked if I was grumpy because I was she-ee-py. We laughed so hard that we were crying and had to pull off the road. That damn sheep became a catalyst in our marriage, and now, whenever one of us picks a fight, we use the sheep reference. Thank you for always making me laugh. It is truly one of the best gifts you give me. I love you even when you're she-ee-py.

To my sons, John, Paul, Mark, and Joey. I love you guys and often think I was as hard on you as my character Valentina, but I see how you turned out and know that, as hard as I was on you four, I loved you with the same passion. There were many calls from you guys to Dad saying I had gone crazy again. If I was out of control, it was because you guys were driving me to the brink of insanity, and you deserved what you got. And that's only for the stuff I knew about. God help you for the stuff I didn't know about. Love you boys to the moon and back.

To my daughters-in-law, Eve and Nawal. You rock my world. Thank you for keeping my boys in line. My respect and admiration knows no bounds. Now, if you could work on the other two getting married, I'd sure appreciate it.

Poor Eve, you thought Valentina should be charged with child abuse, even though the boys were all in their twenties. It is the old way of raising children—spare the rod and spoil the child. I would never condone child abuse, but a good cuff to the head knocks sense into otherwise senseless teenage boys.

Nawal, I know Luca's your favorite, but I couldn't help thinking she is totally dumping Luca for Santino. Am I right? Love you girls.

Isabelle, my beautiful little princess, my precious three-year-old granddaughter who is going on twenty-one. I love that the only one who can paint your nails to your specifications is your dad. You sure keep him in line, and me in stitches. On our weekly family night, you forever ask me to give Tony (my husband insists she call him Tony not grandpa) a hot bum and laugh when I pretend to. Remember, Bella Mia, that your family is your foundation, the basis for every relationship you will have from here on out. And you, my lucky girl, have a group of people who adore you and love you. Love you always and forever.

To my mom. I guess when you say what Lola wants Lola gets because I got you. Love you.

To Ettore De Benedetto the real chef from Tuscany who taught Chloe and Santino to cook. I was in Italy last year with one of my sons and his wife. I love to take a cooking course wherever my husband and I travel, and he graciously indulges me. There was a mess-up with my booking, and through pure luck, we met Monica at a restaurant. She arranged with her friend Ettore to give us a class in her home. Thank you, Monica, you are very sweet. Meeting Ettore was an absolute thrill. The man is a gentleman through and through. His talent and passion for the culinary arts and his family is impressive, to say the least. He's as obsessive about his love for creating amazing food as I am about writing. When I asked him if he would allow me to write him in a book I was thinking of writing, he said, "No"—(my heart stopped)—"I would be honored." I hope in some small way I captured your passion and kindness of a man I met and spent six hours with, but who made a lifetime impression on me. You are an amazing man. If any of you go to Tuscany, visit the restaurant where he showcases his talents, Ristoro di Lamole. It will truly be a highlight of your culinary trip. Introduce yourself to Ettore because this is a man worth knowing. From the bottom of my heart, thank you, Ettore. Go to my website for his caramel panna cotta recipe.

To my beta readers, Sarah, Tina, Eve, Nawal, and Diane. Thank you so much for reading each book and giving me feedback. We have some amazing discussions stimulated by your feelings about topics in the book. I love defending my position and you defending yours, but ultimately, it is my decision. It's so good to have all the power. LOL! I love you girls, and from the bottom of my heart, thank you.

To Kristin, my editor and my bitching sound board. Laughter is truly something that I feed off of, and you make me laugh all the time. I don't know who hated Valentina more—you or my daughter-in-law Eve. I love getting an email during edits to hear how you want to slap her. I always think if I incited that much anger, my job is done. Thanks for the validation and all you do. You are a great mom and a great friend, so you must have a little of Valentina in you. LOL! Thanks for giggling through the she-ee-py part, too, because it means something to me. I missed you and am so glad you're back in my life. Love you, friend.

To Melissa, my copy editor. I thank you for everything you've done. If I had to compare you to anyone, it would be Francesca in the last series and Emmy in this one. You are that damn sweet. You are a storybook mommy with your girls, and they are very lucky to have you, even if they don't want the princess bed. LOL! I can never thank you for always having my back and your positive energy. Calling you my friend is one of the easiest things I do. The one day you finally lose it on your daughters, I want an email so I can write them and tell them to knock it off, because if they pissed you off, it must have been really bad. LOL! Thanks for everything. Love you!

To my readers, especially Annette, Colleen M., Maylin, Enza and her two friends, Jessica, Tina, Joan, Lynn, and Kendra. You make every sleepless night and eighty-hour week worth all the work. In the next series, you are going to learn about the Irish, bad tempers and all. I love history and, because of you, I get to keep researching and learning. Thanks for reading. Love, your indebted author.

To my two besties, Liz and Liz. Without you two, my childhood and adulthood wouldn't have been this much fun. That's even without all the booze. Nah, that's a lie, and you both know it. I feel like I owe you both so much, something I could never repay. You are the sisters of my heart. Love you both to infinity and beyond. Hey, that sounds familiar. Must have been from one drunken Caesar Friday. LOL

Last but not least, to my strega Diane. It began with you, and now you are soon moving on to different things. Will you ever stop impressing me? You teach me every day to keep reaching for things I'm not sure I can do. Rock on, Sista! Love you!

There is No Truth
Chapter 1
Not So Luck of The Irish

"Dad!" Molly ran into the cardiac emergency waiting room. "What happened? Have you heard anything?"

Declan MacKenna jumped up and opened his arms for his frantic daughter. "No one has come out yet to tell me anything." He pulled her tight to his chest. He hadn't realized until this second how terrifying it would be to tell his only daughter that her mom might not make it.

She pulled back. "What happened?"

He took her hand and guided her to some chairs. "The police—"

She yanked her hand away. "Police? I thought you said she had a heart attack?" She tried to stand, but he pulled her back down and held both hands.

"Molly, slow down and give me a minute to explain. The police called and said some guy tried to carjack her. After hitting her in the head with the butt of a gun, he yanked her out of the car. Witnesses said she struggled to her feet, put her hand to her chest, and fell. It scared her so badly that she had a heart attack."

"Oh my God, no! Did you call Jack?"

He gave that look only Irish fathers could give when they were talking about their sons. "I left a message. He's probably out with those hooligans, drinkin'."

Molly yanked her hands out of her dad's and reached into her purse for her phone. "I'll reach him." She stood and dialed her oldest brother, but it only rang before going to voicemail. Walking in circles around the room, she hung up, then called ten more times before he finally answered.

"It better be an emergency, Moll," twenty-eight-year-old Jack snipped into the phone.

"Mom's in the hospital. She had a heart attack! It's bad, Jackie. We're at the Cleveland Clinic. Get here as soon as you can. I'm calling Ronan."

He exhaled loudly, not ready for another family drama. "I'm coming. Did you tell Dad about calling Ronan?"

She hushed her voice, "No." Then she said with an edge, "He has the right to be here."

"I'll call Ronan." Jack knew she was dealing with Dad, so he should make the call.

"No! I don't need you fighting with him. Let me." Molly knew deep in her heart that, no matter what happened, Dad would want Ronan here for Mom's sake. "Just get here as quickly as you can."

Jack hung up without saying goodbye, which ticked Molly off. He always did that.

Her family had gone from close-knit to enemies in a war zone. Molly hated it.

She walked back to her dad, who looked like a little boy who had lost his family. He was scared.

Her dad had always been her hero. The man she adored and the one she compared every man to.

God, she should also call Killian. He would come and help keep the peace.

Killian was the son of one of her dad's best friends. He had lived with them for a year after immigrating from Venezuela before getting his own place. He and Molly had always been close. She had even helped train him for his job in their family business. First, though, she had to let her dad know she was calling Ronan.

She stood in front of her dad, waiting for him to look up at her. "Jack's on his way. I'm calling Ronan." Molly saw the second it penetrated past his fear.

His face twisted in distaste. "I don't think that's good idea. Part of the reason Colette had the heart attack was because your brother broke her heart."

Disappointed, she answered, "Please, Dad, this is about Mom. You know she would want Ronan here."

Molly's guilt trip worked. "Fine. But tell him to keep his distance from me."

Molly didn't dignify his response with an answer as she walked back to the far corner of the semi-occupied room. Her heart raced as she searched her contacts for Ronan's number. It rang twice before he picked up, snarking out, "Did Hell freeze over?" At twenty-six, Ronan was two years older than Molly.

"Hello to you too. I don't want to fight. I'm only calling to tell you that Mom's in the hospital. Someone tried to carjack her, and she had a heart attack. We're at the Cleveland Clinic." She heard his gasp, but he didn't respond. "Ronan, did you hear me?"

"I'm on my way. And thanks, Lil' Moll. I'll see you soon. Bye."

"Bye." She smiled to herself. That was the brother she knew and loved.

Her next call was to Killian.

"Hello, reinita. To what do I owe this pleasure? Have you finally come to your senses and you're calling to ask me out?" He had always called her reinita, the Spanish word for little queen.

"I need you. Mom's in the hospital."

"Cristo, Molly. Tell me where you are." The genuine concern was a relief. She knew without a doubt he would side with her and keep tempers in check.

She recited the same story she had to her brothers, and then Killian said he would be there as soon as possible and told her to stay strong.

Molly felt better. He would make it better. He always did.

She settled in beside her dad, tucking herself into his arm and laying her head on his shoulder. "They're all coming. Jack, Ronan, and Killian. Dad, promise me you won't pick any fights. Do it for Mom."

Declan twisted his upper body, placing a hand on her head as he kissed the top. "I've been sitting here thinking. You're right. I don't want to upset your mom. I promise I'll be good as long as Ronan does the same. I know your mom loves him."

She squeezed his bicep. "So do you, Dad. You're just angry and disappointed right now. I've said it a thousand times—it just doesn't make sense. Ronan has to be innocent."

He made a humph sound. "So much for the luck of the Irish. Lately, it's more of a curse."

Molly couldn't help silently agreeing. The family had gone to hell in a handbasket in the last year.

Their family was very successful, and it showed, but none of them had ever had anything handed to them. They worked hard, sometimes double the hours of most of their friends. When her dad had immigrated to America, he had landed not knowing a soul, and with only a few hundred dollars in his pocket.

There was a story behind Dad and his best friends' sudden departure from Ireland, but they never talked about it, and he never returned to his homeland. When both of Molly's paternal grandparents had died, Dad hadn't even gone home to attend their funerals. Money wasn't an issue, and Molly knew they had been close—her grandparents had visited every year, and it was evident they had adored their son.

She and her brothers had always speculated it was something really bad, but they had nothing concrete to go on. Even Mom, who loved to gossip, was tight-lipped on the subject. She also hadn't ever gone back to visit anyone after she had immigrated a year after Dad had settled in.

They had all heard the stories over the years of how Declan and his three best friends had been closer than blood brothers growing up in a suburb of Dublin. They had gone to school together and lived on the same street. Everyone had called them the four amigos, and distance and time hadn't changed that.

One stayed in Ireland, but the other three had immigrated to different countries. Declan in Chicago in the US; the others to Vancouver, Canada; and Caracas, Venezuela.

Molly had studied all about the great migration of Irish settlers in school. Chicago had a huge influx of Irish immigrants in the early 1900s after the great potato famine of 1845. It all but dried up in the '50s, but during "The Troubles" in Ireland, the last great wave of Irish settlers immigrated to Chicago in the 1980s, her father included in the tail end of that trend.

Chicago had a huge Irish Catholic population with a smaller Protestant one. Her dad was a proud Catholic who had worked construction during the day and served soft-serve ice cream in the evenings at the Dairy Cream. Mr. O'Leary, the owner of the Dairy Cream, had immediately taken a shining to Declan after he rented the apartment above the store, and offered him an opportunity to be his night manager with a chance to buy into the operation because the man was childless.

Thirty-four years later, Declan owned the three flagship Dairy Cream stores and franchised the business across the country. All his kids, plus Killian, had worked for the business until last year, when Ronan was caught embezzling. Because of it, he had been thrown out on his ass, and Dad and Jack refused to speak to him.

Ronan swore on his life that he was innocent, but the evidence was stacked against him. Still, her brother believed his family should take his word for it, regardless of what the books said.

Molly often felt like grabbing each of the stubborn males in her family and smashing their hot heads together.

Irish people were known for their sense of humor and easygoing personalities, but if they thought they had been wronged, they would write you out of their lives as soon as look at you. They were a prideful bunch, which drove her to the brink of insanity. If they would have just approached it with level heads, the dumbasses could have spent the last year trying to figure out how the books got so screwed up, and money was transferred, instead of believing one of their own had turned against them. Molly just wanted her family reunited, and for them to rally around their mom.

If that wasn't bad enough, six months ago, Jack's wife of a year and the love of his life had announced she was pregnant with one of his newer friends. Molly had to peel her brother off the guy, terrified he was going to kill the loser.

Her soon-to-be ex-sister-in-law, being the stupid cow she was, might have thought her brother's temper was scary, but she had better keep one eye open—nothing was fiercer than a little sister scorned.

That cow would pay.

It was as if thoughts of defending Jack made him appear as he came flying through the door.

All her girlfriends went nuts over her brothers, often comparing them to the Captain American actor, Chris Evans. Molly had gotten the same thick brows as her brothers, but hers were dark auburn. She was so thankful for being born during the invention of tweezers, because they were such a contrast to her strawberry blonde hair. If that wasn't bad enough, the light freckles that softly dotted her face pulled it all together. But nothing indicated her Irish background more than the bright green eyes she shared with her brothers and the MacKenna side of the family.

Her brothers got the height of five-foot-eleven, which was tall for the Irish, considering their dad was only five-foot-eight, but she had stopped growing at five-foot-four, thanks to her mom. Whereas her brothers were stubborn, Molly was hot-tempered. No one crossed the fiery little firecracker and lived to tell about it, as her ex-sister-in-law would find out when the time was right.

"How's Mom?" Jack asked before he even made it through the door.

Dad stood and hugged his son. "We haven't heard anything yet. She must still be in surgery."

Jack then went to Molly and hugged her tightly. "She'll be okay, Lil' Moll. Nobody's as strong as Mom." Unsettled, he said, "Mom's car isn't brand-new. I don't understand."

Declan looked sternly at his oldest child. "Probably drugs."

Jack rolled his eyes. His dad had found his stash of pot when he was eighteen and was still convinced his son had a problem. The man didn't understand recreational use. Jack couldn't convince his parents that it wasn't any different than his dad's beloved Irish whiskey. Nobody ever commented on the amount of Guinness or whiskey they consumed as a family. Oh, that's right, because it was part of their blessed heritage. God save him from hypocrites.

He didn't share his thoughts, though, because Ronan walked in, and tension filled the air in his wake.

Molly hurried over to greet the black sheep. "Ronan." She pulled his tense body into a hug. "It's good to see you. I just wish it wasn't because Mom was in the hospital."

"Hey, Lil' Moll, how is she?" Ronan asked, ignoring the latter part of the greeting, as well as his dad and brother.

Molly told him what they knew, and that they were waiting to hear from a doctor. Ronan then moved to the farthest corner of the room, looking at his cell phone.

Molly was torn between sitting with her dad or Ronan, so she chose neither, deciding to pace.

Killian walked in ten minutes later, alleviating some of the tension by going to everyone and shaking hands as Molly watched him.

Killian was drop-dead gorgeous. His father was Irish, but his mom was Venezuelan. Molly and all her friends compared everyone to famous people, and they had decided Killian looked like the singer Enrique Iglesias, except with longer hair and penetrating blue eyes. He was taller than her brothers by about three inches, and his facial expressions were as intense as his good looks. When he talked to you, it was like there wasn't another person on Earth. Sometimes Molly felt like he was looking right into her soul. He also had one of those deep, smooth voices with a Latin accent that made her want to cross her legs. The man was the whole damn sexy Irish/Latin package, which was why she wouldn't date him.

Molly didn't want to feel like a bush pig next to his godliness, and she didn't want a repeat of her brother's marriage. Nope. No, thank you.

Killian finally made his way to Molly. "Hey, reinita, how's my girl holding up?"

The concern in his eyes made her want to bawl. In fact, Molly couldn't answer as tears welled up, so she just stepped into his arms. His warm body was as welcoming as his scent.

Killian wrapped one of his hands around her back, the other against her head. "Your mamá's going to be fine. You know she's stronger than all of us put together." When she seemed to relax, he said, "Come on; sit down. And don't worry, I won't leave your side."

Molly had talked to Killian many times about everything going on in her family. He was the only person she confided in, because he had lived with them and knew all their strengths and weaknesses. He had also known all of them from childhood.

The doctor finally walked in. "MacKenna family?"

"Here," Declan said as they all gathered to hear what the doctor had to say.

Killian wrapped his arm around Molly's shoulders, offering support.

"Mrs. MacKenna survived the surgery. She had an aortic valve replacement. With open heart surgery, we had to stop her heart to replace the faulty valve with an artificial one. It was a birth defect that had gone undetected."

Molly gave her father a quick look to make sure he heard that part and would stop blaming Ronan.

The doctor continued, "It was actually lucky for her that help was so close; otherwise, she might have had the heart attack alone. I've placed her on blood thinners because of clotting. In all probability, she will be on them for the rest of her life.

"The success rate for valve replacement is very high, but it was a major surgery, and we had to cut the breast bone, so any number of complications can arise in the next twenty-four hours. We will be monitoring her in ICU with one-on-one nursing in case of a second heart attack or infection. We're also keeping an eye on the hit she sustained to the temple.

"We are keeping her sedated for the next twenty-four hours, and then we'll take her for a CT scan. You can visit as soon as they get her comfortable. I don't want you to be alarmed when you see the equipment needed after the operation. As I said before, we're expecting a full recovery. Does anyone have any questions?"

That was a lot of information in a short amount of time, and the family was so overwhelmed they couldn't think of anything to ask. Molly then piped up and thanked the doctor, and the rest followed suit.

As soon as the doctor walked away, they all hugged, except for Ronan, who went back to his corner and hid his face in his hands.

Molly wiped her tears, then headed toward him, sitting beside him and rubbing his back.

He broke her heart as he struggled to deal with his emotions alone. He had talked to Mom but hadn't seen her after their dad had banned him eleven months ago. He had been the closest to her by far before his excommunication.

"She's going to be okay, Ronan."

He threw his arms around his sister, who had tried everything to keep him in the fold, but because he had been so angry, he had pushed her and Mom away. Molly was so much like their mom.

"Thanks, Lil' Moll. I want you to know I don't blame you or Mom. You two are the best part of this family. I'll need you to coordinate with me to have some time alone to visit her. It's been too long."

"That's an understatement. You broke her heart." Neither one of them had seen Declan approach. He just couldn't let it go.

His fiery little sister stood up and blocked Ronan's view of their dad. Her hands on her hips, madder than a wet cat, she spat, "You heard the doctor, the same as I did. It was a birth defect. You can't blame Ronan.

"If you three would work together to figure out who really embezzled from the business, we could tell Mom this idiocy is finally over. Nothing would make her heal faster than having all her family back together. Ronan is your blood, for God's sake."

Declan had the good sense to look chastised. "Sorry, daughter. You're right. I'm just really out of sorts and can't bear the thought of losing her."

"Aw, Dad, we're not going to lose her." Molly hugged him tightly. "She's going to be fine, but we all have to pull together to help her through the recovery, and that starts by putting all the nonsense under the rug for now. No one is going to upset her, or I swear to the Lord Almighty I'll de-man all three of you." She whipped around, pointing her finger at all of them.

The lethal threat from the smallest and youngest amongst them had them all choking out a little laugh.

"Mighty Mouse, or should we say Mighty Molly, strikes again," Jack sputtered out.

She whipped back to him. "And don't forget it, Jackie."

Killian walked up to her, proud as a peacock. He looked to each man as he spoke. "Reinita has spoken. While you all visit Colette, I'm going to run out and call Aidan; let him know what's happening. He can pass it on to everyone else." Looking directly at Molly, he said, "Give Mamá a kiss from me. I'll be waiting for you when you're done."

Killian was such a good man. What would she do without him?

"No, go back to work. I'm going to stay here for a while. I don't want to leave yet. I'll keep in touch with everyone."

"I'm not leaving," Declan declared. "I'll stay with Molly. Jack, you go back to work with Killian." No one inquired about Ronan, but he didn't give a shit. He had as much right as the rest of them to be there. He wasn't leaving.

Jack's hackles rose as he snapped back, "No way, Dad. Mom just had open heart surgery. I'm not going anywhere until I know she's on the mend. If Killian wants to go back, he can. If not, the business will be fine without us for a day."

"He's right," Killian was quick to add. "We have good people in place."

Ronan wasn't convinced of that, since someone had set him up.

"And I'm not leaving Molly or Colette. I'm sure Ronan wants to stay too."

They all turned to look at Ronan, who nodded. He appreciated Killian including him, but it also pissed him off because Killian wasn't blood. It would be so easy to take his anger out on him, but he had to remember where the blame actually belonged—with his dad and brother.

Before anyone else spoke, a nurse pushed the door open, stepping into the room. "MacKenna family?"

"Yes," Declan said, advancing quickly toward the woman. "Can we see my wife now?"

"Yes, I will take you in. First, let me explain that we have Mrs.

MacKenna on a ventilator and hooked up to a lot of monitoring equipment. It can be a little overwhelming, but let me assure you that it's all very normal."

"Why is she on a ventilator?" Jack asked. "Can't she breathe on her own?"

The nurse explained that all patients with a valve replacement had to have a ventilator during surgery. And some patients required it for up to twenty-four hours afterward, but they were also keeping Colette on as a precautionary measure because she had sustained a head injury.

"With the swelling, we wanted to make sure she was getting enough oxygen to her brain. Follow me, and I'll take all of you in. Just so you know, after the initial visit, I will only allow two in at a time for ten minutes, and then the next two can go in every half an hour after that. Her nurse will be in the room the whole time. We ask that you stay out of her way. It's important to remember that, even though we have Mrs. MacKenna sedated, we still assume she can hear everything, so keep it positive." She turned and led the group into the ICU.

Killian gave Molly a little hug and told her that he would be waiting for her when she got back.

Declan waited for his daughter, then took her arm and followed the nurse.

Molly was thankful her dad was holding her, because overwhelming wasn't the word she would have used when she saw her mom. More like devastating.

Colette was naked from the waist up, with an eight-inch incision along her sternum with iodine surrounding it. Colette's head had a gash, and a deep, swollen purple bruise. There was what looked like hundreds of machines hooked up to her body.

Declan advanced toward the bed, softly weeping as he reached for her hand. "Aw, lovey, what happened to you?"

As scared as he had been before, seeing her like this crippled him. His wife was the heart of his family. He couldn't live without this woman. They had been through so much together. Married thirty-three years, and those years had been the best of his life, but they were only fifty-four, and had so many years still ahead of them.

She kept him in check when his temper got the best of him, and had always used humor to get him out of his funks. She loved him when he didn't love himself.

"I love you. Please dahn't leave me," he cried.

This was the first time any of his children had seen him cry, but he had never been this frightened before.

"Lord, you take me if you need to take someone. Colette, she's de grand one. She doesn't deserve dis. I've never asked you fer anythin, please. Lord, dahn't take 'er frahm me."

Molly had to wipe her eyes. She knew he was past distraught when the thick accent came out. They all knew Mr. O'Leary had implored Dad the first month he had arrived in Chicago to acclimatize to American English and lose the accent. She also knew that, not only would they have to get Mom through this, they would have to get him through it.

"Dad, the worst is over. You know she said she wasn't going anywhere until each of her kids had our own, so they could seek revenge for everything we ever did to her."

Mr. MacKenna chuckled. She said that all the time.

He gently brushed the side of her head where she was bruised, and looked at her bare chest. "Why can't dey cover 'er? She is such a modest woman an' wooehldn't be comfortable wit' de boys seein' 'er like dis."

Jack and Ronan were both blindsided by the comment. Sometimes their old man sounded like he was ninety. They weren't looking at her breasts. Who gave a shit if they were exposed?

The nurse put her chart down and apologized, but explained she had to monitor the incisions for swelling and would place an ice blanket over her as soon as they left.

As the family each spoke encouraging words to Colette, Killian called his brother Aidan, who answered on the third ring. "Hola, Killian. I wasn't expecting to hear from you today. What's up?"

He reached into the pocket of his jacket for a smoke, which wasn't socially acceptable in the US nowadays, but it was still the norm in Venezuela.

As he got one out and lit it, he said, "It's Colette, man. She was carjacked and had a heart attack. I'm at the hospital."

"No way. Is she okay? Do you want me to come to Chicago?"

"Not yet. They say the prognosis is good." Killian took a deep drag, pulling as much smoke into his lungs as possible. On the exhale, he said, "I just can't believe it. I swear, every time I turn around, something worse is happening here. Damn, bro, if I didn't know better, I'd swear there was something evil at work."

"Brother, it's not just there. Stuff is happening here too."

"What's going on?"

Aidan lowered his voice. "I can't get into it now, but I'm starting to think no one is safe from the ugliness of life. First Dermot and now Colette and the shit here? I thought it was only our family with the upheaval in Caracas, but I'm learning life isn't easy anywhere." Their brother Dermot had been murdered during a crisis in Venezuela that led to their dad sending his two other sons out of the country.

Killian looked around at the people pushing loved ones in wheelchairs, getting some fresh air. This hospital was filled with people who were also seeing the shitty side of life. "I guess you're right. But watching Molly go through this is starting to take its toll."

"How is your reinita handling everything? Has she finally agreed to go out with you?"

Killian chuckled. "I'll bet I'm having as much luck as you are with Hanna. Am I right?"

He heard his brother curse. "These North American women aren't anything like Latin chicas. They're so headstrong." Aidan was disillusioned. "Hanna's still dating that loser. I figured she would have dumped him by now. I'm getting tired of waiting in the wings."

"Maybe it's time to move on?" Killian took a last drag, then butted out his cigarette on the pavement.

"I will when you do." Aidan knew Killian was as hopeless as he was.

"It will never happen. Anyway, I better get back inside in case Molly needs me. Take care, and I'll let you know how Colette makes out. Can you call Papá and let him know what's happening? Tell him I'll call later. And keep Colette in your prayers, bro."

"You know it. Touch base soon. Give everyone my love. Adios."

"Adios." Killian pocketed his phone, then headed back inside. Molly needed him, and he intended to show her that she couldn't live without him.

He had spent three years mooning after this woman, and Molly had thwarted him at every turn.

His mind was working overtime. Maybe the key to her heart was discovering who had sabotaged the business. If he could get her family back together, the rest should fall into place.

The family had hired an external auditor, but maybe they had missed something. Jack had wanted to bring the police in and have Ronan charged, but Colette wouldn't allow it, and rightfully so. Killian knew Ronan like he knew his own brother, and was sure he hadn't embezzled from the family. The rest were all caught up in the emotion of thinking one of their own had stolen from them, whereas he could remove himself.

Tomorrow, he would start an investigation himself.

When the family came back to the waiting room, they looked beaten.

Rising to his feet, Killian asked, "How is she?"

Molly unconsciously went to the comfort of Killian's open arms. In an undertone only for his ears, she said, "She looks horrible. I can't imagine how she'll recover from that."

Looking down, Killian tilted her chin up. "Colette will recover because of all of us."

They all stayed until midnight, when the nurse suggested they all go home and rest, reassuring them that she would call if there was any change.

Molly hugged her brothers and Killian goodbye, then led her father to her car. Tomorrow would come soon enough.

Made in the USA
Monee, IL
31 January 2020